MURDERABILIA

MURDERABILIA

CARL VONDERAU

MIDNIGHT INK
WOODBURY, MINNESOTA

First Edition
First Printing, 2019

Book format by Samantha Penn
Cover design by Shira Atakpu

Midnight Ink, an imprint of Llewellyn Worldwide Ltd.

This is a work of fiction. Names, characters, places, and incidents are either the product of the author's imagination or are used fictitiously, and any resemblance to actual persons living or dead, business establishments, events, or locales is entirely coincidental.

Library of Congress Cataloging-in-Publication Data
Names: Vonderau, Carl, author.
Title: Murderabilia / Carl Vonderau.
Description: First edition. | Woodbury, Minnesota : Midnight Ink, [2019]
Identifiers: LCCN 2019008871 (print) | LCCN 2019012474 (ebook) | ISBN
   9780738761701 () | ISBN 9780738761305 (alk. paper)
Subjects: | GSAFD: Suspense fiction.
Classification: LCC PS3622.O675 (ebook) | LCC PS3622.O675 M87 2019 (print) |
   DDC 813/.6—dc23
LC record available at https://lccn.loc.gov/2019008871

Midnight Ink
Llewellyn Worldwide Ltd.
2143 Wooddale Drive
Woodbury, MN 55125-2989
www.midnightinkbooks.com

Printed in the United States of America

Acknowledgments

So many people encouraged and assisted me in making this a better book. Jim Filley and Gary Hassen, of the San Diego Police Department, helped me with a tour of their offices and provided details of arrest processing. Randy Mize and Matt Brainer educated me on the law and how an arraignment and a separate in-chambers consultation with a judge could work. Mark Hayes walked me through processing and housing at the San Diego County Jail. I'm sure I didn't get all of this right, but it is more accurate because of their coaching.

Many people generously gave their time to look at and evaluate earlier versions of the manuscript. Terry and David Brown, Martha Lawrence, Mark Clayton, and Bob Lowe read and helped with earlier drafts. Jackie Mitchard worked with me for more than two years. She suggested so many improvements and even came up with the moniker "the Preying Hands." Among other things, she educated me on pacing, backstory, structure, and the opening. The book is so much better because of her insights. Lastly, my writers' group has evaluated every scene in this book and many that never made it to the final version. They have helped me see the deeper parts of the character and get rid of the boring parts. A huge thanks to Eleanor Bluestein, Peggy Lang, Louise Julig, Suzanne Delzio, Barbara Brown, James Jones, Lawrence Saul, and Walter Carlin.

People in the book publishing industry believed in this book. My tireless and fabulous agent, Michelle Richter, kept pushing until we found a publisher. Terri Bischoff and Midnight Ink saw the strengths in the manuscript and put their time and money behind it. Sandy Sullivan, my editor at Midnight Ink, seems to know the book better than I do. She helped me correct so many things to make the manuscript better. Dana Kaye and Sami Lien of Dana Kaye Publicity, as well as Ellen Zielinski Whitfield at JKS Communications, have helped with great marketing ideas.

Lastly, a great thanks to my wife, Rachel Mayberry, for patiently suffering through the years it took me to finally get published. Without your support, this never would have happened.

I MANAGE SECRETS. SOMETIMES my clients take years to reveal them—hidden trusts for mistresses and drug-addled kids, weddings held up for months or years because someone's beloved refused to sign a prenuptial agreement. Once I helped a dying business owner design an estate plan that forced his first wife's children to be civil to his second wife or they'd lose their inheritance. Over the years I've learned that my biggest value is not my expertise, but my discretion. The clients at our bank count on me to stay in the background but always be close at hand. They appreciate that I buy my suits at Macy's and drive a Camry instead of a BMW or red sports coupe. Of course, there are the usual loan requests—but any banker can handle those. Even the twenty-six-year-olds who honed their sales skills by hawking magazines can get loans approved for the families I work with. But only a special banker can protect a client's secrets.

Our bank sits discreetly on the tenth floor of a modern building, but our offices are designed to look like an old house that one wealthy descendent has passed down to the next. Oil paintings cling to the damask wallpaper beside antique sconces and handmade stands that hold wooden umbrellas and canes. The conference rooms have couches with throw pillows. Coffee table books of Impressionist painters lie open on vintage tables. When our clients visit us, they're supposed to feel as if they're chatting up the kind of trustworthy and cultured friend who would never need their money.

My career—my life—was carefully constructed to appear normal. Until two years ago. That's when a simple cell phone call unraveled the layers of my facade. When I answered, I was standing beneath the glass cupola in our bank's main hallway.

A voice distorted beyond recognition said, "William McNary. That's not your real name, is it, Tex?"

I pushed my palm against the wall to steady myself. "Tex" was my childhood nickname when we lived in Illinois. The name my father gave me.

"Do you ever think about hands? He thought about hands a lot, your daddy did. Right, Tex? You there?"

An electronic warble could have been a laugh.

"Who … who is this?" I asked.

"Your brother. The only one who really knows you."

The line went dead.

I don't have a brother.

I stumbled down the hallway toward the bank's reception area. I could go down the elevators and get some air. But instead I turned and lurched the other direction, toward the fake French doors that led into the banking department. Passing the rows of offices inside, I was aware of Ambrose Hines pitching on the phone, her index finger jabbing each benefit in the air. Everyone else was out seeing clients. I ducked into the cover of my own office. With my door shut, I sank my head into my hands.

The whole country knew of Harvey Dean Kogan, but no one suspected that I was his son. My boss and clients would be shocked. *Why didn't you tell us? What about the bank's reputation?* But worst of all was what this might do to my kids. No child should grow up knowing that monster was part of their family.

I grabbed my briefcase from the floor and stuffed a leather notebook inside. When I reached the garage I saw something jammed under my Camry's wiper. A plain white envelope. At first I thought it was a notice of new parking fees. But nothing was stuck to any other car's windshield. My breath coming faster, I wrenched out the envelope and hit the button for the automatic door locks. I leaned over to check the back seat. Only then did I climb into the driver's seat and open the envelope. A drawing lay folded inside. Or rather, it was a printed copy of a drawing... of hands.

I kicked the underside of the dashboard and shouted. I crumpled the paper and whipped it against the car's windshield. For thirty-one years I'd dreaded exactly this. Someone would find us. Someone would torment us. I just never knew how. Or when.

Everyone has seen that drawing. In the Dürer pen-and-ink sketch, two grayish-blue hands reach out from sleeves folded over into cuffs, the fingers straight and touching in prayer. Only the praying apostle's hands and sleeves are visible, as if his forearms have detached from his body to hover in the air. It's universally known as *The Praying Hands*. In the version that appeared on my car, black words stood out on the light blue background: *Repent and accept your savior.*

I peeled out of the garage. Fifteen minutes later my Camry sat wedged in traffic, San Diego's drought-stricken hills rising like brown hands around me. I had to calm down, to shape-shift into the unruffled father my family knew. I had to stop gulping air.

By the time the traffic released me, I'd stopped sweating. Our neighborhood was full of hundreds of modest ranch-style houses constructed in the 1960s. In front of ours was a honeysuckle hedge. I'd grown it high for privacy from the neighbors and the street. But now I wanted to see behind it. From the driveway I could make out the garage and our miniature, water-starved front yard. My sister Polly and my kids dipped what looked like a hula-hoop into a vat of soapy water. They lifted it into the air and blew out an enormous bubble. I took a long, relieved breath.

Only Polly would show up in the middle of a drought with a toy that required liquid. But her water came from the rain she'd trapped in her cistern. Polly consumed less city water than anyone I knew. Today she'd donned a pirate hat and eye patch and threaded her black tennis shoes with striped green and yellow laces.

Garth and Frieda had their own pirate hats. As the bubbles' rainbow colors vibrated in the air, all three jumped up and down with toy cutlasses in their hands. Polly was so petite that she looked like one of the kids. Jill, long and willowy, sat by the orange tree and oohed and ahhed. I didn't want to say a word. The soap bubble floated to the yellow and brown grass, popped, and disappeared.

My seven-year-old ran to the spot where the bubble had vanished and beat the ground with his toy sword. After the sixth whack, Jill pushed herself up and draped her arms around him. Garth froze but didn't look at her. For a moment, I worried more about our unusual child than the phone call and the drawing.

Jill saw me and waved. Garth returned to beating the same stretch of dried-out grass.

"Hey, banker man," Polly yelled.

Jill and Polly deserved to know what had happened, but not with the kids there. As I skirted the palm tree, Polly asked, "Did you bring me something nice from the bank's vault?" When I was silent, she said, "Any hot new *bankerettes* I should meet?"

I tried to muster a smile. Frieda, my five-year-old, ran to me, her mop of brown hair cut short like her Aunt Polly's. She grabbed my suit and pointed to Polly's soapy water. "Millions and millions of drops in the bubbles," she shouted. "Million" was her new favorite number. I hugged my little girl a bit harder than usual.

Jill stared at me, a question in her eyes. Why was I home so early? "Okay, my pirates," she yelled. "Time to wash off the monster slime."

Garth broke into a gap-toothed grin. I'd been only one year older when an army of FBI agents yanked away my father.

Our kids galloped inside and Jill followed. She turned back and squinted. Cocked her head so her blonde locks hung down lopsided from the Padres cap. Once again I was grateful for my strong wife. If anyone could withstand this, it was Jill.

Polly stayed outside with me. She pulled off her pirate hat and patch. The skin around her eyes furrowed into spidery creases. She and I shared too many secrets to hide anything from one another.

"Someone knows who we are," I said.

Polly's whole body tensed. She knew exactly the kind of sicko I was talking about. "Did he say his name?"

I shook my head. "He called me Tex. He said he was my brother."

Her hands bunched into fists. "Fuck, fuck, fuck…"

Polly's fury always sucked the air out of mine. I dug the copy of the Dürer drawing out of my suit pocket.

"It's like *him*," I said. "It's like he escaped from prison." But he couldn't have. It would have been on every news site and TV station.

My sister turned her spotlight stare on me, her spiky brown hair sticking out. "As if prison could ever hold the devil."

The devil. Harvey Dean Kogan. My father. Everyone had heard of him, but few had studied his history as much as I had. He'd killed his first victim more than forty years ago in a suburb outside Chicago. Bonnie Sendaro had berated a clerk and yelled at another woman's child inside a Montgomery Ward Department Store. Kogan decided she needed to be punished. It was ten o'clock at night, and no one else wandered through the store's parking lot when Sendaro walked outside. He knocked her out with his wrench and laid her on the torn back seat of his van.

Harvey Dean Kogan didn't possess Sendaro through torture or rape. In the ten minutes it took to strangle her, the Dürer drawing he'd seen at the library flashed into his mind. "That's when I became an artist," he later told a journalist. In an abandoned park, he severed her arms with a hacksaw and scissored off the sleeves of her blouse. Super Glue held her hands together in prayer. He used the same glue to attach the turned-up blouse sleeves to her arms. Kogan mounted his creation on a tree limb with baling wire.

In that darkness, Harvey Dean Kogan must have set up a tripod and adjusted the camera to a wide aperture. Maybe a fifteen-second shutter speed. A cable release would have stopped it from shaking. In the final image, a big part of the tree stood in an otherworldly haze of light, as if he'd shone a flashlight on it during part of the exposure. The *Chicago Sun-Times* received that black-and-white photo. Bonnie Sendaro's praying hands seemed to float palely between two dark branches, the stars and moon slightly blurred in the black expanse behind them. There was no sign of blood; blood would not taint his art. The press recognized the reference to the Dürer pen-and-ink drawing and began to call him "the Preying Hands."

He made that photograph when he was nineteen, seven years before I was born.

2

INSIDE OUR BEDROOM I slipped off my banker's clothes: the shined shoes and pressed suit, the gold cuff links. Home was where I pulled on jeans, an old work shirt, and beat-up running shoes, where my children's cleansing voices seeped in from the rest of the house.

I joined them in the kitchen for dinner. Opposite me, Polly had changed into another black T-shirt and Doc Martens. She'd slipped on her silver bracelets and watch, the crystal so big you could tell the time from across the room. Polly followed more issues than most people could keep track of. Tonight she ranted about counterfeit natural foods and the evils of antibiotics, then the sins of families with three cars. "And why does everyone have to flush toilets every time?" she yelled. "We've got a drought, people." My kids started to giggle and she slapped palms with them.

Next to Polly, Frieda opened her fairy-tale coloring book. Her brown bear, Micky Marvin, was snuggled beside her. On the other side of Polly, Garth landed his plastic space ship, his jet engine shushing through the gap in his teeth. As usual, he'd lined up half the cutlery drawer in careful rows in front of him. Garth was the largest kid in his class, the one his playmates picked after the girls for their teams.

Neither child had any idea who Harvey Dean Kogan was. But I'd always known that someday ... someday some stranger would bend down and smile at them in the park. "Do you know who your grandpa is? I'll bet you're just like him."

Jill was picking at her pasta. She said something beside me, but I was still churning through my thoughts. "Did you hear anything I said?" she asked. "Anything at all? Some of the rest of us had an awful day too."

I wrenched my mind back to Jill. Her eyes looked tired. "What happened?"

She turned to the kids. "A half hour of TV. That's it. I mean it."

Garth and Frieda scampered to our bedroom in the back of the house. When the door slammed shut, Jill said, "They suspended Elizabeth."

Elizabeth Morton taught at the same elementary school as Jill. One of Elizabeth's fourth graders had stuck out his foot and tripped her. They both fell. When Elizabeth got up, she yanked the boy up as well. The next day, he showed up at school with his arm in a sling and his mother beside him. She clutched a lawyer's card.

I was actually relieved to talk about someone else's nightmare. "He was in a sling," I said. "What choice did the school have?"

Both women slowly turned to me. How could I be so tone deaf? This could be the end of Elizabeth's teaching career.

"It's terrible," I said.

Jill swept her eyes over Polly and me. She lifted some plates and noisily rinsed them in the sink. When she returned to the table, she said, "What's going on with you two?"

Polly chose that moment to take a drag from her asthma inhaler. She fumbled with one of the diamond studs in her ear.

When you tell someone about a disaster, it doesn't really matter where you start. As I talked, Jill's frown slowly tightened. She and I had fastidiously kept Harvey Dean Kogan out of what our friends knew about us. We'd tell Garth and Frieda about the Preying Hands when they were teenagers, when they could separate themselves from the Preying Hands' abominations. Jill didn't worry about being outed as much as I did. She hadn't lived through what a small town could do.

When I finished, my wife sighed and hooked blonde strands behind her ears. She said, "It's not like we haven't expected this."

"But I don't have a brother."

Jill's eyes widened. How could I be sure?

"No journalist has even hinted at it," I said.

"Then who could this be?" When I raised my shoulders in a shrug, Jill slammed her hand on the table. "You must have some idea."

I thought about the websites: *The Art of the Preying Hands, A Walking Tour through the Preying Hands' Photos, He Killed His Own Sister.* My father had been fourteen when his sixteen-year-old sister, Magnolia, disappeared. "I won't say I didn't do it," he said to the prison psychologists. An uncountable number of death hags, basement dwellers, and night crawlers idolized him for that. No one had ever found her body.

"Hopefully the reporters won't get wind of it," Polly said.

"Are you kidding me?" Jill said. "Is that what you're worried about?"

She didn't understand how miserable the press could make our lives. They'd ask if she'd been afraid to marry the son of the Preying Hands. And that would be just the starter question. I still remembered the hacks aiming cameras through cracks in our doublewide's curtains. Headlines leaped out from every newspaper. Then the fans, the crazies, who drove and hitchhiked from other states to kneel in the yard outside our trailer.

My career was a whole other issue. "Son of a serial killer" wasn't in the job description of a private banker. And this bank could fire me "at will." Our savings might last three months.

"Look, I came into this family with my eyes open," Jill said. "I won't let some bastard harass us."

How could I *not* squeeze her hand? Jill had seen her share of darkness. Before we married, she'd helped street kids in Colombia. If you ever want to see my wife turn into a warrior, threaten a child.

"We fight this jerk," she said. "Tomorrow we go to the police."

Polly walked around the table to hug her. "William, you are so lucky to have this woman."

I stared down at my wife's hand. The simple, delicate face of her watch looked up at me from the inside of her wrist. The wives in my business made entrances draped in fistfuls of gems. I loved Jill's watch and its weathered leather band. She wore it practically, so she could read to her third-grade class and gauge the time she had left.

"Kogan only attacked women who *abused* children," Polly said. "That's what his art was all about."

"Is that supposed to reassure me?" Jill said.

After dinner, Polly and I stood beside the orange tree outside my front door. For a moment we both took in the perfect San Diego temperature and starry September sky. Even the starved grass gave off a delicious smell.

Her bracelets jingled and she put her hand on my shoulder. "Is it possible we're overreacting?"

I thought of the wacko who'd sponsored an internet contest: "A Hunt for Kogan's Kids." Then, the "Pyramid Power" woman who, twenty years before that, had concluded she was my father's soul mate. Hoping it would reach us, she told the *Chicago Sun-Times* that "I want to be your sister and stepmother."

"You know as well as I do that we're not overreacting," I said.

We walked to her pickup in the driveway. A passing car's headlight beams raked the honeysuckle hedge and lit us up. Polly clasped my arm, her tight grip like an extension of her gaze. "You know, I can't ever remember our father comforting me. Even his hugs didn't seem natural."

We both avoided saying his name. Saying his name made him real again. "Mama wasn't a hugger either," I said.

"Mama's a whole other story."

I looked up the street at the silhouettes of bikes and balls on the lawns, at the driveways with shadowy basketball hoops or boats. Would those children still play with Garth and Frieda? Maybe not after their parents learned about our past and the kinds of fans that our history attracted. Or, worse, perhaps those kids would never stop asking our children about their grandfather.

"Could our father have had another lover?" I asked. "Maybe we have a brother. Mama would know if it's even possible."

"He kept bigger secrets than that from her," Polly said.

Thirteen secrets. That number hid behind everyone's lips in Blue Meadow, Illinois. Maybe Mama could have been unaware of one or two or even five victims, but thirteen? Even Polly at thirteen years old, and I at eight, should have noticed something. When the local kids burned 666 into our lawn on Halloween, we had to kill the grass around the number to erase it. Mama drove to another town to buy groceries at ten o'clock at night. School was the worst. None of the other kids talked or looked at us. It was as if we were caked with stink.

I used my fists to make them feel me. Even before the fights started, I wept with rage. Once, three sixth graders held me down until Polly swooped in to pull them off. The school wanted to send me to a psychologist, but Mama refused. She thought that psychologists and psychiatrists peddled the kind of thinking that only took you farther away from God.

Beside me, Polly glanced at her left arm, at the blue dolphin tattoo with a halo that peeked through her bracelets. The tattoo covered the patch of skin she'd started cutting three months after our father was arrested.

"No matter how hard we try, we can't stop remembering, can we?" Polly said.

I pulled her close. She threw her arms around me and squeezed. More cars passed, mothers and fathers grinding home after late nights at work.

Polly said, "I'm a grown woman now. I'll survive. Even reliving it."

I didn't think even she was sure of that. I wasn't.

She set the play pirate hat on the passenger seat of the truck. Her hand dug into her pocket for her Wonder Woman key ring; my sister never carried a purse.

"I'll follow you home," I said.

"Like hell you will. I'm not letting this cocksucker change a single thing in my life."

She was the only gay woman—maybe the only woman—I knew who called people that. "Just be careful," I said.

Her ropy, elfin body climbed into the pickup and she roared off. The truck flashed red under a streetlight. I couldn't imagine anyone hurting Polly. It had taken her thirty-one years, but she was indomitable.

And if anyone tried, I'd tear him apart.

3

THAT NIGHT, LYING IN bed next to Jill, I remembered my father. I could still see those unblinking amber eyes as he gripped a hotdog in each hand. Then he rose to his giant height above the dinner table. The trailer door slammed. I could feel him even now. He was a darkness that hovered over our house.

My home office stood on a hallway of bedrooms off our open kitchen and living room. It was where I retreated when Harvey Dean Kogan kept me awake. I unlocked the bottom desk drawer, but not the metal strong-box inside. A bottle of bourbon, a vape pen, and a silicone ball sat next to the box. I opened the ball and dabbed marijuana extract, like maple syrup, into the open cavity of the vape pen. The pen's coils heated up. I breathed in the marijuana and expelled the gray-white mist. Jill didn't know about my medication. Nor the thoughts I was blotting out. Some nights it was the only way I could sleep.

I turned on my laptop and pulled out the bottle of bourbon. First I looked at emails from work, then sports pages and other news. A half hour later I moved on to the websites devoted to the Preying Hands. It had been thirty-one years since we'd changed our name and moved to California, but his fans were still searching for us. Tonight there was no mention of Harvey Dean Kogan's family. Whoever had traced us to San Diego didn't boast on the internet.

I took a shot of bourbon. Then another.

At midnight the computer pinged with a message that contained no subject line. I didn't recognize the sender. My finger stayed poised over the mouse. No words, only an internet address: www.preying hands.com.

I clicked on the link. A black screen contained a single prompt that asked for my first name. I entered it and the blackness transformed into a text screen surrounded by charcoal sketches of hands: long fingers and jagged lines on the palms, blackened and manicured nails. Two hands were folded in prayer like the Dürer drawing. Text glowed red underneath.

> *Do you really think he isn't inside you? Your mama can pretend that's true, but you know better. Your daddy also couldn't sleep at night. Even your photography is like his. Right, Tex? Imagine what an art show I could put on for your neighbors.*

I jumped up from the chair. I rushed to the kitchen and its window. All was black in the yard outside. I hurried to the living room and its full-length windows. Nothing was visible, not even the outline of our garden or the orange tree. But I could feel him out there in the dark. He knew my fears. Even the horrible photos that I'd shot all those years before. And he was laughing.

My breath still coming hard, I paced back to my office. The message still lit up the screen.

> Don't you know I'm just having fun teasing you, little brother? With a simple conversation, all this will go away. A few words won't hurt you. Go to Kate Sessions Park at 12:30 tonight. Jill, Garth, and Frieda will be sleeping like kittens in their little beds. I'll be waiting at the end of the road by the turnabout. Don't be late. This is just between you and me and our father. No one else.

Kittens. In prison my father had said that he'd started killing cats as a teenager. It was practice for women. My hand struck the mouse. The site disappeared.

Gradually my thoughts came into focus. There was no reason to panic. I could persuade this deluded fan to leave us alone. One way or another.

I clicked on the link again. But the server informed me that I wasn't authorized to enter the website.

I'd tried most of my life to escape Harvey Dean Kogan's legacy. All I wanted was to live normally and savor the small joys of raising children. My family had been so careful. And still someone had found us.

It was 12:08. If I called the police, what could they do? Threatening to reveal someone's true identity wasn't a crime. By the time the police showed up, no one would be at the park.

I had to handle this myself. Right away. The alcohol and marijuana only strengthened my resolve. I'd confront the harasser. Force him to understand that my children's lives could not be corrupted. I'd do anything to stop that. Anything.

Ten years earlier, when the internet crank had offered a reward to find us, I'd purchased a Colt .45 handgun. Now I took down the lockbox from the closet, dialed the combination, and slid out the pistol.

The edges of the stippled black rubber grip pressed coldly into my hand. The magazine could hold seven rounds and the chamber one. I put in the shells, one by one. I'd never been to a gun range or even shot the pistol. But I wouldn't need to. It was just a prop.

I set the alarm and locked the doors.

4

KATE SESSIONS PARK SAT on the eastern edge of Pacific Beach, up in the hills near Highway 5. The gate stood open but the unlit park seemed deserted. The dark expanses of picnic grass bordering the left side of the road were clear. But anyone could hide in the cement restroom on the right.

I squeezed the wheel of my Camry and stared beyond my headlight beams. There was no sign of a car or an SUV. No one walked outside. The only sound was the growl of the car's engine and the hiss of my breath. After a turnabout, I emerged onto another short road. A hundred yards farther on, Cyprus and eucalyptus trees abutted another turnabout.

He'd written that he'd be waiting at the end of the road. Where the hell was he?

I parked and turned off the lights. Clutched the revolver. Perhaps he wanted me to stand on the road. But the land sloped down into dense brush and trees where he could be waiting to jump out with a knife or a gun. Maybe with a drug that would incapacitate me more quickly than the Preying Hands' chloroform. The houses bordering the park were too far away for my shouts to reach them.

I opened the window and listened for the sounds of footsteps stirring the underbrush. Nothing but the drone of crickets. Overhead an incomprehensible swarm of stars.

The flashlight was in the dashboard compartment. I aimed the beam into the brush.

No one.

Nothing.

I wiped the sweat from my hands onto my pants and looked at my watch. 12:45. He'd ordered me not to be late. But it was after midnight when I'd read the message. It was possible he'd already shown up and left.

Maybe he wanted me out of the house. Maybe he wanted my family alone.

I yanked out my phone and started to dial 911. And stopped. What if police cars roared up, their sirens screaming, and no one but my family was inside our house? I set the phone on the seat. My Camry would get there much faster than the police.

The wheels squealed on the blacktop. Roaring down the road, the Camry hit a pothole and the headlight beams jerked and shuddered. I reached the highway and peeled east beside San Diego's shadowy hills, then down deserted residential streets.

I saw our house. The lights were still off but something looked different. Our garage door was open. I was sure it had been closed when I left.

Pulling into the driveway would make too much noise. I parked a few houses away, behind the boat trailer bearing our neighbor's Boston Whaler. Pistol in hand, I ran silently over the lawn. At the side of the orange tree, I caught my breath and took in our front door and full-length windows. Why hadn't I let my children get a dog, a mutt that barked like crazy?

Something white hung from the door. I crept forward, swiveling my head to take in the yard around me. An envelope with *Tex* typed on the front was taped to the door. I tore it open, reached inside. A photo. My flashlight beam revealed a close-up of a dish drainer in a kitchen. A woman's severed head sat inside the rack.

I gasped. Then recognized the blonde hair woven into maiden braids. It was Leslie Miller, the Preying Hands' last victim.

Jill was also blonde.

I started to jab my key into the door lock. But bursting in was what he'd expect. And if he lurked inside, hovering over Jill with a knife …

A fence with a backyard gate separated our property from the neighbor's. I unlocked the gate and slipped along the side of the house. Peered through each window. No lights or shadows moved inside.

In the back yard, I crept past the swing set and stepped over the toys strewn about the grass. Each of my shoes eased onto the deck. The sliding door to the kitchen was locked. I stuck in my key and slowly pushed it open.

The alarm pad blinked, still armed. I set the flashlight on the table. The gun stayed in my right hand as my left punched in the code.

I tried to slow my breathing, tried to silence my own fear. If he'd somehow demobilized the alarm, he could walk around freely. But then he couldn't re-set it, could he?

The grandfather clock clicked in front of me in the dark open living room. The refrigerator thrummed beside me. I inhaled the basil from the pesto sauce Jill had made that evening. My eyes now could pick shadow from shadow.

I skirted the table and tiptoed to the hallway on the right that led to my office and the bedrooms. The door on the left to Frieda's room stood open. When I'd left, it was closed.

I covered the space in two huge steps. Crouched in the doorway, I pointed the gun with two hands into the room. All was darkness. My flashlight still lay on the kitchen table. I slid open her closet door and turned on the light inside. The house shifted. I whirled. I was pointing a pistol at my youngest child.

Frieda lay on the bed. I listened to the slow breaths of my five-year-old's heavy sleep. She cuddled her Micky Marvin bear under the "Girl Power" coverlet. Her dolls stared out from the bookshelves. From a picture, Frieda and Polly smiled in Halloween witch costumes with Garth beside them as a warlock. My child's innocence could be shredded with a single shot.

Perhaps Jill had woken up and looked in on her. I padded to the hallway and along the wood floor to our bedroom at the end. Jill softly snored.

I turned on the hallway light and made my way back to Garth's room on the other side of Frieda's. His breathing rippled out from his superhero comforter. He still wet the bed, but tonight his pull-up was dry. On the carpet, toy soldiers stood in the same battle lines beside a block castle and rolling train. From the poster on the wall, Hulk Hogan flexed in all his 1990s glory.

My family was safe. I blew out air. Forced my heart to slow.

Only the garage was left. I crept back to the kitchen and through the side door. Turned on the light. No one hid behind the boxes and bags. No one was by the driveway or slinking across our neighbors' yards. My tormentor might have opened the garage door, but he didn't turn off the alarm. There wasn't any conceivable way he'd been inside.

My rage ignited. I kicked a Goodwill bag, punched it, and kicked again. The bag split and clothes spilled over the floor. With the light on, the neighbors could see me melting down. He could be out there laughing.

I closed the garage door and banged in the keypad code to re-set the alarm on the door to the house. Back inside, still trembling, I made sure every window and door was locked. But I knew that nothing would ever seal my house from this man. The Preying Hands' fans didn't listen to reason. I leaned against the hallway wall and took in my wife's calming snore. Neither of my children made a sound. Somehow my family hadn't heard me. And if this freak had really opened the garage door and wandered outside our house? They hadn't awakened to that horror either.

Back in my office, I circled the carpet and swore. I sat down and unlocked the bottom desk drawer. My legs were jiggling. My body needed the vape pen and the bourbon. But for my family's sake, both stayed in the drawer.

Beside my "medicines" lay the strong-box. I opened it with a key and pulled out a bundle of photographs. His photographs. My talismans to ward off his evil. These were his secret sins, which I kept caged in that box and never looked at.

I pulled out the photos and the old rubber band burst. His terrible images spilled over my desk. A familiar revulsion gripped my stomach. I hadn't seen these pictures for years and yet each image was familiar.

I found Leslie Miller. In the black-and-white photo, the long window above her kitchen counter framed the shot. Leslie Miller's severed hands were clasped in prayer and jutted through the front wire supports of the dish drainer. Her head stared out from behind her hands. In mid-depth on the left sat an open can of Budweiser, its tab in the air. Above and behind the rack, on the windowsill, one naked foot pressed into a Tupperware container, the toenails painted a darkish color. Her other foot stood on the other side of the windowsill, to the right. Outside. The photo taped to my front door was identical—even the layering.

Harvey Dean Kogan butchered Leslie Miller just before he was arrested. He'd decided she deserved to die because she'd lost her kids due to her alcoholism. After composing her picture, the Preying Hands slid her fingers, one by one, into a Trix cereal box and sent it to the *Chicago Tribune*. *Trix are for kids*, he wrote. Eighteen days later, police cars and FBI vans roared down the gravel road beside our doublewide trailer. I never saw my father again.

Maybe something lighter than bourbon could take the edge off my dark thoughts. Walking would stop my legs from shaking. Gun in hand, I made my way to the kitchen and the bottle of Chablis in the fridge. Something stood in front of our dish drainer by the sink. It was an opened can of Budweiser.

I hadn't opened that beer can.

We had no beer in our house.

5

I **WAS A CHILD** when I last spoke with the police. The day my father was arrested they gave me a Coke at the station and called me Champ. "I'll bet a husky guy like you likes football," they said. I sat on a chair to face them, my feet dangling above the floor. A lady counselor sat beside me. All their smiles disappeared as soon as I spoke about Pop. The men's big torsos—even their eyes—stiffened. "You didn't hear or see anything?" they asked. "Nothing at all? Are you sure?" Even an eight-year-old could pick up the anger and suspicion behind those questions. There was a reason they'd separated me from Mama and Polly. To hurt Pop. To hurt our family.

I go out of my way not to speak to the police.

Now there was no choice. Not after that beer can appeared in our kitchen. But what would they say when I called in the middle of the night? "Your alarm was set?" "The only evidence is a beer can?" It would be best to wait until morning to tackle the police.

I changed the house alarm code and stacked cans of food in pyramids against the front door and the side door into the garage. A half broomstick jammed the deck door closed. I checked twice that the windows were latched shut. Only then did I sit down on the couch, the revolver in my lap.

At five a.m., I made coffee and stuck the food cans and broomstick back in a closet. I stared out our window and watched the sun burn through the morning coolness. Jill's alarm blasted her awake at six fifteen. While she banged plates in the kitchen, I slipped into Garth's room. Peeking through the blinds, I searched the front yard for footprints, displaced flowers, a wrapper or a piece of paper inadvertently discarded. I saw nothing.

Garth watched me from bed. "Morning, big guy," I said and gave him a hug. He wound his arms around me tightly. Too tightly? I stepped back. "Are you okay?"

He nodded dreamily.

"Did you have trouble sleeping last night?"

He shook his head, crinkling his eyes in the way his mother did. I couldn't discern any fright in his sleepy expression.

Frieda lay in her bed with her stuffed bear. Above her a painted fairy princess and her pet dragon flew across the wall. I tried to sound the same as every other morning. "Did you and Micky Marvin sleep well?"

She pointed to the window overlooking the front yard.

I spun around.

"*El sol,*" she said. *The sun.* It shone through her blinds.

I wrapped my arms around her. She was so small compared to Garth. "I've got two bears who speak Spanish living in my house," I said.

She pulled away from me. "We're *osos*."

"Did Mommy teach you that word?"

She shook her head and grinned. "School." She pointed to her other two bears. "If Wanda has two babies and Beatrice has two babies and Micky Marvin has two babies…"

"Yes?"

"I'll have nine bears."

Threes fascinated her. I played the same game as a child. Then fours and fives. My love of nines lasted a whole year.

I stroked her hair. Both my children were safe.

As the kids ate breakfast, I motioned Jill into our bedroom. She closed the door. Before I could say a word, she said, "Garth's teacher called."

Our son loved his make-believe worlds much more than he liked school. The other kids had started to tease him. "He'll grow out of it," I said. "I did."

Jill cocked her head. She knew something was wrong.

"I have a hankering for beer tonight," I said. "Do we have any?" It was a clumsy way to ask the question. She didn't drink beer.

"What's going on?"

"Nothing. I just want some beer."

My fruitless trip to the park now seemed idiotic. I looked at my watch. Jill had to leave for school. It was not the time to panic her. Better to tell her after I talked to the police, when I could assure her that they'd protect us.

"It's about my harasser," I said. "But I'm taking care of it. We'll talk tonight." I wrote down the new alarm code and gave it to her.

She stared at the piece of paper. "Now you're scaring me."

"It's good to change the alarm once in a while," I said.

6

MY FATHER KILLED AND photographed six women before I was born. To find him, the police set up a special unit that screened thousands of people. They picked up men recently released from mental hospitals and previously arrested for sex crimes. They visited photography studios and clubs, searching for anyone taking kinky photos. The city had to hire extra people to crosscheck the fifteen thousand tips. But no one got close to Harvey Dean Kogan. Except one. Me. The same huge hands that had cradled his victims' heads cradled me.

A year after I was born, the Preying Hands chloroformed a woman who regained consciousness. She escaped before he could steal her away. Fingerprints on live skin disappear quickly, but because she ran to the police, they managed to extract the image of an index finger from her cheek. It didn't help. Harvey Dean Kogan had never been arrested and his prints weren't on file. He'd never even registered for the draft. A strand of his hair had fallen onto her blouse collar, but DNA analysis didn't exist then. When asked for a description, the woman said she was so panicked she never saw him. My father still lay low. He was a planner, what the experts call an "organized killer."

I'd often wondered how he controlled his urges, sometimes for years. I used to believe that his restraint came from more than just a fear of getting caught. Maybe he resisted his secret life because it would tear his family apart. Now such speculation seems like delusion, a delusion not unlike Mama's willful blindness.

After a few months, the Preying Hands killed again. Police teams fanned out across Chicago. Their twenty-five-thousand pages of interviews and statements could have formed a pile eight feet high. Thousands of hours of taped interviews sat stacked in lockers. By then, the FBI's National Center for the Analysis of Violent Crime had offered some theories. The killer suffered from a mother-hate complex. He murdered to repress his homosexuality. The killer was a woman who'd experienced sex as a punishment. As if anyone could really think the Preying Hands was a woman. The FBI analyzed the timing of the slayings and deduced that the crimes weren't influenced by the phases of the moon or the anniversary of some event. They were completely flummoxed.

Eventually the FBI admitted the Preying Hands might be anyone in the community. Maybe a married man with a job and children. His profession must have enabled him to slip away to attack women in both the daytime and the night. Neither the FBI nor the police attempted a composite sketch or physical profile. No living person had seen him. Any medium-sized man could subdue a woman with chloroform. The police must have been desperate when they consulted a psychic. Leonora Delavito saw black hands pressing in on Chicago from the outside, but she never narrowed down the "outside" to a small town like Blue Meadow, Illinois.

All of Chicago was spooked. One woman shot a boy who knocked on her door for directions. Another said she killed her husband because she was sure he was "the one." Investigators soon learned that "the one" also owned a large life insurance policy and was having an affair. As the paranoia increased, late night talk show hosts and magazine writers made jokes that men discreetly passed along to other men: "Don't just pray—give God a hand." "Be careful when you go to your photographer for a headshot." Outraged women condemned the "typical male coarseness" in long newspaper editorials.

My father watched it all, never giving us a hint of his secret hobby. When he emerged from his photo shed, his enormous hands only clutched color shots of Mama, Polly, and me. As I remember that period in my early childhood, his moods stand out. Some days he could barely speak and didn't stir from the couch. On others, he'd pick flowers for Mama, and Polly and Mama would bake cookies. The smells of butter and chocolate filled the doublewide. He'd wrestle with me and we'd throw rocks at monsters in the creek. During those happy times, Polly and I wanted to spend every moment with him. It turned out that those days were the ones after he'd killed someone.

7

I'D NEVER TOLD ANYONE at work about my father. In our bank, gossip was a currency and my father's identity would be gold. One casual announcement from me, and in minutes most of my colleagues would be whispering into their phones. By morning the reporters would ring our doorbell at home and show up at the bank. Soon my clients would complain to Vanessa, our CEO. Where were the discreet financial services they'd been promised? Of course it wasn't right, they'd say, but negotiating a loan with the son of a serial killer made them uneasy.

Now was not the time for the great reveal at the bank. The best course, until Jill and I figured out what to do, was to go to work as if nothing had happened.

I shut myself in the smallest conference room. With its antique moldings, Victorian lamps, and fold-down mahogany card table, it looked like the den in a dowager's house. For five minutes, I closed my eyes and tried to focus.

I called Polly and told her about the emailed link and the trip to the park, not mentioning the beer can I'd found in our kitchen. Polly would have exploded if she suspected that someone had broken into our house, and I was too exhausted to deal with one of my sister's outbursts. Predictably, her first shouted question was whether I had a gun. She had two. She'd also studied kickboxing and karate. But even after a feast, my sister didn't reach a hundred pounds. "You be careful too," I said, knowing my warning was pointless. Polly wasn't about to let some man scare her into changing her routines.

After I hung up, I stared at the bronze angel clock and relived the night before. The light from the window burned my face, as if the small room were a tastefully decorated oven. By the time I picked up the phone again, I was so angry I had to stand.

The police transferred me to someone in the crime squad. When I divulged who my father was, he said, "*The* Harvey Dean Kogan? No wonder you changed your name."

I couldn't tell him that someone had broken into our home. Not when the only evidence was a beer can. Instead I described the copy of Harvey Dean Kogan's photo taped to our door.

"Some people might call that a threat," he said. "But I'm not sure a court would agree."

"We need protection," I said.

He actually chuckled. "Haven't done that for years. No budget."

How could the police not even consider protection? I glared at the striped-cloth chair and the fold-up antique table. I imagined flinging them against the wall. We couldn't afford private security. And what would this man do to my family the next time he broke into our house?

"I'll tell you what we *can* do," he said. "Send someone out to talk to you."

As if talking with a policeman would stop this man. But what choice did I have? I gave him my address at the bank.

The next call went to our alarm monitoring company. Jill had refused motion detectors and cameras in our home, but that was before last night. The man at the company said the earliest anyone could upgrade our system was the next afternoon. No extra alarm would protect our house that night. Except me.

My head felt full of wadded-up Kleenex. I left the conference room and strode down the main hallway, veering through the French doors toward my office. Bob, our rainmaker, stood inside the office across from mine. He leaned over his desk, one arm resting on a stack of tax returns. A light blue handkerchief peeked out of the pocket of his pinstripe. Even he called himself "Bullshit Bob." Bob could sell you something you didn't even know you wanted. The only person better at it was the man I didn't like to think about. My father.

As usual, Bob's deep voice boomed out over the phone. In the office next to him, Ambrose stood and closed her door, not even pausing as she spieled her client.

Bob hung up and his phone rang again. "Thanks, Kathy. I'll be right there." His eyes widened when he saw me. He hung up and moved to intercept me. "We have to talk," he said. "Massy's here. He asked to see me. I didn't call him."

Lawrence Massy was a well-known La Jolla ophthalmologist whose business I'd almost won before I left my previous bank.

Bob sped by me and opened the French doors. Massy stood in the main hallway. His hair shone dark black against his cherry-red eyeglass frames.

Perhaps something *had* changed at the bank. Was Bob stealing my prospect?

8

Two hours later and still no word from the police. At least Jill and our kids were safe at school. I had to take a meeting.

This conference room was called the "living room" because of its faux antique wainscoting and green and rose floral couches. Vanessa Barksdale, my boss, sat opposite Jim Poderovsky at the pearl-inlaid table. She was barely five feet tall and, as usual, draped in pearls. Maybe it was Jim's husky body, or the fake Louis XIV chair, but that morning she reminded me of a blonde child queen. A queen who was the best schmoozer I'd ever worked with. She remembered the names of every client, their children and their grandchildren. She knew what schools they attended, what they liked to do for entertainment, and who had decorated their houses. I'm sure she also knew about Jim's father and his reputed mob connections. But Jim didn't let his family tarnish him. He never even brought up their names. And I wasn't about to hold his father against him.

I sat next to her and tried to smile away the night before. "So nice to see you again," I said to Jim.

Jim's big body seemed taut, even as he rested his loafers on the table's paw legs. He wore a suit rather than his usual khakis and polo shirt. Even his smile looked strained. As he rambled on about his latest safari, Vanessa's eyes widened and narrowed. Her face crinkled as her voice bubbled into a laugh. She was reeling him in. I wondered what the prize was.

She poured coffee from the silver tea set. "So how's Cheryl?" she said.

Jim examined his coffee cup as if evaluating the bone china. He sipped and slowly set the cup in the saucer. "She's in Hawaii with Megan." Megan was his young daughter.

"I'm so jealous," Vanessa said.

That was misdirection. Vanessa knew as well as I did that Jim's pause before answering hinted at something. Four weeks earlier he'd brought his new estate planning attorney to the bank—without Cheryl, his wife of six years. She'd always joined the meetings. Then Jim wanted to sell some nicely performing apartment buildings, despite having no apparent need for cash. I thought about the Four Ds that made our chief credit officer twitch: drugs, dementia, death, and divorce.

Jim jerked forward and the wooden chair groaned. "You know, I think you shouldn't need Cheryl to sign on the loans anymore. I mean, look at my track record."

He was getting divorced. I was sure of it. Jim must have just found out that Cheryl wouldn't guarantee any more of his business loans. The issue was how, after the carnage from the settlement, he'd repay our line of credit. Cheryl would hire a pit bull lawyer and Jim might no longer own any assets that he could sell to repay us. That's why we had to keep her on the hook for the loan.

I should have spewed out some vague words about lending principles and fanatical banking regulators. But I was so frazzled I couldn't muster the energy. I had to get back to my office to be available for the police.

Vanessa picked up a coaster. Apparently deep in thought, she fondled our gold-pillared emblem. "Well, maybe we could manage something."

Heat crept up my cheeks. There were lots of financial numbers I could massage—debt ratios, historical income, recurring cash flow, even what we count as liquidity. But releasing a wife from a loan guarantee? I forced myself to take a deep breath. There are few things that will cut short a career faster than publicly contradicting your boss. Now was not the time to get fired.

Vanessa sculpted her hair, as if further pondering Jim's request, and said, "William, why don't you talk with Chad about this?"

Chad, whom we called Chad the Impaler, was our chief credit officer. I knew what he would say. *Are you crazy? He's getting a divorce.*

I tried to be diplomatic. "Chad is going to have a few questions," I said.

Her miniature hands set down the coaster. She gave me an icy blue stare: *Don't you dare screw this up.*

Jim didn't need his mob-boss father to push through his deals. He could set up his ambushes all by himself. The real reason for this meeting was to get Cheryl's name off the guarantee. Jim had invited Vanessa, the relentless business developer, so I couldn't say no. My hands squeezed the sides of the fake antique chair. I tried to cover up my annoyance with a smile. Unsuccessfully.

Vanessa rose. "We'll find a way to get this done," she said and looked at me.

Jim's whole body seemed to sink into his grin. "Of course you will."

Our chairman evaluated Vanessa based on how many new loans she put on the books—not their quality. If this one went bad, I'd take the fall, not her.

A thought flashed in my mind. I almost laughed. Just a few words, that was all I needed to end this farce. *Guess who my dad is.*

We dropped off Jim with Tom Mullen so Jim could pretend to be interested in Tom's investment strategy. If another bank offered to remove Cheryl's name from the guarantee, Jim would move those investments out the next day.

But I had more important things to worry me. I returned to my desk. Officer Mortimer of the San Diego Police had left a message that they couldn't see me until tomorrow. "Now listen," he'd said. "We'll have a patrol car drive by your house a few times tonight. If you see anything that doesn't look right, you call 911."

I collapsed in my chair and grabbed my phone without any idea who to call. 911?

———

None of the Preying Hands' victims ever managed to dial 911. They'd never seen him coming. He purchased the chloroform illegally years before and stored it in steel drums we thought were full of photography chemicals. When those women awakened, he told them what he was going to do. "Once she's bound, I never lie to her," he confided to the prison psychologists.

Despite his moniker, he didn't like to use his own hands. A ligature offered more control. He gently wrapped something personal around their necks like a stocking or belt or bra—once, a taffeta dress. Eleven pounds of pressure on the carotid artery rendered a person unconscious in ten seconds. He was so precise that fractured hyoids or broken necks never disfigured his victims.

When Jeff Nelson, the journalist, interviewed him in prison, Harvey Dean Kogan said he loved the colors in their faces as they died: azure, light sky, cobalt blue, and even indigo. Capillaries burst in pinpoint splashes of red on their eyelids or cheeks. The jagged petechiae in their irises were like fireworks as their eyes faded and the last bit of breath sighed away.

But the Preying Hands' real joy came after death. He lingered for up to five hours in the victim's apartment or house, draining the body in a bathtub, measuring and sawing off appendages. He carefully cut so the ligature marks on their necks wouldn't show. If the hemorrhages had been massive, he covered them up with the victim's own makeup. An hour or more could be spent just on lighting. He had to get just the right angles and intensity, sometimes using windows or shaded lamps or, once, covering a handheld flash with a white shirt to soften the intensity. Most of the time he'd already composed the scene in his mind and had picked out the props. But each element had to be arranged at just the right angle. He claimed to experience a kind of bliss while he created his shot. "All your senses jingle and jangle," he said. Afterward he prolonged the ecstasy in the darkroom of his photo shed. "That's when I truly possess her."

———

The rest of the morning I stewed over the night before and searched the internet. Harvey Dean Kogan's fans liked to brag. But there were scores of sites and thousands of acolytes. I got through a third of them and still found no mention of us. By lunchtime my stomach was so pent up that eating was impossible. I took a walk outside by the fake pond. I didn't feel any better when I returned.

A message from Vanessa was waiting for me. She wanted a chat in her office—not a good omen. When I got there, she asked me to close the door. I sat in front of her desk. I felt like a kid in the principal's office.

"What's wrong with Poderovsky?" she said.

I was sick of tiptoeing around her. "He's getting divorced."

Her nostrils pinched. "You don't know that. There's absolutely no reason to even bring that up."

"Come on, Vanessa. Chad will be all over this."

Her small face sagged into a frown that combined disappointment and resolution. "Then you have to convince the Credit department that it's not an issue. That's your job, you know."

The rumor was that the chairman had given Vanessa a year to boost loan growth. By the time this deal blew up, her fingerprints would have disappeared. "William brought in that dog," she'd say. "Didn't he know what kind of reputation that family has?"

Vanessa sighed and stared at the antique shelves that held books like *A Winning Team* and *Where is Your Value?*

"A divorce is the first thing Chad will suspect," I said.

A tight white line encircled her mouth. The pearl bracelet rattled. "William, Charles only wants people who can make this bank grow."

Vanessa liked to pretend that Charles was making the threats. Our chairman ran our bank according to two immutable formulas: Loan Growth and Return on Equity. Anyone who didn't make both equations hum was shoved to the street.

"My numbers are above plan," I said.

She shook her head sadly. "Our employees need to perform way beyond plan. Like Bob Morgan. That's who your model should be."

I was so tired the words came out before I could stop myself. "Bullshit Bob?"

She drew back and frowned at my indiscretion. "Charles is going to make him an SVP."

Senior Vice President Bob. One of the unpleasant truths in banking is that expertise is cheap. Only people who make sales get promoted. And Bob could sell anything to anyone.

Vanessa leaned as far forward over the desk as her petite frame permitted. "I know you can do this. I tell Charles you've started executing all the right strategies."

That was supposed to intimidate me: my boss having to defend me to the chairman. But after the night before, her threats no longer made me wince. "I appreciate you looking out for me," I said.

Vanessa always offered a carrot after she pressured someone. Today she volunteered to transfer some of her clients to me. "Just get Poderovsky done," she said.

I wasn't immune to bribery—I needed the loan volume. And if Poderovsky's loan went belly up because of the divorce? That was several paychecks and maybe a bonus into the future. I just needed time. Time to find this freak.

"My clients will be glad they finally have someone competent covering them," she said.

Instead of her? I couldn't even respond to that kind of false modesty.

"You always behave like the perfect banker, don't you?" she added. "But toeing the line isn't going to get you noticed here. You have to push the limits. I think you're capable of much more."

All CEOs squeezed their reports. But Vanessa was a master. Sometimes her words were as dense and multilayered as haiku. You'd leave her office feeling both supported and afraid. I sometimes wondered what she was like at home. She'd exiled her daughter to boarding school but her husband often showed up at the bank. Bernie was technically an accountant. At social events he stood silently beside her. It was only when he slipped over to the bar that I got a taste of his wit.

"She's given me an extra foot of leash tonight," he once told me, his eyes expanding mischievously. "No choker if I'm good."

Vanessa was staring at me. "Is there something going on in your life?"

How did she know? I shook my head too hard. "I just didn't sleep well," I said. At least that was true.

"I know you'll be smart about this." She reached for the phone and fiddled with some papers. I was dismissed. As I left her office, she yelled, "Harry. How *are* you?"

A year earlier, at my interview, Vanessa had nodded and exclaimed at each of my morsels of insight. At the time I was toiling seventy hours a week at a mega-bank and her words had resonated for days. "No bus lines in front of our tellers," she'd said. "When clients come into our office, the first thing they get is a smile." I soon discovered that smiles were a kind of language to Vanessa. They could radiate delight and laughter, or disapproval and menace. She'd gaze at clients as if they were the most interesting people in the world. But when an employee displeased her, her eyes hardened and her smile became as sharp as a knife.

I returned to my office and closed the door. I sat and let the exhaustion pour through me. A message blinked on my phone. Reluctantly I hit the replay button and braced for the electronically disguised voice. But the caller was Lawrence Massy, my old prospect that Bullshit Bob had been talking to. In his rich baritone, Lawrence said, "William, I'm so sorry. I thought you'd be at the meeting today." He sighed. "Could you come out to the house tomorrow morning? I finally need to borrow some money. And William...please don't bring Bob."

Doctors didn't have time for salesmen. Particularly Lawrence Massy. He wanted his banker to provide quick diagnoses and prescriptions, the same way he managed his patients. Maybe I didn't need Poderovsky's bad deal after all. No one was a more perfect banker for Massy than I was. I was whistling as I went through my inbox.

In the middle of the pile was a plain brown envelope with no return address. For several seconds, I didn't touch it. Grabbing a Kleenex, I picked up the envelope and cut open the bottom edge. A photograph fell out.

I steeled myself for a picture of my family. But the photograph was a glossy black-and-white image of a can of Budweiser. This picture didn't display any of the Preying Hands' exquisite staging and lighting. Even the centered framing was amateurish. But I couldn't take my eyes from the dish drainer next to the beer can. It looked like the one in our kitchen.

I grabbed my phone. Punched in the number for Jill. She was in the middle of parent-teacher conferences and her cell skipped to voicemail. "Don't walk in the school parking lot by yourself," I said. "Under any circumstances."

I called the Haven, Polly's restaurant. The hostess said Garth and Frieda were sitting at a table right in front of her. Polly was prepping in the kitchen.

My family was safe.

9

PART OF MY FAMILY'S shame is that the Preying Hands started the serial killer "murderabilia" market. Fans began purchasing his pictures soon after he went to prison. They revered him as a genius at technique and maintained that his photos demonstrated a "raw yet sophisticated power." His pictures must have inspired Elmer Wayne Henley, a man who tortured, raped, and murdered twenty-eight teenagers. Henley's pen pals curated the first public auction of his landscapes. Those sales led to others—a rendering of tulips by Charles Ng, psychedelic paintings with crosses and swastikas by Charlie Manson, and poetry by Jeffrey Dahmer. Many aficionados don't have the money to collect the "art" of famous killers. But they can still buy painted greeting cards, prison wall calendars, and murder crime scene photos from other, less notorious murderers. I think owning something created by a killer empowers people. They want to feel their own darkness without unleashing it.

Some of these fans think the Preying Hands is an icon. For college credit, they listen to learned "scholars" theorize about his "complex psychology" at the Expo of the Depraved in Las Vegas. They read academic essays that analyze how his images referenced famous old pictures, or why he only photographed one of his victims in color. Murder tourists can trek to the Murder Museum in Chicago to study replicas of his photography hutch and our "haunted" trailer house. I've seen that recreated Redman doublewide. It's so accurately detailed that I had to flee to a men's room to recover.

Even museums own Harvey Dean Kogan's work. The Chicago Institute of Art purchased a photo of a trestle bridge's skeleton shadow rippling over the Chicago River. "We don't exhibit corpse photographs," the Institute proclaimed. Of course, Harvey Dean Kogan's notoriety had nothing to do with that purchase, did it? The Museum of Architecture owns another photograph. It features a barn roof destroyed by fire, the endless sky glowing through the charred latticed struts. I think the real reason the museum made that purchase was the title: *Abused Child*. It was the only photo my father named.

Online traders and brokers have made good money dealing in his "art." Some claim to have original negatives they're willing to unload for the low price of ten thousand dollars. They offer certified copies, complete with commentary about each kill and the careful planning that went into the "re-assemblies" and lighting choices. That leads to another disturbing question. How does a person become an expert in certifying the work of a serial killer?

Most people just go to the internet to take in the black-and-white pictures of women's severed heads, hands, and feet. They take virtual tours and role-play his killings. To participate, fans attest that they're at least twenty-one, the same cut-off age as on a porn site.

Over the years I've come to know more than I want to about his "art." My education began in high school, when I holed up in the public library to read about him. Sometimes my whole body shuddered from what he'd done. How had Mama, Polly, and I not suspected it? I'd go home telling myself I'd suffered enough. But after a day or two, or maybe a week, I'd come back to slide into the same carrel in the same shadowed corner. My fascination with my father's terrible secret life was both addictive and repulsive.

There were hundreds of articles. The journalists wrote little about the victims, usually not more than a few sentences. They saved their eloquence for my father, joyfully inventing nicknames like the Fiend of Photography and the Prince of Perversion. In one article, an interviewer claimed he was like John Wayne Gacy, Jeffrey Dahmer, and even Ted Bundy. He said my father was as empathetic as a water bug. Harvey Dean Kogan skimmed across the surface of emotion but felt nothing underneath. What did that say about the family who loved him?

I believed his compulsion had to be driven by a wound, something so deep and painful, so uncontrollable, that he hid it from us. Whatever it was, it was buried in his terrible photographs. I sent away for copies advertised in *True Crime* magazine. Month after month they arrived at our house in brown envelopes. I pored over those images, absorbing them in study hall, on busses, and at night in my room while everyone else slept. His pictures taunted his victims for cruelties to children that he mostly imagined. There was a sick playfulness about how he staged those women's heads, hands, and feet next to props, even about how he sometimes lit them at odd angles. But I found no answers. Only a frightening question. How could such a fiend seem like a normal father?

Eventually I discovered the non-victim photographs. In one that was published in *Newsweek*, a morose young boy of about six stared out the window of the Chicago Elevated train. He looked abandoned and without hope. Beside him, a blonde woman, her image blurred, had turned away. Some "experts" said that photo was an homage to the famous Robert Frank trolley picture. In Frank's photograph, the boy was older, wore a bow tie, and didn't appear sad. It was the black man behind the boy who stared out with melancholy. *Newsweek*'s caption below my father's photo said, "What kind of childhood?" They'd researched Harvey Dean Kogan's family and mentioned his terrible, abusive mother. But what most struck me about my father's version was how lonely that young boy looked.

In an image printed in *Photography Art*, Harvey Dean Kogan planted dolls on top of a six-year-old's cemetery plot, as if he felt that he'd never survived his own childhood. That awful period also seemed reflected in the shot that appeared in *Landscape Photography*, and was later purchased by the Chicago Institute of Art: the trestle bridge casting a skeleton shadow onto a river of roiling gray textures, the darkened sky above. His pain and isolation were obvious. And yet that childhood couldn't explain how he'd come to mutilate those women.

I suppose it was inevitable that I took up photography. It was a way to use his own medium to separate myself from him. My pictures would tell stories about life and survival, not death. They'd be in color. Of course, Mama rejected the idea and refused to buy me a camera. I had to make one disappear from the display counter of a photo shop downtown. My high school had a darkroom and I never needed to pay for development or bring my work home.

With a camera, I immersed myself in the lives of people without getting too close. At night, from behind the corners of buildings, I caught images of men and women happily kissing in front of bars and jumping into taxis, then people trudging home alone. In the Saturday pictures, children laughed and yelled at bowling allies and on the swings and monkey bars of parks. Sundays told more forlorn stories. Once I hid in the bushes across the street from a funeral home to shoot people's unbridled anguish and, in one case, the hidden joy as they emerged from the service.

My art teacher pinned up my work. "How did you get the eye?" he asked. He was always nudging me to talk about my past.

"No idea," I said.

Of course, Mama eventually learned what I was doing. She never asked how I obtained the camera or why I'd adopted that hobby. She didn't want to consider that kind of "mortal error." "When you look through that lens," she said, "find God's goodness."

"Is that the lens you saw Pop in?" I asked.

Mama rarely wept. That day she did.

10

THE UNIVERSITY HEIGHTS NEIGHBORHOOD announced itself in a giant, red, trolley-shaped billboard. On its main street, an alternative medicine shop and yoga studio faced a liquor store that might have been built in the seventies. You could get your hair styled at a hair salon or nip to the other corner to a little market with a psychedelic-yet-Disneyesque mural on its wall. The restaurants offered California food alternatives—Mexican vegetarian, gluten-free pizza, Thai, and even West Coast Abyssinian. But the queen of the restaurants was the Haven. The whole community hung out there to discuss local ordinances or to soak up cocktails while watching sports on TV. Dinner could be vegetarian, but pork was not a dirty word. The Haven celebrated the kind of California tolerance that the rest of the country mocked. Their baseball team was called the Switch Hitters.

My sister's pickup was parked outside the restaurant. I couldn't see anything through the white half-curtains and the stained-glass iguanas and donkeys on the window. I pushed open the front door. My children sat at a table near the kitchen. Frieda talked to a waitress wearing a baseball jersey, her hair spiked into a bleached-blonde hatchet blade. On the other side of the table, Garth puckered his lips and sounded the jets as his spaceship took off. I'd known from my telephone call that my children were safe. I still felt relief.

Frieda saw me and pointed to her teacup and a cookie on a flowered plate. "We're having a gluten-free tea party," she said.

"Caffeine-free too," the waitress said. She nodded and her bladed hair cut the air. Her skateboard leaned against the chair next to them.

"It's a *fabuloso* party," Frieda said. She was soaking up Spanish words almost as fast as numbers.

Garth's voice made an explosion. His ship took off from the lines of knives and forks. Next to him, a cook in a tight muscle shirt flew a plastic superhero from a pile of coffee mugs to Garth's mother ship. Is there a more wonderful place than a seven-year-old's imagination? Until my father was arrested, I'd also lived in that world of pretend.

Polly's restaurant welcomed families, particularly those with children. A padded floor in the corner was surrounded by a plastic barrier. Inside its confines, wooden boxes brimmed with coloring books and crayons. She thought that outlawing tips would further heighten the family atmosphere. Sharing the 18 percent service fee with the kitchen would improve the cooking and transform the waiters and waitresses into "food ambassadors." Instead, her staff grew most animated when they played with the kids or talked about art, local politics, or the Padres. Getting the food out was a low priority.

Thin arms encircled me from behind. I turned to give my sister a peck on the cheek. She'd bleached a fringe of her hair blonde and it looked like a single bright flame.

"Staying late to count all the bank's money?" she asked. When I didn't answer, her smile froze.

I followed Polly. Her running shoes padded through the swinging door into the kitchen. We passed the great stoves with their sixteen burners, then the scrubbed counters filled with chopped vegetables and blocks of cheese. The draining boards for curing bacon stood near the back door opposite the walk-in fridge. She heaved open the big steel portal and closed it behind us. The fridge was the only private place in her restaurant. Racks ran along each of its four sides and slabs of ham and beef hung down from the ceiling in the back. She draped paper towels over the cold metal of two empty shelves. We sat next to bins of butter, sauces, and dressings.

"Tell me what happened," she said.

I retold what had happened the night before, then showed her the photograph of the Budweiser can my stalker had sent to the bank. I didn't mention that the dish drainer in the photo was the one in our kitchen. As soon as she learned that, she'd be camping out at our house with a loaded pistol.

Polly shivered. She fingered the double-bladed axe of her labrys necklace, her symbol of strength. "The beer can photo must be a copy of his," she said.

"Pop's?"

"Don't call him that."

"What do I call him then?"

"Asshole. Cocksucker. Satan. Look, some nutcase dug up one of his pictures from some perverted website."

But the composition was all wrong, the lighting amateurish. I kept quiet.

She rose and hugged herself. Her wrinkled hands seemed to have become old overnight. She turned and her head sank to one of the metal shelves. But she didn't cry. I hadn't seen my sister weep since she was thirteen.

I stood up and gave her a hug. She pushed me away and the old guilt rushed through me. My whole life, I'd never been able to protect my big sister from what our father did.

Even now, the memory floods over me—Polly about twelve watching *Star Trek* beside Pop, his hand enveloping the peanut butter jar, their two spoons inside. Three kittens meow on the porch. Pop fetches a dish and pours some milk out of a half carton from the fridge. Opening the screen, he kneels in his dungarees on the stoop. His bull shoulders are as high as I am. He coos in his high voice. As the kittens slurp the milk, he raises a burlap bag from outside the door.

Pop thrusts the kittens into the bag. They wail and thrash inside. Now he's standing, huge and grinning, a hank of blond hair flopped over his forehead. Polly and I are yelling. "But they'll be happier at the park," he says. His amber eyes are as unblinking as a dog's. Walking away, he pulls a red apple from his pocket and takes a crunching bite.

Years later, Polly told me what happened—and that Mama had refused to believe it. Polly circled back to secretly follow Pop. He carried the kittens out behind his photography shed and dumped the bag into a barrel. When he lit it, they screamed like children.

"I can still smell the gasoline," Polly told me.

11

I DROVE TO JILL'S school. Frieda and Garth walked inside with me to the crowded gymnasium. There, among the parents and teachers, Jill leaned forward in a somber discussion with a worried mother and father. I texted her a reminder to walk to her car with a male teacher.

We returned home and, for a half hour, I retreated into our bedtime ritual. Lately Frieda had grown fond of my wooden-handled brush. She insisted I use it on her *pelo* so it would look more "shiny." Then the questions. How many hairs were on the brush? How many hairs on her head? How many on my head?

I managed to slip in with Garth before he fell asleep. We lay together on his bedspread of superheroes. Our boy was so quiet compared to his sister. "How's school?" I asked.

"Fine." His soft voice barely registered.

I rose to my elbow. "What's going on, big guy?"

He sighed. "Nothing."

I lay back beside him and stared up at the glow-in-the-dark constellations on the ceiling. What had he seen?

"Kyle wants me to sleep over," he said.

I wedged my arm under his head. His grandfather also was a bed-wetter. It's one of the strongest markers for serial killers. But lots of normal people also wet the bed as children.

"You know, I had accidents at night when I was your age." Sometimes a lie is the kindest gift to a child.

"You did?" His voice rose.

"Sure did."

"Did Hulk Hogan wet the bed?"

"He might have."

Garth pushed himself up. I couldn't see his face, but I knew he was puckering his lips in thought, his eyes crinkled like his mother's. At last he laid his head back on the pillow. Soon his breaths eased into long waves. I closed my eyes. Garth had his own seven-year-old terrors.

My father sometimes lay in bed with me, his legs stretching over the end of the mattress. Because I loved cowboys, he called me Illinois Tex. Some nights he sang to me to soften the dark and I smelled the wood shavings on his clothes and the developer chemicals on his hands. Outside our trailer, a chorus of crickets accompanied his soft tenor voice. He said he could hear frogs and beetles singing with him, then the raccoons clapping their paws. He could hear the goodness beating inside my heart. When I think about those nights, I believe a part of him was kind and that, once, he reflected God as perfectly as Mama had imagined.

After I left Garth's room, I slipped outside the front door to stare at the night. Only a few stars flickered through the clouds. The air felt damp with the promise of rain. For a few minutes I tried to extend the night's calm.

I heard crickets.

———

By the time Jill arrived home, I was pacing through the kitchen. We sat across from each other at the table.

"This freak sent me a photo," I said.

It took her a few seconds to make the connection. "Oh my God."

"A can of beer," I said.

Her head jerked back. She must have remembered that I'd asked her about beer that morning. "Just a picture of a beer can?"

"You might need a glass of wine," I said.

When she'd poured a generous Chablis, I held her hand on the table. She silently listened. I told her what had happened the night before, except for the can of beer inside our house. I couldn't. Not yet.

After I'd finished she wrenched her hand away. "Are you crazy? How could you go to the park with a loaded gun? Why the hell didn't you tell me?"

"I didn't want to scare you."

"And what are you doing now?"

Jill strode to the kitchen counter. She squinted through the little window above the sink at our dark backyard.

"The police are doing drive-bys," I said.

She sat back down at the table. "Listen, you can't cut me out. No matter how bad it gets. You hear me?"

That was the theme of our marriage: facing things together. In our eight years we'd fought plenty, but I'd never slept on the couch. Jill had spent many nights alone with her parents, but not because she was angry. No matter what happened, we scrapped our way through it. She deserved to know the rest.

But admitting calamity had always been difficult for me. I grew up in a family that believed you didn't talk about bad things. Giving words to those thoughts gave them the power to make you sick. We kept our misfortunes to ourselves and denied their existence.

I fought my impulse to say nothing. Keeping Jill in the dark wasn't going to make my tormentor disappear. I took a breath. I told her about the beer can beside our dish drainer.

Jill's arm shook but her eyes boiled. "That bastard was in our house?"

I nodded.

"While we slept?"

"He'll never get in here again," I said.

She stared at me, shook her head, and walked to our bedroom. The door clicked shut. I put my head in my hands.

She returned five minutes later. Glaring at me, she set down the revolver on the table. "It's time you learned how to shoot," she said.

12

MAMA NEVER ACCEPTED THAT I'd inherited my father's insomnia. "You're not going to spend your life creaking around at night," she'd said. One of many things she was wrong about. For three hours I combed through my father's photos and the serial killer sites. The Preying Hands' work was everywhere, but I didn't find an image of a lone beer can.

I slumped on our nubby couch in the dark, the pistol in my lap. Every car light beam stabbed through the blinds. Every shift and tick in the house made me flinch. At three o'clock in the morning, I resorted to a dose of bourbon and some puffs of marijuana.

The next morning, I tried to rouse myself with a giant mug of coffee. My stomach ached from adrenaline, yet my mind crawled. I wanted to call in sick. But Lawrence Massy had asked me to discuss a deal at his house, a deal that might make Vanessa back off. I followed Jill's car to school and watched as she parked next to the empty space assigned to Elizabeth Morton. I sat alone in my Camry. The building's glass door opened and closed.

Soon I was driving up the hills surrounding La Jolla. I took in the big palms and pine trees and the high walls and hedges that insulated these homes from the rest of the world. Up here even the air felt professionally cooled. The owners kept their lawns emerald green and only planted sage brush and cacti for decoration. Some of these houses could see the ocean swell all the way to Mexico, where the gardeners, nannies, and tradespeople came from.

Dr. Massy's white English Tudor stood behind a vine-covered wall. When I turned into the entrance, the electronic gate swung open. I followed the unistone driveway past the carport where he'd parked his black Maserati. The last time I'd visited him was more than a year earlier, when I'd still toiled at my other bank. In the interim he'd sculpted the yard to match his neighbors' estates. A terra cotta brick walkway bisected purple lilacs and white flowering pear trees.

Massy waited outside a beveled glass and mahogany door. In his early fifties, he was always fastidiously groomed. Today he wore a custom-tailored shirt with ruby cuff links that matched the cherry-colored frames of his glasses. He grinned and slapped me on the back, the cuff link digging into my shoulder. "William, it has been too damn long."

He led me inside in short, careful steps, as if balancing on a ledge. In the living room, an acrylic painting took up most of a cream-colored wall. The painting's yellow letters proclaimed *Peace = Mind*. Massy abhorred violence—even football. As I followed him, I remembered Harvey Dean Kogan telling a reporter when he'd reached his own blissful state of mind: photographing his victims.

Massy pushed open French doors at the back of the house and stepped under the archway to the patio. Flowers draped the herringbone-patterned brick walls beside a saltwater pool. It was the kind of expensive landscaping that a thriving ophthalmology practice could pay for.

He leaned into me and said, "Do you want to know the secret to a beautiful yard?" He put his finger to his lips. "A landscape designer."

We sat at a teak table under a yellow awning on chair pads that would never get old enough for the sun to fade. He glanced down and drew his head back.

"My, you really must do something about those shoes. You might as well tramp around in a couple of boxes." Massy always wore hand-crafted Italian loafers.

"I'm a banker," I said. "It's part of the uniform."

"That car doesn't help either. It looks like something a college student would drive."

"It's practical. I don't like to waste money."

Massy slipped a pink handkerchief from his shirt pocket and polished the lenses of his glasses. "Are you trying to give me a message? That you'll also be careful about *my* money?"

I smiled as if he'd seen through my subtlety.

Massy slid a folder across the table. On top of piles of tax statements, a diagram showed a trust in the Bahamas owning a corporation and a labyrinth of interlocking limited liability companies. Without even looking at the details, my body deflated. Chad would only draw one conclusion from that diagram: Massy's ownership structure was a warren of lawyer tricks to shield him from creditors. At my other mega-bank, Massy hadn't needed any offshore entities. Something had gone wrong.

"Let's not make the obvious complicated, shall we?" he said. "Malpractice liability."

I looked up and tried to appear enthused. "Excuse me?"

"In my profession, one slip means that some swindler will try to grab every stick I have. So I own everything in the Bahamas."

Malpractice insurance was just an *hors d'oeuvre* for the ambulance chasers who'd go after Massy. But if his assets were domiciled in the Bahamas, they'd have to sue him there. An almost impossible process.

"It's a shame, but when you see so many colleagues brought down, you have to give up believing in karma."

"Or at least hire an attorney to protect you from it," I said.

Massy chuckled and slipped his glasses back on. "Monique really would love that bit of humor. I'm getting married, you know."

I hadn't known. In the living room, I'd seen pictures of a striking redhead filling a mahogany hutch. The new fiancée. I'd soon have to restrain myself from wincing at the alliteration of Monique Massy. Hopefully he'd close on the loan before the wedding. That way I wouldn't have to get her to guarantee the loan. "That's wonderful news," I said.

He gave me a thin smile and passed over the second folder. The pages inside detailed the deal he wanted me to finance. One of his competitors was selling his practice after a lawsuit came perilously close to destroying him. Massy would use the loan proceeds to buy the doctor's customer list.

"I don't think he'll have time to spend it all playing golf," he said. "He's another cream-filled and glazed Midwesterner. The man must weigh over three hundred pounds."

He passed me a folder with pictures and financial figures for the collateral, a storage facility in Julian, a tourist town in the mountains northeast of San Diego. Massy's balance sheet was a jewel: little debt and lots of liquidity, progressively more equity in each of the three periods shown. He earned more in a year than I made in ten. In my head, I calculated a few liquidity, debt, and cash flow ratios. The numbers were beautiful. Who cared how much he overpaid for the client list? Even Chad the Impaler was going to like this.

The Impaler. I almost shivered.

Massy gazed at the blue water lapping softly in the pool. "I hope you'll excuse me for saying this, but I wouldn't want to take a deep dive in your colleague *Bob's* pool."

"Bob is a very aggressive marketer," I said. "He brings in a lot of business."

"Do you know what he said? Your competitors would poke out their own mothers' eyes for a deal."

Had Bob forgotten that he was talking to an ophthalmologist? "Sometimes his humor gets carried away," I said.

"When I asked him about his protege, you know what he said? 'At least Ambrose is pretty.'"

I'd warned Bob about the dangers of his loose, sexist talk. There hadn't been a complaint for months.

"Thank God Monique wasn't there," Massy said.

Yes, thank God. Then it hit me. Lawrence Massy was finally getting married. I had a strange thought: What would a father like Massy have been like?

I followed him back through the house and out the front door. After all that effort at my prior bank, then a year of solicitation at this one, I was finally winning Massy's business.

Nothing compared with driving back to the office with a deal. All was possible. I could smash my bank targets, win big bonuses, and beat out Bullshit Bob for the annual sales award—even buy a new house. I reached the tenth floor and was strolling under the cupola toward banking when my phone rang. Jill's number.

"There's a camera in Garth's book bag," she yelled. "Pictures."

I couldn't breathe. I stepped inside the large conference room. Collapsed hard on a chair. "Were the pictures ..."

"She's alive, William. Some model with a goddamn dog collar around her neck. A dog collar."

Somehow I managed to keep my voice calm. "Stay at school until I get there," I said and hung up.

I pushed through the French doors to banking and lurched to my office. My arm shook so much I could barely punch in the number to Officer Mortimer. The call went to voicemail. All I could do was yell a message into the phone.

The name came to me after I disconnected. Winnie Dover. Harvey Dean Kogan had followed her home because she blew up at a child in a mall. Dover lived with a German shepherd in a building on the south side of Chicago. The next afternoon Kogan walked through the unlocked stairwell entrance and up to the third floor. The dog snuffled on the other side of her apartment door, but Kogan was prepared. He slipped meat laced with sleeping pills underneath. A bump key opened the lock.

The picture is infamous. Winnie Dover's severed head rests on top of the dog collar as if she's wearing it. Each of two dog dishes contain one of her feet. The dead animal itself is lying down and intact. One paw grasps the loop of the leash attached to Winnie Dover's collar. A blown-up, pink bubble of gum protrudes from its mouth. When Kogan sent the photo to the *Chicago Tribune*, the accompanying note said, "Sorry about the dog."

And now his disciple was hunting my son.

13

A Detective Lund called back five minutes later. They had new information. Could I come to the police station right away?

I bolted from the office. My Camry ran every yellow light. If the police stopped me, I'd demand an escort.

The station, a six-story modern building with microwave dishes on top, was on a part of Broadway I never visited. I threw some quarters into a parking meter and rushed inside. In the reception area, people filled out forms around a blue plastic table with a haggard plant. Others lined up at the front counter. Two men stepped from behind it as if they'd been waiting.

"Detective Kevin Lund," the taller of the two said in a deep, radio announcer voice. With his perfectly combed gray hair and crisp gray pinstripe, he looked more like a private banker than I did.

The other, younger man's head was as big as a boiler, his crown buzzed down to a stubble. But his eyebrows bristled with hair. He stuck out a meaty hand and said, "Ben Hempel." His hoarse voice sounded as if it came from a cement mixer.

"Is my boy in danger?"

"Not yet," Hempel said.

I let myself relax a little. These men would have ideas about how to keep my son and the rest of my family safe.

The detectives nodded at some fellow officers and led me to the back of the building. We boarded an elevator to the fourth floor and a door that said *Homicide*. I stopped and made sure I'd read it right. "Has this man killed someone?"

Hempel shrugged his thick shoulders. "We'll talk about that."

We'll talk about that?

The Homicide Department was a sea of cubicles with half-walls. Organization charts of suspect photos overlaid two of the windows. Both the men in the photos and the detectives sitting at the desks grimly stared at me.

Lund led me back to an interview room the size of a cave. Old paneling rose up half the wall, with the rest painted a Girl Scout green. We sat at a pressed-wood table, a smudged whiteboard mounted on the green wall in front. The erased writing must have prompted the box of Kleenex on the table. My leg began to jitter.

"Nothing's happened to my family, right?" I said.

The wrinkles around Lund's eyes and mouth softened his bony face. "We sent an officer to keep an eye on them." Compared to Hempel, his deep voice was like honey.

Hempel, jacketless and chomping on a piece of gum, pushed in an office chair on castors. Three cans of Coke and some files sat on the seat. He gave a Coke to each of us. My can was warm, almost hot.

Lund frowned. "For God's sake, at least give Mr. McNary a cold one."

Hempel grimaced and collected the cans. "I just grabbed the nearest ones," he said.

"It doesn't matter," I said. "Really."

"Won't take a minute," Hempel said. He hurried out the door.

Lund said, "He has the strange idea that people like their soft drinks hot."

I gave him a courtesy smile. "Why aren't we talking about what happened?"

Lund held up his hand. "Not until Ben gets back."

We waited. My legs shook. My feet fidgeted under the table. Lund turned his gold-filigreed ring, rubbed his gold silk tie. His thoughts seemed far away.

"I need to know what's going on," I said.

Lund gave me a pained half-smile. "We have to do our interviews in teams these days. Detective Hempel must have had to visit the men's room."

Patience, I told myself.

At last Hempel pulled open the door. He gave each of us a freezing can of Coke, then picked up the files from the rolling chair seat and set them on the floor. One of the files was thick. They'd been chasing this man for a long time.

Hempel sat. In the small room, the cedar and rosemary scent of Lund's cologne bled into the minty odor of Hempel's gum. The combination unsettled my stomach.

On my left, Lund said, "Take off your coat. No need for suits around here."

"Can we please get going on this?" I said.

Lund nodded. He stood, shucked his own pinstripe jacket, and draped it over the chair. His gold cuff links flashed, then his ring. He sat. Popped the tab on his Coke can and drank. He looked as if he were relaxing on a coffee break. My suit coat remained on.

Lund pointed to the black bubble on the ceiling in the corner. "That's a camera. New policy. We're taping all our interviews now. That way we can use them in court, if we need to." He pointed to the doorway behind me. "This is only a discussion. You can leave anytime you want through that door."

That was a strange way to start the interview. The door was opened to a slit.

"Tell me why I'm sitting in the Homicide Department," I said.

"We'll get to that," Lund said.

We'll get to that? "Look, he broke into my house. He put pictures in my son's book bag. Terrible pictures. I need to know what kind of danger we're in."

On my right, Hempel took a few chomps of gum. He said, "Slow down and have a drink. When you're stressed, the worst thing you can do is get dehydrated."

I remembered another Coke in a glass bottle. I'd sat on a rolling chair, my feet not touching the floor. Those policemen also had smiled and reassured me.

I didn't touch the can.

"Let's start at the beginning, shall we?" Lund said. "For my benefit. Tell us about why you went to Kate Sessions Park."

Finally.

I told them about the phone call, the drawing of a hand jammed under my car's windshield wipers, then the emailed link and the trip to the park. "I thought I could talk some sense into this guy," I said. "Persuade him to leave us alone."

Hempel raised those overgrown eyebrows. "At least you were armed when you went there."

63

That made me wonder how dangerous my stalker was. I'd been a fool to drive off to that park by myself.

Lund said, "Fortunately, you never had to take out the revolver, right?"

I'd never said I was armed. "I didn't get out of my car. No one showed up."

"You just sat there all alone in the park?" Hempel's blue eyes stared into mine, his mouth slowly munching. His Coke sat on the table in front of him, untouched.

"I gave up and went home. This was taped to my door." I dug out the photo of Leslie Miller's dismembered body. "Is this what he wants to do to my family? Make us into one of the Preying Hands' photographs?"

Their faces were as stiffly blank as mannequins. Hempel pulled latex gloves over his thick hands and slipped the picture into a plastic bag. He turned and squinted at me. "You didn't see a single person at the park? A dog walker or some kids, maybe?" His voice was like sandpaper.

"You already asked me that." Both legs were fidgeting. I shifted in my seat. I knew I had to calm down, but I couldn't.

"We have our own protocol we have to follow," Lund said in that calm, deep voice. "I'm sure it's frustrating to you. But it's our way of jogging your memory. Maybe you'll think of something that will help identify this man."

I wondered if they already had a suspect. But I couldn't tell from their faces. "What about my son? A photo on my door is one thing. But putting a picture like that in a child's school bag? It's a threat."

"You're upset, Mr. McNary. So maybe you didn't hear me before." Now Lund's voice was almost creamy. "We've got an officer looking after your family. He's with them at school."

"How did you know which school?"

Lund interlaced his fingers on the table. The sun had mottled the tops of his hands but his nails were filed into perfect white crescents. "You told us."

Maybe I'd mentioned the school when I'd talked to him earlier, or when I'd called. I couldn't remember. My mind was bouncing and spinning.

Hempel drew himself closer across the table. "I still don't understand something. If you changed your name and kept your dad a secret, how did this stalker find you?"

I raised my palms. "What difference does it make?"

"Elizabeth Morton is a teacher at your wife's school, isn't she?" Lund asked.

Both men studied me. My insides twisted. "What about her?"

Even Hempel's sigh sounded hoarse. He said, "We found her body in Kate Sessions Park. It was cut up in pieces."

I looked at Lund's thin, furrowed face, the gray hair perfectly parted, then at Hempel's wider face, his thin mouth chewing. Lund, then Hempel, then Lund. Nothing about their expressions contradicted what Hempel had said. My arm started to shake.

It hit me then. "I'm a suspect."

They drew back at the same time. Lund's shirt was so starched that it barely dimpled. He leered as if I'd said something crazy. Hempel scratched the stubble on his head.

Lund said, "Look, William, with TV, everyone gets a false impression about detectives. They think if we're talking with you you're a suspect. That's all fiction. You have no idea how many people we interview in a case like this. It could end up hundreds. What we do is collect as much information as possible. We talk to all the people near the crime scene."

I worked in a world where the sales pitches were more convincing. Unless they'd arrested someone, how could I *not* be a suspect? I should have bolted from that little box right then. But I hadn't done anything wrong.

"William, easy," Lund said. "We're just questioning you."

He bent down to pick up a notebook on his side of the table. I hadn't seen it when we came in, but it must have already been there. He flicked some pages.

"You're our sixth interview today," Lund said. "And that's just us. We've got four other detectives working this case."

"Have you got a suspect?"

Both men silently stared at me, their faces as still as photographs. This interview had never been about Garth—only Elizabeth. They actually thought I could have killed her.

"Do you think Elizabeth Morton hurt that kid at school on purpose?" Hempel said.

My mouth opened and I gaped at them.

"What do you think?" Hempel said.

"The boy fell when he tripped her. When she got up, she pulled him up by his arm a little too forcefully. It was just a mistake."

Lund said, "Your wife worked with her. What did she think?"

"I just told you."

Hempel's big face crimped into a grimace. "Come on. Jill had to be at least a little pissed off at her."

I'd never told them Jill's name. "What the hell are we doing here?"

Hempel said, "Look, you were in the park. Your wife teaches at Elizabeth Morton's school. Of course we're gonna talk to you."

"What would your father have thought about her?" Lund said.

There it was. Even after thirty-one years, the police couldn't consider me without bringing in Harvey Dean Kogan. "You already know what he would've thought."

Someone knocked on the door. I looked up and a woman leaned through the opening. "The chief wants to see you."

Hempel said, "Tell him we'll be there in ten minutes."

He leaned down, picked up the thick file, and consulted it. He swiveled his big head like a turret. "Maybe you can help us understand something. Elizabeth was wrapped up in a garbage bag. And this bag"—he raised his dense eyebrows at me—"had your fingerprints on it."

I stopped breathing. My fingerprints were on the bag? How?

Lund said, "We took your prints off that can of Coke."

They'd given me a warm can just so I'd give it back.

"For the record, you told us you had a gun but you never pulled it out. Right?" Lund spoke as if he were confirming a harmless detail.

I'd never told them about the gun. This was some kind of trick. I stood. "I'm not a goddamn killer."

Lund felt the silk knot of his tie. He nodded. "You can leave, of course. You can also have an attorney—even if we have to pay for it. You don't have to tell us anything. But then we have to stop talking. We can't share what we've found."

Something about what he said sounded familiar.

"I don't see what the big deal is," Lund went on. "You already told us about the gun. And you registered it."

How did they know I'd registered it?

"It's public information," Hempel said.

They couldn't have known that I'd brought the gun to the park. They were making this up. I could see the ploy now. If I admitted to taking a weapon there, they'd accuse me of using it to make Elizabeth cooperate. But how did my prints get on the garbage bag? The answer came to me like one of Mama's "angel thoughts." The killer had taken a garbage bag from our house.

I slammed my hand on the table. "This son-of-a-bitch set me up!"

They flinched. Then stared at my hand as if it might hold a weapon.

Hempel said, "Let me tell you a few more details you'll want to hear. Park workers found the body this morning. The chief got the

DNA analysis through real fast. That's what happens when the vic is a young white schoolteacher." He flipped through pages in the file, slowly munching on the gum, the paper scratching. "Man, there're a lot of connections to you in here."

He read off a long list: my shoe prints, fresh rubber on the road that matched my Camry's tires, dirt in the wheelbase from Kate Sessions Park. So much evidence told me one thing—they were lying. The police couldn't have done all that analysis in one morning. They would have needed a search warrant. They were trying to rattle me so I'd confess that I killed Elizabeth.

"Hear us out, William," Lund said. "We've got a witness. I guess you didn't see him, but he saw you. He found it suspicious that you drove into the park after it was closed and took down your license plate. What's interesting is how fast you left. Why were you in such a hurry?"

I could explain. Explain it all. But I needed a lawyer first.

Hempel pointed to the Coke in front of me on the table. "Why don't you sit down and have a drink? You really need to take your time and help us think through this shit."

I glanced back at the open door. But my feet wouldn't move.

Lund leaned back in the chair and massaged his tie. "The way she was cut up looks like torture. That's called a 'special circumstance.' In California, they give you the needle for that."

Needle. My thoughts skittered: alone and strapped to a gurney; never seeing my children grow up; Garth and Frieda hiding their humiliation, denying I was their father.

Rage shot through my chest and shoulders. It shook my arms. "I didn't kill her!"

Hempel pulled a picture from the file. He stood, his jaw muscles bulging around his pinched mouth. He thrust the photo in my face. "Look at this."

In the blown-up picture, I made out a naked body on top of forest undergrowth. The body had no head. No hands and no feet. Bloody wounds gaped out where she should have had breasts.

My legs jerked and I stumbled. I hit the half-partitioned wall.

"What happened to her?" Hempel said. The blood in that photo slushed through his voice. "Tell us what happened."

My stomach turned. I bent over and Lund's manicured fingers slid a wastebasket under my face.

Gradually my stomach stopped churning. I no longer hyperventilated. Straightening up, I pushed myself away from the wood paneling and stared at the sickeningly green walls. My mouth tasted of stomach acid.

Both detectives sat in their chairs. The cedar smell of cologne mixed with the stench of my vomit. Lund twisted his gold ring. Hempel slowly unwrapped another piece of gum.

The picture lay on the table like an accusation. I'd die before I'd let my children think I was the Preying Hands.

I had to leave. Find a lawyer. Prove just how wrong they were. "With all your games, there's one thing you missed," I said.

"We're all ears," Hempel said.

"I'm innocent."

"Don't go," Lund said. "You won't have another chance to explain." Not a single gray hair had shifted on his head.

I shuffled toward the door. Opened it wider.

No one arrested me.

———

I don't remember reaching the Camry. My feet guided themselves across the traffic on Broadway. Inside the car, I gripped the wheel. I was the prime suspect for Elizabeth's murder. I could be thrown in prison for life. Or worse. A brownstone and stucco apartment building stretched up beside me. A plane glided above it, a nail in the blue sky. The plane descended to Lindbergh Field. Another took its place.

I needed to get to Jill's school. Make sure they were safe and tell her in person. Then find a lawyer.

A knock on the glass jolted me in the seat. Lund stood outside my window. Next to him, Hempel slowly munched on his gum. Two other men framed them. Policemen. They'd drawn their guns.

"Put your hands in the air where we can see them," Lund said.

My hands? What did they want with my hands?

"Put up your fuckin' hands!" Hempel shouted.

I raised my arms.

The door opened and the four men stepped back.

"Out of the damn car," Hempel said.

14

THE MORNING MY FATHER was arrested, our trailer smelled of bacon, scrambled eggs, and ripe apples. Polly had just taken her asthma pill, the pill we didn't talk about with people from our Christian Science Church. As usual, Mama slipped the bottle into the paper bag and hid it in the old wooden kitchen cabinet. She was thin then, her teeth jutting out like rectangles of chewing gum.

"No matter what happens, remember that God is your *real* father," Mama said.

Mama often told us we were the children of God so I didn't pay much attention to her. I watched her open the drapes and take a deep breath. She looked as if she were inhaling the light.

We heard the roar before we saw the five cars tear down our gravel driveway. The men yanked open the door of our doublewide and yelled at us to lie on the floor. "Where's Harvey Dean Kogan?" they shouted.

We stayed on that old floor for what seemed like hours, my head against the cool linoleum. Then a man led us outside to our yard. Lucky lay absolutely still in the shade beside Pop's photo shed. She should have been barking and growling.

"You killed my dog," I shouted.

A lady shook her head beside us. She was younger than Mama and her FBI hat looked like a Chicago White Sox cap. "Don't worry," she said. "We just gave her something to make her sleep."

I never saw Lucky again.

We had to get inside a blue van. The lady sat in the front cargo seat and I in the back between Mama and Polly. The upholstery smelled like cigarettes and I expected Mama to say something about the false pleasures of tobacco. But she just stared down at her clasped hands.

Through the van's windows, I counted six cars. Two men in identical blue windbreakers stooped to shine a flashlight at the concrete slab underneath our doublewide. Others shuffled over the yard and studied the grass as if searching for a lost diamond ring. A tall, gray-haired man raised up my broken cowboy action figure that Pop called "the one-armed gunslinger." Another climbed the ladder to scrabble inside my fort in the apple tree. Others tramped through the goldenrod that sidled against our property.

Mama had shut her eyes, lost inside her silent prayer. I put my hand on hers. "God will make it okay."

She gave me the kind of smile that only held back tears. Patting my hand, she said, "We need all your good thoughts today, Willy."

Polly said, "They took Pop away in handcuffs."

How could she say that? Polly, who held me when I fell and fought like a furious bird when anyone dared to pick on her. Why wasn't Mama declaring God's Truth about Pop?

The tall, gray-haired man plodded out of the photo shed, aiming each foot in front of the other. His gloved hands held a glass jar as if it were a bomb. I made out something floating in a liquid inside. It looked like a hand.

Polly lowered her head and her long hair covered her face. She pushed her palms against her mouth to muffle the sounds, but her shoulders trembled. Her fingers slid up her forehead and curled into tufts of brown hair. Her nails scratched her scalp.

The FBI lady in the front seat said, "This has nothing to do with you. None of this is your fault. Don't ever forget that."

Tears stained Mama's cheeks. "It's my fault," she said. "All of it."

How could Mama think it was her fault?

The truth hit me so hard I gasped. Mama's bad thoughts, her mortal mind, had caused Pop's arrest. If she had just reflected God, Pop wouldn't have been taken away.

The FBI lady's eyes turned hard and she stared at Mama. Later, I saw the whole town look at us with the same flinty crow's eyes. It was the "blaming" look.

15

HEMPEL REPEATED THE FAMILIAR words of the Miranda warning. One of the cops twisted my palms behind my back and the metal handcuffs bit into my wrists.

Lund, a foot from my face, said, "This is your last chance. We can help you if you come clean and tell us what happened."

I felt as if I were inside a hallucination. I shook my head. "Lawyer."

The two policemen maneuvered me across the street. Cars slowed. On the sidewalk, passersby stopped and gawked. We walked through the door to the front reception area, four cops and a killer. People looked up from their forms and the room grew silent. The two officers behind the front desk eyed me, their folded arms barely containing their disgust. Beside them stood a tall woman with short brown hair.

"I want a lawyer," I said to her.

The woman didn't say a word. Her gaze slid over me as if she were searching for something no one else could see.

We walked down a hallway. The elevator doors stood open while a policeman held down the button on the console. We descended to the basement floor. A man behind a counter asked questions that I only half registered. I signed a Miranda statement. Then on to the garage and an upraised cement slab in front of black-and-white police cars. Two policemen guided me to a chair. Its fake brown leather hissed under my body weight. They unlocked the handcuffs and made me shed my suit coat and roll up the sleeves of my shirt.

A policeman with a pockmarked face stared into my eyes. His ears jutted out below his shaggy hair. "I'll bet it feels different when somebody wants to take *your* blood, doesn't it?"

"You've got the wrong man," I said.

Hempel glared at the policeman who'd spoken. "Shut the fuck up." He turned to me, his blue eyes steady. "We got the right to draw blood because we arrested you."

For my own self-respect, I had to resist. "You said that you already had my DNA." I started to rise out of the chair.

Still chewing his gum, Hempel extended his blunt hand and shoved me back down. The man with the pockmarked face strapped my arms and chest to the chair. Another man tightened a rubber hose around my arm and flicked his finger against the vein on the inside of my elbow. He jabbed me and the blood drained into a tube at the end of a needle. Removing the tube, he attached another. Bound in that chair, I imagined him stacking the tubes on the concrete floor in a pyramid. I started to hyperventilate.

"Calm down, William," Hempel said. "We're almost done."

A whiff of rosemary and cedar. Lund's sun-splotched hand with the gold ring pressed my shoulder. "You'll get an opportunity for a lawyer ... after we've processed you."

They'd made a terrible mistake. I'd never done anything violent in my life. But it was too late for that.

When the man had finished drawing blood, Lund said, "Are you going to cooperate now?" His voice, the way he slightly tilted his head and raised his eyebrows, made him appear as if he were confronting an obstructive child. He waited until I nodded my head, then released the straps around my arms and chest.

I lurched shakily to my feet and Lund stood to the side. The four men watched me as if I were an animal they were herding from one cage to another. Lund directed me to a machine that looked like an ATM.

The pockmarked cop with the jutting ears rolled each of my fingers on a glass screen and my fingerprints appeared on a monitor. "Now we'll see all the dead women you've left your prints on," he said.

"I thought you already had these from the Coke can," I said.

"We like to have lots of prints. All your fingers."

"You won't find a damn thing," I said.

"Shut UP," Lund yelled. He glared at both of us.

The loudmouth, Lund, Hempel, and I strode through a door marked Office 138 and into a room with old linoleum floors and faded white wall tiles. A big, thick-necked policeman was waiting. He handed me a white plastic cup with some kind of powder inside. "You know what to do," he said.

I turned so they couldn't see me. Lund grabbed my shoulder and shook his head. "We have to witness it."

"I guess humiliation is part of the process," I said.

"We got no choice," Hempel said.

I pretended I was standing over a urinal.

After I finished, the big cop ordered me to spread my nostrils and open my mouth. Without touching me, he peered inside with a flashlight. I had to stick out my tongue and shift it from side to side, then scrape a cotton swab against the insides of my cheeks. He ripped open another package and removed what looked like nail files. A separate file scraped under each of my fingernails.

Another policeman stomped into the room with his cell phone against his ear. "So far so good," Lund said to him.

They were performing a ritual with my body, something they'd practiced over and over. I was the only one who didn't know the sequence. But I knew the last step. It was when my heart stopped.

The big cop unrolled a piece of white material resembling butcher paper and laid it on the floor. I stood on the paper.

Lund said, "We need you to take off your clothes."

By then I wasn't surprised. It was just another part of my official debasement. Still, I hesitated.

The pockmarked loudmouth rolled up his sleeves. "You guys hold him and I'll get his clothes off."

Hempel leaned into me and I smelled his minty gum. "Look, we have to do this. So you have a choice. Either you maintain your dignity, or we hold you down and yank off your suit. In which case, we're likely to tear something."

"Thanks for the choice," I said.

I undressed. Hempel folded my suit, shirt, and tie—even my underwear—and slipped them into a paper bag. I covered myself with my hands and stepped onto the blotter. It stuck to the undersides of my feet.

Something flashed. The thick-necked cop set down the camera and slipped on latex gloves. "I got to search your body," he said.

He ran his fingers behind my ears, then on my head until bits of loose hair fell to the white blotter. Backing up, he said, "Lift your balls."

Maybe there was a purpose to all this—to make me feel some of Elizabeth's suffering. Goose bumps broke out on my arms. The loud-mouthed cop smirked. I had to say something. Anything. But words had slipped out of my mind.

The big man picked up a knife about the size of a spoon. He ran its cold blade down my trembling arms and chest, down my groin and legs. Bits of residue fell from my body and stuck to the paper. I pretended I was in a dream. A dream where a policeman feathered a knife over my skin before he cut me apart.

"Bend over," he said.

———————

An hour later, a police officer handed me a thin white paper suit with paper ties in the back and no underwear. Then plastic booties. With both my hands and ankles cuffed, I shuffled past four scowling, cross-armed officers. We boarded a police car parked in the garage. Hempel and Lund sat in front on the other side of the car's mesh. We pulled forward. An iron gate opened.

Outside, TV cameras pointed at us. A man in a leather jacket stepped to within a hand-length of the car and pointed a camera at me. I twisted away, but it was too late. Garth and Frieda would see me on television. I pushed my face into my shoulder. I wouldn't let them see my tears.

The car drove through the unfamiliar neighborhood. In the sinking afternoon light, I saw a Salvation Army Center, then the Church of Steel Body Piercing and Tattoos. On the sidewalk, a woman in purple sweats lugged a guitar strapped across her back. The trolley clacked past a row of bail bond offices on C Street: red and blue neon signs, blaring yellow and red billboards. All the sights I'd have ignored only a day before. A block away stood the Westgate Hotel, where

Harry Dillard, an estate planning attorney, and I had sipped cabernet on antique couches next to gilded mirrors.

I thought of Elizabeth Morton: petite with shoulder-length, chestnut-colored hair. Every time I saw her, she'd said, "I love teaching kids." Then I remembered Harvey Dean Kogan's rusty saw, the same saw he used to cut metal fence posts. That was what the world would think I'd done to her.

Jill couldn't believe that, could she?

The patrol car stopped in front of a tall building with a façade of frosted glass cubes and an entrance marked *Sheriff's Intake*. An iron gate opened. We followed a bus with tinted windows and emblazoned with gold reflective stars. When the car stopped, Hempel opened the door. He and Lund walked on either side of me, my paper suit crackling, the manacles chafing my wrists and ankles. I stared down at the pavement. Watched my feet make each shameful, chain-jingling step. Someone on the bus shouted, "Why that motherfucker get to go first?"

A jail deputy joined us. I limped beside the three of them through two pneumatically locked doors that made me think of a spaceship. Then room after room of stainless steel counters, barred windows, and wooden benches with shackle rings. Hempel presented my sheaf of papers like a business card to each clerk. I posed for mug shots and answered endless questions about my health and prior injuries. Did I want to hurt myself? they asked. Good question.

I grew numb to the humiliation. With each stop, I felt stronger. Jill would learn what had happened and she and Polly would find a lawyer, a lawyer who spoke in words the men in here would have to listen to. Just a few more hours.

Eventually we met two burly deputies in green pants and khaki shirts. Their belts held canisters of pepper spray. The deputies riveted a yellow plastic band with a barcode and my picture to my wrist.

"This is where we leave you," Lund said. Now I saw the hatred lining his face, the rancor that he'd hidden beneath his pinstripe suit and honeyed voice. "This is a capital case so we're remanding you to county jail," he said.

My eyes bore into his. "I hope I get to see you after you learn what a mistake you've made."

"Save it," Lund said. His voice wasn't so melodious now.

Hempel edged his wide face and caterpillar eyebrows closer. "Just a little warning, my friend. The men in here don't like people who cut up schoolteachers. Some of them think that's as bad as child molesting. So watch your back. We want you to go to trial." He gave me a cruel smile.

The deputy with the shaved head led me to a cell with a heavy steel door and a thick safety-glass window. He fit in a six-inch brass key that looked like something forged for a medieval prison. The cell measured about six feet by eight from one white concrete wall to the other. A stainless steel sink and water fountain connected to the top of a stainless steel toilet. In here the same appliance handled both functions.

I sat on the room's bench. Alone at last, I wanted to lower my head and give in to desolation. But a video camera's plastic bubble stared at me. I wasn't going to let it see me come apart.

Something plastic hung on the wall. A phone. A sign above it said all calls would be monitored. The law required a free phone call. This had to be it. I picked up the phone and heard a dial tone. I dialed Jill's cell number. No answer. School was out so why the hell didn't she pick up? Reporters must have been hounding her. Maybe the police came to her class. Maybe Jill didn't *want* to talk with her husband.

I left a message. "Jill, Detectives ... ah, Kevin Lund and Ben Hempel. They've ... arrested me. I'm in jail." I closed my eyes and took a great breath. "It's about Elizabeth Morton. She's been … she's been murdered, Jill." I opened my eyes and stared at the locked door of the cell. "These men say they sent an officer to school. To keep all of you safe. But … but I don't … Just get to your father's house. And Jill, you better find me a lawyer."

I hung up and took a breath. Dialed another number. When Polly answered, I said. "I'm in jail."

"Jail?" Her hoarse yell sounded like a screech.

"They think I killed Elizabeth Morton."

"What?" She sucked in a wheezing breath. "It's a mistake."

I paced toward the back of the cell, but the short cord jerked the phone out of my hand. I picked up the receiver. "Her body was … cut up. It looks like what *he* would do."

The air shuddered in and out of Polly. She was trying to tamp down her oversized emotions.

"Look, I think he got inside our house."

"What?"

"You remember the picture of that can of beer? It was taken in our kitchen. Somehow he disabled the alarm."

"Fuck."

"What if this asshole wants me out of the way so he can … Just get Jill and the kids somewhere safe."

She inhaled and I heard the high-pitched whistle from her asthma. She was angry. That was when she was strongest.

"Look," I said, "you've got to fight for me. Can you do that?"

"Yes."

"Can you find me a lawyer?"

"I know … a good one."

"Tell Jill not to believe the news reports. Help her protect Frieda and Garth from all of this."

But how could our children go unscathed? Not after they learned their father was arrested for dismembering their mother's friend.

"It's starting." She took a scraping breath. "Again."

"You've got to hold yourself together."

"I'm on it." She hung up.

16

THIRTY-ONE YEARS BEFORE, IN order to stop the press from hounding us, one of my father's defense attorneys rented an apartment under a fake name. It was a two-bedroom unit buried in the basement of a brick building. The rooms remained in shadow all day, but Mama still shut the curtains. "Let's keep all those evil thoughts outside," she said.

"It's a little late for that," Polly said.

I was eight years old but still knew that Pop had done something terrible. We couldn't speak with him and Mama wouldn't even tell us where he was. At night, we were allowed to walk outside. Mama and Polly were so short and thin that the streetlights made our silhouettes look like triplets. We'd trudge past a *Sun-Times* or a *Chicago Tribune* in a coin machine and Pop's picture would stare out from the front page.

He looked huge, bigger and broader than the policemen who stood beside him. He seemed to be laughing at something I couldn't see. Mama wouldn't let me get close enough to make out more than the photo and the headlines. Once, THIRTEEN covered the top of the front page. Thirteen—my sister's age, the number of hearts in a deck of cards, twelve disciples plus Judas, the unlucky number thirteen. "Thirteen what?" I asked. That just made Mama's lips tremble and Polly's hands fist up. "Thirteen" was too dangerous to say out loud.

Every afternoon I slid a chair along the apartment's tiled floor, stood on it, and peeked through a crack in the curtains over the window. I counted the kids my age as they passed the gnarled oaks outside. They rode their bikes or scraped along the walk on skateboards. A basketball bounced forty-six times from one end of the block to the other. I couldn't say a word to them. If I played with those children, I might let my name slip. Someone might recognize me. Then the dreaded reporters would swoop onto our doorstep and aim their cameras at us. The reporters were the worst at spreading false beliefs, Mama said. If they found us, we'd have to move again. "It's like Anne Frank and her family," Polly said.

During our two weeks in that apartment, Polly and I didn't attend school. Someone had given Mama a story-problem book and, for an hour each day, I resolved a part of the world into numbers. Then I'd think about my dog Lucky and where she might be. I'd wonder if she missed me. In the afternoons, Polly and I lay on the floor in front of a dilapidated TV on a rickety stand. We watched cartoons and game shows and even episodes of *Family Ties* and *Highway to Heaven*. Mama made sure the Chicago news never reached us, even as she cooked macaroni or Oscar Mayer hotdogs in the little kitchen. We could be in the middle of a show, and if a bulletin mentioned Pop, she'd turn off the set.

One afternoon Mama made us sit down at the little kitchen table and lock hands. We recited the Lord's Prayer and then Mary Baker Eddy's Scientific Statement of Being.

"Don't tell me how Pop is the image and likeness of God," Polly said.

I expected to see Mama's explaining smile, the smile that said she was more patient than we were and we might as well stop arguing. But she just blinked and wiped her eyes with her hand.

"What did he do?" I asked.

"He's a monster," Polly said. "Our father is a monster."

"He mistook his animal instincts for Truth," Mama said.

As usual, her explanation didn't explain anything. "What did he *do*?" I shouted.

Even Polly wouldn't tell me. Mama just repeated what she'd been saying every day. "The real part of Pop reflects God. That's the part that loves you, Willy. The other part, the false part, is where his sick thoughts live."

"That's mortal mind," I said.

Mama smiled, but her lips quivered. "If you don't believe in it, mortal mind will disappear," she said.

"Is 'thirteen' part of mortal mind?" I asked.

Mama's whole body seemed to teeter on the chair. I thought her crooked teeth would bite right through her lip. Polly must have seen it too because she stopped arguing. We both knew that any negative thought could push Mama over and make her sick. We had to hold our doubts and questions inside ourselves. Secrets to keep each other safe.

Each afternoon, while Polly and I watched TV, Mama set down a bottle of Diet Coke on the kitchen table. Good Christian Scientists didn't drink coffee or alcohol, but Mama didn't know of any commandment against Diet Coke. She drank it all day long, especially while she pored over the Bible and the *Science and Health with Key to the Scriptures*. Sometimes she crooked the black telephone receiver on her shoulder and talked with Betty Treeble, the practitioner, in her low, holy voice. But even a professional Christian Science healer like Betty couldn't heal our family. During one of those phone calls, Polly closed the bathroom door and snipped off her hair.

When Mama saw Polly, her shoulders slumped and her eyes squinted up. "You had nothing to do with this, Polly. You didn't know."

"Tell that to those dead women," my sister said.

I couldn't ask about Pop; such talk might open us up to the power of illness. But at night, corrupting thoughts rampaged through me. Maybe Pop had killed my third-grade teacher, Miss Seckel. Or the nice cashier at Jewel Foods. Pop, who'd hoisted me on his shoulders and called me Tex, who got down on his hands and knees to wrestle or play with toy soldiers. Once he pretended to fight my dog Lucky. He wrenched her leg until her whines made me want to cry. "I didn't mean to," he said. "Honest, Tex, I didn't." I believed him.

Years later Polly told me her own secret. She also couldn't sleep during the lonely two weeks inside that apartment. Late each night she tiptoed out of the little room we shared. She padded over the tiled floors and knelt in front of the TV. Turning it away from Mama's bedroom, she lowered the sound. I imagine how she leaned forward to rest her ear against the little speaker. That way no voices could escape to Mama's room. She must have seen the news announcers. Their expressions would fill with revulsion as they described what our father had done to those thirteen women. Then Pop's photo would brighten the screen as his acts seeped into her.

Each morning Mama saw her pale, bleary face and said, "Polly, you reject those thoughts. Look what those thoughts are doing to you."

"That's because I'm human," Polly said. "At least one of us is."

"Don't listen to mortal mind," I said. "It'll make your asthma come back."

Polly ran into the bathroom and slammed the door.

Mama sat down at the kitchen table and closed her eyes. I knew that she was reciting a silent prayer. When Polly opened the bathroom door, her wrist dripped blood. She clutched a pair of bloody scissors in her other hand.

Mama jumped up and rushed across the kitchen. She pulled the scissors out of Polly's fingers. "What have you done?" she said. Drops of blood splattered against the floor. Mama grabbed a kitchen towel and pressed it against Polly's wrist. She stroked her hair until the bleeding stopped. "God's children don't need to cut themselves," she said.

Later that day Mama sat us down with a plate of sliced apple. While we chewed the sweet wedges, she leaned into Polly and told her how much she loved her.

"How could we love *him*?" Polly said.

Mama hugged her. Kissed the top of her head. "That's the Godly part," Mama said. "That's the real part of him that you loved."

"The other part was the *real* part," Polly said.

Mama's whole body stiffened. She pulled away from Polly. "Listen to me, young lady. You always have the choice about what's true. Don't you forget that."

Polly's eyes widened. She raised her bandaged wrist to her face. "Did you know?"

Mama slowly stood, her arms rigid, her face full of Truth. "Polly Kogan, you reject that thought. That thought is not part of you, do you hear me?"

I still hear Mama's high, fluty voice telling Polly to push away her false thoughts—when Polly dyed her hair so it looked like purple yarn; when she used a doll's leg as a barrette; when she shaved half her head and dyed a red lipstick kiss on the other side; or when she wore two different-colored shoes to school and made a bra from electrical cords. By then, she was cutting red spidery designs across her ankles and forearms. She hid those wounds from Mama with long shirts and pants. I kept her secret.

Beginning from that day, Mama refused to talk about Pop or even say his name. I knew that he'd killed thirteen women, but I had to find out more. One night, Polly and I snuck out while Mama slept. I pulled a newspaper from a garbage can and uncrumpled the pages to read the headline. *HE CUT UP THEIR BODIES FOR PHOTOGRAPHS.*

Polly held me. "Breathe," she said.

A car passed by. The streetlight hummed through the night's heat. The crickets chattered.

"But he's Pop," I said.

She rubbed my hair with her fingers, then the nape of my neck. "He's not our father anymore," she said.

I tried not to love him. But I couldn't stop myself. When we left that apartment and returned to our trailer, I thought I heard his heavy footsteps just outside the door. "Pop!" I yelled and put my hand over my mouth. His big indentation was still in the cushion of the chair with burst springs, his woody smell just behind the door to Mama's bedroom. When I was sure that no one could see me, I closed my eyes and breathed him in.

17

ALL THE GREEN WINDOWS I'd seen on the outside of the jail were fake. Inside, the sun didn't exist. For most of Module E, daybreak came when the main florescent lights and the bulbs behind the unbreakable glass blazed on sometime in the early morning. Even alone on the mattress in my own cell, the funky odors reached me. Someone yelled in another part of the cellblock. Then other men. The shouts went on and on, the unrecognizable words reverberating through my head as if they were part of the smell. I remembered Hempel saying that the other men would treat me like a child molester. What they might do to me blended into those howls. Maybe I didn't have a cellmate for my own safety.

My back ached. In my underwear and a T-shirt, I slid from under the itchy army blanket and off the bunk. The day before, two deputies had given me a hygiene kit with a three-inch toothbrush, a miniature plastic container of toothpaste, and a bar of soap as small as a hotel sample. I brushed my teeth. By closing my eyes, I didn't have to think about the toilet attached to the sink and drinking fountain. My new jail clothes lay splayed out on the floor: a short-sleeved, forest-green T-shirt and elastic-waisted green pants embossed with *San Diego County Jail*. As I dressed, I felt as if I were slipping on tattoos.

The shouting had stopped, at least momentarily. I stepped into the jail-issued rubber sandals and strode to the door. The murky safety-glass window resembled a diving bell's thick glass. My cell stood on the second level. On the other side of the door, a steel catwalk led to stairs that descended to a common area with a high ceiling. I saw four stainless steel tables, a few stools, and a TV mounted on the white concrete-brick wall. Even with my head against the door, the TV voices were muffled. I wiped the floor with my towel and lay down next to the crack below the door. The sounds of the TV seemed clearer but were still unintelligible.

Heavy footsteps and men's voices echoed through the concrete walls. The metal flap on the door banged down. Someone pushed a tray that seemed made of egg cartons through the door slot. I saw a bare arm and then a snatch of forest green. A prisoner was serving me, not a jail deputy. "Enjoy it, asshole."

The tray smelled like boiled waste. It contained a breakfast of runny eggs, fried potatoes, toast, and a small carton of OJ. The eggs shone with a gob of spit. Besides thinking I was as low as a child molester, the other prisoners also probably knew that I worked with primped-up rich people, the kind of people they hated and preyed on.

I had to eat something to maintain my strength. The toast seemed safer than the eggs and potatoes. As I chewed, one slow bite at a time, I imagined Jill, Garth, and Frieda in hiding. A young substitute would teach Jill's class and pull the desks in a circle to discuss what had become of poor Ms. Morton. She'd never mention Jill's unspeakable husband. At the bank, Vanessa would say, "It's hard to believe that the William McNary we know could do something like this." Soon I was pacing inside the cell, three steps to the wall and three steps back.

Would I ever see Garth and Frieda again? I stopped and turned my back to the cell door and its window. I covered my eyes with my hand. No one could interpret my tears as weakness if they didn't see my face.

"This is not you." It was Mama's voice, strong and high, the way I'd heard it as a child. "There is no number big enough to measure God's power."

I sat down on the lower bunk bed and remembered more words from my childhood. "God always has met and always will meet every human need." When I was eight, I'd repeated that phrase as a prayer.

More men spoke and laughed. The deputies had released some prisoners into the common area below the cells. I looked through the door's thick window. A few men slapped dominoes on a steel table by the television.

A face appeared close up on the other side of the safety glass. The blue and red hues of a tattoo blotched his forehead. "How ya doin' in there, my man?" he said.

I didn't answer.

"Lean down to the bottom of the door so you can hear me."

I stepped farther away.

"I can help you. Stop some tree jumper punkin' your ass."

A brown liquid spurted through the small space underneath the door. I jumped back and stumbled into the steel bunk bed. Pushing myself onto the bottom mattress, I curled up my legs. I wouldn't make a sound. Not even a breath.

"I didn't know if you were thirsty or hungry," the voice yelled. "We'll talk about how you cut up that girl later—just you and me."

The smell reached me at the same time as loud laughter and cat-calls. "Eat shit. Eat shit. Eat shit."

Gradually the din died down. I stopped shaking. I stared at the glass window in the door. No blue tattoo, no grinning man. A stack of Styrofoam cups stood over the sink. That was how he'd carried his waste.

Malevolence was the source of strength in here. I hugged my legs and sucked in the stench of hate.

18

I DON'T KNOW HOW much time spooled out. The odor of the disinfectant softened the odor of the excrement. After a while, the door slid open and a deputy informed me I had a half hour in the common room. Then he saw the floor.

"George," he shouted. "This guy got gassed." He glared at me as if it were my fault. "Who was it?"

Even I knew the first rule of jail was to never snitch. "Didn't see," I said and stepped over the mess.

I followed him down the metal walkway. Two large white men smiled as they stood in the doorways of their cells. The one who'd gassed me blew a kiss. The tattoos on his forehead were the cleanest parts of his face.

We clanked down the metal staircase and the deputy led me to the front open area where the TV blared above the tables and stools. Clear glass fronted the common area and a guard tower stood on the other side. Beside me, a Monopoly board lay on one of the tables, the game pieces made of pieces of tin foil and cardboard.

The deputy pointed to a telephone on the sidewall and gave me a prepaid calling card. "This is from your lawyer," he said.

"Who is he?" I asked.

"How the hell should I know?"

Apparently there were no more free phone calls now that I was housed in a regular cell. I put in the codes and called Jill's cell phone.

"William. Are you all right?"

The warmth of her voice should have been a relief. But it made me furious and I didn't know why. "I'm in a fucking jail."

Muffled explosions and fractured music from a cartoon came from her side of the call. A door shut. Then Jill was weeping. No sound could make me feel worse.

"I'm safe," I said. "Are *you* all right?"

She took big breaths. Gathered herself.

"Why in the world didn't you answer your phone before?" I said.

"I had no choice. The reporters were calling every five minutes."

I could imagine the press trucks camped out in front of her school and the house. "Did you go to Polly's place?"

"They followed us there. We had to draw all the curtains. William, they were ringing the neighbors' doorbells."

I knew exactly what she was trying to survive. "You're doing the right things," I said.

"I have no idea what the right things are. We're in a motel. We can't even use our own names."

Just as Mama, Polly, and I had hidden. "Are you safe?" I said.

"We're not allowed to go home. Our home is ... A CRIME SCENE!"

Her shout made me feel powerless, responsible. I had to help them, but how? "Someone is framing me," I said.

I didn't like how quiet she became. "But why?" she asked.

"If you don't believe in me—"

"How can you think that? How can you possibly think that?"

Her outrage helped me breathe again. "It has something to do with my father. Maybe because we renounced him."

I heard her breathing, knew that she was trying to arrange her mind around it. Jill didn't know that nothing about my father made sense.

"Oh, William. I *know* you didn't do those things."

Her words enabled me to endure anything.

I heard her walk back inside the motel room to put our kids on the line. Jill would never let them speak with me if she thought I'd killed Elizabeth.

"Hello," Garth said.

"Hey, buddy, how's school?" How could I ask that? Jesus.

"We're in a motel."

"Does it have a pool?" I sounded so unnaturally chirpy. I was afraid it would upset him.

"I'm watching *Ninja Turtles*."

"Good. Good for you. Are you okay?"

The phone scraped against something.

"Daddy, where are you?" Frieda asked.

How could I tell her where I was? "I had to go out of town."

"Where did you go?"

I was lying to my own child. "Out of town," I said.

"Is it far away?"

A sob filled my chest. I had to hang up before she heard it. "I love you."

"*Hasta luego,*" she said.

I disconnected and rested my head on the phone. Pushed back the despair. All the men in the two rows of cells above me were watching. *Don't weep. Whatever you do, don't weep.*

They started cheering. The brown-haired woman who'd nodded at me at the police station was on the TV. A caption identified her as Jessie Foster, District Attorney.

"We've arrested a suspect," Foster said, and paused for the photographers. She didn't even have to identify the crime.

Behind her, the chief of police nodded but no one looked at him. Someone shouted from the crowd in front.

"Our people have collected the evidence thoroughly and carefully," Foster said. "We have an extremely strong case."

Another indecipherable shout. The next voice was plenty clear: "Is it William McNary, the banker?"

Foster stared at the camera. "We're not releasing a name at this time." She stepped off the dais.

A prisoner shouted from a cell somewhere in the block. "We gonna cut him up just like her."

Laughing and jeering erupted in the other cells.

I looked down at my green shirt and pants and the yellow bracelet on my wrist. The colors all meant something that I didn't understand. But the District Attorney knew. She and Hempel and Lund and the whole police department had already decided I was guilty.

On the television, I saw myself in a police car turning from the camera. The inmates yelled and pounded on the doors of their cells, the din bouncing off the concrete. I thought of Frieda and Garth. What kind of world would allow children to witness their father cowering in a police car?

Shouts and catcalls echoed through the cement walls. Men banged on the metal doors. Someone started a chant. I put my hands over my ears but the words seeped through. "Chop Him Up. Chop Him Up. Chop Him Up."

I thought of Algeria.

19

IF **I** HADN'T BEEN twenty-two years old, I probably never would have ventured to Algeria. The army had cancelled an election that the Islamic party won, and rebel groups and the army were slaughtering one another. They were also killing journalists. That meant no photographers were covering the conflict. My advisor at San Diego State warned against going. The State Department said to stay away. I never asked Polly or the few friends I had. As far as I was concerned, Algeria was a perfect place to freelance my way into photojournalism.

The first day after I arrived, I wandered through Algiers. The streets were lined with blue-framed windows and wrought iron balconies. The side alleys smelled of grilled lamb and coffee. People in suits bustled next to women in hijabs and blue or black burkas. At some point the traffic stopped in front of two cleared blocks while men set down their prayer rugs. Out of respect, I put away my camera until they'd finished. I felt strange in my own skin. I was so foreign and so alien, but it was the way I was supposed to feel in this city.

The danger wasn't apparent. No one threatened me, even as I shot roll after roll of film. I'd taken two French college classes and many people spoke English. Everyone I talked to was appalled by the atrocities and just wanted to live in the same peaceful way as Americans. "Don't go outside Algiers," people warned. The *Groupe Islamique Armé* was slaughtering whole villages that had supported the government. Killing a *kafir* like me would generate the publicity they dreamed about.

In my second week, five grim soldiers in green camouflage fatigues arrested me. I sat trembling in the back of their truck while the soldiers drove me to their base. How could I have been so naive? The Algerian military would have their own reasons for killing a foreign journalist. Particularly one not protected by any news outlet.

The soldiers brought me to a wood-paneled office. Colonel Laribi, a gaunt man with cropped gray hair and slanted cheeks, smiled. But I saw no mirth in his flat eyes. He barked out orders in Arabic. I wondered if he was arranging my torture or my execution. A few minutes later, a soldier served us sweetened tea in china cups.

"You want to be a photojournalist," Laribi said in English. It was not a question. Before I could ask how he knew, he said, "I will help you. You will show the world what happened at Béni-Messous last night."

"What happened?" I asked.

Colonel Laribi sipped from the rose and blue-flower teacup. "Do you know about the *Groupe Islamique Armé?*"

We boarded a jeep in a convoy of military transports and black-clad *gendarmes* on motorcycles. We drove south through the thick Algiers traffic and into the hills and ravines above the city. At a military checkpoint the soldiers saluted. The transports stopped beside rows of abandoned white houses bordering a forest. But that village didn't smell of pine and eucalyptus. The stench was putrid and sweet, an odor I knew instinctively came from corpses. The only sound was the buzzing of flies.

I'd never seen a dead person except in photographs. I was afraid that my stomach would convulse and I'd be unable to frame or focus. But Laribi nodded me forward.

"We count on you to tell the world," he said.

We rounded the front of the houses and came upon the first bodies. Eleven dead men lay sprawled on the dirt road. Inside a house, disemboweled women and headless children lay on the floor. The rotting bodies and fecal discharge drove all other smells out of the room.

I pinched my nostrils and walled off my senses. The Nikon was jammed so hard into my face that it bruised the flesh around my eye. I stopped noticing my shoes squelching in the pools of blood. The smells dissipated and I no longer imagined the screams. My hand stopped shaking. The world narrowed to light and color, shutter speed, framing, depth of field, and angles. I focused on how to shoot images that could convey the horror and still appear in newspapers and magazines.

In the breaks between rolls of film, I searched for an explanation. Why did the massacre happen? The reason had to be both bigger and more primitive than politics and religion. Maybe it was rage or impotence. But no matter how many rolls I shot, I couldn't comprehend that carnage.

The colonel followed me silently. He refused to let me take a single shot of him. "Only the dead want to be photographed here," he said.

I thought my pictures would bring justice to those slaughtered families. One shows a woman from the perspective of the floor of her home. You can see her covered feet and ankles, and then her out-of-focus burka cut in half. Her upper body is at right angles to her waist, her covered head facing the camera. In a second photo, a shadow on the wall looks like a doll being held in the air by a stake. It is not a doll. Another picture shows flies so thickly enveloping a hand that it looks like a black glove. But the most famous picture, the one that appeared on the cover of *Time* magazine, presents the backs of men's dark-haired heads. They sat neatly in a row on a whitewashed wall, the sun casting their shadows onto the road that runs parallel. *God is Great* is written in Arabic in red below them.

When I got back to the jeep, I lowered the camera and the smell overpowered me. I vomited.

"Tell the world," the colonel whispered. "Tell the world what men will do in the name of religion."

He drove me back to Algiers. We picked up my duffle bag from my rented room and he put me up in a nice hotel with white columns and security guards in blue uniforms.

"This hotel is my gift to you," he said. "Your gift will be to help stop Algeria's suffering. Then we will become normal people again."

I never saw Colonel Laribi after that night. I flew home the next day.

The photos appeared in *The New York Times*, *The Wall Street Journal*, *The Times* of London, *Newsweek*, and *Time*. Even *The Economist* used one of my shots. I could have parlayed those images into a long career in photojournalism, but there was something monstrous about a person who could become so dispassionate behind a camera.

The press reported that religious fanatics butchered at least eighty-seven people at Oued Béni-Messous. A few weeks later, I learned that a military barracks a few kilometers away could see the village. The base heard nothing that night, even as a reported band of fifty howling men and one woman ran from the forest's pine trees with knives and machetes. As those marauders broke down doors, the people inside screamed and banged pans in the hope that the soldiers would help them. No one did.

By the time I learned those facts, the rumor had already started: the officers at the base had paid money to robed men with long beards. Human rights journalists that I trusted charged the army with orchestrating the massacre in order to turn the country away from the rebels.

Maybe the sacrifice of more than eighty of the town's men, women, and children helped save Algeria. But putting a value to that slaughter was like admiring the artistry in the Preying Hands' pictures.

20

LATER THAT DAY, MY ankles chained, I limped between two deputies to meet the attorney Polly had found. We walked out of my cell block and into a part of the building with a meeting room. A steel table and two chairs bolted to the floor barely fit inside. One of the deputies uncuffed my right hand, the signing hand, and attached my left to the chair on the prisoner side of the table. Even this little room smelled like unwashed men.

After a few minutes, the door opened and my lawyer stepped through. Short, thick hips, and black hair threaded with wisps of gray. Late forties, I guessed. I rose and the handcuff snapped me back to the chair. She shook my other hand and her gold hoop earrings swayed on both sides of her wide face.

I soon realized why Polly had chosen her. Marta Gutierrez had only been a defense attorney for four years but had previously spent fifteen years as a prosecutor. She knew every angle or trick the other side would use. She'd even worked with the two detectives who'd arrested me. I was pleased until Gutierrez told me her track record. Of the seven murder cases she'd taken as a defense attorney, she'd won three. I wasn't sure I wanted to bet my life on those odds.

"Think about it," she said. "If you're not comfortable with me, you can get somebody else. The important thing is that, right now, you need someone on your side."

No argument there. Not after what had happened that morning. "My sister's recommendation means a lot," I said.

She pulled out a Bic pen and slowly tapped it on a legal pad. "Polly's offered to help pay your fees."

My sister would sell everything she owned to keep me out of prison. I took in Gutierrez's conservative white blouse and stocky body. Her wedding ring was crowned with a single, discreet diamond. I, more than anyone, knew that "flash" was overrated. A jury might identify with her.

She passed me a form to sign. I used her Bic. "Now let me ask *you* something," she said. "Are you okay?"

"They threw shit at me this morning."

She tapped the pen. Unrattled.

"I guess someone told them who you were," she said.

"Wait until they find out who my father is."

She nodded. Polly must have informed her. I wondered if my father's notoriety might have been one of the reasons she'd taken my case.

"We'll get you some extra protection," she said.

"Is that even possible?"

104

She expelled a long sigh and said, "Look, I'm not going to sugar-coat this place."

And she certainly didn't. Module E was where they put San Diego's worst criminals. That's what the green jumpsuit and yellow bracelet meant. Most of the men here had started in juvenile detention and were more at home in jail than on the street. This was what the world now thought of me.

But something more important gnawed at my stomach lining. If Marta Gutierrez had kids, she'd understand. I told her about the camera and photos the killer had put in my son's book bag. "It's not just me he's after."

She stared back, her face blank.

"Do you actually think I'd put those pictures in my son's bag?" I said.

The Bic tapped the legal pad like a metronome.

She said, "No one knows which hotel Jill and your kids are in. Right now, I just want to hear your side of what happened. From the beginning." She extended her hand for me to start.

I talked and she scratched notes, her scowl never changing. I told her how I'd called the police, and Lund and Hempel had persuaded me to come to the station. They'd used a can of Coke to capture my fingerprints.

She screwed up her eyes and groaned. "Hasn't anybody ever told you about homicide detectives?"

They hadn't. I'd avoided crime TV and police procedurals. Too many serial killers. No one in our family talked about detectives. "They lied to me," I said.

"They're allowed to. They can lie to *you* but you can't lie to *them*. It's one of the perks of the job."

And yet, part of me had suspected their bullshit. I'd sat there any-way in that tiny interview room. That's what a banker was supposed to do when he talked with detectives.

"Was any of what they said true?" I asked

"Good question. Someone must have seen your car tearing out of the park and marked down the license plate. That's how they identified you. So there's a witness."

"The detectives only invited me to the station because they suspected me."

"They needed probable cause. That meant matching your prints to the ones on the garbage bag the body was wrapped in."

According to Gutierrez, using a can of Coke to get my prints was an old trick. Along with leaving the door open a crack and saying I could leave. Standard deceptions to make me think I wasn't a suspect. And to convince a judge that they didn't intend to arrest me when they started the interview. "That way they don't have to give you your Miranda warning," she said.

It had all been a play: Lund's reassuring bass voice telling me my family was safe, the Act II surprise of Elizabeth's body in the park, then, *You're not a suspect, Mr. McNary.* They'd saved the sledgehammer for last—those terrible photos of Elizabeth.

"You know the murderer set me up," I said.

Gutierrez stared at the ceiling, her pen swaying in her fingers. Had she even heard me?

She said, "Someone must have run that Coke can to the lab. When the tech matched your prints, you became a suspect."

"They took my prints again later."

She shrugged. "That was an official full set of prints."

"How about the Miranda warning?"

"I'm willing to bet they gave you some form of Miranda and you didn't know it. The courts aren't as strict about that as people think. The detectives don't have to use the exact words. As long as they communicate the content." She winced and shook her head, the earrings swaying. "And you still didn't demand a lawyer."

106

That sounded like a reproof, but I ignored it. "What were they hoping to get by talking to me alone?"

Her eyes widened. She dropped the pen on the pad as if I were being deliberately stupid. "Anything. Any kind of admission. Even a lie. Something they could make you think isn't that bad. Then they pick at it for ten or twelve hours. They drill you until they get you to admit something they can prosecute."

"I never confessed to anything."

Her mouth flattened into a line. "I hope not."

She tapped the yellow pages of the legal pad. Her nails were flesh-colored. Nothing about Marta Gutierrez was ostentatious. Just like me.

"Why the hell did they let me leave the station?"

She laughed. Now my ignorance was cute. "They needed a warrant for your arrest. Someone from the District Attorney's Office must have been standing beside a judge. As soon as the lab matched your prints from the Coke can, the judge signed the warrant. That's when they made the arrest and remanded you to jail. Believe me, you were being watched when you went back to your car."

More nail taps. She looked almost bored.

"They told me they already had DNA analysis," I said.

"That takes weeks. Usually months."

"How about the shoe prints and tire treads?"

"More smoke. But your arrest allowed them to get a search warrant for your house. God knows what they found there."

"Nothing."

She studied her legal pad. "We'll find out in discovery."

I thought of the garbage bag the murderer had stolen from my house. My whole body flinched.

She made a check mark on the legal pad. "From now on you don't talk with anyone but me about this case. Not law enforcement, not detectives, not other inmates or even your family on the phone. Just assume that every corner of this place is bugged."

I thought of my telephone calls to Polly and Jill.

"William, this case couldn't *be* more high profile. Not after what was done to the victim."

I liked how direct Marta Gutierrez was. No lies. No fake optimism. Maybe that's why I spoke without thinking. "You know Elizabeth was on probation. She hurt a boy in her class."

She slammed down the pen. Her eyes flared and I glimpsed the kind of force she could project. "Don't you *ever* talk about knowing that woman. All it takes is one remark, just one, and the news hacks and prosecutors have a motive."

"I didn't do it," I said.

Not a single line of warmth curled the skin around her eyes. Her irises were the dark brown of acorns. "So what you're telling me is the killer manipulated you. He tricked you into driving to the park. A few yards from where the victim was buried."

"I can't explain it. I'm just saying, I've been set up."

She sat back in the chair, her broad face sinking almost to the height of the table. I steeled myself.

"You need to understand what you're up against. If the DA can establish kidnapping, or that there was any kind of torture, it'll be a death penalty case."

The needle. My stomach seized and I shifted in the chair. I fought off the panic. "I didn't touch Elizabeth," I whispered.

She set her arm on the table and leaned closer. "The District Attorney herself is trying you. First time in more than twenty years. You know why?"

"Because of the victim."

She shook her head. "She wants to use this trial to launch her campaign to be mayor."

"And what do you get out of it, Attorney Gutierrez?"

She frowned and sat back. "That's a good question."

"I'm sure you'll have a good answer."

"Look, I won't deny that my practice will get a huge jolt from the publicity. But Polly's a good friend. I would have taken you on regardless."

Something else gave me more assurance than her words. Polly trusted her. "Ms. Gutierrez, there's something that keeps getting lost in everything you've told me."

Now I waited. She nodded.

"I'm innocent."

She studied me. The Bic bounced on the legal pad. I knew what she was thinking. There was only one way I'd avoid the needle.

"Do you think I should plead guilty for something I didn't do?"

She gave me a sad smile, her eyes soft at last. "Just think about everything. We've got plenty of time. Your arraignment is on Monday. You can plead innocent then."

"But I *am* innocent."

Some things were more important than my life.

21

ON MONDAY, TWO DEPUTIES tethered my handcuffs to a chain wrapped around my waist. They snapped shackles around my ankles that forced me to shuffle like an old man. It was time for my arraignment.

We rode an elevator to the second floor and jangled down a hallway to a sky bridge that led to the court building. The two men chatted about football. We reached a line of more deputies and chained prisoners outside the courtroom. A door opened and a man in a blue jumpsuit stepped out, swearing. The next man shambled and jingled through. The door closed. Five minutes later it opened and the man limped back. It was impossible to tell if he'd gotten bail.

And what about the man accused of slicing up a school teacher? Marta Gutierrez was going to have to conjure a miracle to get me out of jail.

A half hour later, the door clicked shut behind me. I stood inside a booth of frosted glass. On one side, a small open window allowed me to see in front of me. The judge, a flaccid-cheeked, gray-haired man in his fifties, perched behind an raised paneled desk. A court reporter sat next to him. I couldn't see the gallery to my right, but its steady murmur made my breath come faster. I could feel how packed the courtroom was. Everyone wanted to see the freak.

A guard in green pants and a belt full of weapons stepped beside the window and yelled, "William McNary."

The door opened. I strode out to stand just in front of the wooden booth, between the judge and the gallery. A line of cameras clicked and whirred to my right. Behind them, people completely filled the rows of seats and others peeked in from the entranceway. The room snapped into silence. All eyes focused on me like a single spotlight. My legs flinched with a sudden urge to run. Did anyone here believe I didn't cut up Elizabeth Morton? I searched for Jill and found her blonde hair in the fourth row. Her eyes crinkled and she mouthed, "I love you."

Those silent words buoyed me. I straightened my shoulders and turned to face the judge. He'd pressed his lips into a righteous frown.

My attorney came to stand beside me and said, "Good afternoon, Your Honor. Marta Gutierrez on behalf of William McNary." The rest of what she said flooded out in a torrent, a practiced ritual of words that ended with a plea of "Not Guilty."

"Jessie Foster, on behalf of the people."

I recognized District Attorney Foster from the police station and the press conference I'd seen on the jail's TV. Today she stood out as a statuesque and very angry attorney. Her short brown hair was perfectly coiffed and an elegant green dress only emphasized her long legs. In black heels, she towered over Gutierrez. I had no doubt who would dominate the news tonight.

The judge said, "It has been some time since we've seen you in this courtroom, District Attorney Foster."

"This case is very important to the people, Your Honor. The crime is particularly horrific. The victim, Elizabeth Morton, was a dynamic teacher of young children. Her young students adored her."

She'd said "young" twice so no one would miss it.

Gutierrez said, "Your Honor, the victim's profession is no more relevant than the fact she was under review for hurting one of the children in her classroom."

Clever. Foster must have thought so too because she didn't respond or even glance at Gutierrez.

"Your Honor, Elizabeth Morton's head, breasts, hands, and feet were cleaved off," Foster said. "They were dumped in a garbage bag in Kate Sessions Park."

As if he didn't know, the judge's eyes widened and he scowled at the cameras.

Foster bowed her head and released a sigh so long and loud that even those outside the courtroom must have heard it. "I'm saddened to say that this is one of the most heinous crimes I've ever seen in San Diego. That's why we propose that no bail be offered."

The courtroom wavered and rippled in front of me. *No bail!* My eyes sought out Gutierrez. She was already talking.

"…maintains his innocence of all charges. He has two young children and his wife is in this courtroom today. He's a successful banker and a well-regarded member of his community. Mr. McNary has no prior convictions or even arrests. He's been a resident of San Diego since he was a child and is not a flight risk."

"Counsel is aware that this is a particularly horrific crime," the judge said.

"Particularly horrific" was the same phrase that Foster had used. My eyes sought out Jill. I didn't want her to connect those words with me. But her head was bowed. Her hand shielded her face.

Gutierrez said, "We suggest that bail in the amount of one million dollars would be appropriate."

I let myself breathe. A million dollars wasn't hopeless. We could put up our house as collateral for the bail bond.

Foster drew her head back as if she'd been insulted. "Your Honor, there's an enormous amount of evidence that ties the accused to the evisceration of this young teacher. We submit that if any bail be considered it should be at least ten million dollars."

An airy murmur rose from the public gallery. My heart pulsed through my ears. I glanced at Gutierrez. *Say something!*

Finally she spoke. "My client has a total net worth of one point three million dollars. To demand a bond of ten million is the same as refusing bail. He'll never find enough collateral to get the bond issued."

The judge studied Foster and Gutierrez. But he spoke too quickly to have considered their arguments. He must have made a decision before he even came into court. "Bail will be five million dollars."

Five million dollars! I would rot in Module E. I'd never hug my family again. The madman would attack them. My legs felt as if there was nothing inside them.

The judge turned to Foster, who said nothing, then to Gutierrez. "Do you waive bail review?"

She shielded our faces with her hand so no one could read our lips. "Don't waive the review," she whispered. "Then he'll have to give us a shot at reducing the amount within a few days."

"A few days?" My voice was so loud I covered my mouth. I stared out. Every eye in the gallery focused on me. Except Jill. She'd now buried her face in both hands.

"You have no other options. I'll make sure nothing happens to you in there. Courage, William." She turned to the judge. "My client does not waive the bail review, Your Honor."

The judge nodded as if he'd expected that answer. "We'll have a review in three days."

I remembered the man with the tattoo like a purple scar on his forehead. Even if I survived three more days, I didn't have that kind of collateral.

"Next case," the judge said.

A deputy grabbed my arm. He opened the door to the booth. As I stumbled through, I heard weeping. Jill.

22

FOR THE NEXT TWO days, I retreated behind my cell's reinforced safety glass and ate by myself. All day long the shouts and laughter from the other inmates echoed through the thick cement walls. At night, the shouts turned more forsaken and angry. My only break from the din was an hour alone in the common room each morning. As I walked down the passageway toward the stairs, the smells of body odor and disinfectant assaulted me. The other inmates yelled to come closer so we could talk. But I didn't go near those thick windows or the open space below the doors. I scanned 360 degrees around me. Even in the common area someone might be waiting, someone whose cell door had been "inadvertently" left open.

I only spoke by phone once with my attorney. Marta Gutierrez was waiting for the evidence from discovery. But she managed to have the *San Diego Union-Tribune* delivered to the jail for me. Sometimes it even arrived without being torn up or spit on. Maybe she'd started to believe in me. The *Union-Tribune* hadn't. My picture stared out from the newspaper's front page just about every day.

It was hard not to fill that empty time with worry. There were so many ways a psychopath could attack my family. Not to mention the terrible shame my arrest had brought down on them. At night I could block out the shouts from the other prisoners, but I couldn't stop the scrape of my thoughts. I needed the vape pen. I needed the bourbon. Rage at my killer became a kind of distraction.

On the afternoon of my sixth day in jail, Attorney Gutierrez and I met again in the same small, stark room. Without a word, she plopped down opposite me at the steel table and flicked through a thick file.

"What happened?" I said.

She gave me an icy stare. "The forensics investigators found someone else's hair on Elizabeth Morton's body. Along with your hair. More of both in your trunk."

"I don't know how my hair, or anyone else's, got there."

"That's not all. Drops of her blood were in your trunk."

"Do you actually think I had an accomplice?" I said.

Gutierrez's arms thudded against the table. "The report says you never denied carrying your revolver to the park."

"I never denied that because I'm innocent. And I did carry it."

"Jesus, William. You don't have a concealed weapon permit and you went within a few hundred yards of a school. The DA could throw you in jail just for those two things."

She wasn't finished. Not even close. Armed with a search warrant, the police had found dirt from the park in my closet. Footprints next to the body matched a pair of my shoes. They'd also found the shovel used to bury Elizabeth. In our garage.

It was as if I'd been an accomplice to Elizabeth's murder without knowing. I imagined the horror on Jill's face and my whole body jerked. Gutierrez shrank back, eyes flown wide. In that flinch, I saw just what my attorney really thought of me.

She squinted as if in pain. "For God's sake, William, we've got to try to save your life now. For your kids." She curled up her fingers as if she wanted to slash me with her flesh-colored nails.

"I told you. He was in my house."

Her black eyebrows rose to show just how ludicrous I sounded. "Look, maybe I'm not the right attorney to represent you. Maybe you need someone more famous, someone who's fought these kinds of cases."

"An attorney who can work with a guy like me—someone who likes to get together with his buddy and cut up women?"

Her resolute stare condemned me as thoroughly as any words. I was even going to lose Gutierrez. My leg jiggled under the table. *Needle* circled through my mind.

I forced my shoulders to relax. I had to be an analytical banker. "Look, I don't mean to tell you how to do your job, but let me lay out some things."

One shoulder gave a half-shrug.

"Let's think about the actual evidence."

She folded her hands on the table, as if forcing herself to stay in that room.

I spoke as I would to answer a tough question in loan committee. "Let's just imagine what could have happened. A man somehow gets the code for our alarm. He sneaks into our house while I'm at work and my family's at school. He steals an old pair of shoes from my closet. There's a shovel in my garage, and he takes that too. Then he snatches a bag from the garbage can outside. He grabs Elizabeth Morton. Kills her. Moves her body to the park. All while wearing my shoes and using my shovel. He picks the lock on my car and drips the blood inside the trunk."

She didn't say anything. I went on. "He cut her up. Where the hell would I have taken her for that? I go to work and I come home. That's it. No one's mentioned finding a strange woman's blood in my house, right?"

Nothing. No reaction. The same stiff face and back. Did she believe even a part of what I'd said? Her nails softly tapped the stainless-steel table.

I continued. "At the park, he covers her with just enough dirt that the body will be found in a day or two. And the coup de grace ... he places her in the garbage bag he stole from me, a bag with my fingerprints on it."

Gutierrez picked up her pen and stared at it. "And then I assume he takes the shoes back to your closet and puts the shovel in your garage."

"Yes."

She half smiled. Tapped the pen against the steel table. "The tip to the police about your car ... it was anonymous."

My eyes widened. My head straightened. "I'll bet it came from a throw-away phone bought at some convenience store."

She nodded. Studied her pen. "But what about the second person's hair? Is it his?"

He was too careful for that. Saying it was his hair would sabotage my whole theory about his meticulousness. Unless ...

"I think I know what happened there too," I said.

118

23

THE BAIL REVIEW TOOK place the next morning. In the spectator part of the courtroom, Jill sat glumly behind a wall of newspaper photographers and TV men. Marta Gutierrez and I faced the judge from the defense table. Marta's face looked puffy, dark ridges under her eyes as if she'd had little sleep. So much for my confident attorney.

We'd settled on a "creative" strategy, something she'd never tried before. "If it doesn't work it's only the bail review, not the trial," she'd said. But her assurance didn't calm my stomach. If we didn't get the bond amount lowered, I wasn't getting out of jail. Which would give the men in Module E months to figure out how to slice me up.

Ten feet to our right, District Attorney Jessie Foster stood in a dark blue dress and severe heels. She aimed a righteous stare at the crowd and the cameras. No notes. Only a slim leather briefcase sat on the prosecutor's desk. She looked like a movie heroine about to bring justice to all the women in America.

We sat and faced the judge, the gallery behind us. The judge started to speak and my lawyer interrupted him. "Your Honor, may we meet in chambers?"

The judge raised his eyes to the ceiling. "You don't *really* want to talk with me in chambers, do you, Counselor? In this courtroom that rarely turns out well."

We hadn't even gotten past the first part of our strategy and the judge already resented us. I stole a glance at Jill. Her mouth pressed tightly shut.

"We have further evidence best discussed privately," Marta said. She gave a quarter-glance at the row of press behind her to make her point clear. Neither the DA nor the judge would want them to hear what she had to say. That worried the judge enough that he raised his eyebrows at Foster. She shrugged.

"Your Honor, I need to be present," I said. I'd already told Marta that I wouldn't stand in front of the press while my lawyer privately discussed my case.

A murmur bubbled up in the spectator section. Camera shutters clicked. The judge glared at me as if I were a heckler.

Marta said, "Your Honor, he has a point. A bail hearing gives the defendant the same rights as a public trial does."

The bailiff behind me groaned.

The judge frowned at the district attorney, who nodded. He turned to Gutierrez. Without looking at me, he said, "Mr. McNary, not a word out of you unless I ask for it."

The bailiff checked my wrist and ankle shackles. He accompanied us through a door adjacent to the courtroom. As I shuffled, my chains chinked. The cameras furiously ticked.

The judge's chambers contained a big desk behind a leather couch and two leather chairs. No one sat. Even in heels, Marta Gutierrez was six inches shorter than the rest of us. With her wide hips and gray-speckled hair, she looked more like a mother than a slick defense attorney. But flamboyance wouldn't matter with only the four of us in chambers. In here, no one had to perform for the press. At least that was the plan.

"Your Honor," Marta said. "We have further explanation to support a reduction in the bail amount."

The judge gave her an austere look. She stared back, her jaw set. No one was going to intimidate my lawyer.

She continued. "Mr. McNary has offered reasonable explanations for all the physical evidence. What that shows, when looked at properly, is that he was set up. The killer stole and wore a pair of Mr. McNary's shoes. He took a shovel from his garage. He even stole one of his garbage bags, food particles still clinging to it, so as to put Mr. McNary's fingerprints at the scene."

She'd stated it well, and, more importantly, no one had cut her off.

"Counselor, we didn't come in here so you could present your case," the judge said.

My stomach recoiled.

Marta said, "I'm just pointing out that there are reasonable explanations for the evidence found and that my client deserves a reasonable bail."

"I'm losing patience," the judge said. "Is that the extent of what you have to say?"

I couldn't keep my body still. I shifted and the shackles jingled. All three turned to stare at me. I started to apologize and clamped my mouth shut.

Marta said, "I also want to add that, despite all the circumstantial evidence so conveniently found in William's home, the investigators still haven't located the saw used to cut up the victim. Nor have they found the place where she was dismembered. They don't even know how William could have kidnapped her."

She was indefatigable. The use of my first name made the judge see me as a person rather than a criminal. He nodded and Marta almost imperceptibly nodded back. I took in a long, slow breath.

"What do you say to that, Jessie?" the judge said.

Jessie? The district attorney was on a first name basis with the judge?

Foster said, "I would like to draw your attention to the fact that Mr. McNary has already admitted that he was at the park. It was during the same window of time that Elizabeth Morton was buried there."

The judged turned back to Marta. "You started this line of discussion, Counselor. So how did Mr. McNary happen to be at the park that night?"

Marta explained how the internet message had lured me to Kate Sessions Park. "He never got out of his car, Your Honor."

The judge chuckled. Is there any worse feeling than when a judge laughs at your explanation?

Even Foster half smirked. She leaned in toward the judge and said, "The victim's blood was found in Mr. McNary's trunk."

Marta stood a little taller. "The blood didn't pool in the trunk the way it should have. It was in drops—as if from an eyedropper."

It was crucial information but she was speaking too quickly. I couldn't find an inconspicuous way to signal her to slow down. Not without crossing the judge.

"Utterly baseless conjecture," Foster said.

But she didn't refute it. That was progress.

"As long as you brought up the blood," the judge said, "how about the hairs and the DNA analysis? I presume that we have the usual delay?"

Marta cleared her throat. "The hair samples contained very good follicles. District Attorney Foster gave the DNA analysis special priority."

The judge turned to Foster. I think she saw the trap snapping shut.

"We'll have explanations for that," Foster said.

Weak.

Marta leaned forward onto the toes of her shoes. "Actually, Your Honor, two types of hair were on the body. Investigators found the same two types of hair, along with the victim's hair, in the trunk of William's car." She slowly swiveled her head to Foster, as if to ask whether the district attorney wanted to contradict her.

My lawyer didn't look so motherly now.

Foster must have realized where Marta was headed, but her face still bore the same severely confident expression. "We're waiting for another opinion," she said.

"Are you saying there's an accomplice?" the judge said.

Marta drew out the silence before she spoke. "Defense asked the University of Arizona to look at some of the hair strands. They have special equipment that can do the analysis in a matter of hours. The university sent us their conclusions this morning. If we put aside the victim's hair, the other two sets of hair have the same genetic characteristics ... as William." Her stare was like a finger pointing at Foster.

The judge's eyes had grown hard and his face started to flush from the neck up.

"In fact, to be more specific," Marta said, "the second person's hair came from William's daughter."

Marta controlled her expression just as absolutely as she had controlled the discussion. There wasn't a single hint of smugness. I was the one fighting to keep my face somber.

Foster said, "Mr. McNary must have picked up and hugged his daughter. Probably on the day that he murdered Elizabeth Morton. His daughter shed a few hairs and those same hairs dropped from his clothes onto the victim."

Now Foster was speaking too fast.

Marta said, "Then you would expect a few hairs from the daughter to show up separately on the body and in the trunk. But every sample of William's hair was intertwined with a sample of his daughter's hair. And vice versa. There was as much hair from his daughter as his own."

The judge was starting to breathe more heavily through his nose. "What is the People's response?"

No more first names now. Foster stood motionless. She didn't shrink from looking at the judge; she didn't stoop or fidget. I had to give her that.

"Pure conjecture, Your Honor," Foster said.

Marta stared only at the judge, as if the district attorney had already been ordered out of the room. Now she was getting cocky. I aimed a warning glance at her but she wouldn't look at me.

She said, "The most logical explanation is that, when the murderer was in William's house, he removed hairs from a brush. The same brush that both William and his daughter used. His daughter likes to go into her parents' bathroom and use her daddy's brush. She's a five-year-old and thinks it makes her hair shinier."

No one smiled at the cuteness of my daughter. The only sound was the hissing of the judge's breaths. Then a car horn on the street.

Marta continued. "William and his daughter have the same hair color and the daughter's hair is short, like his."

Now she was overselling.

Foster said, "Your Honor, this is not the place for this kind of speculation."

She was too late.

The judge raised his hand. "So, Defense Counsel is saying that the killer sprinkled these hair fibers on the victim and inside the defendant's trunk? Along with some of the victim's own hair?"

"Why would anyone possibly do that to him?" Foster said.

Marta drew back, squinting as if the question were absurd. "That question has no more relevance than asking why William himself would commit this kind of crime. The answer is that he wouldn't, and didn't. We contend that he's a highly successful banker with a young family and no history of misconduct. He's an innocent victim set up by the real murderer. And someone who deserves to post a reasonable bond."

The shortest person there had the loudest voice. God she was good.

"Enough," the judge said, but he was glaring at Jessie Foster.

Marta said, "In light of the new evidence, I respectfully request that Your Honor consider a reduction of bail to two million dollars."

The judge turned to her. "Counselor Gutierrez, you have a point."

We walked out of the judge's chambers and the loud conversation in the gallery cut off. I found Jill and gave her a nod. I was thinking about what our family would have for dinner that night.

The judge stared into the line of cameras. "I have carefully considered all the evidence, including the new evidence. Nothing presented so far persuades me to lower the bail previously set. It remains at five million dollars. Please remand Mr. McNary back to jail."

———————

In the cramped conference room of the San Diego County Jail, I felt so numb that I could only stare at the top of the metal table. Marta reached over and grabbed my arm.

"Let me repeat a few facts of life. This judge has big ambitions for the Court of Appeals. The last thing he wants is to look soft on a potentially horrific killer. Or less than deferential to the World's Greatest Prosecuting Attorney."

I raised my head. "There's no way I can come up with five million dollars."

"That's the bond amount. Most bonding companies want more collateral than that." She examined her nails. "Then there's the bond commission, typically ten percent."

"Five hundred thousand dollars?"

"You know, William, there happen to be a few people out there who believe in your sorry ass. And I managed to get the commission down to five percent."

Two hundred and fifty thousand dollars. We didn't have that kind of cash. Then I thought of Randall, Mama's dead second husband. She'd inherited his retirement portfolio. Also his real estate, including a medical office building. If Polly also put up her house and restaurant as collateral...

"Your mother and Polly are betting the ranch on you, William. Don't let them down."

I had to look away so she wouldn't see the tears. Then I realized what Marta had said. I slowly turned back to her. "Do you really think I'd run?"

"Plenty of people would with these charges hanging over them. But you're not going to, *are* you?"

If I fled, the bail bond company would seize the collateral and Mama and Polly would lose everything. "No, I'm not going to run. Do you know why?"

We locked eyes. She looked down.

"Because I never want my kids to think I could do something like this."

"Polly told me you'd say that."

She'd made sure, anyway. Polly and her network had recommended the right attorney. Marta Gutierrez had just the toughness I needed.

She pulled some papers from her cracked leather briefcase. "I was up most of the night because I knew we only had a small chance of winning in there. I've never drafted one of these before."

She held out the sheets: quit-claim deeds to pledge all the real estate that my sister, Mama, and I owned. I knew at least ten attorneys who could have helped her, but when it came to the law, Marta was strictly self-reliant.

"You'll be out of here in a few hours," she said. "The judge was so pissed off at the World's Greatest Attorney, he's not even making you wear an ankle bracelet."

She was laughing.

24

SIX HOURS LATER, A policeman led me out of my cell and I changed into a suit Marta had brought. Outside, we pushed through a mob of shouting reporters and photographers and jumped into a limo with tinted windows. The driver sped us away. He cut across lanes and made quick turns to lose anyone following.

"Get used to it," Marta said. "They goad you for the cameras so you look like Hitler. Then, when you're found innocent, they'll photograph you like Jesus."

"Where the hell is Jill?" I said.

"I saw no reason for her to deal with those crazies."

"The press will assume she thinks I'm guilty."

Marta put her hand on my arm. "William, you can't control what the hacks write. We'll just have a chat and then you go see her. She's with your kids."

The limo dropped us off in front of a small refurbished brick building. It stood a block away from King Stahlman Bail Bonds and two blocks from the jail and the courthouse, but there was no sign of reporters. I watched the trolley clank by. The air gave off a hint of the ocean. I closed my eyes.

"Nothing like being out, is there?" Marta said.

The entrance of the building led to an open-air courtyard, the darkening sky visible above the four floors. We boarded an ancient elevator with metal accordion doors and lurched and hummed to the top floor. An unlit outdoor walkway reached a plain wooden door.

"Here's my luxurious office," she said.

Inside I saw bare white walls, a half partition, and two old laminate desks. Marta picked up a UPS envelope from under the mail slot and we walked across the balding Indian rug. The scent of leftover popcorn made the place smell like my living room. It seemed Marta was barely hanging on. But that didn't stop her from taking on Jessie Foster and the whole District Attorney's office.

She poured coffee from a pot into two mugs and buzzed them in the microwave. We carried the mugs and the UPS envelope to an office in the back. Files were piled up on the credenza, the desk, and the table. She dropped some of them onto the carpet to clear off two wooden chairs and said, "Someday I'm going to really move in here."

We sat at the table. Metal-framed photos stared back from some bookshelves: a huge Latino family at a celebration, and a photo of a teenager and a man that had to be her daughter and husband. Instead of wearing big hoop earrings like Marta, metal rings pierced the daughter's lip and eyebrow.

"My daughter's gay," she said. "Polly helped her a lot."

There was the connection. My sister had helped a lot of young people with coming out.

Marta pulled a thick file from her battered briefcase and dropped it into an empty space on the table. "Do you have any idea how much shit you're in?"

"But we explained the evidence."

"Trust me, Foster will figure an angle. And my old friends, Hempel and Lund? Once they put their weight behind a case, they don't back down. That would lower their testosterone levels."

So I could still go to prison for the rest of my life. Or worse. "Thanks for your optimism," I said.

She jabbed her finger at the heavy file. "Why the hell would someone so carefully frame you?"

I had a theory, but it seemed too strange.

"Spill it, William. I'm your attorney, for chrissake."

"Well, this guy must admire my father. Maybe he murdered Elizabeth to get his attention. You know—'Your son pretends you don't exist, but I can make him *feel* your suffering.'"

Marta drew back. She started to speak and shook her head.

"You wanted to know."

She drummed her fingers on the file. "We have to construct a narrative. Something that's better than what the World's Greatest Attorney will saddle you with. It all begins with 'Why?'"

I had no other ideas.

She slid a disposable cell phone across the table to me. Her number was marked on a piece of paper taped to the back of the phone. "It's our own private hotline," she said.

As I slid the phone into my pocket, she examined the UPS envelope. It was from the *Union-Tribune* and addressed to me. "Get used to it," she said. "The reporters are like flies around a case like this." She shook it. "It's light." She slit open the envelope and slid out a smaller, pale rose envelope with my name in flourished script.

We both stared at the envelope on the table.

"This wasn't sent from the newspaper, was it?" I said.

She crinkled her mouth and thought. Then pulled a Kleenex from a box and handed it to me. "Don't get fingerprints on it."

I slit open the bottom of the envelope. A card fell out. On the front was a picture of champagne bottles and streamers. *Congratulations!* Something was inside the fold. I took a wary breath and looked at Marta. She nodded. I removed a black-and-white photo.

It was my father's work. Kim Johnson, a teacher, had hit one of her student's wrists with a ruler. In the shot, Johnson's head sits on a small blackboard, her blonde hair splayed out and her pale face looking up at the camera. Chalk-drawn children's faces look out from the corners of the blackboard. One of her hands holds a ruler and the other grasps a book: *The Giving Tree*.

"Oh my God." Marta jumped up. She scrambled back from the table.

The woman in the picture was too young and thin for Kim Johnson. She was Elizabeth Morton.

25

I **STARED AT THE** motel from the rental car. Jill was locked in a room on the second floor, a revolver in her hand, as she watched over our kids. They were safe, but the man only needed one unguarded moment. I remembered Marta jumping back from the photo on her table, her hand over her face, her terrible high moan. Later, Detective Hempel as he slipped the image into a plastic bag. He looked pained but didn't say a word.

Now, sitting in the car, I realized that the murderer had taken Elizabeth somewhere to kill her and cut her up. He'd snapped pictures, then put her dismembered body in the garbage bag and took it back to the park. All in a few hours. Just like Harvey Dean Kogan.

I had to face Jill. I tramped up the motel stairs and heard cartoon voices yelling from behind the door of their room. Behind me the relentless groundswell of cars swept over the highway. A haze of motel and highway lights blocked out the stars. I knocked and stepped back so my wife could identify me through the spy hole. The door stayed closed for a long time.

The lock rattled. She pulled back the handle, and the light from the doorway touched a fringe of her blonde hair. She threw her arms around me. I relaxed into the familiar contours of that embrace. But when she drew away I saw uncertainty in her eyes.

A lamp dimly lit the room. Garth clutched his spaceship and stared from the bed. Frieda stood beside him and cradled Micky Marvin the bear. How could I describe what the world thought I'd done? All I could do was hug them.

After, Frieda tugged at my arm. She pointed to the pizza box on the desk.

"There are twelve pieces," she said. *"Una docena."*

"A *docena*?" I said. "How many pieces would be in two pizzas?"

"Two *docenas*." She pulled me down closer to her face. "It has pepperoni. Polly can't have that part."

Our child sounded so normal, as if I'd slipped away on a business trip and just arrived home from the airport.

We sat together on the bed, the TV murmuring in the background. Jill stared at me from the other side of the bedspread, the conversation we needed like a veil between us. I pried a piece of cold pizza from the box and pretended to savor it. As long as I lingered over that soggy crust I wouldn't have to tell my children about my arrest and Harvey Dean Kogan.

"Your face looks sad," Frieda said. "Why aren't you happy?" She threw her bear onto the floor and pushed her head into the bedspread.

My five-year-old had no idea why she was suffering. I pulled her into my arms and reached for Garth.

Jill said, "You have to tell them. You have to tell them everything."

Even if it would twist away their innocence? But if I didn't confide in our children, they'd learn the ugly things I'd been accused of later at school. I picked up the remote and turned off the television. Now the room was even darker.

"Daddy," Frieda yelled.

After today, our children would never see me the same way. It didn't matter if I was innocent. "I'm going to tell you something that's not nice."

Frieda's mouth closed and her eyes grew uncertain, as if she were preparing to burst into tears again. "Did Grandma die?"

"No no no. Grandma Rose is fine."

"It's about the police," Garth said.

My perceptive, fragile boy had heard something. He too was struggling and needed reassurance.

"Do you remember Grandma Rose's first husband?" I said.

"He's in heaven," Frieda said.

"It's not true."

Both our children's mouths drew open.

They didn't need to know all the horrific details. They had the rest of their lives to face those. "My daddy did some very bad things. They put him in jail so he'd never hurt anybody. We haven't spoken to him for more than thirty years."

Frieda's eyes expanded and her mouth slid open. "Six times me."

"He killed people," Garth said.

How did he know?

The bed creaked and Jill's arm draped around me. She rubbed my back, as if I were the child she had to comfort. My wife gave me courage.

"The problem is, the police think I did some bad things. They think I'm like my daddy."

Both my children stared as if they were watching a part of me disappear. Garth's shoulders, so huge beside Frieda's tiny frame, seemed to curl in on themselves.

"They think I hurt Ms. Morton at your school."

"They're wrong," Frieda shouted.

Her tear-filled face made me want to erase what I'd said. But it was too late.

Jill drew her arm tighter around my shoulders. "They're completely wrong." She stared from Garth to Frieda to me, as if daring any of us to think I could do such a thing.

Our kids gave me a bear hug. I leaned back and felt myself uncoil, as if my whole body were relinquishing a burden.

Garth jerked away and pushed himself off the bed. "They think you killed her. They think you killed Ms. Morton, and now they're going to kill *you*."

Jill pulled him into her arms. As he wept, she stroked his hair. "No one is going to hurt your daddy," she said. "Your daddy is innocent. Don't you ever think any other thing."

I wondered if there was anything in the world so brightly fragile as our children.

Something rapped against the door. I pushed myself away from Frieda. Jill walked toward the sound. "Wait," I said.

"What's wrong?" Frieda yelled.

Jill reached for her purse on the table and withdrew her revolver. She looked through the keyhole. *"Tu tía está,"* she said to Frieda. She opened the door.

"I hope Micky Marvin didn't put pepperoni on my pizza," Polly said.

26

JILL AND I STARED through the rental car's windshield at the lit-up second floor motel room. Garth, Frieda, and Polly were playing Crazy Eights inside. Beside us, the cars scudded along the freeway, their lights burrowing into the night. We didn't look at each other. We had to talk. But what would those words—and all the thoughts behind them—do to our marriage?

Jill said, "Do you know what I thought when those detectives showed up at school?"

There was no good answer to that question.

"I thought this lunatic had killed you."

I reached across the seat compartment between us to touch her shoulder. She moved away.

"The next day they brought a policewoman with them. You know why? To stay with Garth and Frieda. So they could talk with me alone."

"To tell you I was—"

"I knew you couldn't have murdered Elizabeth."

What, then?

She turned. The motel lights reflected the tears in her eyes. It hit me. "Did they talk to you about my home office?"

She looked down at her lap. So here we were, finally at the core of what loomed between us. I imagined Hempel showing her the bottle of bourbon, then lifting the vape pen and the container of marijuana extract. Finally, the coup de grace, the copies of my father's pictures. I could almost hear their questions. *Did you know about the marijuana? Why didn't he tell you about those pictures? How are your husband's relationships with women?* At that moment, I hated those detectives as much as I hated the killer.

"I knew you were drinking in your office at night," she said. "I could smell the alcohol on you. Sometimes I thought I caught a whiff of marijuana. But I figured you needed those things. Because of your insomnia."

I didn't know how to begin.

"Say something," she said.

"I can't imagine what you thought."

"You can't imagine? That's it?" She let out an exasperated sigh.

I said, "At night my whole body feels what he did."

She nodded. Waited.

She said, "Your mother taught you to hide your hurts and worries, didn't she? But not with me. Please, William."

I looked up at the motel room where my sister watched over our children. I said, "At night I wonder if he escaped and I don't know it. So I go on the internet. I look at the websites and make sure he's still in prison, still at Stateville. I make sure one of his crazy fans doesn't have a bead on us. But even when I know we're safe, I feel him hovering. It's like his evil is fidgeting and pacing in my body. All the guilt and shame just pours over me. It's even worse since we had children. What if his genes are hiding inside Garth and Frieda? That's why I have the bourbon and the vape pen."

She stared up at the roof as if she were trying to see through the car to the stars. I knew what she was thinking about. Something far worse than bourbon and marijuana. But my mouth wouldn't move.

She said, "I get how everyone has secrets. Shit, it wasn't like you didn't tell me about those photographs. But that was in Colombia. Years ago. Why would you have those things in our house?"

I had to get out of the car. My fingers snatched at the door handle. She set her hand on my shoulder. It was the lightness of her touch that stopped me. Her face was tender.

"Talk to me," she said.

A terrible shame infused my cheeks. There were no words for such an old and disgraceful obsession.

"Please," she said.

I had to say something—for the sake of our marriage. "I haven't looked at them in years."

She put her hand on my arm. "Is this your punishment? Each time you open your desk and see that steel box … you force yourself to face up to what he did."

I swallowed. Forced out the words. "Those photographs prove I'll never be like him."

She slowly shook her head and turned to face the window. A sadness floated between us. We watched a car rumble through the parking lot and turn off its lights. A noisy family clunked up the stairs to their room.

"And you couldn't talk to me about it?"

"What would you think? No normal man would keep those things close to his family."

I felt her eyes reaching for me but I couldn't look at her.

"You still believe you carry him inside you, don't you?" she said.

The fear, the guilt, the shame, the years I'd tried to untangle my past … they were all woven into those photos. But most of all, his darkness lived there, the darkness that might also lurk in me. I said, "All his monstrous thoughts are locked inside that steel box. It's as close as I can get to controlling what he did to my life."

She sighed. We stared up at the motel room with our kids inside.

She said, "You've been trying to figure this out since you were a child, haven't you?"

"I try to put words around it. But they're just words."

She reached across the space between us and her fingers caressed my hair. "Those women weren't the only victims. He really messed you up too."

"And Polly."

She shook her head. "Thank God you two have each other. You know, when you were arrested, Polly insisted I bring the kids to her house. She said we had to deny the hysteria. She wouldn't even let us turn on the TV. I was actually happy to hear her spout her opinions."

We smiled. It encapsulated what we both cherished and couldn't stand about Polly. "Don't tell her this," I said, "but sometimes she sounds just like Mama."

Jill's palm touched my cheek. "Polly says everyone believes *she* suffered the most because of your father. But she thinks you were more hurt. She wears her wounds, but you bury yours."

My generous sister.

"When those detectives talked to me, I couldn't believe they were describing my husband. This was the person I knew better than anyone in the world. How could I have thought that about him?"

I might not have heard what hid inside that last sentence but for the way Jill's eyes flinched open and framed her betrayal. She leaned across the space between the seats and threw her arms around me. She began to weep. I looked down at her blonde hair, her face pushing into my chest. She held me as tightly as one of our children would.

A terrible fist clenched inside me. Would we ever love each other in the same way again? I told myself that thousands of betrayals can creep into a marriage and still not break it. How was her doubt any worse than the pictures I'd hidden inside our house? I put my arms around her. But something still balled inside my chest.

When we drew apart, our fingers interlaced. I stared at her watch, with its simple leather band. Jill's eyelashes were as translucent and delicate as moth wings. I should have told her about the picture the killer had sent to Marta's office. But I couldn't. Not tonight.

27

JILL AND I HAD met in Colombia. It was supposed to be an easy assignment, one that would help me cast off the demon that had possessed me in Algeria. The photo exposé would be called "Colombia after Pablo." Éscobar had lived in Medellín, but he'd also terrorized Bogotá, the capital. That first morning, wisps of clouds twined around the gray Bogotá skyscrapers and hovered above the clay-tiled roofs of the houses. A cable car ascended to a white church that shimmered in the green Andes Mountains. The only guide I could afford proposed carting me around on the back of his Yamaha motorcycle. When I told him I'd just photographed a civil war in Algeria, he said he knew just the place for me to shoot.

The next morning, I rode behind him to Cartucho, the underside of Bogotá that the government had surrendered to drugs and prostitution.

Crumbling three-story concrete and brick buildings leaned over little alleys paved with mud and litter. Addicts slept on the sides of the streets. The more fortunate ones huddled inside structures cobbled together with rotting wood, plastic tarps, and newspaper-filled garbage bags. Most mornings the sun rose over at least one new murder victim. As I gazed at that gray street of suffering, I realized that I'd fled Algeria only to gravitate to the darkest corner of Colombia.

I stuck my eye against the Nikon and, in seconds, absorbed myself in the lines and layers of Cartucho. The figures crumpled on those streets were so covered in dirt that, in the soft morning light, their images appeared black and gray. I was snapping quickly with a telephoto lens when I saw her. Tall blondes stood out in Bogotá. In a red baseball cap and a gray *ruana*, she knelt next to a street kid. The boy's hair was shaved down to a nub above his dirt-blackened face. Grime completely covered the original colors of his pants and shirt. But his spotless blue Reeboks looked new. She pulled him close to give him a hug. It was a perfect shot: Cartucho as a backdrop, the dirty urchin with new shoes clutching the woman with her blonde hair hanging out of her baseball cap.

She let out a yell and ran toward us. My guide revved the motorcycle. "Wait," I said.

The morning light and her anger lit her green eyes. When I apologized in my primitive Spanish, she shouted back in English that I had no right to take pictures without permission. I explained that I was a photojournalist. My job was to document the underworld that people didn't want to see. That quieted her. Her pale cheeks looked so angular compared to the wide faces of the Colombians. She was still angry but accepted my lunch invitation.

That afternoon, my guide dropped me off at a café near the city hall to meet her. Plastic-covered tables, a red counter, and a refrigerator full of soft drinks and beer crowded the little room. Salsa trumpets and a loud bass throbbed through good speakers. When she arrived, she called out a greeting in Spanish to the owner. Even as I stood up, she pulled out her own chair and sat. Her hair shone white in the café's tungsten light. I wondered if she'd let it down for me.

"Are you really a photojournalist?" she asked. I expected a sardonic smile but saw only curiosity.

"The cover of *Time* a month ago," I said. "Photos of a village in Algeria."

Her eyes spread open. "The massacre? You took those pictures?"

I heard disgust in her voice, or maybe it was just surprise. In those days, I felt recrimination in most conversations. Motioning to the street outside, I said, "It looks like you found another kind of hell right here."

Her body stiffened under the bulky *ruana*. She glanced at her cheap watch with its scratched leather band. "Some of the best people I've ever met live in these blocks."

Jill Bartlett spoke the idealistic words of a college girl, yet her voice and face seemed tired, as if she'd suffered a great deal to maintain that optimism.

"I came here for a semester," she said. "That was two years ago."

The owner set down plates of salad, rice, beans, and *arepas*. She waited for him to leave, then leaned across the table to tell me why she stayed. More than a hundred thousand families had fled to Bogotá because of civil war and the hard life in the countryside. But in Bogotá there were no jobs and no food and the fathers abandoned their wives and children. To survive, the wives took up with new men, and the new men rejected the other men's offspring—especially the boys. As young as five, these children were pushed onto the streets. Alienated, they developed their own forms of Spanish. At night, to keep warm, they slept in packs on newspapers in the sewers. During the day, they robbed the vendors and shopkeepers. "The shopkeepers pay the police to kill them," she said. "They call it 'rehabilitation.'"

"They murder children?"

"Five of my kids in the last year." Above her furious scowl, her eyes blinked back tears.

Had the outrage made her stay? A blonde *gringa* taking on the dark excesses of Cartucho? "How do you keep going?" I asked.

She nodded for five seconds, as if congratulating me on the quality of my question. "I don't work alone. Father Nícolo has a whole organization."

"But what can *you* do?"

"I hug them. I tell them they're important. Sometimes all these little boys need is hope." She frowned. "You have no idea what it's like to help a child dream, do you?"

The question seemed condescending, yet I didn't feel accused. The usual sarcastic words didn't flare up in my mind. Instead I felt as if I were soaking up her strength.

"Tell me why you're really here," she said. She crinkled her eyes and I saw softness, a willingness to sympathize, inside her fierceness.

I was exhausted, far from home. I assumed I'd never see her again. But it was more than that. Being confronted with her honesty, I didn't want to hide anymore. In that little café, I told her about the hell I'd photographed in Algeria. Before I knew it, I revealed the atrocities my father had committed, and what it was like to grow up in my crazy family. My whole life, I'd had to define myself as someone different from him.

She shook her head and tendrils of blonde hair shifted and glowed in the café's lights. "No one could think you were like him."

"*He* could have taken those pictures in Béni-Messous."

She didn't cringe. She didn't retreat to the bathroom. Her eyes crimped up and she reached across the table to cup my hand. "You were abandoned too," she said.

The unexpected truth of it knocked the air out of me.

"The whole world must have been talking about your father. But now he was a stranger."

I expected to see pity in her sad smile but spotted a different, more discerning kind of sympathy. Instead of running from my history, she wanted to understand it.

I told her how I'd tried to comprehend my father by studying his deviant photos, how Mama pretended that her husband had died and moved us to California, how she steeped herself in religious platitudes and wouldn't even talk about him.

"Maybe religion gave her the strength to protect her two kids," Jill said.

We quietly chewed on the salad. Conversations and laughter crested over us. Someone had turned off the salsa music. She took a deep breath and hunched over that table to stare into my eyes. "You might have some of your father's darkness. But that doesn't make you *like* him."

The kitchen door of the restaurant opened and her eyes lit up like malachite. The brass pre-Colombian figure on her leather necklace was beautiful. When we parted that afternoon in Bogotá, I gave her Mama's address. She kissed me on the cheek.

Three years later, I'd left photojournalism and resolved to live a life that could never reference my father and his photos. Excitement in banking came only from deals and achieving a business plan. It was a profession where I could get to know the lives of my clients and their families without ever revealing my tortured past. My colleagues didn't need to become my friends.

Jill sent a postcard to Mama's address. "Remember me?" Her father worked at Camp Pendleton, and she'd moved to be closer to her parents. She was studying to be a teacher. We met at a Korean restaurant. She wore another cheap watch with a different leather band and I wore a banker's suit. I kissed her that night.

My family loved Jill almost as much as they loved me. Mama admired her optimism. Polly liked her spunk. "A blonde in the slums of Bogotá," Polly kept saying. Then, "William, I adore this woman." And finally, after I'd dated Jill more than three years, Polly said, "Are you gonna grow some balls and propose, or what?"

28

MY SISTER WAS IMPULSIVELY courageous. I was the only one who could talk her into being more careful. That would mean leaving Jill and our kids in the motel room. But Jill had already stayed there for days. Before she'd even checked in, she'd tested the lock and double bolt. She had a revolver and could shoot better than I could. I left her with our kids and followed Polly's truck back to Normal Heights.

Polly's home, one of the few two-story houses in the area, stood at the end of a road that overlooked a protected canyon. When she'd purchased it, the structure was a wreck; that was the only way she could afford it. For five years, she oversaw work on the new roof, windows, kitchen, and bathrooms, often pounding away herself at midnight or later. The people next door didn't appreciate her diligence. They also didn't like the honeybee hives she bought for the backyard.

Lawyers got involved and Polly ended up driving the hives to a farm. Then there was the problem of her bright green grass. San Diego was in a drought and the neighbors thought she was illegally using too much water. When the city inspector arrived, she gave him a tour of her gray-water plumbing system and the cistern buried in the back yard. When he left, he clutched a coupon for a free dessert at the Haven.

Tonight, we stood on the wooden landing and peered through the front door's red and blue stained glass. She pointed to the wrought iron bars over the windows. "He'd have to cut through those to get in. Then there's the alarm."

"He disabled my alarm," I said.

"Shit."

She unlocked the door and punched in her code. A skateboard leaned against the side of the wooden staircase. Above the stairs a friend had drawn a mural of yellow female silhouettes, their faces blurred, flying above a pitched roof. Tonight, their obscured expressions seemed angry. On other days, they looked sad or sagely confident. "But never, ever afraid," Polly always told me.

My sister boiled water and poured it into a French press. I followed her into the dining room with its bamboo floors and rows of framed Panamanian *molas*. Five Wonder Women dolls lounged on the glass top of her china-filled hutch. She set the press next to her computer on the table. I glimpsed a half-written blog, her latest food opinion, on the screen. My sister wrote about local, naturally produced farm-to-table food and the perils of poison-for-profit agribusiness. She or someone on her staff drove her pickup to organic farms for untainted vegetables and meat from hormone-free animals. "Factory food is a delivery mechanism for empty calories and sugar," she said. At least five times a day.

She poured the coffee, thick as oil, into mugs. Tonight, the house seemed too big and quiet. I said, "You really shouldn't be here alone."

Polly fished out a handgun from her backpack. My sister carried around a loaded revolver while she zoomed through San Diego in her truck. Without a concealed carry permit, of course. If she ever pulled out that gun in public, she'd be arrested. "Laws have about as much effect on the crazies as algebra or calculus," she liked to tell me, the brother who was good in math.

"Can't you get a roommate for a while?" I said.

She placed the pistol beside her inhaler on the table. "I sleep with these," she said.

"Polly, this bastard is aiming at all of us. You need protection."

Polly was proud of her ability to defend herself, even if it was mostly a fantasy. She shook her head, sipped her coffee, and closed her eyes.

The one thing that consistently gave joy to my sister was the first taste of a fresh cup. I let her savor it. She was looking more and more like an elf, wrinkles and folds giving new dimensions to her neck and hands. The spidery circles around her eyes only intensified her gaze. She had adorned her ears with diamond studs in the nineties, and now, as gray crept into her hair, she still wore them. And that watch as big as a clock? "At least I don't need glasses now," she'd insisted after she bought it. "Glasses are so ugly."

After her third sip, I said, "You told Marta about Pop."

"Pop. God, I hate that name."

"I'm glad you told her. Apparently the press doesn't know he's our father."

"It's inevitable, William."

"Do you think the killer is trying to reach Harvey Dean Kogan through me?"

The coffee moment was over. She reached across the table and clutched my arm. I looked down at the dolphin tattoo on her wrist, the faint cutting scar underneath.

"You know what he wants to show the Preying Hands?" she said. "That, even after all these years, we can't escape."

"Why kill Elizabeth?"

Her short fingernails dug into my skin. "She was at the same school as Jill. Your kids knew her. That cocksucker would have loved those details."

That cocksucker. Our father. Pop. The man who killed and cut up women and then came home to play with us.

"But who knew we were his children? Jill's the only one I ever told."

She withdrew her fingers from my arm and chafed her hands against the ceramic cup, her silver bracelets jingling. "A lot of people have been looking for a lot of years. So, one of them found us."

"It's as if this person—I assume it's a man—"

"It's a man."

"It's as if he's trying to reach the part of me I fear the most."

"Yeah, I think he is."

I hadn't expected her to agree with me so quickly. "But why?"

She cocked her head as if it were obvious. "He wants to punish us for disowning our father. You know the best way to do that? Turn you into the Preying Hands."

I stared down into the dark coffee. My sister had articulated what I'd suspected, but it was still too warped to get my mind around.

The world's ugliest cat ambled down the stairs and she cradled him. He hung from her arms, fixing those cold, lemon-shaped green eyes on me. He didn't blink. Homer was furless and always looked like a giant rat to me. She'd bought him because he was supposed to be hypoallergenic. I thought she'd chosen the name because he was a Sphinx cat and Greece lay close to Egypt. But I was wrong. "Homer

Simpson," Polly told me. "Our Homer lost his fur because he lived next to the nuclear plant." One of his huge fleshy ears was half bitten off from a lifetime of fighting. Ridged scars extended from the pink wrinkled skin of his neck to the loose folds of his potbelly. I often wondered why she'd picked a predator as the only male allowed in her bed. Then I remembered the kittens our father had burned when we were children. Homer bore the scarred flesh of a warrior survivor.

Polly put him down and he rubbed against her leg. "How are Jill and the kids holding up?" she asked.

"Jill never knew how the world would punish her. Just for joining our family."

"She'll get over this. She's a strong woman. You just make sure she and the kids stay safe."

I sipped the coffee and felt fatigue pulling my body inside out. "The police refused to give us protection. No budget."

"That's bullshit."

"Not if they think they've already caught the killer." Just saying it made the old anger hit me, hard and fast. "Goddamn it, we've spent most of our lives running from what he did. And we never did anything. Ever."

She formed a bitter smile. "Tell that to the people in Blue Meadow. Tell them how Mama tried to heal the evil out of a serial killer."

"Mama had no idea what he was."

"She didn't *want* to know. But deep down … she knew the devil slept in her bed."

The argument was so old—and so hopeless. I repeated what I'd been saying for years. "Mama's different now."

"William, I swear, sometimes you're as delusional as she is."

"Maybe it's you that hasn't changed."

"Next topic."

We were both angry. I should have waited, even just a few minutes. Instead I told her about the photo of Elizabeth Morton's head, knowing how it would puncture her. Polly pushed her head into her hand. Her frail body seemed to shrink more.

I felt cruel then. I got up and walked around the table to hug her. "We're going to find this bastard," I said. "We'll prove to the police it's not me. This is going to end."

It was an old method for dealing with tragedy in our family: denial by optimism.

———————

After Pop's arrest, Mama, Polly, and I had moved back into the trailer. But we could no longer face all the people in our town and huddled inside our home as if we were in a spaceship. A month later, Mama decided that we should reject our "belief of isolation." She insisted that Polly go to the middle school dance and, as an incentive, bought her new jeans from Walmart.

The night of the dance, I sat in the car's front seat with Mama. Polly made us park three blocks away. As the door creaked open, our mother's shrill voice rose above the ticking engine.

"You just open yourself up to good things, Polly Kogan. Fun is part of God, you know."

"God made those kids nice," I said.

"And he made Mama's scraggly teeth too, didn't he?" Polly said.

Mama's mouth slacked open, then snapped shut. Her crooked teeth would contradict anything she said.

Polly ran for almost a block. Then she trudged so slowly I wasn't sure she was still moving.

"Your sister is going to have a good time," Mama said. "I prayed on it with Betty Treeble."

That night, only one boy asked Polly to dance. During a slow song, the boy leaned in and whispered in her ear. At first Polly thought he said he wanted to kiss her. Then she made out names. "Bonnie, Kim, Winnie, Barb ..." He recited the other nine victims, his voice growing louder as my sister fled across the gym. "Did your daddy teach you how to saw up a body?" the boy yelled.

Polly was sitting at the edge of the parking lot when Mama and I picked her up. As she slid into the back seat, Mama said, "Whatever *some* of those kids did to you, there're others who know it was wrong. The others will be your friends, Polly."

I said, "It's like Daniel in the lion's den. You can't give in to fear."

Polly normally would have sneered. But she just pushed her face into her pulled-up knees and wound what was left of her skinny body into a ball. She wore black ankle boots with bits of beads and ribbons tied to elaborately knotted white laces. Between the ankle boots and her jeans I saw lines of thin scabs where she'd cut herself.

At home I retreated to the sweet smell of our apple tree. If I stayed out of sight, maybe Mama and Polly wouldn't put me between them. Maybe they'd forget that I was there. But the memory of my sister's collapsed body roiled my insides. How could God's perfection feel so much like pain? I heard Mama's voice in my mind. She was telling me to correct my thinking. But I couldn't. Polly had tried to be friends, just as Mama told her. And look what happened.

Later, Polly told me that she dreamed about her classmates after the dance. They held her down and slowly cut her apart, starting with her toes and fingers. I hugged her then. I was five years younger, but I tried to comfort my big sister.

I felt guilty for not reflecting God enough to heal her. I still feel guilty. But now it's for not having forced Mama to love Polly for who she was—and is. When Frieda or Garth scurry to our bedroom, their bodies bursting with fear from some terrible dream, I can't refuse them. I hoist them into our bed and welcome our children inside the little cave of blankets between Jill and me.

And I think of my sister.

————

I left Polly and drove toward the motel, then made a sharp U-turn. I had to go home. By the time I arrived, it was ten o'clock at night. Even the yard looked gutted. The police had ripped out the ground cover and much of the jacaranda from the garden. They'd torn away the skirt of ivy around the palm tree, as if the vines might have grasped a hand or a foot. I strode into the backyard. Boards that had been pried off the deck lay stacked on the grass.

Inside, the mail was piled up like a deck of cards thrown down below the slot. The police had stripped the bed in our room and set the mattress, with probing stab holes in it, against the wall. My suits, still on the hangers, lay stacked on the floor next to plastic bags of clothes. Except for the smell of the cedar chest, our bedroom didn't seem like ours.

The neatness of my children's rooms was a bigger violation. All Frieda's bears and dolls sat beside a pile of central air grates. I picked up a plastic bag and her miniature tea set clacked inside. In Garth's room, his stripped mattress leaned against the wall. The investigators had removed the plastic cover and now his old yellow urine stains—his shameful secret—were revealed.

I needed the medicine in my office. The police must have searched my desk, but maybe they hadn't taken everything. The bottom drawer was unlocked. The bottle of bourbon lay on its side by the empty steel box, but the vape pen had disappeared. The police had also confiscated the marijuana extract, the red pocketknife, and the copies of Harvey Dean Kogan's pictures. All my secrets would be revealed at trial.

My father gave the pocketknife to me the night of my seventh birthday. We'd helped a woman on a dark road change a tire. He pointed out how she'd sucked in her lips and her pupils had widened when she saw us. "The body grows scared before the mind," he said. When she'd driven away, he placed the pocketknife in my hand. It was the best gift ever. I still remember the pungent odor of the June hyacinths.

I grabbed the bourbon, went to the living room, and turned off the lights. The soft warmth of the alcohol slid through my body. It was what I needed, what I deserved after the hell I'd been through. I lay down on the couch like an unwanted guest and waited for my thoughts to shut off. But they wouldn't. People I didn't even know had torn my family's house apart, and I'd been absent.

A specter coiled in the drunken air above me. "I always knew this is what you'd become," it whispered.

I drove back to the motel and curled in beside Jill on the double bed. Maybe if I held her tight enough I could recover my home.

29

I WOKE JILL AT six in the morning. Outside, under the landing's spot-lights, her hair fell like a sheet of water to her shoulder. I tucked strands behind her ears, putting off what I had to tell her. We both watched the sun rise and shimmer off the cars on the highway. All those people hurtling from somewhere to somewhere else.

She pulled away. The skin around her eyes furrowed into a question. I reached down and caressed her hand. I told her about the picture of Elizabeth that the murderer had sent to my attorney's office. Her mouth opened. "Had he ... had he ...?"

I nodded.

She collapsed her elbow onto the railing and covered her face with her hand. I looped my arm around her and drew her limp shoulders to me. I told her she needed to take the kids to her parents' house in

Leucadia, where her father had a collection of guns and a state-of-the-art alarm system. It was safer if I was alone while I looked for the killer.

She turned her face to me. "This is exactly what this bastard wants. To rip us apart."

My wife is an optimistic person. When she grows depressed, I find myself manufacturing hopefulness. "We're a strong family," I said. "We'll get through this."

"Will we?" She pulled away. Hunched her shoulders into the wooden rail and looked down at the parking lot of empty cars. "Garth is in trouble at school."

It wasn't a surprise. My sensitive boy had to react to the crises swirling around him. He'd held a pencil under another boy's seat and the boy sat down on the point.

"Intentionally?" I asked.

Her eyes fired. She pounded out the words with her wrists on the wooden railing. "HE DIDN'T STAB HIM."

Her shoulders shook. I tried to pull her to me but she pushed away. Jill would battle even me to protect her son. On her outstretched arms, I saw her watch. The crystal had cracked.

I'd met Jill's parents when her mother asked me to dinner two months after we started dating. Mike, her father, had seen terrible things up country in Vietnam. That night we avoided talk about Southeast Asia, Algeria, and Harvey Dean Kogan. After the meal, he and I sucked on cigars and sipped port while Jill and April, her mother, cleaned up. Mike broke the silence. "You know all the awful things you can't get out of your mind in your twenties? Well, those memories get fuzzier in your thirties. By your fifties they might even fade away." Later he said, "I served with a few men who enjoyed killing. Those men all had kids. And those kids turned out just fine." We were friends for life after that.

Mike arrived at the motel wearing a holster. At sixty-six, he still was imposingly tall and fit, his head full of blond hair. His khakis and shirt were perfectly pressed, his shoes buffed to a military shine. He hugged Jill and our kids and shook my hand. Grasping my arm, he leaned in and whispered, "If the police don't get this son-of-a-bitch, you and I will."

Without kissing me goodbye, Jill climbed into her father's Lexus with Garth and Frieda. She didn't look back as Grandpa Mike drove away. I watched the cars that trailed them. It was pointless. Mike, the soldier, would protect them better than I could.

A half hour later, I still held the motel's railing. The sun was sucking up the last of the morning breeze and beginning to bake the parking lot's blacktop. My cell phone rang.

I recognized the detective's grating voice before I pulled in his name. "We've still got your suit at the station," Ben Hempel said. "You better come get it. Otherwise somebody at the Salvation Army is gonna look like a banker."

That didn't seem too ominous.

"And we want to show you a letter the *Union-Tribune* just got," Hempel said.

"From who?"

"Who do you think?"

I stopped breathing. The killer would only send a letter to take credit for the murder. The letter could exonerate me.

"If you want to see what he says, come to the station. And William, let's leave your lawyer at home, okay?"

158

30

"BEN, HOW THE HELL are you?" Marta said. We stood in front of the blue plastic seats in the reception area of the police station on Broadway. My lawyer carried an enormous purse as big as a briefcase.

"Just dandy," Hempel said, his voice like gravel. He wasn't at all perturbed that I'd brought Marta along. Today his white shirt tugged at the buttons, as if he'd borrowed it from a younger, less broad-chested version of himself.

Marta reached over to touch his striped tie. "I've missed you, Ben."

He grinned. "We keep hoping you'll reject the devil and come back."

"To be a prosecutor again? How is that rejecting the devil?"

They chuckled as if I weren't there.

We strolled past the gate at the reception desk. On the other side, Marta said, "How goes the battle?"

"Twenty days," Hempel said.

"Damn. We're rooting for you."

I had no idea what they were talking about. Was Hempel in AA?

We reached the elevator in the back. On the fourth floor, Hempel led us into Homicide and to the same interview room they'd stuck me in before. Just looking at those ancient wood panels and the sickly Girl Scout green walls made my stomach tighten. I sat at the same place at the table, the box of Kleenex in front of me and the whiteboard on the wall above. But this time Marta was beside me. Hempel sat next to her and gnawed on the inside of his cheek.

There was a knock. Lund leaned against the doorjamb in a tailored gray pinstripe. "Look who's here." His bass voice rolled out like an announcer at a charity gala.

"Why, if it isn't the best-dressed detective in San Diego," Marta said.

Lund grinned and flashed his gold cuff links. "Only the top of my game for you, Marta."

The Old Home Week banter was as grating as Hempel's voice. "Can we talk about the letter?" I asked.

Lund shut the door behind him. Today he wasn't trying to convince me I could leave at any time. He handed me a folder and sat on the side of the table opposite Hempel. We were so tightly packed together, the cedar and rosemary scent of Lund's cologne seemed to suck up all the air.

Lund said, "The *Union-Tribune* got it in the mail this morning."

Inside the folder was a photocopy of a typed note with no signature. Marta and I read it at the same time.

My Dear Public:

Does anyone who wears yellow sneakers deserve to live? That sin was almost as bad as her wrenching a child's arm. At least

160

Elizabeth Morton loved *The Giving Tree*. She loved it so much that I made her a part of the story.

Now you know the punishment for an evil woman who assaults children. Justice is a tornado that slips across the empty cornfields and hurls itself upon the icy lake.

By the way, publish this letter and I will delay punishing another child abuser. Some would consider that a Hobson's choice, but I'd classify it more as a dilemma.

Your friend,
The Defender of Children

My father could have written the first paragraph before he was arrested. Even the second paragraph's poetic twists sounded like his. But the third paragraph showed off the writer's education. As if he were saying that he was the next, more enlightened Preying Hands.

"Well?" Lund said.

I told him what I thought. He nodded as if I'd revealed something he didn't know. I doubted that. Maybe he believed I'd explained the note so well because I'd written it.

Something else was hidden in that text, something familiar I couldn't quite pull in.

"Are you sure this isn't some nutcase?" Marta said.

Lund frowned. "There were pictures. 'Before' and 'After.'"

I tried to block out those images, but I still saw Elizabeth's eviscerated body. The killer had cut her up the same way the Preying Hands would. With one significant difference. "Harvey Dean Kogan never cut off breasts," I said.

Lund raked his hand through his hair. The layers of gray sprang back into place. "How do you know that happened with Elizabeth?"

"Because you showed him the goddamn picture when you arrested him," Marta said. "The World's Greatest Attorney even mentioned it in court. Cut the bullshit. Now why the hell hasn't the DA dropped the charges?"

"Based on one letter to a newspaper?" Lund said.

"The pictures," Marta said. "Whoever sent them murdered Elizabeth Morton."

Hempel drew back, his broad face squinting and frowning. He looked as if he still believed I was the killer.

Lund said, "You used to be on this side of the table. Let him help us."

Marta shook her head. "I like you guys, but that doesn't mean I'm gonna go all stupid. Just give him back his clothes so we can go."

Neither Hempel nor Lund moved in their chairs. Hempel unwrapped a piece of gum and shoved it in his mouth. They had a bigger agenda than gauging my reaction to the letter.

Hempel scratched the nape of his neck and met my eyes. "The killer's gone through all kinds of hoops to pin the evidence on you. Why the hell would he send this?"

To punish me for abandoning my father. But I couldn't say that. Besides, I knew what Hempel was really driving at. "What's the postmark date?" I asked.

Hempel said, "Day before yesterday."

"It would be pretty hard for me to mail it from jail," I said.

Hempel and Lund both slowly nodded, as if they hadn't thought of that.

"Unless someone mailed it *for* you," Hempel said.

Marta reached below the chair. She heaved up her purse with both hands as if she were getting ready to walk out. "Ben, you know why the killer sent the letter. It isn't enough for him to do the deed and frame William. He has to make sure the whole world knows how clever he is. He has to tell everyone he's the second coming of the Preying Hands."

Lund stared at the half-paneling encircling the room. He pushed back his chair and hiked one pinstriped leg over the other. "Well, there is something that could help us all get on the same team."

"Team," the word people pulled out when they intended to use you.

"I can barely stand the suspense," Marta said.

"A polygraph," Lund said. "Then we'd be able to tell the chief how much you're cooperating."

"And maybe he'll make an exception and approve some protection for your family," Hempel said.

I was innocent. What did I have to worry about from a lie detector test?

Marta was chortling.

"I'd fly through it," I said.

"Let me tell you something," Marta said. "Christ himself would fail a polygraph if you gave it to him on the wrong day." She was talking to me but looking at Hempel and Lund. "Which these fine detectives know perfectly well."

Lund grinned.

"I'd be disappointed if you didn't try," Marta said to them.

It hit me like one of Mama's angel thoughts. I remembered where the first sentences of the letter came from.

"'Justice is a tornado that slips across the empty cornfields and hurls itself upon the icy lake,'" I said.

Marta and the two detectives slowly turned to me.

I went on. "Harvey Dean Kogan used exactly the same phrasing to describe what he did to Bev Holland."

"Bev Holland?" Hempel said.

Marta grabbed my arm and shook her head. I was displaying too much familiarity with my father's murders. To the detectives, she said, "Look it up."

"You sure know a lot about his victims," Lund said.

"Just give us his damn clothes," Marta said.

Hempel reached below his chair and handed me a paper bag. Inside were my cell phone and the suit and shirt I was arrested in. "We all know you're innocent. We just have to prove it." Hempel almost looked as though he meant it.

I took the bag, wondering if a listening device and GPS tracker were sewn into my suit.

Once in my car, Bev Holland came back to me. Twenty-six years old and a single mom, she'd made the tragic mistake of letting her child wander into a swimming pool. To punish her, Harvey Dean Kogan stole her bike and advertised the sale of another on the bulletin board of her apartment building. She met him in a Sears parking lot to take a look at the "almost new Schwinn."

I was eight months old. Probably asleep in an infant seat next to jars of baby food. Why else would Holland step inside that van? She'd come by bus and Harvey Dean Kogan offered to drive her and the bike home to her Schaumburg neighborhood. When she climbed inside, he chloroformed her.

In the photo, the Preying Hands set her head on top of my car seat, her hands wired in prayer in front of her face. Her shoes sat on either side of the hands, the feet and ankles still in them. When Harvey Dean Kogan sent that picture to the *Chicago Sun-Times*, he glued a shot of a swimming pool below it. That was the only time he used a diptych method. Newspaper type spelled out the message across the blue of the pool: "Buckle up when swimming."

I'd always wondered if I had sat inside his shed while he composed that picture with her body. Maybe what he'd done to Bev Holland festered in parts of me I didn't even know existed.

31

MAMA HAD ALWAYS DREAMED of living in a house in La Jolla. She ended up within ten miles. When Polly and I were young, she would have considered a home with four miniature rooms and a two-car garage a palace. She inherited her new house from Randall, the man she married sixteen years after her first husband was arrested. A fellow Christian Scientist, Randall showed Mama how much fun it could be to only partially reflect God. His money gave her the material comforts that Christian Scientists thought were just illusions but still loved to acquire. Eight years into their marriage, despite Mama's healing powers, poor overweight Randall keeled over from a heart attack. Mama consoled herself by retreating to his kitchen. She lingered over his out-of-date Formica counters and dark-stained laminate cabinets. Her fingers ran over his seashells and model sailboats. She seemed to listen for his cackle on the other side of the wall.

Polly and I met there on Sunday night. I'd spent the weekend hiding out at my in-laws' house and reconnecting with Jill and our kids. But now it was time to ask Mama about the first husband she'd tried so hard to forget. We needed clues from the man the killer was copying. I brought Garth and Frieda along so Jill could have a night alone with her parents. By the time we arrived, Polly's red pickup already stood in the dark driveway. As usual, Mama had left her front door wide open. She wasn't going to fear the killer. That only gave him power.

Mama used to be coat-hanger-thin, but had grown a belly over the years. "My body reflects how my thoughts are flourishing," she'd say. I was never sure it was a joke. Tonight, she sat on her living room couch next to Polly. She wore a spotless white shawl draped over a plain blue dress—Mama did not wear pants.

When Polly saw my kids, she jumped up, twirled Frieda, and slapped palms with Garth. Mama rose to give me a hug. "William, I knew they'd let you go. It was just mortal mind controlling the police."

Mortal mind. Over the years she'd tempered her use of Christian Science vocabulary, but the old expressions still slipped out. When Polly and I were children, Mary Baker Eddy's words made their way into most of Mama's conversations.

"I guess your prayers made the police see the error of their ways," Polly said. She couldn't resist rankling Mama. That was probably why she wore black pants, a black shirt, a green bow tie, and a green vest.

Mama pursed her lips, her form of disapproval. "How's my Garth?"

Garth shrugged and looked at the floor.

"Young man, when someone asks how you are, you say you're wonderful. You know why you say that? Because, in fact, you are *perfect*."

Mama could make you feel like the image and likeness of God—and small at the same time.

She ran her hand through her stiffly sprayed hair. "Honey," she said to Frieda, "when you grow up, just remember, you don't have to dress like a man to be different."

Frieda, in a red dress and pink barrette, stared at her aunt. "I don't think you look like a man."

Polly winked.

Garth tore off, whooshing like a jet, Frieda trailing behind. Mama watched them go and flashed her perfect smile. Randall had persuaded her to let an orthodontist make her teeth reflect God's symmetry.

I eased into the floral couch next to her and Polly sat in a chair across from us. For a while we talked about Frieda and Garth. Then how happy I was to be free. That let me segue into what I really wanted to discuss.

"You know who I felt like in jail?" I said. "Pop."

Mama's mouth turned as rigid as her hair. "You were never like him. Never."

"Well, somebody is," I said. "We hope you'll help us with that. Maybe you remember something about Harvey, something to help us find the man copying him."

She rose and strode over the parquet floor and onto the linoleum in her open kitchen. Polly shook her head and raised her hands. I knew what she thought. Mama's determination to be silent about her first husband was as unchangeable as the kitchen's old counters and cabinets. But I had more faith in her.

Mama lifted out a bottle of Diet Coke from the fridge and poured it into glasses. Christian Science admonished its adherents to avoid caffeine, but Mama was religiously flexible when it came to soft drinks. Eight or ten bottles could be stashed in her old cabinets. I liked to imagine that she also hid bourbon up there.

She returned with a tray and set down full glasses in front of us. When she sat back on the couch, the Diet Coke trembled in her hand. She gazed up at the yellow ceiling and closed her eyes.

Then she said, "Do you know what Harvey's mother told him? She said he was an embarrassment, that she wished he'd never been born. Even when we went to see her, Harvey would stand there, two times her size. But the power of that idea, that he was worth less than a dog…"

Polly and I didn't dare comment. It was the most that Mama had ever told us about our father's relationship with his mother. I couldn't remember the last time she'd pitied someone.

"What else did she do to him?" I asked.

She shrugged as if to say, *What else matters?*

Polly and I waited. Randall's ship clock softly ticked on the mantel. Garth and Frieda yelled and giggled in the bedroom.

"You have to think about what kinds of thoughts a person's mother puts in him," she said. "Your father's mother did it to him. And to his poor sister."

"You don't think he killed Magnolia?" I asked.

Mama drew back and curled her mouth as if I were being obtuse. "He loved his sister more than anyone in the world."

She drank, one careful sip at a time, and stared through the transparent sides of the glass. "Harvey told me that Magnolia adored thrushes. You know, those birds that hide in the woods. The hunters have to scare them out into the open to shoot them. After she ran away, she probably changed her name and hid somewhere."

Polly grinned. "Maybe her new name is Magnolia Thrush."

Nothing could close up Mama like sarcasm. I shot Polly a look.

My mother ran her hands over the sides of her glass. "Perhaps this misguided man has the belief he had a terrible childhood."

Later, I'd spot the perceptiveness hidden in that sentence. But at the time I couldn't get past the convoluted Christian Science syntax. It was how Mama would have spoken thirty years earlier. I could read in Polly's cold smile what she thought. Mama believed our childhoods would have been fine if we could just change how we thought about them.

Garth dashed in from Mama's bedroom, a towel flying behind his back like a cape. Polly jumped up out of the chair. "It's Superman," she yelled, tickling him. "Do you feel the kryptonite?"

Frieda stood in the doorway. She'd removed the bow barrette from her hair and attached it to the collar of her dress. The barrette looked like Polly's bow tie.

Polly grinned at Frieda and dug her hand into her pocket. She pulled out her Wonder Woman key ring and puffer. Her long, noisy lungful of medicine was a middle finger pointing at Mama and Christian Science.

Polly said, "I have to go."

The longer Polly lingered with Mama, the more likely they'd argue. They disagreed on most topics and, over the years, had learned to stick to the surface of things. Polly liked to get out fast, before she did too much damage.

Her cowboy boots clumped on the slate walkway outside. The door of her pickup slammed shut. As her headlights raked the curtains, Mama sighed. "She's so good with children."

My mind automatically interpreted: *She'd be such a good mother if she'd just stop being a lesbian.* Part of me, the father part, knew that wasn't really what Mama meant. I think she loved her daughter so deeply that she'd accepted her sexuality. It just took twenty-five years.

Garth and Frieda ran giggling to the bedroom with the TV. A smile burst from Mama. It was a beautiful smile, a smile not encumbered by Godly thoughts. She ran her wrinkled fingers over the green and orange blossoms on the cushions. She loved flowery chairs and couches.

"You know, after a while, the past becomes just like any other conception," she said. "It's not *what* you remember but how you *choose* to remember it."

I was startled by her words. In one sense, they were vintage Christian Science. But tonight, their meaning seemed deeper. As I tried to take them in, she continued.

"I think of your father shoveling snow or cutting wood for the older folks at church. I think of him loaning out tools and helping people fix things. Remember the tree house he built? The dollhouse? In the winter, he'd sit in that van and warm it up for you and Polly."

The van was warm because he'd trolled all night. In that van, Polly once discovered a woman's glove stuffed between meticulously cleaned seats. I'd found a roll of duct tape. Still, I was as crippled by the good things he did as Mama was. Even as I remember the tape, I picture him calling me Tex and bouncing me on his knee as if I were on a bucking horse. "Hannibal, it's time to ride your elephant," he'd yell. His lips buzzed and he'd set me on his shoulder. And then we'd wrestle and he'd pretend he was André the Giant and let me pin him. Or, in the autumn, he'd heave me ten feet into a mountain of raked leaves. He'd wrestle Polly, too, holding her against the floor and tickling her. Sometimes he didn't stop until she cried.

Mama was peering at me. Her eyes said, *Even you know there were times he reflected God.* If only she hadn't tried to heal his black parts. Or tried to heal Polly into how she imagined God's child. Then maybe she would have seen both of them for who they were.

32

I WAS SEVEN YEARS old when Mama decided to heal Polly's asthma. She'd been leading up to it for months. Every morning she stood on a chair and took down the paper bag she'd hidden in the melamine kitchen cabinets of our doublewide. She'd pull out the asthma medicine bottle and, as she gave Polly a spoonful, say, "There's a reason this stuff tastes so awful." Then she'd hold up the liquid to me and say, "We're not going to mention this bottle of false belief to anyone at church." Medicine was our family's secret spiritual failing. But Mama was going to erase our shame. If Jesus could heal a cripple, she could heal Polly's asthma.

That fall Polly was thirteen. During the months most of the world knew as ragweed season, she suffered from what Mama called an "errant belief in the power of oxygen." One morning in September she started to cough, and by afternoon, the air scraped like stones in and out of her lungs. That evening, Polly's face turned the red of our place mats. Strands of her long brown hair trembled with each rasping breath.

Mama sat with her on our saggy couch. "God's love is like air," she said. "It flows through you, Polly Kogan." She turned to me. "You too, Willy."

"God is not air." Polly's voice hissed out like a ghost's.

Mama frowned. Then she corrected herself and smiled. Her jutting teeth hovered over her lower lip. "Young lady, does that sound like a thought from God?"

Pop had scrunched his big body into the green chair with the burst springs. "Let me tell you what *real* motherly love is," he said. "Giving your daughter medicine and taking her to the doctor." His big face nodded at each of us, but his amber eyes fixed on me.

Mama didn't seem to hear him. It was dark outside, but she still rose to close all the drapes in our trailer. "Let's shut out mortal mind,' she said and sat down again next to Polly on the couch. "Do you know what I'm thinking right now? I'm thinking about all the ways I'm grateful that you're my daughter. God's perfect child."

My sister's face looked pleased then—and sad at the same time.

Mama retrieved a new bottle of Diet Coke from the fridge and sat at the fold-down card table under the kitchen light. Her hands moved to her holy books—her left on the Bible, her right on the *Science and Health with Key to the Scriptures*. She opened the *Science and Health* and I could almost hear the swish of drapes encircling her. I knew better than to interrupt when she was reflecting God.

Pop knew better too. He lifted Polly as easily as one of her stuffed bears and carried her to her room at the far end of the doublewide. I followed and watched him prop her up on pillows. After settling her, he walked past Mama. She sipped from a Sleeping Beauty glass and flipped a page.

In the living room, Pop turned on the TV to *Magnum, PI*. The whole couch sank under his girth. When I sat beside him, I felt as if I were about to slide down a hill. His hands smelled of photography chemicals and I wondered if that sour odor was making my sister sick. Then I chided myself. Such bad thoughts might prevent Mama from healing Polly. To make up for that false thinking, I prayed silently, just as Mary Baker Eddy recommended. In my mind, I repeated the Lord's Prayer, then the Scientific Statement of Being. "There is no life, truth, intelligence nor substance in matter." But I couldn't remember the rest, so I whispered, "God is Love" over and over. Then, "Love heals all." But Polly's coughs grew louder.

Pop bent down to pick strands from the burgundy carpet. After a few seconds, he lurched to his feet, took two steps to the bookcase, and gazed at the pictures of our family. His thick finger grazed over the warped wood, then our few volumes of World Book Encyclopedia—A through F.

He sat back down and the couch sank to tilt my body toward him. He lowered his head close to mine. "You know, you could be a detective someday. William Kogan, Private Investigator."

Those unblinking eyes could convince me of anything. But how could I consider something so wondrous when Polly was gasping for breath?

Pop strode to the kitchen. He stared down at Mama at the card table and said, "I can see it in you, Rose. You don't want to ignore the sound of your own daughter suffering."

Mama looked so small next to him, her teeth sticking through her sad smile. "Harvey, someday you'll realize that God's way is more important than what *you* want."

He stood over her. The air seethed through his nose. His hands clenched into fists as big as cans of baked beans. Without a word, he walked to the bathroom and slammed the door shut. The whole trailer rattled.

"Willy, don't let anybody change your good thoughts," Mama said. She picked up God's books, her bottle of Diet Coke, and the Sleeping Beauty glass. She dragged the telephone with the long extension cord into their bedroom. The door clicked shut.

I wondered if she'd left me alone because she'd heard my bad, sickness-causing thoughts. She wanted to shield herself from both Pop *and* me.

When Pop got back from the bathroom, I said, "Is Polly going to die?"

His whole face pinched into a scowl. Then his eyes turned gloomy and his face softened. "I think you're the only one who can save her."

"I'm praying as hard as I can. I'm knowing the truth."

"You're the best person in this family. You're our Magnum, PI. I know you won't let your mama ignore your sister."

"Mama's reflecting God to heal her."

His great head slowly shook back and forth. "Polly'll die unless she goes to the hospital."

A sob welled inside me. "Why don't you drive? You could take her."

He pushed blond hanks of hair off his forehead and squinted. My own pop, the biggest, strongest man I knew, was holding back tears.

"She's got my keys, Willy."

A body couldn't be mended in a hospital. If I thought it could, I'd weaken Mama's positive healing thoughts. But if I didn't convince Mama to let Pop take her, Polly would die. Something lurched and twisted in my stomach. It's mortal mind, I thought.

"Maybe your mama should stop being so proud of her holy beliefs," he said. "I think she's drunk. Drunk on God. Do you hear her muttering away like some nun in there?"

I couldn't hear anything. "Pop, call 911."

"She's got the phone." He bit his lip. After a few shuddering breaths, he said, "You're the only one who can convince her."

My father could have bashed through the flimsy door and taken the keys. He could have grabbed the telephone. But Mama had so filled herself with God, I couldn't imagine him overpowering her.

I ran across the kitchen linoleum to their bedroom. The phone cord snaked underneath the door. "Mama," I yelled. "God wants you to take Polly to the hospital. She'll die if you don't."

Mama was reciting something inside. It had to be Mary Baker Eddy's words.

The door was locked. I pounded on it. "Mama, please." I started to cry. "At least give Pop his keys. Let him call 911."

"William Kogan, you listen to me. Your father put those beliefs in you just to hurt me. Don't you give in to that. Your sister is in no danger." Her voice was as calm as air.

"Please give Pop his keys. Please let him take her."

"I don't have his keys."

On the couch, Pop shook his head and his eyes crinkled. He pushed the remote control button to turn off the TV. To the blank screen he demanded, "How could I expect a woman like her to do the right thing?" He turned his unwavering eyes to me. "She loves God more than her own children."

"Mama, give him the phone."

Pop gathered the newspaper. I followed him through the kitchen to Polly's room in the back of the doublewide. He sat on the floor beside her bed. His head reached above the little side table.

She sat on top of the covers, her lower body limp, her back upright and sunk into the pillows behind her. "Where's the medicine, Pop?" she said.

Pop reached up his arm but he didn't hold Polly's hand. He never did. His palm covered the base of the Snow White lamp on the table.

Polly smiled at me. Just moving her lips stirred a small cough. "I love you, Willy." She took a big wheezing breath and covered her mouth with her hand.

"Maybe we should fold our hands and pray," I said.

Polly shook her head. "Never."

Pop's laugh, long and hard, sounded like its own loud cough. Polly stared at him, her eyes watery.

I went to the bathroom. Two of Mama's pink towels lay in strips on the floor. Pop must have torn them up. In Christian Science you're not supposed to talk to God like a person, but I did anyway. As I relieved myself, I prayed. "Help me heal Pop and Mama so we can heal Polly. Don't let her die. Please. I'll be a better Christian Scientist."

Back in the kitchen, I heard Mama's low phone voice murmuring through their bedroom door. She must have called Betty Treeble, the practitioner. I set my ear against the cool plywood.

"I know it's true, but it's not helping," she said. The next phrase came from Mary Baker Eddy. It was a phrase we'd recited in Sunday school. "God did not give us the spirit of fear, but of power, and of love, and of a sound mind."

From Polly's room, Pop yelled, "How can you expect to heal her when you're afraid?" He could hear every word—even if it was whispered—in that trailer.

Polly coughed so hard I thought she'd throw up her insides. In the in-between silences, the newsprint crinkled as Pop turned pages. Then a ticking noise too irregular to be a clock. It sounded like his camera. I buried my head in the couch. I prayed with all the words I remembered from Sunday school.

When I awoke, sunlight slanted through the windows. I listened for Polly's cough. Nothing. Our house was silent. My eyes filled with tears. God had not healed her and she was dead, dead because I'd selfishly slept instead of praying.

But the drapes were drawn back. Mama had lit the stove. The air was filled with the most wonderful smells—pancakes and bacon.

And then I saw Polly in the kitchen. I jumped up and ran to her. "You're healed," I shouted. "Mama, you healed her."

"There's not a spot where God is not," Mama said.

Polly gave her the kind of grimace that she'd later transform into a sneer. She turned away from Mama and wrapped her arms around me. Her breath sounded scratchy, as if part of the false belief in asthma still clung to her.

"Willy, we only have each other."

I tried to pull away. I wanted to see in her face what she meant. But Polly held me tight.

At last she let go. I looked up at Mama. Her lips pressed tightly over her teeth. She was staring at Pop as he walked out from Polly's room, his camera cupped in his hand. A pile of torn-up newspaper strips lay on her floor.

A thought descended over me, a thought so twisted it had to be mortal mind. Maybe Pop had healed Polly by taking pictures of her. In the pictures, Polly was the image and likeness of God.

Polly left the trailer and slammed the door.

"Harvey, I'm so proud of you." Mama was beaming up at him.

"What?" he said.

"You only made Willy say those things because you loved your daughter. It was the way you reflected God's love that healed her. It shined right through you, Harvey Dean Kogan."

Mama touched my head. Her hand was so light it must have been filled with God's Spirit. My whole body tingled.

"Willy, your love helped heal her too," Mama said.

"Maybe we should all get in the van so we can ascend to Heaven," Pop said.

Mama gave him her warm smile, the one that said you weren't being nice but she loved you anyway.

"Each of us gets closer to God in fits and starts," she said. "God will tell you where to find a job, Harvey. You just have to listen."

Pop reached into his pocket and pulled out the keys to his van. His eyes met mine and slipped away.

"Just where I knew those keys would be," Mama said.

Something stuck in my throat—words my mind couldn't grab hold of.

Pop yanked open the front door and slammed it behind him. I stared at that door, my whole body stinging. I still hear his keys jingling.

"Willy, let me tell you something about your father. He thinks he'll feel stronger if he destroys my faith in God. Today he learned he can't. I think this is another healing."

Mama went to her room and shut the door. I looked at the plate of pancakes and bacon on the kitchen counter. I wasn't hungry anymore.

A sound came from Mama's room. It was so strange I wasn't even sure it was her. I put my ear to the door. She was crying.

I went outside but didn't see Pop or Polly. Pop's hatchet leaned against the elm tree. I picked it up and reared back. After a few blows, I flung away the hatchet and kicked the tree until it bruised my feet.

Pop had only pretended not to have his keys. What kind of monster would try to destroy his wife's faith by manipulating his son and risking his daughter? It took me years to craft that question. Probably Polly was never as sick as my young mind thought she was. Or maybe Mama really did heal her—as hard as that is for a skeptical banker to believe. In any case, she only channeled enough of God into her daughter to cure her asthma and not her spirit. Christian Scientists would say that's impossible. They'd say that's why the asthma came back. Even at seven years old, I knew it was only half a healing.

Years later, I found out what Pop did after he left that day. Katherine Miller made the mistake of jogging in a park while her husband looked after their sunburnt kids. The Preying Hands' photo recreated the famous Rodchenko picture of a black trumpet player. He photographed Katherine Miller's severed head from below, her makeup-darkened cheeks puffed out by wads of Kleenex. Instead of a trumpet, she blew a whistle. Next to her face he'd placed a tube of Coppertone with the picture of a dog pulling down the little girl's bathing suit. "That picture made all my senses jingle and jangle," he told the prison psychologists.

To Mama, a body was nothing but a kind of metaphor, a reflection of a person's thoughts. My father believed the same thing.

33

MAMA AND I WERE still talking when Frieda ran in from the bedroom. "We saw a ghost." She was crying.

I leapt up. "Where's Garth?"

"At the swings."

We'd been talking so intently we hadn't heard Garth and Frieda go out the bedroom's sliding door to the yard. How could I have let that happen?

I ran into the kitchen, grabbed a hammer from the tool drawer, and tore through the guest bedroom and out the door. I leapt over the deck's railing and onto the flower bed beside it. Garth was a frozen shadow in front of the chain-link fence that separated Mama's yard from a ravine. I ran to him and dropped the hammer to pull him into my arms.

"A man," he said.

I carried Garth to the deck and snatched a flashlight from Mama's hand. Branches broke and thrashed as someone clambered through the underbrush down the hillside. With the hammer in one hand and the flashlight in the other, I pulled myself over the fence and sprinted after him. His path left a trail of trampled branches and flattened leaves. The brush scraped and crackled around me. I just had to get a glimpse, enough of his face to identify him. And if he turned and attacked me? I'd crush his skull.

The path spilled out onto the road at the bottom. A lone car sat parked about forty yards off. As I bolted toward it, the engine roared and its tires sprayed gravel. The car sped away, lights off. I couldn't make out the license plate or even the model. In seconds, I heard nothing but crickets. Whoever it was had run like a man, not a ghost. A man who was watching my children.

————————

Hempel and his forensics guy showed up an hour later. Hempel nodded as if he believed my story, but his blue eyes still gleamed with doubt. I would always be a suspect until we captured my father's admirer. The forensics investigator searched through the undergrowth of the ravine. He only found a few smudged footprints. No clothing, no hair or skin that had been scraped off. Except mine.

Jill's father picked up Garth and Frieda. Mike was armed; he'd always be armed now. Tomorrow morning, Mike would drive them to school. At three o'clock he'd be waiting in the parking lot, checking his mirrors, a revolver on his lap.

It was up to me to safeguard my mother and sister. When I called Polly, she assured me that she had her pistol in her hand and that her alarm system worked perfectly. Mama, as usual, refused to budge or take any precautions. Talking with Mama made me want to go buy a new vape pen.

But I didn't. I was done with vape pens.

34

I SLEPT IN OUR deserted house. In the morning, I watched the sun singe away the thin layer of moisture on the back lawn. For a few peaceful minutes, I read the *Union-Tribune*. On page 3, a reporter analyzed the killer's letter. He noted similarities to letters Harvey Dean Kogan had written more than thirty years before. The press hurricane was about to strike. But I didn't have time to worry about that. Vanessa had ordered a command performance at the bank that morning. Over a week had passed since I'd straggled into work.

We met in the boardroom, our most severe conference room. Just beyond the reception area, this space contained no couches or art books. Only a long wooden table and an empty cabinet that we used for serving food. There were no snacks today.

Vanessa swept in, her strings of pearls clacking, and sat opposite me. She looked no bigger than Garth. But there was nothing childlike about her thin frown. I'd learned to gauge her tone by the colors of her shoes. For our meeting, she wore gleaming red pumps: *aggressive*. A child queen about to render a sentence. Maybe that's why she'd left the door to the conference room open. This was to be a public execution.

"Would you like something to drink?" she asked.

We only made that offer to prospects and clients. With those few words, she was telling me that I no longer belonged there.

"William, we know you couldn't have done this terrible crime."

One of Vanessa's great skills was misdirection. In fact, she'd been so certain I was innocent that she'd never once reached out to me in jail. Which also explained this meeting. Our clients detested controversy—especially from their bankers. I could imagine our chairman wanting to soothe their concerns by cutting all the bank's ties with me. But I would never get another job with a murder charge hanging over me. Without my income, our family would lose the house.

I wasn't about to meekly slink off. "It's really wonderful you're behind me," I said. "Only a good employer would take that stance."

"Of course we're behind you." Her face softened to a kindly smile, but her eyes were as hard as slate. "When's the trial date?"

"The charges are about to be dropped." It was wishful thinking, but how would she know?

Vanessa leaned over the table. Her hand slowly descended toward the polished wood. I smelled her perfume—a disorienting mixture of flowers I couldn't identify, familiar yet distant.

"Your performance hasn't been what we expected," she said.

She didn't need a reason to terminate me. I was employed "at will." But I'd done my research.

I said, "I understand how you have to protect the bank. But fire me now? My attorney thinks you'd be crazy to do that." As if Marta knew anything about employment law. "I mean, after all the turmoil my family's been through?" I shook my head and hissed the air through my teeth. "What would the board think if you fired me and the press turns against the bank?" What would her boss, the chairman, think?

"Your legal issues have nothing to do with this. Our business relationship just hasn't worked out. We're parting company, that's all. Amicably."

Amicably. As in: *Your reference is at stake.* But my reference was already printed in newspaper headlines. I wondered if she'd bragged to the chairman that she could shove me off the roof without my severance package.

"I'm not sure the public is going to see it as amicable," I said. "And certainly not the press. I think they might use one of the 'W' words." I mirrored back her own soft smile. "'Wrongful,' Vanessa. As in 'wrongful termination.'"

"I think you're exaggerating."

"Not in California. The state Labor Code is pretty specific. It says you can't take action against an employee when his arrest doesn't lead to a conviction. In my situation, the charges are about to be dropped. By the way, that's section 432.7. I'm sure you'll want to look it up."

Vanessa wedged herself into the back of the chair, her arms stiff at her sides. She hadn't expected such fierce resistance from me. "I seriously doubt anyone would see this as 'wrongful termination.'"

"Maybe. But then there's the 'D' word. 'Discrimination.'"

"Discrimination?" she yelled. I was male, white, well-educated, and only thirty-nine years old.

"You'd be surprised how a clever lawyer can play with that term. I suppose we should also talk about that terrific offer letter you wrote. It was what persuaded me to leave a job I liked in order to come here. I'm sure you recall that the letter included a severance payment of three months if it didn't work out."

No reaction. Evidently Vanessa had been so confident she could slough me off that she hadn't even consulted an attorney. If she had, she would have offered a leave of absence or administrative leave. That convinced me to push it a little further.

"Pretty severe penalties if you get it wrong," I said. "Triple damages plus court and legal costs."

I saw her mind calculating. She was going to have to pay me in either case. Why risk a press backlash or a court case by firing me?

She shrugged. "If you want to stay, we can keep you on for a while. It's the least we can do."

Only one word resonated in that sentence: *least*. I was so caught up in our verbal jiujitsu, so indignant, that I fired a last bullet without thinking. She deserved it. "Just one more thing."

Her shoulders shifted a fraction of an inch.

I waited an extra few seconds. "As it turns out, my father is pretty famous. He's in prison in Illinois."

She actually sucked in her lips.

"His name is Harvey Dean Kogan."

A phone jangled in reception area. Clients talked and laughed.

"Oh my God," Vanessa said.

I'd never seen fear widen her eyes. That was the power of my father's name. For a moment, I just took it in. Savored it.

I rose, towering over her. "Nice chatting with you."

My legs walked by themselves from that conference room. I wanted to go straight through reception, board the elevators, and find a bar. Instead I turned toward the banking department. Just before passing under the cupola, I reared back and kicked the wall. Even if they fired me, that dent in the damask wallpaper was going to stay.

Remorse hit when I closed the door to my office. I slid into the chair and lowered my head into my hands. My legs began to jitter. I'd actually enjoyed the fright in Vanessa's face. Just as Harvey Dean Kogan would.

———

By the time I left, Vanessa had gone for the day. As I crossed the reception area, someone called my name. It was Lawrence Massy, the ophthalmologist I'd visited in La Jolla the day I was arrested. He rose from the couch, the shelves of unused books behind him, and peered at me through his red-framed glasses.

The words felt weak even as I said them. "They're about to drop the charges. The whole world knows I'm innocent." I wasn't sure what made me seek his affirmation.

His dark eyes deepened with a long inhale of disappointment. "William, you have to be careful about the way you talk. If you say you're not guilty too loudly, people think you're lying. Be confident. There's no need to prove your case to anyone."

It was perceptive advice. "I'm glad I've got you in my corner," I said.

He hitched his neck. Pushed back the collar of his blue blazer. "It's Monique. I know, it's ridiculous, but she's about to become my wife." He frowned down at his Italian shoes.

"Your fiancée thinks I'm guilty?"

"I'll change her mind. It's just a matter of time."

Then why was he here?

Bullshit Bob strode from the main hallway through the entryway. "Hi William," he said, his voice as warm as a robot's. "We need to talk later."

Massy followed Bob, with his short, careful steps, toward the conference room where Vanessa had tried to fire me. "Can I offer you something to drink?" I heard Bob asked. The conference room door swung shut.

I stared after them. On a nearby wall, next to the bookshelves, a watercolor painting depicted the San Diego cliffs jutting above the ocean. Maybe it wouldn't be so awful to hit a client. Or a colleague. My career was already over.

"I'm sorry," Kathy said from the reception desk. She'd taken off her headset and looked like she wanted to hug me. "Some people are just plain disappointing."

But Bob and I liked each other. He'd never tried to steal a client. Massy must have called Vanessa because his fiancée asked him to. Vanessa wouldn't have hesitated. I could even imagine what she'd said: "William is the only one who doesn't know he no longer works here."

I went to the garage. Sitting in my car, I stared out the windshield at a concrete wall. I felt as if I'd never escape what people thought I was: a killer like my father. What would it be like to take my family and disappear? We'd pack our belongings inside a trailer, attach it to the Camry, and drive the ten miles to the Mexican border. Just keep going south. Jill already spoke Spanish, and in weeks, Frieda and Garth would be fluent. We'd change our last name and construct a new life, thought by thought. Just the way Mama, Polly, and I had thirty years before.

Delmore Shepherd, the First Reader in our little Christian Science church, had helped us escape from Blue Meadow, Illinois. A lanky, bald man with a hairy Adam's apple, Delmore used to teach Sunday school class and once told us how he'd healed a brain tumor—his own. At the end of his story, his voice fractured and he pointed to the *God Is Love* sign on the wall. Tears slipped from his eyes. Polly waited until we'd reached the church parking lot, then said, "How could God heal such a dork?"

A few weeks after Pop went to prison, Delmore showed up at our trailer. "You don't deliberately stay in the lion's den just so you can prove you reflect God," he said.

Polly thought Mama only listened to Delmore because he'd healed a brain tumor. I think she took us away to save Polly and me from that town's hate. The congregation raised a collection to pay the first three months of our rent. Somehow our old Ford towed a trailer all the way to San Diego. I thought we'd fled to an exotic jungle, where palm trees grew between pines and huge flowering bougainvillea.

Our family could only afford to live in National City, a town just south of San Diego. But Mama had her eye on somewhere that better reflected God's perfection. That first Sunday we drove to a huge white Christian Science church in La Jolla and tried to believe that we belonged. Polly and I talked with kids our age and I even played soccer in the parking lot.

I expected Mama's face to reflect God's joy that day. But when we got home, she sat us down at the kitchen table and poured glasses of Diet Coke. "You have to be careful with friends," she said. "They want to know things. It's natural that you want to tell them."

"About Pop," I said.

Mama sipped her Diet Coke. "Sometimes it's all right to make up stories. You know why? Because they better reflect God's world."

She stopped and shifted her eyes between Polly and me to make sure we understood. I had no idea what she meant.

"We should say your father died six years ago. He had the false belief of a heart problem."

Pop dead? If God was Truth, how could Mama make us tell such a lie?

Polly said, "We can say that Pop keeled over from a heart attack. Then Mama tried for a week to heal him back to life."

Mama pursed her lips. "Polly McNary, that is not funny."

McNary. I winced. Why did our new name have to be so ugly?

"We have to be very careful with friends," Mama said. "We don't want to have to move again, do we?" She aimed her eyes at Polly.

"I can't have friends?" I said.

Mama combed my hair with her fingers. "Just for a while. Just until we settle in."

"Who do I play with?" I said.

"Who needs friends when you have God?" Polly said. She gave Mama an innocent smile—her newest weapon.

I expected Mama to snap at her. Instead she said, "Polly, I've always known you reflected God. But sometimes I'm just amazed. Even you don't understand the truths that fly out of your mouth."

That took the smile off Polly's face.

"But who do I play with?"

"You have Polly," Mama said. "Your best friend."

That fall I thought of Pop launching me into piles of red and yellow leaves. I thought of my dog Lucky barking and scampering after me. At Christmas, because I missed the soft squish of our boots outside, Mama bought fake snow and we spread it under the tree in the apartment. Most nights, when I was supposed to be in bed, I looked out my window at a corrugated metal hut beside the complex. The fat padlock on the steel door looked like the one Pop had hung on his photo shed, his "Fortress of Solitude." I thought that any day the apartment's shed door would creak open. Pop would step out in his steel-toed boots. His hands would brim with photos.

35

I HEARD THE SOPRANO singing *Carmen* even before I pushed open the Haven's heavy wooden door. It was three thirty, a slow time, and Polly always put on opera in the break between lunch and dinner. Mike had dropped off Jill and the kids, knowing that Polly and her staff would watch over them while he ran an errand. One by one, I identified each member of my family. In the corner play area, Polly and Frieda jumped up and down clutching junior hockey sticks. Jill and Garth, holding their own sticks, shook their heads at a ball rolling inside a plastic net and goal. They were playing Haven Hockey. All were safe.

I exhaled.

A new picture hung from the ochre wall beside me: two women with big hair in leather pants, black muscle shirts, and red heels. Each held the hand of a little boy. The boys looked like twins with their spiked hair, dirty pants, and Superman capes. It was the family Polly had always wanted. Instead, she'd adopted ours.

Jill waved tentatively at me. She must have noticed my somber expression and came over. Jill, Polly, and I sat at a table under a bird mobile. Polly poured the coffee into three baseball mugs from her Padres collection.

"What the hell is wrong with *you*?" Polly said.

I wasn't sure I wanted to tell them. Outside the half-curtained windows, a car cruised by and a rapper's voice cut into the baritone from *Carmen*. The rap faded. Three staff emerged from the kitchen's swinging door with boxes of cutlery for the tables.

"Well?" Polly said.

It would be so easy to keep it secret. Just make up something. But I didn't. I told them about my meeting with Vanessa. "I just wanted to freak her out," I said. "That's the only reason I told her who my father was."

"The bitch deserved it," Polly said.

"But I liked it."

Polly shrugged, her bracelets rattling on the table. "We all like to intimidate assholes."

Jill jerked back. "Jesus."

"Well, maybe it wasn't your best moment," Polly said.

"After it was over, I wanted to come get you all and run away. Just like thirty years ago."

We listened to the alto's solo and sipped the coffee Polly had brewed. As usual, it was thick as sludge.

My sister set down her mug. "I think you wanted to run away from *him*, from the similarities you saw in yourself."

I shook my head. "I wanted to run away from the bank and everything else that's happened."

"But what you actually did was come here to be with us," Jill said.

Polly pulled at the diamond stud in her ear. She gazed at the little barriers around the play area. "Sometimes I wonder if he's inside me too."

Jill slapped the table so hard her coffee spilled. "Will you two just move on?" She swiveled her head to take in both of us. "A killer was inside our house."

My wife's glare bored into us. Polly swallowed. Her neck reddened and her mouth opened. Then shut.

"We need to take precautions," Jill said. "Especially when my dad's not with us." She opened her purse so we could see inside. A handgun sat next to her makeup mirror. I'd already seen the pistol at the motel. Before I was arrested, Jill had always kept her guns locked up.

Frieda squealed and our heads jerked. I swept my eyes to the front door. Back to the kitchen. Just one of Frieda's dolls. It had fallen from a produce box they'd cut and drawn into a space station. I rolled my head and shoulders. My body was as tight as a bow.

Polly said, "I've got staff and customers who'll look after me." She patted her backpack. "I'll keep my Glock within snatching distance."

They both slowly turned to me. I was the weak link. My bail prohibited me from carrying a firearm. I said, "If I identify him ... I won't need a gun."

Jill shook her head. "What if *he* has a gun?"

I said, "If he has a gun, you think you'll get to yours fast enough?"

Polly kicked her boot on the bamboo floor. "Shit."

"None of us is doing anything stupid," I said. "If we ID him, we call the police. Right?"

Jill nodded.

Polly said, "Unless we have to shoot him in self-defense."

Polly had only used her guns at a shooting range. I thought of all the karate classes she'd taken. Her bluster was bigger than she was.

The soprano's voice crescendoed to a high note that cut through the restaurant. Our eyes shifted to the play area. Garth rammed his spaceship into a block castle. Frieda had moved to a play house. Her doll walked on the roof's edge.

"How are their classmates treating them?" I asked.

Jill shrugged. "They're all curious. But the teachers keep a lid on it."

"No spawn of the devil stuff?" Polly asked.

Jill winced. "That was *your* childhood."

Something wasn't right with Garth. He clutched a block like a cudgel and stared at the entrance door to the Haven.

Frieda shrieked.

A man in glasses peered through the door. He held a Nikon camera. His mouth slacked open as he stared at our screaming daughter.

We knocked over the plastic barriers around the play area to get to them. Jill hugged Garth. Frieda sobbed in Polly's arms.

"It was a different camera," Jill said to our son. "Not the one in your book bag."

"No one is going to hurt you," Polly said.

Frieda was so tuned in to her brother that she'd screamed before she even knew why. She aimed her stricken eyes at me. "Are the police … going … to take you again?" She pushed away from Polly and wrapped her arms around my waist.

"No one's taking me anywhere," I said. "I won't let anything happen to you."

"Was it the man from Grandma's house?" Garth asked.

"No," Jill said. She hugged him harder and stared at me. Her pupils were dilated, the whites too large. *That's how you know a woman's afraid*, Harvey Dean Kogan had once told me.

What had this bastard done to our family?

36

JIM PODEROVSKY, THE CLIENT who wanted to remove his estranged wife's name from the loan guarantee, called me the next day. "You need friends," he said.

I chose to meet him at Wired Café, a little European coffee house that was dark even during the daytime. It was almost never crowded, particularly at three o'clock in the afternoon, and I'd never seen anyone from the bank there. Today a soft violin concerto wafted from the speakers. A few women ate French pastries and sipped chardonnay while a man in a suit bent over his newspaper and nursed a cup of coffee.

I spotted Jim in the back in his preferred attire: khaki shorts, a Hawaiian shirt, and flip-flops. The barista set down two espressos on his table and Jim's eyes followed her all the way back to the wooden counter. I sat down across from him and picked up one of the espressos. Still admiring the waitress, Jim barely looked at me.

He said, "I thought my old man was fucked up."

I put down the cup.

"I got a call last night from your friend, Vanessa. Seems that Bob Morgan is my new account manager." He turned and gave me a tight-lipped smile. "Vanessa likes to talk so it wasn't hard to pull the rest out of her. They're still gonna fire you, you know."

"I'm a private banker. It's unforgivable to be embarrassing."

"Then maybe it's time you did more of it." He lowered his barrel chest over the table and gripped my forearm. His hand nearly encircled it. "At least get in a few kicks before they shove you out the door."

He released my arm and leaned back, his shoulders straining the top of the Hawaiian shirt. He raised his demitasse as if listening to the violin music. "You know my old man had mob connections."

It wasn't a question; everyone in the bank had heard the rumor.

"I know what it's like for a family when the father gets arrested," Jim said. "Everyone treats you like you should be in jail *with* him. I think that's what pushed my brother into it."

Why was he telling me this? There was no reason. But Jim always had an angle.

He chuckled and jiggled his espresso. "Look, I don't expect you to say anything right now. When private bankers hear something they can't deal with … all of a sudden they become great listeners."

Maybe I was just being paranoid. Maybe he was really trying to be a friend, one of the few I had left.

I told him about the letter and pictures of Elizabeth the killer had sent to the *Union-Tribune*, then about the stranger who'd slinked outside my mother's house while my kids were playing. "The police aren't doing anything," I said.

Jim swirled the espresso. "Why is this guy doing this to you?"

Everyone asked the same question the police did—even the ones with mob connections.

Jim put down his cup and scratched his big palm. Without looking at me, he said, "You know, there's one bastard who might really understand what's going on."

The man I hadn't seen for thirty-one years. "But I'm not allowed to leave the county. It's part of the bail condition."

He looked up and squinted at me. "Since when has bail ever stopped anyone from leaving the county?"

I didn't know what to say. Behind me, the man with the newspaper turned a page. One of the women giggled. The espresso machine wheezed over the violins.

"Don't look so shocked," Jim said. "This is how the real world works, the world outside your fussy little bank."

Maybe. But I didn't want to hear it from a client.

"Think about what you need," he said.

What I needed? I had no idea. To fill in the silence, I latched onto the first question that came to mind. "So how is Cheryl?" Before he could see me wince, I said, "Your little girl is doing well?"

He stared at the espresso cup. "I guess you've figured out we're separated."

"It's why she and Megan are in Hawaii," I said.

He looked up. "I'm counting on you keeping that just between us."

And to get Cheryl's name off the loan guarantee. In exchange for him helping me. Or was there something else?

No, it couldn't be Jim. My gut told me it was impossible. Maybe that was why I'd listened to him so calmly.

He looked at his watch and drained the last of his espresso. Then lumbered to his feet. Proposal delivered. We left for the strip mall's parking lot and I watched him get into his van—a Mercedes.

Once in my car, my suspicions seemed worse than paranoid. But I was in no position to ignore them.

I drove into the bank and rifled through his financial statements. Like most developers, Jim primarily owned buildings and land. He was worth fifteen million dollars but only had about $100,000 in liquidity, all invested at our bank. If he were the killer, he'd need funds for an escape. He should have liquidated his investments and mortgaged his house to get more cash. But Jim's house was free and clear. Everything about him testified that he was just a tough real estate guy—despite his father and brother.

Outside my office window, huge gray clouds had gathered. After weeks of dryness, the meteorologists warned of a deluge. But afterward the drought would continue.

I drove home to make sure our house was battened down. I still hadn't put the inside back together after the police search. In the bedrooms, our clothes were in bags on the floor. In the kitchen, everything that had been stored in the cabinets lay on the counters. I didn't feel like putting anything away. Sitting at the kitchen table, the center of our home, I couldn't stop myself from listening for the sounds of our children. My eyes drifted to the glass sliding door and the dark backyard with its swings and toys. An envelope was taped to the glass.

Sliding open the door, I looked around. No one. No sound. I peeled off the envelope and tore it open. Inside was a black-and-white photograph. But no terrified woman stared out. No severed hands or feet. The photo looked as if it had been shot from a telephoto lens. Next to a white dog, a small girl kneeled in front of a school. The girl was Frieda.

37

I CALLED MIKE'S HOUSE and told him about the picture. "I'm wearing my firearm and watching Frieda every second," he said. Next I called the detectives. They didn't answer their phones so I left messages. Then a voicemail for Marta.

There was nothing to do but wait. My revolver was still in a police evidence locker so I sat on my couch with a carving knife. With the lights off, I listened for any sound in the house. I stared through the picture window at the black sky. The night felt trampled and empty.

The bottle of bourbon lay next to the empty steel box in my desk drawer. I could buy a new vape pen, hook up with more marijuana, and be back in an hour. But I stayed on the couch.

The rain started in a soft splatter. Within minutes, it was rattling the picture window and falling in such torrents I couldn't make out the orange tree outside. I opened the front door to take in the roar and the smell. The kitchen knife still in my hand, I slogged across the mushy yard. On the street, the water overflowed the drains and swirled like a river. The palm trees bent as if their spines would break. A few cars swooshed slowly by, their wipers waving furiously above the foggy beams of their headlights. I let the storm envelop me, my head raised to the clouds. Rivulets ran down my face and chest. I closed my eyes.

By the time Marta arrived, I'd gone inside and changed. She was drenched and lugged a broken umbrella. I went to get her a towel. When I returned she was staring at the knife on the table. She dried her hair and neck before she spoke.

"Put the knife away. You don't want to look like you're falling apart."

"What the hell else could I look like? She's five years old."

Marta gripped my shoulder. "He knew this would freak you out. That's why he did it."

"That picture makes it pretty damn clear what he wants to do."

Her dark eyes bore into mine. "We'll keep your kids safe. That's job number one. Now go put those dishes away in the kitchen. And make coffee. Hempel and Lund like it thick as dirt."

For a half hour, I slowly put the foodstuffs away and clanked the pots, pans, and dishes into the cabinets. The coffee was steeping in the French press when the bell rang. The two detectives stood back on the front stoop so that the light clearly illuminated them. I opened the door.

Shadows darkened Lund's eyelids. The storm had beaten up his perfect hair. "I thought we'd float right off the road," he said.

Hempel, unshaven, carried a metal attaché case. "Whatever evidence there was is washed away by now."

They slipped off their rain coats and I led them to the living room. The picture of Frieda lay on the coffee table. Lund sat in our ragged chair opposite our ragged couch. He smoothed out his hair. Hempel lowered himself onto the couch beside me and set the attaché case on his knees. He put on plastic gloves to look at the picture.

"Well?" Marta said. She'd perched forward in the other chair beside Lund.

"Looks like a home printer job," Hempel said. Tonight, his voice sounded like a door whining open.

Lund leaned over to take in the photo upside-down. "Maybe our techs can identify the printer."

"And then all we have to do is figure out where the printer is," I said.

Lund poured coffee for us from the French press. He sipped from his mug and nodded. "Now that's good java."

"There could be a drop of sweat on the envelope," Hempel said.

Lund took another sip and shook his head. "I doubt it. Probably not any fingerprints either. This guy is too careful for that."

I hated the deep resignation in his voice. "That's not good enough," I said.

The detectives barely glanced at me. Hempel took a big gulp of coffee and fished out a pack of gum from his pocket. He tapped out a piece and stuck it in his mouth. "Look, if he's like Kogan, he doesn't attack little kids."

"Suppose he's decided to be different than his hero?" Marta said. "What if he's interested in children now?"

Hempel chewed. He downed another slug of coffee like medicine. Chewed some more. What a waste of good coffee.

Then he said, "We'll go back to the chief. Try to persuade him to make an exception and get you some protection."

I wondered if I was the only one who realized the obvious. "What about asking the guy he's copying?"

All three of them stared at me.

"Our folks in Illinois say Kogan won't talk with anyone," Lund said.

"But I'm not anyone. I'm his son."

The detectives regarded me as if they'd underestimated how dangerous I was.

Hempel shook his head. "I don't see the judge letting you slip out to Illinois. The press will say you're bragging to your daddy. Comparing kills."

Daddy. His voice made the word sound full of phlegm. "How about if I go incognito with one of you?"

Their silence gave me the answer.

Hempel said, "Why don't you give your dad a call? We'll come out here early tomorrow morning. Listen in while you talk to him. We can help."

Talking with my father while the detectives listened would be a disaster. He'd hear them whispering in the background or pick up from my hesitation that they were coaching me. He'd hang up.

"I'll think about it," I said.

Hempel slipped the photo and envelope into a plastic bag and into his briefcase. I walked the three of them out. Their cars pushed like boats through the flooded street, palm fronds skimming over their wakes. I closed the front door. Locked it. Checked the rain-battered windows.

It was one o'clock in the morning in Illinois. Too late to call. I debated driving to Leucadia, but my family was already asleep. I lay on the couch and tried to doze. The name Polly had invented for Kogan's missing sister drifted into my half-consciousness: Magnolia Thrush. It was a joke she'd thrown out at Mama's house. But it also made a kind of sense.

At six in the morning, eight in Illinois, I telephoned. Inmates at the Stateville Correctional Center could only return calls at designated times, so I had to leave a message. With nothing else to do but wait for him to call back, I slouched down in front of my home office computer.

No one had ever found Magnolia's body. Was it possible my father didn't kill his sister? That was what Mama thought. It was a long shot, but something about the name "Thrush" stuck with me. A Google search pulled up sixteen people named Magnolia Thrush across the country. I found telephone numbers for the ones on the East Coast, where it was now nine thirty. No one had ever heard of Magnolia Kogan. I moved on to the Midwest. On the seventh call, a woman in Chicago answered with a deep, breathy voice.

"Are you, by chance, Magnolia Kogan?" I asked.

She gasped.

38

TWO HOURS AFTER I spoke with Magnolia Thrush, an inmate from Stateville called. "Nobody understands this killer like your father," he said. "But Harvey Dean Kogan's help only comes in person." He hung up before I could argue.

After thirty-one years, my father still knew how to work me. If I was desperate enough to telephone him, I was desperate enough to go see him.

I called Marta and she contacted the judge. He categorically refused to authorize the trip to Illinois. "Don't you go sneaking out there," Marta said to me. "They'll throw you back in jail. And you know what else? You'll be looking for another lawyer."

My attorney's sensible advice was no longer useful. Not after the killer had taped that photograph of Frieda to my door.

I drove to meet Jim Poderovsky. On the streets, city trucks and bulldozers cut and lifted trees limbs and palm fronds to cart them away. The sun was already sucking up the moisture.

At Wired Café, Jim was on his second espresso and evaluating another waitress. After I ordered, he said, "You know what you need to do now? Shake up the bank. Grow a beard, or even better, go out and buy a light green suit. Now's the time."

I told him about the photo.

"Jesus," he whispered. "I'd kill that guy."

I wanted to. But I had to find him first. For that, I needed my father's help and he'd only talk face-to-face. My espresso came. As soon as the waitress retreated I said, "I have to break bail."

Jim shrugged. "Stateville has so many visitors they'll have no idea who you are. But you'll still need a new ID. And the police probably red-flagged your name with the airlines."

He sipped and swished the bitter coffee in his mouth. Then again.

"I know an artist," he went on. "Holograms, magnetic strips— even fonts that'll fool the TSA. You can use the new ID and someone else's credit card to buy the airline ticket."

"Isn't using a fake ID at the airport a felony?"

Jim turned the metal salt shaker. It looked like a child's toy in his hand. "You could always do nothing. Sit back and watch those detectives pretend to work the case."

The waitress shimmied by on the way back to the bar.

"I can get it done for five thousand," he said.

Five thousand dollars was nothing to Jim. He expected a favor in return: I'd have to lie about his divorce and get his soon-to-be ex-wife's name off the guarantee for his line of credit. And that would only be the start. Soon I'd be discussing felonies with the rest of his family.

———

Nothing happened. No call from Jim. Marta went dark. The detectives might as well have been working in another city. Two days of waiting and worrying while San Diego cleared the storm detritus and returned to its normal desiccated self. Then Jim called.

We met in his "inconspicuous" Mercedes van with mag wheels. He wore reflector sunglasses and a shirt with the sleeves cut off. Grateful Dead blared through his fifteen speakers. Jim handed me an envelope. Inside were a new birth certificate, a plastic-laminated Nevada driver's license, and an airplane ticket to Chicago. I was now Pete Jones. Another envelope contained more than two thousand dollars of cash.

Jim laid out the facts and my countervailing steps as if they were the details of a real estate deal. I'd need a credit card for the rental car companies and using one of my own would ping the police. That was the reason for the cash. After landing in Chicago, I was to take a taxi. The best day was Sunday, when prisons were stuffed with families. He knew entirely too much about spoofing the court system. But I couldn't afford to ponder that thought. Or to consider all the felonies I was committing.

"You have no idea how easy this will be," he said. "Since the courts started using ankle bracelets they've gotten lazy. You're one lucky bastard not to have to wear one of those."

"Why are you giving me this much help?"

He waited until the end of the Grateful Dead song before he spoke. "I have a daughter too. And I know what it's like when the assholes in blue go after a family."

It still didn't really make sense. But I couldn't solve that now. I went home and left a message for Harvey Dean Kogan at Stateville. Pete Jones would be visiting him tomorrow.

If Jill knew that I planned to jump bail to see my father, she'd try to make me stay at home. We'd argue and fight and then I'd go anyway. And what would happen if I was arrested at the airport or at Stateville? Jill and the kids would continue to live with her parents. Mike would keep them safe. Only I would be in danger, back at the San Diego County Jail.

I called her when I knew she couldn't answer the phone. "I need to be alone for a couple of days," I said to her voicemail. "Incommunicado. I'll be at our house by myself with my phone off. I appreciate your understanding."

What was a lie when our daughter's safety was at stake?

At the house, I retreated to my office and my computer. I looked through Harvey Dean Kogan's pictures to see if someone might have discovered something new, a picture like the one the killer had taken of Frieda. Nothing. Then I saw the image that I hated more than all the others, the one I'd discovered at a public library when I was eighteen.

The police had found the photo in my father's shed when they arrested him. They'd kept it buried in their files. Ten years later, someone on the force must have needed money and sold it. Of course, no magazine would publish the image, but early internet users weren't so scrupulous. I'd had no idea the photo existed until I pulled it up on a library's computer.

The picture is in color. A green field of three-foot soybean plants seems to move—an effect of the long exposure and early morning light. In the vertical middle near the left border, Polly and I hide behind the leafy stalks, only our grinning faces visible. We're maybe four and nine. Above, on the right, is an abandoned tractor next to an amber hayfield that extends to an endless blue horizon. It's what he double exposed on the bottom right foreground that makes the photo famous. There, obscured by green soybean leaves and pink flowers, a severed head stares out with dead eyes.

The owner of that picture proudly announced that it was the only victim photo with the Preying Hands' children in it. Since the dead woman had never been identified, a few "scholars" speculated that she was Harvey Dean Kogan's sister, Magnolia. But no one knew for sure.

What most unsettled me were the greens, ambers, pale blues, and pinks in that photograph. He'd always shot his victims in black-and-white, but his family in color. I'd believed that by using color, he'd walled us off from his killing. But the photo of the soybean field proved that even that boundary didn't exist.

The blonde head at the bottom had to be someone linked to our family. I printed a copy and packed it in my bag.

I looked at my phone. Jill hadn't called. Her respect for my need to be left alone should have been a relief. But I just felt despicable. Lies ruptured marriages.

At one a.m., I lay down in our bed. The neon numbers flashed in slow motion on the clock beside me on the table. At three a.m., I arose. It took twenty minutes to hike to the nearest shopping center. I called a taxi with a new disposable phone. The taxi delivered me to Lindbergh Field at five thirty.

I tried not to hold my breath as the airline agent examined my fake ID. She put the prepaid debit card through her machine, booked my seat, and printed the boarding pass. The TSA officer studied my driver's license. He looked at my face, then at the license. I stared back at him and told myself that he just wanted to process his line. I was no different than anyone else. The officer let me through.

Once on the plane, I closed my eyes and willed myself to calm down. It would be good to sleep. But I couldn't stop thinking of my father. When Harvey Dean Kogan had sneaked off and killed those women, did he imagine himself as another person?

39

My father's Chicago trial lasted only two weeks. Police had found drums of chloroform and hundreds of negatives and prints of the victims in his shed. Fingerprints, hair, and blood from those women dotted the surface of his developing table and the inside of his van. DNA analysis was in its infancy then, but forensics specialists still linked most of the evidence with his thirteen victims.

Harvey Dean Kogan barely spoke with his lawyers. His public defenders knew they'd never persuade a jury to accept an insanity plea—not after the methodical ways in which he'd snatched and killed those women. Kogan refused to plead guilty. At the trial, he sat at the defendant's table and studied each jury member. The women jurors later said they could feel his terrible amber eyes taking them apart. Sometimes he smiled. At other times, he laughed in a single powerful, high huff. The jury took two hours to find him guilty, and then a half hour to sentence him to death. They later admitted that they didn't need that much time.

Periodically my father's life at the penitentiary made it into *The New York Times* or *US News and World Report*—once even *The Wall Street Journal*. A few journalists reported that he sometimes didn't sleep for days. "The Preying Hands dreams while he's awake," they wrote. Most of the reporters also mentioned my father's superhuman hearing. He picked up whispers from other cells and once heard a guard's irregular heartbeat. But I never believed those stories. Several unnamed prison guards reported that he'd borrowed hundreds of books from the library. No one had suspected he could read with such speed and concentration. The guards said he liked art, psychology, and history. He must have also studied the law, because he made his own appeals for more than fifteen years. In the end, Governor George Ryan saved him by establishing a moratorium on the death penalty in Illinois. But one late-night talk show host offered another opinion on why Harvey Dean Kogan was still breathing: "Even God is afraid to meet up with the Preying Hands."

Several articles reported that he was accused of killing an inmate. The man had bragged that his friends had found Kogan's family and were going to make us look like his victims. When the corrections officers discovered the inmate, his head rested on the New Testament of an open Bible. His throat was slit and his tongue sliced off. No other inmate ever threatened his family.

Kogan always had his own cell, but after the inmate's murder, he never exercised or ate meals with the other prisoners. The ten photos he was allowed were his only company. Harvey Dean Kogan wanted images of his family, but we wouldn't communicate or even tell him where we lived. So he tore out photos of us from old magazines and glued them to cardboard. On a table next to his bed, Polly and I forever remained thirteen and eight years old. Despite our abandoning him, despite all the years we'd been separated, he still wanted to be our father.

40

MAGNOLIA THRUSH LIVED IN Rogers Park, a neighborhood on the northeast side of Chicago. Her building was jammed into a long row of brown and red brick apartments about a half mile from Lake Michigan and a quarter mile from a cemetery. By the time the cab pulled up to the building, the sun had moved to an early afternoon position and some kids were heaving a football on the street. She buzzed me in and I plodded up the stair's threadbare carpet to the third floor.

Even stooped, Magnolia was tall—nearly six feet. Her hair was blonde, like her brother's, but streaked with gray. It hung past shoulders that were broad, like her brother's and mine. She seemed both older and younger than her late sixties. I gave her the bouquet of lilies and took her hand in both of mine. It was large like my father's, the skin cracked and dry.

"I can't remember the last time someone gave me flowers," she said.

Magnolia motioned me inside. She might have bought her faded nylon pants from a secondhand store years before. Our shoes squeaked across the old wooden floor of the front room. I sat on a brown upholstered couch in front of a warped wooden coffee table. Framed needlepoint pictures decorated the walls. Who did needlepoint anymore? It seemed like something from the seventies. She sat in an armchair across from me. My father's square chin stood out in her long face. But her eyes, soft and milky blue, were nothing like his.

"I hope you like chamomile," she said. A teapot steeped beside two unmatched ceramic mugs.

She poured and handed me a mug. Individual packets of sugar and expired creamer sat in a basket on the table. A practical woman, I decided, one who had very few guests.

I produced an envelope from my pocket. "Pictures," I said. "Mine, not his." When she still didn't open it, I said, "Of your niece and my family. Maybe someday you can meet them."

Her long fingers slipped the photos out. She examined them away from her body, as if she were farsighted or not sure if she should look too closely. It must have been strange for her to be presented with a family that she'd never thought she'd be a part of. When she saw Garth's picture, she broke into a grin. She too had a gap between her front teeth. As I talked about our kids, she turned the photos and ran her clipped nails over the shiny surfaces as if touching their faces.

"They're beautiful," she whispered. She picked up the mug and breathed in the chamomile.

Already I was drawn to her gentle restraint. "My sister drinks coffee the way you drink tea," I said. "The first taste is always the best."

She smiled shyly. "Your eyes are round like Harvey's. You're not as tall, of course. He was a giant."

Like Mama, she referred to him as just Harvey. They were the only two people in the world who saw him as a large and awkward boy.

I began with a soft question to draw her out. I didn't want to scare her and risk that she would shut down. "What have you been up to all these years?"

She pointed to the needlepointed birds, flowers, and butterflies on the walls. "Just my hobby and doing people's books."

I wondered how many hours of solitude those images contained. An old computer sat in the corner, but no TV. She must have cut herself off from the news. Still, she had known about my arrest.

"Well, I don't think you came all this way just to give me flowers and pictures." Both kindness and dread filled her eyes.

"I know this is probably hard," I said. "But I want to talk to you about your brother."

"My brother."

"What was he like?"

She set down the mug as if it were fragile. She sighed. After fleeing her past for so many years, I wondered if she was reconsidering her talk with me.

"I'm sorry this is so difficult," I said. "But I really need to know."

A telephone rang in another apartment. Someone pounded on the floor overhead.

"Harvey wasn't … he wasn't at all like the newspapers told. Just … a normal boy." She fished out the words as if dragging them from some hidden place. "That child's mind—" She shook her head and smiled. "He was just full of stories. Elves and dragons and talking skunks, even dolls."

After thirty-one years of serial killer accounts, it was hard to imagine Kogan as a child inventing stories. But he'd told me some of those tales. Owls that only ate wayward mice and cats that understood the world better than we did. The key was the woman who raised him.

"What was your mother like?"

Magnolia sipped the chamomile tea and pinched her eyes shut. "The first thing you have to know is that Mother had three pairs of shoes. And she liked to use them all to whip us. Especially Harvey. Sometimes she'd be pounding him and I'd hear the train whistle over the bridge at Wilson's Creek. Harvey said he used to imagine he was inside that train, chugging over the trestle bridge. He'd get so far away from Mother he didn't even cry."

I remembered his photo: the bridge's skeleton shadow rippling over a river's swirling water, water that was gray in the black-and-white photo. None of the experts at *Landscape Photography* or the Institute of Art had connected its sad isolation to those beatings and the train.

"He had a dog named Lucky. He loved that mutt."

I drew back. Why had I never known? "My dog was named Lucky."

She nodded. "One day his dog got into the garbage and Mother killed it with a shovel. Harvey had to watch."

I heard the shovel clang like a bell. It was so brutal it made me shiver. "I see why you had to get away from that mother," I said.

She nodded slowly, sadly. She stared at her needlepoint on the wall. "Mother wouldn't tolerate a boy like Harvey. Do you know what she said to him? 'You're not only a bed wetter, but you're stupid.' When he had his accidents, she locked him in the metal tool shed for the whole night. And that was after she scrubbed his privates with a Brillo pad."

I tried to push the thought of Garth out of my mind. "She was …" I stopped. "Monster" was what everyone called her brother.

"Mother destroyed us all in different ways. Harvey was lucky he never had to stay in that shed when it was really hot. Not like his brother."

His brother? Scores of writers had excavated Harvey Dean Kogan's past and no one had ever mentioned a brother. A brother changed everything.

The killer had claimed to be *my* brother.

Magnolia wrapped her long fingers around the warm mug and stared into the amber tea. Even now she could barely bring herself to speak of him. "Jonas Mark Kogan. None of us knew who his father was."

I needed to be gentle and patient. I needed to coax out the story. "What a pretty name," I said. "A Biblical name."

She nodded. "Even at five years old, Jonas had spirit. He loved to roam the woods around our house and search for buried treasure." She sipped on the tea as if drawing strength from it. "One night he stole Mother's chocolate chip cookie. When she found out, she slapped and poked and cussed. She tore the aerial off the TV to whip him. By the time she dragged him to the shed, his face was full of bruises. 'This is nothing next to what your daddy done to me,' she yelled. She locked Jonas in there with only a Bible."

Tears had pooled in her eyes. It seemed too cruel to be possible. "For eating her cookie," I said.

"There was no way to reason what Mother did. She wouldn't even let us bring him water." Magnolia swallowed and wiped her eyes with her broad, creviced hands. "At midnight I tried to go to him and she whipped me with that TV wire. 'Don't you dare mess with God's justice.'"

I already knew the end of this story. Magnolia couldn't possibly have foreseen what would happen to her little brother, but the guilt was carved into her face. You could push that self-recrimination under your skin, but it would never go away. I touched her arm and she stared at my hand.

"How old was Harvey?" I asked.

"Fourteen. Mother didn't even reach his shoulder, but she had all the power of the devil. Harvey just curled up around himself in that little bed of his. He didn't say a word or cry or even plug his ears. Jonas bawled and screamed most of the night."

I could hear those screams. They were the wails of my own children. "And then his voice stopped," I said.

Her face trembled as she held back a sob. "It was so hot ... as hot as it gets in Illinois. And that shed, it was all metal. I thought Jonas had fallen asleep." Magnolia covered her face with her big hands, hands that, if she'd had a mother like Jill, could have played piano. She took a great, shuddering breath. "Jonas had never even been to school."

Why hadn't she gone to someone for help? But I knew the answer. She couldn't imagine a life outside the spell of that leviathan. Just as Mama couldn't imagine a life outside of her husband and our Redman doublewide.

Magnolia straightened her shoulders. She took a sip of the chamomile. She stared down at the table as if parts of her past were scratched into that dried-up and faded wood. "Mother was afraid of the police. If they found out, they'd throw her in jail. She said they'd throw Harvey and me in a different jail for helping her." She shook her head. "I didn't know anything."

I wanted to whisper that it wasn't her fault. I wanted to say that my children would help her recover, just as they'd helped me. But I couldn't say a word.

She continued, the words coming faster as if she were trying to get them out and behind her. "Mother made Harvey carry Jonas to the graveyard. She'd wrapped him up in a trash bag. A trash bag! It was the middle of the night and they'd just filled in a fresh hole over someone's body. Mother gave Harvey a shovel and told him to dig. Then she made me dig. After an hour, she decided we'd gotten far enough. I set my own little brother inside that hole. 'Pray for this child of Adam,' Mother said. I never even knew whose gravestone covered him. She told us we never had a brother. That's what we were supposed to say.

217

And you know what she did that night? She bleached the gray out of her hair, bleached it as blonde as the angels."

The woman in the soybean field photo with Polly and me was also blonde. It seemed too depraved. But no more so than what that mother had done to her child. Could Harvey Dean Kogan possibly have preserved his own mother's head? Then put it in a picture with his children?

The bright afternoon light from the back window lit up the smoky blue of Magnolia's eyes. She gave me a sad, hopeless smile. "Jonas had never been anywhere in this world but that falling-down shack and the woods around it. He was a boy who liked sticks and throwing rocks. He liked to search for buried tin cans." She took a slow, labored breath, as if even the air ripped and clawed at what was inside her. "Two weeks later I ran away forever."

I walked around the table to hug my aunt. Her hands, so big and yet light as paper, barely touched my back.

"The world would have been different if I'd taken Harvey with me," she said.

41

SUNDAY MORNING, A TAXI drove me forty miles southwest of Chicago and across flat fields to the Stateville penitentiary. The endless gray-brown concrete walls and guard towers of the prison reminded me of the barricades and turrets of a giant castle. Behind the high walls, long poles with huge night-lights lanced the sky. A water tower looked like a metallic gray-and-white mushroom cloud. This otherworldly fortress and its neighbor, the now-closed Joliet prison, had confined some famous killers—Leopold and Loeb, Richard Speck, John Wayne Gacy, and Harvey Dean Kogan.

The cab stopped and I walked through the parking lot to the gatehouse. The crowd inside wore jeans and T-shirts or cheap printed blouses. They looked as if they'd just come from running weekend errands. I was the only one in a starched white shirt and shining wingtips.

I took a clipboard to fill out a Prospective Visitor's Interview form and lied that I had no outstanding warrants or pending charges. At the counter, a woman behind a glass window scrutinized my fake driver's license and birth certificate. My IDs had passed TSA but I had no idea if they'd fool anyone else. I tried to look bored and keep my legs from fidgeting.

She looked up. Her eyes were not friendly. "Prisoner's registration number?"

"I … I have no idea."

She gave me an exasperated sigh. "What's his name then?"

"Harvey Dean Kogan."

She swallowed and bent into her computer.

"You hear that, *ese*?" said the man in line behind me. "This *huevón* talking to the Preying Hands." He had a shaved head. His cheek was inked with a black teardrop and his biceps with Jesus wearing a crown of thorns.

"He the dude that chop up *beeches* and take pictures?" the other man asked. A heart with horns and wings adorned his forearm.

"Yeah. *Hee's* not all bad."

As they laughed, I tapped my finger on the counter, beaming to the clerk to hurry up.

She looked up. Now there was alarm in her eyes. I glanced around. Maybe I could get lost in the crowd of visitors.

"Why didn't you say you were his lawyer?" she said.

The whole line of visitors quieted. It had to be unusual for a lawyer to meet with his client on a Sunday. But if I denied it, I'd never see him.

"Sorry I didn't mention that." It wasn't precisely a lie.

Now she wouldn't look up from her computer. "You've got an attorney's visiting room. This is your first time, so you should know he'll be restrained."

The man behind me laughed. "Restrained."

The clerk leaned in. "For your own safety, there's a video camera. But no sound."

So they wouldn't listen or record any audio, preserving attorney-client confidentiality. He'd designated me as his lawyer to make sure we'd be alone.

Reaching into a drawer, she pulled out a form and slid it across the counter. The page certified that I was his legal representative and released the prison from any liability for my being alone with him. But he was in his sixties, weak from all those years in prison. He'd be "restrained." I signed.

The clerk handed back my IDs and paperwork and gave me an entry badge. After I stowed my wallet and keys in a locker, a corrections officer stamped my hand and I passed through metal detectors. Another officer searched me—even inside my shoes. Two more officers accompanied a group of other visitors and me across a courtyard and up some stairs. We made our way through more checkpoints and down other stairs into a large visiting room, where maybe fifty tables of families all seemed to be shouting. Everyone in my group found the inmate they were looking for, even the two tattooed Latinos.

An officer grabbed my sleeve. My body tensed. "Come with me," he said.

But he didn't put me in handcuffs. He didn't lead me back to the waiting room. I followed him down a hallway and through a wooden door to a meeting place so small that a table and two chairs barely fit. I sat at the table with my back to the wall. That way, the camera mounted behind me, aimed at the door, couldn't view my face.

"No handshakes," the officer said. "No hugs. Stay on your side of the table. When his voice gets soft, don't lean in. This is for your own protection."

The officer left and shut the door in front of me. The little space reeked with the cleanser they'd used to scour the floor. It reminded me of the slightly sweet smell of stop bath and developer chemicals. His photo shed had been bigger than this room.

I wanted to get it over with. Maybe he'd just stare at me and not say a word. Suppose he told the guards who I really was? My wingtips dug into the concrete.

Metal jingled. Men spoke outside. My arm quivered and I pushed it under the table. The door squeaked open.

I gasped. His great shoulders had sunk into their bones. Once-thick hair had thinned to frayed strings of blond and gray across his pale forehead. His hands were chained to his waist and his ankles shackled together. He was so much smaller and thinner than the giant of my childhood.

I should have gotten up but I couldn't move. My fingers squeezed into knots. Even as he shuffled and clinked toward me, his luminous eyes took me in. He wore a blue denim shirt. When he sat, the chains gave him enough slack that his hands reached the middle of the little plastic table. Gaunt, straight fingers pushed against each other, his palms together as if he were about to pray.

"No closer than three feet," the officer said. The door moaned and clicked shut.

He didn't blink. I'd forgotten that. How could I have forgotten? The whites of his eyes had become yellowish and blended into the amber irises.

"You agreed to help if I came here," I said.

Not even a nod to acknowledge he'd heard me.

"Say something," I said.

"I still love you."

My mouth fell open. Anger—or was it shame?—flushed through my face.

"I understand." His high voice and even his hurt, wincing sigh were almost tender.

"What you did ... Mama had to protect us."

He rattled the manacles and I flinched. My foot jittered.

"We each are chained to our own burdens, aren't we, Tex?"

Tex. "Because of what you did," I said.

He pursed his thin lips. They were covered in cold sores. "What a handsome, strong man you've become."

He was appealing to the little boy part of me, the part that had once longed for his affection and approval. He pushed in closer and his mouth slacked open. A dead stench laced his breath. My head inched away. His teeth were shades of brown and yellow, his tongue flecked with spots of gray. I fought the urge to lean back. Was he sick? Mama would say his thoughts had rotted his insides.

"Did you ever want to see me?"

The soft tone so close to me—even the way his mouth curled—seemed full of longing. I reminded myself that he'd once used crutches to get beneath a victim's defenses.

Harvey Dean Kogan didn't blink as he sat back into the plastic and metal chair. "I can hear your heart, Willy. It's thumping like a locomotive. You don't really think I'm going to hurt you, do you?"

When I was a child, he'd never once raised a hand to me. Now he was restrained, his thin body stooped, and yet my legs pushed into the concrete floor.

He gave me a friendly smile. "So you're a banker now?"

"Yes."

He had enough slack to cross his legs and drape his hands over his knees. "You're still that little boy who doesn't know who he is. Even in the newspaper photos I could tell."

His flat, appraising eyes soaked up my confusion, as if he were feeling all the creases and edges of it. Maybe that's why I tried to hurt him.

"Mama got her teeth fixed and remarried."

"So Mary Baker Eddy couldn't straighten Rose's teeth?" His face didn't show any hint of sarcasm.

"Polly owns her own restaurant." I paused so as to better gauge how the next phrases would pierce him. "She lives alone … just hasn't found the right woman yet."

His broad brow fractured into pale crevices. "Do you think I hate homosexuals? I know you want to hurt me, Willy. Who wouldn't? I'm the one who ruined your life."

I was prepared for him to hurl guilt at me for abandoning him. I expected excuses for his atrocities. But I wasn't ready for sympathy. I perused his face, the sores on his thin lips and the cracked yellow skin around his mouth. There were vestiges of the man I used to love—the strong chin and those eyes.

"Polly's been trying her whole life to get over what you did," I said.

He didn't flinch. I saw no hitch in his long, slow breaths. "And that's why she lays down with women?"

"That's what Mama thinks."

He shook his head at the absurdity of it. "I'm sorry I wasn't there to stop all that. I didn't want either one of you to suffer because of me." The chains on his wrist rattled. He set down his foot and shifted forward in the chair. "I tried to resist my urges—I really did. Once for two years."

"I guess that was as much as you could do … so your children wouldn't suffer."

He sighed. "We still had good times in between the bad ones. I'll always remember the tree house we built. All those donuts your mama didn't know we ate in the van. Remember how we laughed?"

My foot was still now, my body locked into what I needed to do. I had to be hard if I was going to get information. Still, it would go smoother if I acknowledged him.

"I remember," I said.

He slowly rubbed his bony hands together. The flesh on his wrists hung as yellow and frail as old wallpaper. I tried to ignore how ancient he'd become.

"Show me a picture of your children," he said.

He'd somehow learned about our kids. But I wouldn't allow his corruption near Garth and Frieda. I shook my head.

He leaned across the table, his lips inches from my ear. I smelled his putrid breath. "Do you want to know a secret we share? The secret is, we'd both do anything to protect our offspring. Anything." He slowly leaned back, his face slack and expressionless.

"I won't talk about my children," I said.

"But life is always about children. It's the child who's the father of the man."

His bullshit had gotten philosophical. "Are you going to help me or not?"

He cocked his head and shrugged. "Of course I am. You're my son. Tell me how he punished Elizabeth Morton for hurting that boy."

I wondered just how much he already knew. But I decided not to probe that possibility yet. "Park workers found her."

"How about blood?"

"No blood in the park. Eight pieces and no blood."

"You always were a boy who liked numbers."

I needed to pretend I was talking about a stranger, as if I were seeing Elizabeth from behind a camera's lens. "He cut off her head, hands, and feet," I said. "Even her breasts."

He pinched his eyes shut and tapped his pointed yellow nails on the table. His hands looked like the talons of a hawk. "He needed a private, lighted place for the carving."

My spine tightened like a wire. The carving. That was the way he'd always described butchering a woman. I took a breath and forced myself to continue. "After he cut her up, he put her dismembered

225

body back in the park. Inside a garbage bag… a bag he got from my house."

Kogan pinned my eyes with his own, his amber irises digging into me. That unblinking stare made me feel as powerless as a child.

A copy of the killer's letter to the *Union-Tribune* was in my pocket. I set it on the table.

My Dear Public:

Does anyone who wears yellow sneakers deserve to live? That sin was almost as bad as her wrenching a child's arm. At least Elizabeth Morton loved *The Giving Tree*. She loved it so much that I made her a part of the story.

Now you know the punishment for an evil woman who assaults children. Justice is a tornado that slips across the empty cornfields and hurls itself upon the icy lake.

By the way, publish this letter and I will delay punishing another child abuser. Some would consider that a Hobson's choice, but I'd classify it more as a dilemma.

Your friend,
The Defender of Children

Kogan sat back. "Our killer shows himself even here."

"That he wants to be your disciple?"

He squinted at me as if he couldn't believe I didn't understand.

"Tell me," I said.

"Say something about his photos." His soft, high voice shivered through me.

Somehow I described the pictures of the can of Budweiser and of Elizabeth's severed head on a blackboard.

"Just a can of beer?" he asked.

I nodded.

"He actually centered her head? On a plain black background?" His whole face screwed up into a grimace.

"He was copying your photo."

My father shook his head and closed his eyes. "Not with that framing."

I fought off my disgust. "He doesn't have your talent."

He broke into a smile so gentle it made me recoil. "You've studied me, haven't you?"

"I never learned anything from you."

"Death is as beautiful as life if you know how to frame and light it. You should try black and white. The graininess, the contrasts, they make you view the world differently. Like you're a child again."

He was playing with me. I had to fight through his feints and parries. "Why did the murderer recreate the Kim Johnson photo?"

He seemed to inhale the image of the teacher that he'd made all those years before. The air hissed softly in and out of his nose in long, unhurried breaths.

He said, "You know, I looked you up in *Time* magazine. Those shots of that village in Algeria. I was proud. The odd angled views, the lines those bodies formed in the frames, the juxtaposition of beauty and death. You have the eye, Willy. Polly didn't get it, but you did."

"I hate those pictures."

He pursed his injured lips and tapped his sharp nails on the table, the slow beat of a clock. "Not everyone can look so close. Most have to avert their eyes. They don't have the stomach to get down in the blood. It must have seemed as if her body had been split apart just for that photo. Even the light was perfect. Soft, so the blue of the burka offset the red blood. I loved the way you shot her covered feet and ankles. Sharp and detailed. But you kept everything else out of focus. It was a glorious composition, Tex. Soulful, even. I congratulate you."

227

Even now, after thirty-one years, he knew how to reach inside me to my worst fear. I felt as helpless as the eight-year-old boy I was the last time I'd seen him.

"Tell me what the note to the *Union-Tribune* means," I said.

He shook his head at me. "If you're going to catch him you have to see life like he does. Our killer fantasizes for a long time about what he's going to do. Every detail. The killing becomes a beautiful play he's rehearsed."

"Tell me about the letter." My voice trembled.

He leaned forward, his yellow eyes like spotlights. "Then there's the power of the gag. For him, the gag filters out all the lies. The words are in the expressions on her face and the birdsong of her moans. That's when he feels their souls twine together. That's when all his senses jingle and jangle. He sees God when he tightens that ligature."

"Stop it."

He nodded and leaned back. His unblinking eyes took me in. "I know this is hard. No normal person thinks this way. It's even hard for me now."

His mouth relaxed into a sweet smile, a smile that, when I was a child, could persuade me to do anything. "There's so much I wanted to hear about you and Polly. All the parts of your growing up. But I missed that. So tell me about my grandchildren. You can let me be part of your life, can't you?"

For Garth and Frieda's sake, I pushed my sacrum into the chair and hardened myself. He must have known he had me rattled. Now, when he thought I was weakened, it was time to go on the offensive. "Why did you pretend your sister was dead?"

He blinked and cast his eyes down at the table. His shoulders hunched forward and the chain chimed against the hard plastic. He hadn't expected me to know.

"Why did you make people believe you'd killed her?"

He gazed above my shoulder as if he were watching the wall behind me open, as if he saw something he distantly remembered. "Only if you tell me about your children."

I pressed on. "You never said a word about your brother. Did you love him as much as your sister?"

"I think I'm growing tired. And I always want to be at my best when I see my son."

He was going to stop the interview. I'd broken bail for nothing.

I yanked out the picture I'd copied from the internet: the green soybean field with Polly and me as children. Setting it on the table in front of him, I tried to inject warmth in my voice. Tried to remember him as my father. "I need your help, Pop."

His eyes blinked once, twice.

"Why did you take this in color?"

He raised the photograph as far as his shackled hands would allow. "It's quite beautiful, isn't it? The green flowing into the tan of the next field. Then the blue horizon that takes up half the frame. Like eternity. I can see why you like color work. I really should have done more of it."

I pointed to the head double-exposed over the green soybean stalks in the bottom corner. "Who is she?"

"Her barrette was a purple butterfly. You would think she was a child with that barrette."

"Is she your mother?"

He drew back.

"Is she?"

He formed a sad, disappointed smile. "My mother died in a car crash before you were born. Crumpled up inside her old Pontiac. No, the woman in that photo is not *my* mother. Think of teachers. Think of children."

229

"Is she Kim Johnson?"

He slowly shook his head. "This teacher liked to school her children at home. She never got out much in the daytime."

I couldn't recall a single victim who was a home schooler. "Who was she?"

"You know, soybeans are very nutritious. Particularly in Fullerton."

"What's in Fullerton?"

"He wanted nourishment. That's why he cut off her breasts."

Harvey Dean Kogan rose and shook his head, his face full of the same reluctant disappointment I saw when I was eight years old. "Tex, our artist is a Midwest boy, like you and me."

I slammed my fist on the table. "Do you know how much I risked to get here? Who is he, goddamn it?"

His head sprang forward. The chains clinked on the table. His eyes were wide and furious. "Think. The letter to the newspaper. How many tornados are there in Southern California? It's only the great Pacific Ocean they talk about there. Empty cornfields beside icy lakes? Those are in the Midwest. In California, they call sneakers tennis shoes."

He sighed and his fury dissolved as quickly as it had flared up. "There's so much I could have taught you."

I closed my eyes and played over what he'd said. I tried to connect Fullerton, California, with the Midwest. Maybe the killer had lived in both places.

Something touched my hand. I slammed my back against the chair. His face hovered a foot away. His hand lay on mine, the skin hot and rough like sand paper. He'd leaned over the table. His chains hadn't made a sound.

"It's been so long since I got to touch my son. You can't blame me for that, can you?"

I jerked my hand away.

"The next time you come here, I want you to bring something."

"We're not finished yet. Tell me who he is."

His eyes had grown soft. "It's such a little thing I want. Just a lock of hair from your beautiful wife. You can do that, can't you?"

The door burst open. An officer jerked Harvey Dean Kogan away from the table and pushed him out of the room. His chains clinked and rattled in the hallway outside the door.

"A lock of Jill's long blonde hair," he yelled.

I'd never mentioned her name. How did he know she was blonde?

42

BEFORE HE WAS ARRESTED, my father made our world into a strange play yard. He converted a cattle tank into a swimming pool and rescued a discarded arcade game that only he and I played. Once he tied me to the Tarzan swing and pushed me so high I thought I'd flip over the maple's branch. And then he was gone. Replaced by lit-up yellow eyes.

I stewed about Fullerton, California, on the way to O'Hare Airport, then on the late-afternoon flight to San Diego and in the taxi. I went home rather than to my family in Leucadia. I wanted to feel my own house around me. Standing outside in the dark, I picked an orange off the tree and rolled it in my hands. Overhead, the stars blazed in the cloudless, hot night. The smells of the grass filled my long, slow breaths.

Inside, the grandfather clock made its empty click. I listened for the familiar beeping of the house alarm. Nothing. With my family away, there had been no reason to arm it. I turned on the lights. Without the sounds of children, all I felt was emptiness.

In Garth's room, I looked at the plastic bags where the police had stuffed his rolling train set, blocks, and action heroes. But something was different. Garth's mattress, stripped of his plastic cover, had been turned so his old yellow urine stains no longer faced out.

He'd been inside my house again.

I forced myself to think. If I called the police, they'd say I'd forgotten that I'd moved the mattress. Even if they believed me, they wouldn't come for hours. And then I'd have to explain where I'd been. I retrieved a hatchet from the garage and searched every room and closet. The only thing out of place was Garth's mattress.

Why the fascination with my son? First the camera, and now he'd turned the mattress. The killer was both reaching out and sympathizing, as if he wanted a relationship with him. Just the thought of it made acid dribble down my stomach. I remembered what Kogan had said just a few hours earlier. *We'd both do anything to protect our offspring. Anything.*

I turned on the alarm and called Jill's parents. Mike answered the phone. "You found that asshole yet?" he said.

"I just want to make sure everything is okay."

"Of course it's okay. You think I'm an amateur at this? Look, Jill's in the shower. You want to talk to the kiddos?"

He put Garth on the line. "Grandpa gave me a BB gun and pocket-knife," my son said. "To defeat the villains."

Weapons to make him feel safer. Something his father wouldn't do.

"We're going to the rifle range," Garth said. "Grandpa's teaching me how to shoot."

Frieda took the phone and declared herself *fabulosa*. She said more, but I only heard the inflections of her voice.

After I hung up, I trudged to my office and opened the bottom drawer. The bottle of bourbon was still there. It was half full. I peered through the brown glass sides and contemplated the warm alcohol sliding down my stomach.

I put the bottle back in the drawer. I had work to do.

My computer found thousands of hits for Fullerton, California. But the city had virtually no farming. The only reference to soybeans was a food processing plant. It would take me years to figure out any connection between that plant and the soybean field in Illinois.

Maybe sleep would clarify what Kogan had told me. Our bedroom was so hot I had to open the windows. I made the bed and collapsed into the familiar softness. The little breeze flowed like solace through the screens. I inhaled the smell of clean sheets. My children's happy voices floated into my mind.

I should have been afraid that he'd sneak into our house while I slept. But he no longer held any terror for me. Beside me, under the pillow, was the hatchet. Let him try to cut through the bedroom screens and creep into our house. Just let him try.

When I was eighteen years old, I'd sneaked out of our apartment to take night photos. The bus dropped me off in the neighborhood around the University of California. I took shots of young people a little older than myself strolling out of a building. At about one o'clock in the morning, a brunette in jeans slammed that door. She weaved unsteadily on the sidewalk and swore at someone she imagined, her head jerking up and down. Drunk or high, she didn't notice me behind her. Every few paces I snapped a photo. After five blocks, she stomped into another building. I stayed outside in the dark.

A light flashed on in a second-floor corner apartment. It was a hot night and I saw her slide open the screen door to her balcony. A strange question occurred to me. Would her face strain with the same turmoil as she slept? The balcony overlooked a dark alley. I waited thirty minutes before I stepped on a garbage can and pulled myself up to the balcony's cement base.

Her bed stood just on the other side of the screen mesh of the door. I listened to her soft snoring. Sometimes the sheets swished as she stirred her feet or arms. The light from her bathroom paled portions of her face. I used the top of a balcony chair to steady the camera so I could take a longer exposure. On the other side of the screen, she looked peaceful. Not a single sign of distress marred her face. I imagined my father setting his body on her, pushing his hand over her mouth, using chloroform or choking her unconscious. What would that feel like?

For ten minutes, I photographed the sleeping woman, waiting for some unknown and uncontrollable compulsion to explode inside me. But all I felt was shame. Even to watch her was a violation. As I lowered myself back down into the alley below, my shame transformed into relief.

I still cringe when I think about what I did. Not even Jill or Polly knows about that night. I locked the film inside the steel box with my father's pictures. A year later, I burnt the undeveloped film of that woman. But I kept my father's photos. It was better to keep his evil trapped in that box.

Sunlight awoke me. I didn't want to get out of bed, but the safest way to conceal my trip was to continue living my life like it was a regular workday. I went outside to retrieve the newspaper. A neighbor's cat with half a tail eyed a hummingbird floating beside the Bird of Paradise flowers. I scared them both away. There was enough death hovering around our house.

A pink envelope was lodged in the crease of the newspaper. I made coffee and tore it open at the kitchen table. Inside was a watercolor print of a home with a white picket fence. A folded, typed page was beside it. I steeled myself.

My Dear William,

What a most disturbing few days you've had. I hate to deliver more bad news, but are you aware that the mortgage on your home almost equals its value? And your interest rate is about to reset! As a banker, shouldn't you have known the perils of an adjustable-rate mortgage? Particularly when your job at the bank has become so, shall we say, tenuous? I'm very concerned that Jill's teacher's salary will be insufficient if something should happen to your employment status. From what I could see in your files, your meager savings will only satisfy the bloodsuckers—I mean the bank—for a few months. Just a few months to find a job at another financial sweathouse, despite having "accused murderer" as one of the accomplishments on your resume.

As you well know, the world is not kind to people from the Kogan family. At least your dear children can move permanently into Grandpa Mike's gun compound. And Jill, too, of course. Too bad Mike wasn't in that Algerian village.

Please know that I am deeply concerned and often think about you and your family. As I do about our father. Did you have a nice visit with him?

Sincerely,
Your Brother

I jumped to my feet and heaved the coffee cup. Black liquid trailed behind it across the kitchen. The cup shattered. I collapsed back into the chair and reread the letter. The police needed to see it, but then they'd know I'd been in Chicago. They'd throw me in jail for breaking bail.

I paced around the house. The letter's words caroled inside my head. Without us ever noticing, he'd shadowed my whole family and looked up Mike's name from his address. He even knew that I'd gone to Chicago. But the worst part was that he'd referenced the Algerian massacre. Women and children had been slaughtered there. It was in the same paragraph in which he'd talked about Jill and the kids.

I had to think of something, do something. But what? I slipped the watercolor and the letter into my briefcase and sat down at the kitchen table. My thoughts swirled like leaves in the wind.

At eight o'clock the doorbell rang. Standing on my stoop were two men. One of them was gray-haired and tall. Detective Lund.

43

I OPENED THE DOOR and tried to smile, but my whole body was locking up. As usual, Lund wore an impeccable suit and every strand of his hair was sculpted in place. The second man might as well have searched for the plainest brown suit, tie, and shoes he could find in a catalogue. He toted a thin brown-leather satchel.

"Thought we'd drop by for a chat," Lund said. "We figured you'd rather do that here than at the bank."

There was that syrupy voice again. I wondered where his scruffy younger partner was. "I'm calling Marta." I started to close the door.

"How did you like Stateville?" Lund asked.

The door stopped, my hand on the knob.

"We could cuff you right now," Lund said.

There had to be a reason they weren't immediately arresting me. As for the quiet, second man, below his cropped gray hair, something was wrong with his ears. The right one had no upward curve. The left was even more shriveled. He hadn't gotten those injuries working at an office.

"Now you're really giving me a reason to call Marta," I said. But I didn't shut the door.

"Bankers love facts, don't they?" Lund said. "So, let's just review the facts. Contrary to an order from the court and a specific instruction from the judge, you left the county. That makes you subject to arrest. You also used a fake ID at the airport, which is not only a violation of an act of Congress but a felony. Then you pretended you were an attorney inside a penitentiary. Just state law for that one."

The more he talked in that smarmy voice, the better I felt. His words sounded less like a threat than a sales job. These two had shown up unannounced so Marta couldn't parry their tricks. I could see an advantage in letting them underestimate me. And where there was a stick there had to be a carrot.

I turned to the second man with the grizzled ears. He was short and stocky, at least ten years younger than Lund. His gray eyes seemed both curious and wary. "Who are you?" I said.

"Let us come inside and I'll tell you." When I didn't open the door, he said, "I promise this will have nothing to do with Elizabeth Morton's murder."

"We actually need your help this time," Lund said.

My curiosity overcame caution. I pulled open the door.

Lund raised a white paper sack. "We brought coffee. From this really good Italian place."

We trooped through the living room into the kitchen. Three men around our table made it seem small. Even the air was stuffy. I strode to the sink and opened the window to let in a breeze from the backyard. Their heavy eyes were like hands on my back. But I was prepared for their ploys.

Lund took out three Styrofoam cups of coffee and set them around the table. My cup and my empty chair faced the new guy. It seemed that he wanted to study me, with Lund at his side to confirm his diagnosis.

"Black, am I right?" Lund said, lowering himself into his chair. "By the way, I meant to tell you before, this is a really nice house."

He not only looked like a private banker but bullshitted like one. Now he pointed his chin at the floor by the counter. "Who broke the coffee cup?"

I ignored the question to focus on the new man. The melted flesh around his left ear shone in the morning light. Wrestlers had ears like that. He reached into his pocket and pulled out a card, not getting up. I had to walk over to him to take it.

I absorbed the information. Special Agent Blake worked in the Chicago office of the FBI. The FBI wouldn't fly someone all the way to San Diego if this meeting was only about breaking bail.

"What happened to your shirt?" Blake said.

I looked down. My white shirt was stained with a collage of brown spots. "Coffee spill."

"I guess something made the cup fly out of your hand," Blake said. He slid out an iPad from his satchel and set it up so the screen faced the chair meant for me. I saw a wedding band on his finger. What kind of woman could get past those ears?

"Have a seat so you can see this," Blake said.

Lund raised his coffee with his sun-mottled hand. "Really good java. You should try it."

I sat. My own kitchen seemed to shrink into that miniature Homicide room.

"Don't say anything until you see it all," Blake said. He pressed the screen and I saw myself walking through Lindbergh Airport, then through Chicago's O'Hare. I squirmed in the chair. No lawyer could argue against that evidence. The judge would throw me back in jail, and then what would the madman do?

"The warden told us that Kogan put a new visitor on his list," Blake said. "The guards turned on the video and the microphones when Pete Jones showed up. It took about five seconds to make you."

I hid my face by sipping from the Styrofoam cup. There had to be a deal or I'd already be in the back of a police cruiser.

"The folks at Stateville—they pretended you were his lawyer," Lund said. "And, of course, seeing as you weren't really an attorney, they could still turn on all the electronics. The sound was a lot better in a private room."

They'd *wanted* me to break bail to visit Kogan.

"Looks like you're going inside for some serious time," Lund said. "I'm afraid your days in the financial industry are over. You won't even be able to clean the offices."

He was goading me into begging for a way out. He'd probably contacted the FBI before I went to Stateville and never told me. Then the FBI listened in at the prison to see if I would admit to Elizabeth's murder. Maybe they thought I'd confess to impress my father. But the way Kogan played with me had to convince them I was innocent.

I pulled out my cell. "Stop blowing smoke. Unless you tell me why you're here I'm calling my attorney."

Blake said, "I told you, putting the screws to him is pointless."

Lund smiled thinly. "I guess I should listen more carefully. Especially to an expert from the FBI."

Those few words told me what had happened. "You were ordered to bring in the FBI, weren't you?"

Lund gave me a Mona Lisa smile. Blake stared at me, tight mouthed, his eyes bright.

"So why did the FBI send you all the way from Chicago, Agent Blake? I'm pretty sure there's an office in San Diego."

Lund started to say something and Blake put up his hand. "Let me fill in the blanks. Just to illustrate how it pays to work with us."

He smiled at Lund. Lund eyed him like roadkill.

Blake continued. "We ran Elizabeth Morton's murder through the bureau's computers. There were twenty-two related killings."

My body jerked. The killer's photo of Frieda flashed into my mind. Frieda as small and delicate as a figurine.

"The murders go back nineteen years. Heads, hands, feet, and sometimes breasts were sawed off. No hands clasped in prayer and no photos sent to newspapers. Except for Elizabeth Morton, no victim was suspected of abusing kids. Still, we probably would have seen a pattern, but our friends in San Diego didn't contact us about you. Or report it to the national database." He smiled at Lund.

I said, "I guess the detectives thought they'd already caught the murderer."

Lund shrugged. He didn't look at Blake.

I could imagine how it played out. After the killer sent his letter to the *Union-Tribune*, Lund and Hempel's boss ordered them to contact the FBI.

"Fifteen murders were spread out in Illinois and Indiana," Blake said. "Then a lull of eight years. The killer started again in California, Arizona, and Nevada. We calculate seven more killings. The only one in San Diego was Elizabeth Morton. Your father was spot-on when he said that the killer was from the Midwest."

I said, "If the killer admired the Preying Hands, wouldn't he have contacted Kogan?"

Blake rubbed one of those ears. Then the other. "You were the first person to visit him in ten years."

Ten years without a single visitor. Ten years alone in a cell. It was unimaginable. "Who did he see ten years ago?"

Blake raised his palms. "It's a long way back for prison records."

He gave me a smile so friendly it made my stomach clench. "We'd like you to help us. Now that you aren't a suspect."

I'd always be a suspect. And if I refused to play … The videos on the laptop informed me of what would happen. That was another reason they'd let me break bail.

I took a sip from the Styrofoam cup. "You know something, Agent Blake? You're desperate. I'm the only one who can get Kogan to cooperate. You know it, Lund knows it, and I know it." I locked onto both men's eyes as if I believed it.

They didn't leave. And they didn't pull out handcuffs.

"I want protection for my family."

"The chief turned us down," Lund said. "But if we could give him something else …"

With Blake there, I was sure it wasn't just a come-on. I had some power. Maybe Blake needed an appetizer.

I got up, retrieved my briefcase, and took out the watercolor and the typed letter from the killer. "Don't say anything until you've read it all," I said, handing them to Blake.

He smiled thinly and slipped on gloves. He studied the letter so long he must have memorized the words. "It fits," he said. "The man wants to torment you. Our profilers think he may be jealous."

"Because I'm Harvey Dean Kogan's real son?"

Blake let the question hang, his thumb rubbing the Styrofoam cup. "He'd like to be his son instead of you."

The more I considered that statement, the more frightening its implications became. "He called me his brother. He wouldn't want to murder his brother, would he?"

"Not if he were a *normal* person," Blake said.

That's why they needed my father. Only an aberration like Harvey Dean Kogan could understand the subtexts in that letter.

"What about Fullerton, California?" I said. "And the picture of Polly and me with that other victim's head?"

Blake released a long, beleaguered breath. "We're running that through our computers."

They were throwing stones into a lake and hoping their computers would interpret the ripples. Blake didn't seem to care if I knew that they were floundering. That was refreshing. There was a certain nobility about not hiding those ears.

"We've been thinking about Magnolia Thrush," Blake said.

So they did have a plan. That was another reason they'd let me skulk off to Chicago. I shook my head.

Lund peered at me, forcing me not to ignore him. "Kogan was playing with you. He knows a lot more than he's saying."

The FBI profilers must have concurred. But exposing Magnolia to her brother and these men would tear her life apart. "She hasn't seen him for fifty years," I said.

Lund crossed his arms. His whole body seemed to frown inside that blue suit.

"A man is totally different with someone he knew as a child," Blake said. "Particularly someone in his close family. Our psychologists think it could shock him into opening up."

"No."

Lund sipped his coffee. Blake changed his cup to his other hand and rubbed it with his index finger. Maybe he didn't drink caffeine. Maybe he was the kind of wrestler who only drank herbal tea.

"The killer likes to do things in threes," Lund said. "That means another murder. Soon. If his sister saw him, Kogan might give up something, something that could save a life."

That was how desperate they'd become.

Blake said, "This man never completely followed your father's pattern. He didn't just attack women with kids. He didn't always dismember his victims in the same way as Kogan did. Our profilers think he might be changing. Aiming at something higher. Like taking the Preying Hands' mantle. And that would mean eliminating all the other pretenders to the throne."

That sounded prepared. It still made my arm shake. I set it in my lap.

Blake picked up his coffee cup and turned it in his hand. He aimed his eyes at mine so his words would reach inside me. "In the note you got this morning, there was a reference to an Algerian village. What was that all about?"

"I'm sure you've seen my famous photos," I said. "Evidently the killer has too. He wants to show me that he knows all about me."

Blake nodded. "But there's something more. Weren't there women and children killed?"

I couldn't tell whether he really believed that my family was in danger or if he was just trying to manipulate me. He must have known it was my greatest fear. I put my other arm in my lap.

"Think about asking Magnolia to help us," Blake said. "The FBI has a bit of influence in San Diego. We could make a call. Maybe persuade the chief to assign a squad car to watch your family."

The letter wasn't enough. I had to persuade Magnolia to face her brother at Stateville. I had no choice. That was the only way my family would get protection. "I don't call her until there's a police car in front of my in-laws' house," I said.

Blake nodded. He set his leather satchel as gently as a baby on his lap. Slid out an X-ray. The light from the window over the kitchen sink illuminated the image. I saw something round and white.

"That's a pancreas." Blake pointed to a spot on the image. "And that shadow is cancer. It's advanced, very serious."

"What does this have to do with anything?" I said.

"This particular pancreas belongs to Harvey Dean Kogan," Blake said. "We need to get his help soon."

44

POLLY AND I USED to dream about our father's death, hoping that someone would obliterate him as he'd obliterated our childhoods. But now that the time had been fixed, what he'd done thirty-one years before, and even how he'd abused me at Stateville, faded away. I remembered him as a father—his great high belly laugh as we rough-housed or played soldiers, the smell of freshly sawed wood as I leaned into him on the couch. Even his infamous green van had been a joy to me. I recalled the sweet taste of jelly donuts while the heater whirred, the scrunch as he scraped the snow from the windshield. Pop was dying. Polly and the whole world would rejoice, but all I felt was loss—for what he was and what he could have been.

I had no time to grieve. Marta would be furious that I'd gone to Chicago. But despite disobeying what both she and the judge ordered, despite all the mistakes I'd made, going to Stateville had been the right strategy. I now had leverage with both the police and the FBI.

My conversation with Marta could best be managed at the bank, where she'd have to reign in her anger. I drove to work and phoned her from my office. As soon as I told her I went to Stateville to see my father, she cut me off. "Stay the hell where you are," she said.

She was there in fifteen minutes, probably because she'd stamped on the accelerator. I ushered my seething attorney into the small "den" conference room and closed the door. She sat opposite me at the antique card table. I kept my voice low, made it sound reasonable. Kogan wouldn't talk to me by phone; I had to do *something*. It wasn't just me in the crosshairs; the picture the killer took of Frieda was a direct threat. In the note I got this morning, he'd mentioned the names of my family and connected them to the massacre in Algeria.

Marta glared at the cloth wallpaper and touched a leaf of the plant below it. "Jesus, even this is fake."

"Less maintenance," I said.

She stamped to the heavy beige drapes and stared out at Cowles Mountain in the distance. Without turning, she said, "Did you really think Stateville would ignore a new name on his visitation list? The first one in fifteen years?"

"They need me. So much so, the police are putting security around my family." I didn't mention what I'd traded in exchange for that protection.

Marta strode to the damask-papered wall. Sneered at an oil painting of a little town in Europe. "God, this whole bank is pure pretension."

"Did you hear what I said? Tonight a squad car will guard my family while they sleep."

"All of that because you saw your father in prison?"

"The FBI thinks the killer's about to slaughter another woman."

She turned, probably to make sure I saw her disgusted scowl. "That's what the FBI always thinks."

"If they throw me in jail, they won't get anything from Kogan. That's why the detectives haven't told the DA about the trip."

Marta's laugh was so cruel it sounded as if it came from another person. "Of course the DA knows. You're a mouse she's playing with."

I'd saved my best information for last, after she'd spent her anger. "I saw Harvey Dean Kogan's sister in Chicago."

Her face froze but her hoop earrings seesawed across her cheeks.

"The FBI wants her to see him."

"These geniuses actually think he'll open up to her?"

I nodded. "We have to do it fast. Because of his cancer."

She paced back to the antique card table and sat down heavily. I explained my father's diagnosis.

More heavy breathing. It seemed like ten minutes but was probably only one. She said, "Don't ever think you're on the same team as these guys."

I accompanied Marta to the reception area and then headed back down the hallway. No one was around. My shoulders deflated and I leaned against the wall. I wasn't in jail, and Marta was still my lawyer.

I returned to banking and packed up to go home. Bullshit Bob stood across the hallway, his office door open. He was loudly setting up his calls for Wednesday, his weekly prospecting day. Every few weeks Bob dressed as a "tribute to the Golden Eighties." Today he wore red suspenders and a blue shirt with white cuffs and a matching white collar. Even his new leather briefcase, with its old-style latches, looked like an heirloom. Next to the case on his desk was a manila file folder labeled *Dr. Lawrence Massy*.

The son-of-a-bitch was getting the last of the paperwork done to close my deal.

I started to laugh. I laughed all the way to my Camry. It was only when I got behind the wheel that it hit me again. Pop was dying.

45

I PEERED THROUGH THE half-curtains in the front windows of the Haven. It was six o'clock and a crowd stood inside for Monday Night Football. I swung open the entrance door and their voices rose from a hum to a roar. Groups of men and women had bellied up to the bar and its TV. The waitress with the hatchet blade of blonde hair furiously shook a martini. Tonight she wore a Raiders jersey. In the front part of the restaurant, families and couples filled the tables. For the first time all day, my neck and shoulders loosened. The Haven felt like home.

No sign of my sister. I slid through swinging doors to the tumult of a busy kitchen night. In the front, a sous-chef chopped vegetables like a samurai at a wooden counter. At the stoves, the cooks shook sizzling pans over the burners. It was the kind of glorious frenzy Polly loved. She stood at a metal counter. Her gloved hands, still wearing bangles, whirled and jingled in and out of containers. She was assembling six salads.

"Not a good time," she yelled.

"I visited Harvey."

Her hands froze while her head jerked up.

"I asked for his help."

She heaved a handful of ingredients onto the counter. The latex gloves followed. Her bracelets somehow stayed on her wrists. She shouted for someone to take over, and, without a word to me, stamped to the back of the kitchen and the walk-in fridge.

I followed and prepared for her onslaught. The steel portal flew open and I clicked it shut behind us. There was a space on one of the shelves, beside cheese and salad dressings, to sit. Polly was too angry to sit or even stand within two feet of me.

"Do you want to ruin your life?" she yelled.

"I met Magnolia."

Her head drew back. "Jesus."

"She's in Chicago. Her new name is Magnolia Thrush. Just like you guessed."

Polly collapsed onto the shelf beside me. Her fury could deflate nearly as fast as it ignited. Only to explode again. She raised her hands in front of her chest and her bangles chimed down her wrist.

"She's tall like he is. She's even got his chin."

"I hate her already."

"You can barely hear her talk she's so shy. Her apartment is like a tomb. She leaves it maybe once a week."

Polly screwed up her whole face. "And now this nice, timid bitch wants to help?"

Sometimes my sister could be so frustrating. I suppressed a sigh. Waited.

"You already ruined my day," she said. "Don't skimp now."

"Magnolia said things about his childhood. About how their mother abused him."

"You already knew that."

"I learned something none of us ever suspected."

She cocked her head at me. Raised her eyebrow. That's when I told her about Jonas, how our father's mother shut her five-year-old son in a shed until he died from the heat. By the time I finished, all she could do was shake her head and blow out air.

"Pop had to bury his own brother," I said. "At night, so no one would know."

"Goddamn it, I've told you, don't call him Pop. And don't you dare feel sorry for him."

"He's got cancer."

Her mouth curled. "I'll bet he told you that, didn't he? In five minutes he was playing with your head."

"Actually, the FBI told me. They showed me an X-ray."

"The FBI? The fucking FBI is involved?" Polly jumped up and strode to the other side of the fridge. Turned and collapsed on the shelf to face me.

"Twenty-two murders. Across the country. All connected to this killer."

"Shit. Shit shit shit."

She was boiling over again. I ignored it. "All the bodies were cut up. Like variations of what Harvey did."

"Don't call him Harvey!"

As if in pain, she squeezed her eyes shut and reached for her Labrys necklace. But she wasn't wearing it. Her fingers found the bangles on her left hand, then the scar.

"He thinks our father is his daddy," she said. "His poor, persecuted daddy."

She was right. My sister knew nothing about the murderer and yet she'd guessed the relationship in minutes.

She drew in a breath—calm but still simmering. "All these years you've kept him out of your life. And now you let him back in?"

The cold wasn't even affecting her. I hugged my arms over my chest and slid forward to make the shelf freeze another part of my buttocks. I told her the FBI thought that only our father could understand the killer. This madman was somehow related to Fullerton, California, and to the picture of us as children in the soybean field.

She listened without uttering a word. Then jerked to her feet and paced to one end of the fridge and back. She squeezed the metal of one of the racks.

She turned. "I'll bet he tried to make you think you have a father again. 'Please forgive me, son. I love you.' He said that, didn't he?"

"He wanted to know about you, about my kids. He asked for pictures."

Her whole body seemed to furrow up in disgust. "He's sucked us right back in."

"And I have no choice but to go to him again for help. The killer was inside our house while I was gone."

"What?"

I told her what I'd come home to. She grabbed a container of salad dressing and hurled it. The plastic burst and the creamy liquid splattered over the shelves.

My sister fought off tears with fury, taking long breaths, self-ventilating, pushing out her rage. She set her hands on my shoulders. The chill from her bracelets seeped through my shirt. "I should be the one to talk to him," she said.

Our father was the only man who'd really hurt her. "Absolutely not."

"I'm tougher than you are."

It was the first time Polly had ever said that. I should have been insulted. I shook my head.

"Goddammit, I have nothing to lose."

"Just your life."

"Look, you're the one with the wonderful wife and kids. I've got nobody, not even a sometime girlfriend. That's what this cocksucker did to me. You know why he'll never pull me in? Never make me think he's my father? I hate him too much."

What a family we were. Polly salving her wounds with her restaurant and all her causes. Mama papering over her own hurt with Christian Science platitudes. And me? I'd covered up my secret pain with numbers and elegant banking manners. At night I'd relied on bourbon, my vape pen, and staring at the steel box where I'd locked up his pictures.

One of her hands lifted from my shoulder and gently pushed back my hair; the same caress had comforted me as a child. "Stay here," she said.

A few minutes later Polly returned with a small cardboard box. Inside was a smashed golden locket in the shape of a heart. A long-ago high school girl might have cherished it.

"Our father gave this to me," she said. "For his 'special girl.' Probably thought I'd put his picture inside."

"Is that why you smashed it?"

She shook her head. "It belonged to Jenny Winston."

It took a few seconds. Then the name flared inside me. When I was four years old, Jenny Winston's car almost hit me in our church's parking lot. Winston lived in a house by herself in the woods. When she came home from work one day, our father was waiting.

Polly said, "I thought he'd bought the locket. After he was arrested I found out who he stole it from. That's when I smashed it against a wall. Then I wondered whose picture Jenny kept inside it." She aimed her glare at me to spotlight what she was about to say. "I keep it so I'll never stop hating him."

The last gift her father gave her.

46

THE NEXT DAY, AFTER a special FBI request to the judge, Blake and I boarded one of the bureau's Gulfstream jets to travel to Chicago. A car was waiting. At midday, we arrived at the blocks of apartment buildings where Magnolia lived. I went up alone.

She stood in front of her door on the third floor. Her gap-toothed smile only shamed me more for what I was about to ask. Magnolia ushered me into the back of the apartment, to a kitchen with tiles that must have been installed in the sixties. She boiled water on an old stove and poured it into a Chinese pot with bags of chamomile inside.

I gave her drawings that Garth and Frieda had made. They weren't just to persuade her to help me. I really wanted her to have them. She reciprocated with two framed needlepoint pictures. For Garth, a brown-and-white eagle. Frieda's picture was a purple, orange, and black butterfly with the word *Mariposa* inscribed under it. I stared at Magnolia, then at the gifts. I couldn't bring myself to make the ask.

She poured the tea into flowered, mismatched mugs. Closing her eyes, she drew in the mist and said, "You want me to go see him, don't you?"

I studied my lap. "The FBI thinks he'll tell you things he won't tell me."

"And what do you think?"

My children were threatened. I had no choice. "We'll be in a private room. He'll be chained to the chair. There won't be any danger."

Her arms pushed into her sides. Her eyes turned to glass. "We'll have to talk about Mother and Jonas, won't we?"

That was the point. His sister and his childhood terror were the shocks that would open him up.

The late-morning sun through the back window lit up her eyes. She gave me a sad, hopeless smile. "Just before I ran away, he told me about a dream. He and Jonas took an axe to Mother."

Her head sank into her hands and her long blonde and gray skeins hung to the old kitchen table. In the apartment above us, footsteps stamped over the floor. A child cried in the overgrown yard below the apartment building.

"I can't do this," she said.

I knew she was right. Once inside that prison room, she'd come face-to-face with her brother as a stooped and broken old man. She'd think once again that if only she'd stayed with him or brought him with her, she could have prevented what he'd become. And that would just be the start. When the press learned about Magnolia, hundreds of the Preying Hands' fans would hunt her down and knock at her door. They'd take pictures through her windows and follow her through the streets.

"I'm sorry," I said.

She still cupped her face with her long, outstretched fingers.

"My children will love the needlepoints," I said. "I'm sorry."

As I left Magnolia's apartment, the sun shone through the white curtains covering the living room window. I closed the door quietly and wondered what I would do. Half the Chicago FBI would be listening to me inside Harvey Dean Kogan's cell. And I had no plan.

47

HE WAITED FOR ME at Stateville, in the same miniature attorney-client room. This time he sat on the opposite side of the table, his back to the camera on the wall. The FBI had suspected he'd position himself so they couldn't video his expressions. To foil that tactic, technicians had installed a peephole camera on the opposite wall.

I sat down. Kogan's sallow cheeks had sunk in the two days since I'd seen him. His prison shirt's sleeves were rolled up and his wrists were cuffed but not chained to his waist. Illness made him smell rancid, like a dog.

"The FBI told me you were sick," I said.

The edges of his mouth curled. He'd probably always assumed I was working with them. "The governor of this great state thought the death penalty was immoral," he said. "But he had nothing against cancer."

When I was young, my father's high voice had seemed so normal. Now it was scratchy and nasal, as ill as his yellow sagging skin and putrid smell. "Maybe we can get you better treatment," I suggested.

"So that more advanced docs can tell me I have more advanced cancer?" He cocked his head and his luminous yellow eyes bore into me.

I gave him the lock of blonde hair the FBI had supplied. He rolled it between his fingers, sniffed it, and let it drop to the floor. "This isn't Jill's," he said.

I'd decided to fight back. Show him he wasn't always in control. "I spoke with Magnolia."

His eyes shut and opened. "How is my dear sister?" His voice was expressionless. But the yellow skin on his forehead tightened.

"She put you behind her. Even what happened to your brother Jonas."

He smiled. "Our artist friend is highly educated," he said.

I'd let him think he'd deflected me. "What profession?" I asked.

"Maybe he's a banker."

I shook my head.

He licked the sores on his lips and leaned back in the chair. "Our friend probably had a father who left when he was young. I know his mother was a sadist."

"How?"

"Tell me about your family."

Again, I shook my head.

"*Thou shalt protect the children*, that's the unwritten commandment, right? Of course, no follower of mine would go after children. Unless he doesn't want to be a follower anymore."

He was mind-fucking me, hinting that he knew something else, something about the killer's plans for my children. "What do you mean?" I said.

He shrugged. "I thought we don't talk about Garth and Frieda."

Their names could have appeared in a newspaper. Or online. Maybe a guard told him. "Are my kids in danger?" I said.

"Let's discuss your wife. She teaches children. And before that, she protected poor little boys on the streets of Colombia. I admire a woman like that."

I couldn't wonder about how he knew. It was too frightening. "You have to tell me if he's after my children. They're your grandchildren, your bloodline."

"If a mother tortured her child, would you kill her?" he asked.

I had to respond to his questions in order for him to respond to mine. "Which mother? Which child?"

"Answer."

"If it was my son or daughter, I might kill her."

"Not good enough."

What did he want to hear?

"Answer."

"Not for someone else's child."

He tilted his head. "A pity. Such mothers deserve to die. Someday their kids would thank you."

I looked away from those sallow eyes. Down to the plastic table. It was pointless asking him to clarify. "You know all about the twenty-two murders across the country, don't you?"

His thin eyebrows arched. "Twenty-two? My, he's a busy little artist, isn't he?" He licked his lips. The handcuffs chimed as he shifted. He examined his long fingernails, stretching them out in front of him. "I would imagine our carver has a collection of handcuffs and leg irons.

261

His pornography is all bondage and no sex." He looked up at the ceiling as if to say, *Did you get that?*

"How do you know?"

"For this man, every word from a woman is the lash of a whip. Actually, he prefers to be alone. Then he can lie down with his fantasies and pretend that he has some power over that mother. He thinks if he can block out the real world he can heal himself. Maybe he's part Christian Scientist. Your mama should get to know him."

"Don't you dare threaten—"

"Threaten? Come on, Willy, when did you ever know me to *threaten*? I'm more an *action* kind of guy. What action would you take to save those children in that little village?"

The Algerian photos. The photos that resembled his.

"Is our visit over?" He shifted in the chair as if getting up to leave.

"It was too late," I said.

"Very clever the way you took the shots of those heads. From above to soften the afternoon light. You must have stood on a wall or a jeep. What shutter speed did you use?"

"One twenty-five."

He nodded as if he approved. "Would you kill those men to save the children?"

It was a crazy question. "Maybe."

He pinned me with his unblinking eyes.

"I've never killed anyone."

His head drew back. He expelled a long sigh. "There's nothing quite so photogenic as a good slaughter, is there? It's amazing how a soft light can make a massacre look beautiful. I like how you managed the shadow of that child on a stake, the large aperture to reduce the depth of field. Was it a boy or a girl?"

"What does this have to do with the murderer?"

"Everything. You knew no one would publish a straight-on shot of all that carnage. That was before the internet made it so common. You had to be cleverer than that. So you photographed those heads on the wall from behind. Amazing how neatly the terrorists placed them there, nicely spaced in a straight line. Even their faces all pointed at the same angle. Almost a black-and-white photo, that one. But there's a wonderful tinge of red—maybe from the blood on the wall. What did that writing say?"

"You know what it said."

"'God is great.' Those words remind me of someone."

I leaned toward him. I pictured my free hand smashing into his luminous eyes and broad nose—a nose like mine. "Leave Mama out of this."

He breathed deeply, as if he were inhaling all the contours of my anger. "You know, the whole world recognized truth in that picture."

"It was an atrocity."

"Is that what you think I mean?"

I was silent.

"Say something, Tex. Otherwise I go home to my cell."

I squeezed my biceps under the table. "I didn't enjoy making it. I'm not like you."

"Is that what you think?"

"Now it's your turn to tell me something."

He leaned in. "First admit what you felt when you approached that town."

I took a breath, filled my diaphragm. He didn't have all the power.

"Such wonderful rage, Tex. And then that control. It's like you're lassoing a tidal wave."

He used my childhood name like a barb under my skin. I had to ignore it. I said, "I didn't feel anything before I got there. I had no idea what I was about to see."

"I can hear that extra rush of blood to your brain. Delusion requires lots of blood. What did you feel when you got close to that town? Tex?"

"You bastard."

"Say it."

"I knew there might be a massacre."

"And that excited you, didn't it? What were you excited about?"

My head felt in a vice. My breath rushed in and out of my nose.

"I can see in your eyes that you want to be honest. Now is the time. Say it."

"I thought the massacre would make me famous." The words came out loud and hurried.

"Ahhh. There's the honest little boy I know. Even the tears in your eyes." He smiled and licked his lips. "All those beautiful reds as the afternoon light softened. All those final, eternal expressions on their faces. Fear, resolve, submission, fury. And that row of heads on the wall, that nice line that paralleled the road and the rows of white houses. Do you know who's really represented in that picture?"

I didn't answer.

"If you expect my help, you have to at least *pretend* you're cooperating. Who is really represented in that picture?"

"The men who killed them. Their rage."

"Ahhh, rage." He tilted his head. His thin lips hinted at amusement. "And what else, Tex?"

I spit out the word. "Pleasure."

"You always were a perceptive boy. But we're not done yet. When you saw all those bodies, what did you feel?"

"I took those pictures so the victims would get justice."

"Tell me the truth."

"I was nauseated."

"The sound of your heart is giving me the real answer."

A strange calm had loosened my hands.

"The light, the background, the composition," he went on. "You walked around those torn-up women and children. You took in the copper smell of their blood and the putrid smell of their flesh. But all you thought about was the shot. You even controlled your breathing to steady the camera. After a while you didn't think about how they'd suffered, did you?"

He slowly nodded, watching for his poison to seep into my eyes and shift my body. But I sat absolutely still. My eyes never left his.

"Oh, but I forgot. You took those photographs to get justice. Of course, that would just require one picture. How many did you shoot? How many rolls? Don't tell me you didn't feel proud when you saw those photographs in *Time* magazine and *The Economist*. Oh, you embraced the abyss then, didn't you, Tex?"

"You know the biggest difference between you and me? I can leave."

He stared at me, his face blank. He knew I wasn't going anywhere. There was too much information I needed.

"I have a question, Tex. What do you get to become if you're a holy man in a holy war in Algeria?" He waggled the fingers of both hands in front of me like a bogeyman. "A serial killer."

"I'm not like you."

He raised his hands toward his face as if he held a camera. He peered through the space he'd made with his thumbs and index fingers. "We're both looking through the same viewfinder, Tex." He clicked his tongue like the sound of a shutter.

I'd brooked the worst of him. I was no longer afraid of what he'd expose in me.

"Did you have any relationships with other women?" I asked.

He leaned in close. "Thirteen of them."

I couldn't imagine anyone wanting to bear his child. And if he'd somehow had another son, he would have bragged about it in prison. He couldn't have restrained himself.

"Why is he tormenting my family?" I said.

"You know why."

"Tell me, goddamn it."

He leaned forward and spread his rotting breath over me. "He wants to heal you."

I forced my stomach to unknot. "When did he visit you?"

He shook his head. "He doesn't communicate that way."

"How does he communicate?"

"Through bodies."

I thought I saw anticipation—even delight—in his face. But I still had to ask. "What's he saying?"

"'Hel-loooo.'"

My fisted hand raised by itself. And stopped. A smile was crueler. "Did you love your brother?" I asked.

He blinked.

"That was as close to love as you got, wasn't it?"

He rose. But he had to walk by me to get to the door. I slid my chair over to block his path. He froze. Shoes stomped on the linoleum floor outside the room. Voices. The sound slowly faded.

"I think you've been talking to the FBI headshrinkers," he said.

"The killer has a kind of love for you, doesn't he?"

"Lots of broken men love me for what I did."

One of them was a man with a past so shattered that he'd murder for him. The killer's mother had to be the key. Kogan had already told me she was a sadist.

"You killed abusive mothers," I said. "That's why he came to you."

He nudged my leg to the side with his manacled hands. At the door, he turned. "Willy, I'm your father. I'm the one who held you when you were a baby and played with you when you were a boy. A father can forgive his son for anything. Even for what he did in Algeria."

He knocked on the door. "Clarence, please take me home."

————————

In the Stateville parking lot, Blake and I sat in the rental car. His shriveled ears were particularly livid in the afternoon light. I touched the nylon car seat and stared at the trees through the dirty windshield. The leaves would turn colors here soon. Fall. Something foreign to San Diego.

Blake put his hand on my arm. "You've given us more than you think. We know the killer's from the Midwest. He's highly educated. Afraid of women. A loner. And you're onto something with Kogan's brother and sister. You can leverage those weaknesses."

"We knew that before."

Blake's jaw clenched and unclenched. "He wants you to admit that you're like him. And that little dig at the end? He says he forgives you, but he really wants you to forgive him."

"He's capable of remorse?"

Blake shook his head. "As soon as you forgive him, he gets power. Power to manipulate you."

I grimaced and squeezed my eyes shut. I couldn't do this anymore. "I've got to get home and protect my family."

He nodded. "Do you think you can do that better than an officer in a car out front? Day and night? Plus there's your wife's father, the soldier. He'd die before he'd let anything happen to them."

"They'll never be safe."

Blake leaned his face closer to mine. His ear lumps seemed to change from red to white and back. He said, "He wants you to feel paranoid. The more you worry about your family, the more you have to come back to see him. So he can play with you."

He reached over the seat and opened his briefcase in the back. He pulled out a picture and gave it to me. "The prison found this."

The photo showed a man with blond hair, a blond beard, and luminous blue eyes.

"Les Filson," he said. "The only person who visited Kogan more than once. The last time was ten years ago."

"Where's he now?"

Blake raised his hands. Ten years was more than a cold trail. Still, how many Les Filsons could there be in the world?

"*Fils* means 'son' in French," Blake said. "*Les* is the plural of 'the.' 'The sons.'"

Another false clue. I said, "He thought the killer's mother was a sadist. I'll bet he was abused as a child."

Blake stared out the window at the trees, their green leaves swaying. "Kogan might have been jerking you around. Using his own twisted past."

Maybe. Then I thought about the killings going on for nineteen years. "Is it possible he met Les Filson before he went to prison?"

"More than thirty years ago? Filson doesn't look that old in this picture."

Unless it was something more twisted. "What if Kogan met him when Filson was a boy?"

Blake grimaced, those beaten-up ears moving farther up his head. "That's even too perverted for me."

He turned the ignition key and pulled the car onto the road out of the prison. Soon we passed a fallow field next to a barn with great fissures in the roof. It was like one of Harvey Dean Kogan's photos.

48

A TAXI BROUGHT ME from the airport to our house. It was still late afternoon in California. The lights were on in our house, and for a moment I thought my family had miraculously returned. But it was just the timer. I went inside and turned off the alarm. It was so quiet: no pans clanking or children squealing and running, no cooking smells. I had put away all the dishes, but the kitchen still felt disassembled. I wondered if it would ever feel like home again.

Something else wasn't right.

I whirled. No movement in the living room. Nothing in the dark hallway. My shoes made slow, soft steps down the wooden floor.

The doors to both my children's rooms stood open, the lights on. In Garth's, his bag of toy soldiers and blocks lay in the same place on the floor. His mattress rested on its side in the same spot against the wall, the urine stain still hidden. In Frieda's room, her dolls and stuffed bears lay on the carpet next to stacked air duct grates. But the bookcase was different. The police had removed the books and pictures to do their search, and now something sat on the shelf.

It was a single framed photo. I stepped closer. The picture was in black and white and showed a child's grave with dolls planted on top. My father's photo. The dead child had been six years old. Frieda was five, almost six.

Breathing hard, I stepped out of her room. Rested my hand against the wall. A faint sour smell came from the far end of the hallway. Even after so many years, the odor was unmistakable. The stench of Béni-Messous.

I flicked on the hallway light. Spots of blood ran down the center of the wooden floor to the closed door of our bedroom.

Frieda.

Suppose he was waiting inside with a knife or some drug? But she could be wounded or dying. The police would take time to get here.

I lay my ear against the wood of our door. No rustling or quiet breathing. Only the putrid smell that was worse than any sound. The metal handle was cool. Softly, slowly, I turned it. The door silently slid open to reveal a crack of darkness.

The smell hit me like a hammer—rotting and palpable.

I kicked open the door and rushed into the dark room. My head jerked from side to side. I whirled behind me. Nothing moved.

I switched on the light. On the bed, the outlines of a body pushed up the covers. Light hair extended over the pillow. Like Jill's hair.

I couldn't think. The smell filled my whole head. I stumbled to the bed.

The head wore pearl earrings. It wasn't Jill. Thank God it wasn't Jill.

Vanessa's blue eyes bulged out. She was so pale, her face like wax. I looked for the blankets covering her to rise with her breathing. Nothing. I threw them off. What should have been her body was an inflatable sex doll reconfigured with Vanessa's head. Jill's Colombian necklace hung between its blown-up breasts.

49

BY THE TIME LUND and Hempel arrived, I sat huddled against the wall near the front door. They gently shook my shoulder and I came back from someplace far away. Then I was outside and sitting under the orange tree, my whole body limp. Three police cars, lights flashing, were angled on the street. Voices chattered like ghosts through the dry night air. A spotlight cast our shadows onto the grass. The crickets trilled in the darkness just beyond our yard.

Lund picked an orange from the tree and turned it in his hand. That melodious voice said, "Whoever did this shut off your house alarm."

I tried to speak. My throat constricted the words. "I just … changed the code."

Hempel clumped over to the entrance to stare at the redwood door and the glass transom above it. Turning back to me, he said, "The alarm is just on the other side of the door, right?"

"On the wall."

Hempel and Lund gave each other a glance. Lund retrieved the ladder from the side of the garage and set it up, rattling, beside me against the orange tree. Hempel slipped off his sports jacket and handed it to Lund. He pulled on latex gloves, turned on a flashlight, and clanked up the aluminum rungs. The light beam slowly swept the rustling branches. I imagined it illuminating Vanessa's pearl earrings and pale face. Her bulging eyes, as big as the oranges, stared at me.

Hempel's ragged voice rose over the crickets and scraped against the night. "It's here."

Lund carried Hempel's jacket to the front entrance and into our house. He closed the door. After a minute, he returned to the tree.

Hempel banged down the ladder. "I could see every stripe on the suit," he said.

"Unbelievable," Lund said. "We searched the whole yard."

Hempel kneeled beside me, his big face inches from my own. "William, there's a video camera in that tree. I'm pretty sure it has some kind of telephoto lens. You can't see the keypad from the walk outside the door. The glass transom is too high. But from up in the branches, and with magnification ... I could make out someone punching in every number."

———————

Two hours later, Marta and I huddled with Hempel and Lund in a police interview room. Hempel wedged a square of gum into his mouth. He held out the pack to me. "It helps you deal with this shit. Distracts your mind from the stuff you can't stop thinking about."

273

His voice reached me like soft static on a radio. Chewing gum wouldn't get Vanessa's puffed-up blue eyes out of my head—and the sex doll wearing Jill's necklace.

Lund said, "Remember, he didn't attack you or your family."

My whole body stiffened. I wanted to jump across the table. I wanted to punch that undertaker's voice out of him. "How the hell is this not an attack?"

Marta put her hand on my arm. "Easy," she said.

I said, "Vanessa's head was in our bed. He left a fucking picture of a child's grave in Frieda's room."

Lund turned to Hempel. "What picture?"

"It's the only damn thing in the bookcase!"

Beside me, Marta squeezed my arm. "Maybe we should put this off."

Hempel picked up a bottle of water. "Have a sip," he said. His thick hand twisted off the cap.

I grabbed the water. What would it be like to heave the bottle against the wall?

I drank. I closed my eyes and willed the anger and panic to slide into the floor.

"What do you think happened?" Marta said.

My eyes sprang open. How the hell should I know? But she was talking to Hempel and Lund.

Lund said, "All we've got is what her husband says. You know how reliable that is. He thinks the killer must have grabbed her at home as she left for work."

I imagined him sticking her with a needle, carrying her to his car. Gently he sets her in the backseat, drives her somewhere, and … and … he carries her head to our bed like a cat gifting a kill.

They were talking to me. "Your colleagues at work say she was trying to fire you," Lund said. "She was an enemy."

"'Enemy' is not the way William would characterize his relationship with her," Marta said.

Lund leaned over the table and set his hand on my wrist. He wore the same gold-filigreed ring, but today his shirt had buttoned sleeves. There was actually a food stain.

"This guy thinks you're his brother," Lund said. "He was protecting you from her."

Killing and dismembering Vanessa to protect me. While threatening Jill and Frieda.

Hempel transferred his gum to a Kleenex and tossed it in the trash can. He popped a new piece in his mouth and opened a manila folder. How could a man with so little hair sprout such huge eyebrows? He looked as if he'd rubbed Rogaine over the wrong places.

"The *Union-Tribune* got photos again this morning," Hempel said. "Brace yourself."

I liked the chafe and scrape of his voice today. It fit everything that had happened.

He set down a black-and-white photo in front of us. Marta started to protest, but it was too late. In the photo, Vanessa's head lay sideways on a counter. Her skin was as sickly pale as milk, her eyes dull stones. Next to the head, her severed hand, encircled by a pearl bracelet, held one shoe. The pointed toe was turned up. The shoe looked like one of the red heels she'd worn when she tried to fire me. It seemed more like her than that face.

"Our techs think they know what he's copying," Lund said. "We thought you could confirm it."

That assumption, delivered in his creamy voice, just made me tired. I set my head in my hand and closed my eyes. More than thirty years before, the Preying Hands had placed a woman's head on its side on a kitchen counter. Next to her face, her hand clutched one of her shined black heels. When he sent it to the *Chicago Tribune*, he called it

Black and White after the famous Man Ray photograph. In that one, the woman was alive and held a mask.

Marta touched my shoulder. Her eyes asked if I was all right.

"Susanna Lopez," I said.

"Your dad made a second photo of her," Hempel said. "Why do you think he didn't copy that one?"

The second photograph was the Preying Hands' own creation: a long line of shoes in a huge closet with her severed bare feet neatly placed at the end of the row.

"I have no idea," I said.

The skin around Lund's eye sockets crinkled and the lines softened his brown irises. I couldn't see any hint of the usual vigilance. He said, "You're doing well, William. Let's move on. Is Jim Poderovsky your client?"

He knew he was.

Hempel scratched his buzz cut. "Poderovsky won't tell us shit without his lawyer."

So Jim had refused to give me up.

"Poderovsky's wife and kid haven't been seen for weeks," Hempel said. His raspy voice conveyed his suspicion as much as his words.

"They're in Hawaii," I said.

"No reservation on any of the islands," Hempel said.

The haze cleared from my brain. I knew where their questions and comments were leading. "Do you actually think he did something to his wife and daughter?"

"We're trying to confirm that he didn't," Hempel said.

They wanted me to arrange a meeting with Jim and bring them along. "I'm not going to ambush him," I said.

Disbelief broke out over Lund's lined face. He raked his hair with those manicured nails. The man had a God-given talent for faking any emotion.

"This isn't an ambush," Lund said. "We just want to talk." When I shook my head, he said, "You know, a patrol car guarding your family is a real exception. The chief was dead set against it."

That syrupy voice belied the threat. But they weren't taking away that car. "No," I said.

"Be smart about this, William," Marta said. "It's your family. You know what Poderovsky's father and brother are into."

"So he's presumed guilty because of his father?" I drove my palm into the table. I had to control something, anything from this horrible day.

Silence. No one had to say what the parallel was.

"Look, I've studied his financials. It's not Jim, goddamn it."

"His financials?" Hempel said. His mutated eyebrows shot up as if I were speaking in tongues.

"It's simple cash flow. The killer knows we're closing in and has to have money to fund his escape. That means a balance sheet with a lot of liquidity. Just the opposite of Jim's balance sheet."

This time Lund's disbelief looked real. But Hempel stopped chewing his gum. He sat back in his chair and nodded.

50

OUTSIDE THE POLICE STATION, I sat in my car with the doors locked. I'd disliked Vanessa and disapproved of her. She'd tried to push me out of the bank while a killer was hunting my family. But she was also a mother. She was someone I'd shared a laugh with. She'd hired me.

Maybe the radio would drown out my thoughts. I punched the button.

"... time we get this scumbag off the street," a talk radio bloviator said. "Did you see the pictures he took in Algeria? He's always been a sick freak. And then that letter. Don't you tell me he didn't write that—"

I hit the "off" button.

My smartphone pulled up the letter from the internet. The killer had left it in the garage of the *Union-Tribune*.

My Dear Public:

Does a sociopathic liar who abuses her child deserve to live?
Her own daughter refused to "friend" her on Facebook.
That's what happens when you abandon your child at a
boarding school and euthanize her dog because it's too much
trouble.

She and I had a truthful and candid discussion. I didn't
think that was possible with someone in the banking
profession. It was a revelation to watch her eyes become
utterly honest.

Ms. Barksdale made an application that I extend the loan
of her life. Unfortunately, our credit committee declined her
request and we had no choice but to seize our collateral.

At least she had good taste in shoes.

Yours sincerely,
Son of the Preying Hands

He'd changed his signature again—from "The Defender of Children" to "Your Brother" and now to "Son of the Preying Hands."

I needed something to remove the taste of bile from my throat.
The lights of a 7-Eleven were close by. Inside, the racks of newspapers
didn't headline anything about the McNary family. But the cashier
stared at me. I turned to see my image in a blue pinstripe peering out
from a mounted TV. Polly appeared in a green vest with the Haven's
restaurant sign behind her. The final connection I'd been expecting
followed: it was a thirty-year-old video of my father, broad shouldered
with a full head of blond hair. He strode forward in handcuffs and
grinned at his guards. The subtitle read, "Is there a murder gene?"

I fled to my car and pulled back onto the street. At least no one
could see my face in the dimming light. I opened the window. As the

night air whooshed over me, I tried to imagine myself flying high above San Diego.

———————

Leucadia, where Jill's parents lived, was a northern suburb of scrubby dry hills and scraggly pine trees. Today a police car sat on the street in front of their neat lawn and the plain, yellow-stuccoed facade of their house. In the twilight—the street lights not yet on—I took in the old-fashioned curtains and American flag. Their home seemed so innocent and otherworldly.

Vanessa's murder weighed on each step up the rutted driveway. When I got to the house, I held on to the side of the doorway to muster my strength. My finger pushed the bell.

The screen door whined open. Jill reached out her arms. "Marta called us," she said. She pulled me close. Everything that had happened, all the deaths and suffering, the anguish over our kids, all swept out of me.

When I drew back, Jill's eyes were both fierce and full of tears. "It's not your fault," she said.

"But ... I ..."

"Everyone in that bank hated her."

I straightened my shoulders. Wiped my eyes. I looked inside to the living room. Polly stood in front of the leather couch. It was the first time in years that she'd ventured to Mike and April's house. She strode across the fake wood floor, her bracelets jingling, and bear-hugged me. I drew in her strength.

I went inside and collapsed on the couch. The leather hissed like a weary exhale. Jill sat next to me and Polly faced me on one of the leather wingback chairs. Between them stood a pine table with a withered plant. Its orange blossoms barely hung on.

Polly said, "He wants you to feel responsible. That's why he struck someone you didn't like."

How could I not feel responsible? If I'd never worked at that bank, Vanessa would still be a wife and mother.

Jill clutched my hand. I said to her, "Tell Mike I'm sorry I'm blubbering inside his house."

"Do you think soldiers don't cry?" Jill said.

Garth's giggle rose from the backyard behind the house. Grandpa Mike roared. Frieda let out a gleeful screech. My children were okay. Thanks to the family around me.

"We're too strong for him," I said. I sounded like Mama.

I stared at both the women in my life. I had to warn them.

"What do you know?" Polly said.

"There's going to be another murder. He does things in threes."

Both women drew back. They hugged themselves.

"We have to really watch each other. The kids too, especially Frieda."

Jill's pupils were enormous. "Frieda?"

My cell phone rang. I started to forward the call to voicemail but saw that the number was from Chicago. I answered.

"I can't bear another poor mother killed," Magnolia said.

51

THE NEXT AFTERNOON, HARVEY Dean Kogan stepped into the attorney meeting room at Stateville Correctional Center, his ankle and
wrist chains rattling. He wore the same blue denim shirt, the sleeves
rolled up. He stopped as if his shoe had stuck to the concrete.

"Hello, Harvey," Magnolia said. She sat beside me at the little
table, facing the door, her blonde and gray hair hanging past her
shoulders. I'd flown in early that morning, again on an FBI Gulfstream
jet. We'd picked up Magnolia in Chicago and headed straight to Stateville.

"Who are you?" Harvey said.

"Magnolia." She gave him a small, difficult smile that revealed the
gap in her upper front teeth.

"Does the FBI think I'm stupid? You're not Magnolia."

She wore a long blue dress that had to be at least twenty years old and fit her like a tarp. She might have worn the same dress when she ran away at sixteen.

"Harvey, they told me you had cancer." Her voice was as soft as the air around us.

He turned away and shuffled and clanked to the door. Loudly knocked. He wasn't even going to speak with her.

Magnolia said, "Remember when you stole that plastic ring and gave it to Mother? You were about five. You thought that ring was the most beautiful thing you ever saw."

He turned.

"But Mother just called you names and threw it away. Then there was that dog of yours, that brown mutt. I can still hear the shovel." She let out a heavy sigh. Her eyes had brightened with tears. "What she did to you when you were a child ..."

He shuffled and jingled to the table and sat in the chair across from us. His face looked thinner and more sallow, as if the cancer had sucked up a little more of him. His chains chimed and he lowered his hands to the plastic tabletop.

"So I guess the FBI dug you up. They thought my old hag of a sister could make me help them."

"I wanted to see you again," she said.

He turned to me and smiled. More cancer sores had covered his lips. "So you finally get to meet your aunt. Better talk to her now before she runs away."

Mama had always pretended that her husband's malevolence didn't exist and highlighted the good in him. That was the way to manage my father. I said, "You knew if people didn't look for Magnolia ... you knew she'd have a new life. That's why you told the world you killed her. It was one of the best things you ever did."

He jerked his gaze from Magnolia to me and blinked. His rotting smell drifted across the table.

"You were a wonderful child," Magnolia said.

"Yes, I'm a child of God, aren't I? Does the FBI think that will open me up? Split me apart like a tin can?"

Magnolia leaned toward him. He drew away.

"I should have taken you with me," she said. "I'll be regretful the rest of my life."

He lowered his head and stared down at the table. Her gentleness and milky eyes, her soft voice, seemed to have melted part of him. "Where have you been all these years?" he said.

She gave a slow, resigned shrug. "In Chicago. Doing people's books. Paying their bills, mostly."

"Did you marry?"

"No." Her voice was so soft I could barely hear it.

"Children?"

"No."

Her long torso drooped until her hair almost touched the table. That whole stooped body formed a single word: penance. Maybe that's why Harvey Dean Kogan's amber eyes gleamed.

"This man killed another woman," she said. "A mother with a daughter who loved her."

He dug his yellow nails into the table. "Did you ever think what our mother would do to me after you ran away? She only had me to beat for what you did."

Magnolia's whole face was squeezing shut.

"Oh, you cry now, don't you? But did you even try to contact me?"

Her long fingers slid in and out of her palms. She could only stare at her lap. "I ... I couldn't bear to think about that life."

His back straightened. He was drawing strength from her anguish. "You knew what she'd do to me and you didn't even reach out. Not once."

Magnolia raised her great hands over her face. She was dissolving. I had to help her.

I said, "Magnolia and Jonas were the only ones who loved you when you were a child. You felt it from Polly and me, too. You can still feel love, can't you?"

He laughed. "Have you been talking with the FBI headshrinkers again, Tex? Or are you reading those self-help books?"

Magnolia's hands dropped. She stared at him, the tears streaming down her face. "Oh, Harvey, what have you become?"

His eyes flared. "Fifty years. And now you only show up for one reason. To help the FBI."

She began to sob.

"You did nothing to save Jonas. Nothing. Jonas, who was better than all of us."

"I ... I didn't know."

"You didn't know? It was a hundred degrees that night. The whole shack was made of tin. How could you not know what that heat would do to him?" Harvey tsked. "Your own baby brother."

I didn't know how to stop him or even deflect his cruelty. I had to say something. "You didn't help him either. You were twice your mother's size, and what did you do? You just lay in your bed. A weak coward who couldn't even stop an old woman."

Magnolia pulled herself up and shook her head. She turned toward the door.

"Sit down in that chair," he yelled.

She sat.

The only way to blunt him was to attack. "You dreamed you and Jonas took an axe to your mother. Cutting up those women ... that was your way of trying to save him, wasn't it?"

He shook his head, the chains rattling. "And here I thought I was the one who lived in fantasies."

It came to me. From nowhere, like one of Mama's angel thoughts. "That first time I came here you told me something. You said the child was the father of the man."

He chuckled. "It's not the child who's the father of the man. It's the man who kills the child's witch mother. He's the real father."

I nodded at the camera behind him. "The man who killed the child's mother," I said.

His face stiffened. He looked away. He'd slipped at last. What had Mama said that night when Polly and I sat in her living room? She'd told me to think about the kinds of thoughts the killer's mother put into him.

I jerked forward in the chair. "The killer is a child of one of your victims."

Harvey Dean Kogan rose and strode four rattling steps to the door. He knocked.

"He grew up to be the brother you lost," I said. "Who is he? What's his name?"

He turned and took in Magnolia's bent shoulders and soft weeping. "If you want his name, Magnolia will have to come back to see me. Just her. All alone. And then we'll have a real conversation."

The door opened.

"Clarence, take me home please."

52

THE POLICE FORENSICS SQUAD had returned our house to us, but Jill still didn't want to live there. And I couldn't stay at Mike and April's house. My research was about something so evil I didn't want it near my family. When I got home that night, I hurried to my office and stared at the bourbon bottle in the bottom desk drawer. With a call, I could score both a vape pen and marijuana extract in an hour.

I sat down, closed my eyes, and thought about the children of Harvey Dean Kogan's victims. My father had said that the killer's mother was a sadist. She'd so abused her child that he grew up to admire the way Kogan cut her up.

The internet provided more background on my father's victims. All but one had offspring, yet the newspaper accounts only published the children's ages and sexes. It was impossible to know which child could have been abused. Twelve women times how many children? I would need the FBI's help to get information on any of them.

My cell phone squawked and I jumped. It kept screeching while I searched through the piles of papers. I found it on the floor.

"You went to see that cocksucker again, didn't you?" Polly said.

Maybe she'd guessed because my phone had been off. "You tried to call me?"

"Why the hell didn't you take me with you?"

"I went with Magnolia."

She was quiet, surprised.

"The FBI thought he'd open up to her. But he was totally abusive. It was awful. She dissolved in front of him."

"You expected something different?"

"He loved his sister. Maybe more than anyone."

"You mean the sister who abandoned him to that mother? The one that let everyone think he'd killed her? That sister? Jesus, she shows up after fifty years—"

"So Magnolia deserved what he did?"

"What I'm saying is, you want something from that bastard, don't walk in with his useless sister."

I told her what we'd learned: the killer was a child of one of Kogan's victims. But I didn't know who. "Tell me if you have any ideas," I said.

"I'll tell you what idea I have. Next time take me with you."

She hung up and I was left again to ponder which victim's child the killer was. I fell asleep in my office chair.

My doorbell rang.

Who the hell would show up at midnight?

I kept the hammer with me now. I padded down the hallway, my arm already cocked. But my assailant wouldn't ring the doorbell, would he?

Someone was pounding the door. "William, open up." Her bangles rang against the redwood.

I let her in. Polly pushed by me. Her boots knocked against the wooden floor as she headed down the hallway. "Get on your damn computer," she said. "We have to find one of his photos."

"I thought you didn't look at those."

"There are a lot of things you don't know about me."

I followed her back to my office. Woke up the computer.

"Find the Robert Frank one," she said.

I quickly found my father's homage to Robert Frank on one of the fan websites. In his version of Frank's trolley photo, the dark-haired child with haunted eyes stared out of the window of the Elevated train. Next to him was the woman's blurred face, looking away as if the child meant nothing to her. The image showed the first letter of the station's name written on the wooden platform. It was an *F*.

"Google the stops for the Howard line," Polly said.

I opened another internet window and did what she asked. On the Howard line, only one of the Elevated stations began with an *F*. "Fullerton."

"Not California," Polly said. "Fucking Chicago."

The train stop where this young boy had desolately stared out at the world. A child who'd grown up to kill in the same way his savior had.

53

THE NEXT MORNING MARTA and I met at Wired Café. The usual Euro techno music wafted from the speakers and the espresso machine hissed like part of the percussion. We spotted Detective Lund at a grungy table in the corner away from the windows. Today his gray suit was full of wrinkles. His eyes closed as he drank from a demitasse cup. Beside him, Hempel was two-fisting a huge cup of coffee. He'd loosened his tie and draped his sports jacket over the chair behind him. They looked as if they'd forgotten what sleep was.

Marta dumped her big purse and battered briefcase on the neighboring table. She pulled out a notepad and a Bic and yelled, "Can we order some coffee?"

Lund gave us a tired grin. "Well, we certainly know when Marta's arrived."

We sat down opposite the two detectives. The waitress appeared and we ordered. Her foreign-sounding English prompted a smile from Hempel. "Love that accent," he said, his rasp almost charming.

After the waitress left, Lund said, "So, William, you're a famous photographer again."

He was referring to the tornado of media coverage. I was almost as famous as Harvey Dean Kogan. We were a serial killer and his son who shared the same hobby—photographing cut-up bodies.

"It'll blow over," Hempel said. "The press can't remember anything for longer than a day."

Until they remembered it again in a week or a month or thirty-one years later.

Marta studied him. "How many days since you stopped smoking?"

Hempel grinned and his overgrown eyebrows shot up to the edge of his buzz cut. "I'm trying not to count." He reached into his shirt and brandished a pack of gum. "Now I'm addicted to sugar." He tapped out a piece and popped it into his mouth.

"Do you know what the worst profession is if you're giving up smoking?" Lund asked.

"Any profession at all," Marta said.

Lund shrugged. Her wrong answer was better than his punch line.

Now I knew why Hempel constantly chomped on gum. Maybe his smoking had scraped away his voice.

"You said you had news," Marta said.

Lund smiled benignly and drank from the demitasse. He set it down gently on the saucer.

"Come on, Kevin," Marta said. "If I have to drag it out of you I'll muss up your hair. Spill it before you burst."

He took another long sip. "Based on what William has put together, we pulled in a favor from some Chicago cops. They went through Kogan's murders and all the victims' kids lives. Couldn't find anything, so they looked at other murders. All the Chicago women

291

over the past forty-five years. Solved and unsolved. It's a pretty big list, but when you look just at the victims who might have abused their kids—"

"It's still a pretty big list," Hempel said.

Lund reached into a folder. With a flourish, he slapped down a photo on the table in front of Marta and me. "This one happens to be unsolved. Alice White. Arrested for prostitution more than forty years ago. She was also hooked on heroin."

The vacant-eyed woman was a blonde with roots showing. I recognized her purple butterfly-shaped barrette. The blonde victim in the soybean field wore the same clip. Kogan had also mentioned it. But maybe that kind of hair fastener was popular at the time.

"Is she the mother of the boy on the train?" I asked.

Lund pulled out a copy of Harvey Dean Kogan's photograph of the child on the Chicago Elevated train. The mother's face was too blurred to tell if it was the same woman. But he said, "The FBI is ninety percent certain that Alice White is both the woman on the train and the one in the soybean field."

Marta's wedding ring clanked on the table. "Ninety percent means they aren't sure. That's some tech afraid to say what he really thinks."

"Now you sound like a prosecutor again." Lund smiled at her. "But we've got more. She had a son, and Protective Services made a visit. It happened so long ago our amigos were willing to unseal the kid's file."

Marta raised her eyebrows. "Sometimes you guys are almost impressive."

"That's as close as our Marta gets to a compliment," Lund said. He reached into the same folder and pulled out a picture of a young boy with brown eyes and dark hair. He put it next to the one of the child staring out of the Elevated train.

The same boy.

"But Les Filson was blond and blue-eyed," I said.

Hempel beetled his eyebrows at me as if it were obvious. "I thought you bankers knew all about hair dye and contact lenses."

It was possible. But it was so elaborate. As if Les Filson had known, even when visiting Kogan a decade before, that he'd someday be a suspect.

"Your hunch was on the money," Hempel said. "A child of a victim. A victim we hadn't identified."

I'd begun to like all the scratches and burs in his words. There was something real about his voice.

"Assuming that Kogan really was the one who murdered her," Marta said.

Lund ignored her qualifier. "Does the boy look like anyone you know?" he asked me.

In the photo, he was so young. It was impossible to tell.

"Here's a bit of trivia," Hempel said. "Alice White disappeared a month before Harvey Dean Kogan murdered Bonnie Sendaro, his first known victim."

For thirty-one years, I'd believed my father killed thirteen women. The very number linked him to the devil. But if that head in the soybean field did belong to Alice White, that meant he'd actually killed fourteen victims. He'd been nineteen years old at the time. His technique for the photo of the boy and the woman on the Elevated train seemed too advanced for someone that age—all those shades of gray, the in-focus and out-of-focus expressions and layering. And he'd referenced the famous Robert Frank picture.

How had he been able to preserve Alice White's head all that time? It seemed impossible. But perhaps before disposing of the body, he'd taken a picture of her severed head. Years later, he could have double-exposed that image with the one of Polly and me in the soybean field.

Marta tapped her teeth with the end of the Bic. "You still haven't convinced me he did this one. Where are the photographs and letters to the newspapers?"

Hempel chewed on his gum and considered the dregs of his coffee. "Kogan was barely a man. He must not have come up with his MO yet."

"A prodigy discovering his technique," Lund said.

"Jesus, Kevin," Marta said. "I think you've been doing this too long."

If it was true about Alice White, that meant that my father had photographed the killer before I was even born. As if he knew that the boy would someday grow up to copy him. That kind of twisted foresight seemed too perfect. Credible or not, the story made me shudder.

"The boy's name was Ronny White," Lund said. "He must have changed it after he got out of foster care. Probably wanted to forget all about his mother and his childhood."

Marta frowned at him. "Don't tell me that Protective Services lost track of him."

Lund winced.

"So no one knows who he is or where he is," I said.

"We're looking," Lund said.

Marta said, "You almost made my day, Kevin. Almost."

The waitress returned with lattes for Marta and me and espressos for Lund and Hempel. The gum still in his mouth, Hempel chugged the last of his tankard of coffee and took a sip of the espresso.

"You're very thirsty," the waitress said.

Hempel beamed a smile at her. He chomped on his gum.

"Ben, we're over here," Marta said.

Hempel said something and the waitress nodded. Her smile lit up her eyes. He was speaking German. Fluently. Every time I met Hempel I discovered another layer. As I listened to them, his scratchy voice seemed to complement the sounds of the language.

When the waitress left, Marta said, "Can we get back to business, or do you want to get her phone number?"

"Come on, you have to take a laugh break once in a while," Hempel said. "Otherwise this shit will drive you nuts."

"You'd better laugh now," Lund said. "The worst is yet to come." He nodded at Hempel.

Hempel's smile vanished. He dug his hand in the sports jacket on his chair and found a green spiral notebook. His bitten-off nails leafed through the pages until he found the one he wanted.

"Like Kevin said, this addict, Alice White, was a working girl. And this young son she had? She was selling him out for drugs. Seven years old."

My mouth fell open. "You mean—?"

"Yeah," Hempel said, chewing. "Everything you can imagine."

I'd seen the picture of that boy staring from the Elevated train for more than twenty years, but I'd never known why his eyes looked so bereft. I thought again of Garth. I shivered.

Hempel glanced up from the green notebook. "Know anyone who might have had that done to him?"

I shook my head. It was the kind of secret people wouldn't talk about. But that child's suffering aligned with something my father had said. "Kogan claimed that the child is some kind of father of the man. That's what made me think about the victims' children."

"More crazy stuff just to throw you off," Lund said. He sipped his espresso and smacked his lips. "This is excellent. Glad you introduced us to this place, William."

"Wordsworth," Hempel said. "'The child is the father of the man.' But it's from a poem about joy and piety."

All three of us drew back.

"I had no idea," Marta said.

Hempel raised his meaty hands. He shook his head as if our surprise was ridiculous. "I went to college too."

"Poetry?" Lund said.

Hempel's face reddened. He chewed his gum a little harder.

A window opened on Harvey Dean Kogan that I'd never expected. Among all the books he'd read at Stateville, the one with Wordsworth's poem had spoken to him. As if he'd yearned for a deeper meaning, an explanation for what he'd become. Or a justification for what he'd done.

"This 'mother'"—Hempel put his fingers in quotes around the word—"just disappeared. No body, nada. Only an abandoned kid in an apartment in Chicago. Someone heard him crying and turned him in to Protective Services. He said he had a mother but no family. Or maybe no one wanted him."

Lund said, "See, William, not all your father's murders were bad."

I couldn't find a single hint of sarcasm in that lined face. The story gelled with my father's soybean picture: a terrible mother—like his own mother—lurking below his happy children.

"No one suspected her case was tied to the Preying Hands' murder?" Marta asked.

"We're the first," Hempel said.

"Maybe the FBI will give you a commendation," Marta said.

"Good one, Marta," Lund said.

We drank our coffee and studied our cups. Hempel spit his gum into his napkin and popped in another piece. Each of us must have been considering Ronny White's sad life.

Finally, Lund said, "We do have one other thing." He pulled a Xerox out of the pocket of his suit. It was a prison visitation form with a scrawl so angular it looked like an EKG. The signature belonged to Les

Filson, or Ronny White. From when he'd visited Harvey Dean Kogan ten years before.

"Pretty distinctive handwriting," Lund said to me.

I shook my head. I didn't recognize it.

Hempel said, "Don't forget he kills in threes."

"We'd better prepare ourselves for another murder," Marta said.

I thought of the head and the sex doll with Jill's necklace on our bed. The picture of a child's grave in Frieda's room. The killer was aiming at my family.

54

I'D ALREADY STARTED MY Camry when the question hit me. How had the killer learned that Harvey Dean Kogan was the one who murdered his mother? Until now, the police hadn't ever suspected Kogan of it. Then I remembered something that had been mentioned by the journalist Jeff Nelson, who'd authored at least ten articles and a book on the Preying Hands. In one piece, Nelson wrote about a prison conversation he'd had with Kogan in which Kogan referred to a victim as a prostitute with a young son.

I stayed in the cafe's parking lot to search for that article on my iPhone. It was buried in the archives of *Deviant Behavior Magazine*. Nelson believed that the murder Kogan described had never occurred. He transcribed the conversation anyway, to illustrate the chilling power of Harvey Dean Kogan's fantasies.

JN: How did you choose her?

HDK: Everyone saw what she was selling on State Street.

JN: So she was a prostitute?

HDK: How much do you think she got for that half hour of proselytizing in the Palmer House Hotel?

JN: I wouldn't know.

HDK: Jeff, Jeff, Jeff. Your whole body tells me when you lie. I can hear it, all that blood rushing to your brain. It's my special skill.

JN: What did it feel like when you followed her?

HDK: What does it feel like to hunt *me*?

JN: Tell me what happened.

HDK: She stopped at a basement window near Cabrini–Green. It seems she wanted a syringe full of happiness for a good night's work. But next door she bought a box of Cracker Jacks. Cracker Jacks, Jeff.

JN: She wanted something sweet? Because of her drug habit?

HDK: Think. A box of Cracker Jacks has a toy inside.

JN: She had a child?

HDK: Ahhh, now you're starting to get it.

JN: How did you break into her apartment?

HDK: You know the kind of place where she lived, don't you, Jeff? The locks on the building's doors are broken. The hallway smells of urine and beer. Do you see the cockroaches scampering along the walls? It's so simple to get inside her little hovel. All I needed was a bump key. The child's bed had a single Cracker Jacks toy on it. A miniature plastic trumpet.

JN: Tell me what happened.
HDK: What did that child deserve to have happen?

JN: It's not for me to judge her.
HDK: No, you're Jeff Nelson, the journalist. It's not your job to save that boy. You only ask what the world did to his mother, the home schooler. How did that poor woman fall so far? You think that's the interesting question, but there's another bigger one. What does that wreck of a mother want most in this world?

JN: What does she want?
HDK: When she came back from the Palmer House, her son was with her. He began to whimper and do you know what she yelled at him? "Eat your Cracker Jacks. Get your prize."

JN: A prize for what?
HDK: What do you think?

JN: Did you do something to that boy?
HDK: I freed him.

JN: How?
HDK: I waited until he was asleep. That's when I opened the closet door and went into the mother's room. *"Surprise."* She

was too drugged to yell. Her eyes were already dead. Maybe her son saw those same lifeless eyes when he was abused. She and I had the conversation then. Right in the apartment.

JN: A conversation about what?
HDK: Everything. And nothing. Even now, I see the tears. Can you see them? Her eyes are alive, so thankful when you drape her belt around her neck. The abyss is a relief for her. Could you end her suffering, Jeff? Do it and that boy will thank you when he grows up.

The interview continued, more pages of Harvey Dean Kogan manipulating and playing with Nelson. Nelson had found no police report of a body resembling that woman. No letter to the newspaper claiming credit. He concluded that the story was a fantasy concealing Kogan's lust for boys. Nelson never did understand him. But in the interview, Kogan had called the mother a home schooler. During my first prison visit, he'd said that he killed another teacher besides Kim Johnson. A teacher who never got out much in the daytime.

Maybe Ronny discovered the article and contacted the man who'd freed him from his mother. She was dead but still haunted him. Kogan would suggest a way to expel her ghost.

55

POLLY WANTED TO SEE me. Right away. I picked her up in front of the Buddha Light Bookstore and Tea Room. She opened the car door and sat in the front. She'd snipped off the bleached blonde flame of hair. My sister was in brunette warrior mode.

I said, "You should be careful on the street."

She crimped her nose. Slammed the door shut. I pulled the Camry out and did a U-turn. We left University Heights and its blocks of hippy cottages. As I drove, I told her about my meeting with the detectives, that they'd learned Alice White was our father's first victim, the one no one had attributed to him. Ronny White, Alice's abused son, was the killer we were searching for.

"Jesus," she whispered. "His own mother sold him out."

I nodded. "Until our father came along and killed his mother. Ronny White was asleep in his room at the time."

She raked her clipped-off nails over her Labrys axe necklace. "I'll bet the bastard woke him up. I'll bet he showed that boy his dead mother."

My eyes blurred. I felt dizzy. This was my father.

Polly said, "Just think if the FBI hadn't caught him. Think of what he would have done to you."

I thought of the woman my father and I had helped change a tire on an abandoned road. He'd given me the red pocketknife that night. The first part of an initiation?

"Ronny White never had a chance," I said.

"You can't feel sorry for them. These bastards suck up pity like blood."

How could I not feel for a boy who'd endured … that?

"Look, you need to be as cold as he is. No sympathy."

My sister was girded for battle. I didn't like it. "Spit it out," I said. "I've waited long enough."

She turned her spotlight stare on me. "We both should go see him together."

That was why she'd wanted to see me so urgently. I stopped the car on the side of the road next to a sidewalk and a block of houses. "You think you'll get more information than I can?"

"Yes."

My hands tightened on the wheel, the heat spreading into my cheeks. A woman hurried by with a stroller and glanced at us suspiciously.

"And how the hell would you do that?" I said.

"For one thing, I wouldn't bring along a sister he can torture for the fun of it."

"Answer my question."

"You know how I'd get him to talk?" She slammed her hand against the dashboard. She stamped her cowboy boot on the front carpet of the car. Ground in the heel. "That's how."

We were silent, as if we'd broken some taboo and poisoned the air. I pulled the car back into the street. We both looked out the windows rather than at each other.

Five minutes later I parked in front of her house. "Come in for a cup of coffee," she said. "I don't want to end the day this way."

I didn't either. We tromped up the walk and onto the wooden landing. She looked through the bars over her door's red and blue stained glass. And froze.

"What's wrong?"

She reached her hand into her backpack. "I don't know."

I latched onto her wrist. "We should call the police."

She jerked her arm free and pulled out the revolver.

"Polly, what are you doing?"

She peered through the window. "Nothing I'd like more than to shoot that asshole." Her voice was so calm.

"This is stupid." But I didn't stop her. A full-grown man and a woman with a gun could end this. Right now.

She unlocked the door. I pulled her back and stepped in first. All was quiet. No movement.

"He fucked with my alarm."

I looked up and saw the stairs. In the mural, the faces of the flying women were blotted over with red. "Maybe it's paint," I said.

Her eyes flared. She took in a full breath and raised the pistol. We strode through the dining room to the kitchen. No one. No sound.

"The mural seems to point us to the second floor," I said.

She nodded, her eyes slitted.

I led the way back through the dining room and up the stairs. Polly stayed behind me and to the side so she could get a clear shot. The old wood creaked with each step.

Her bedroom was first. As usual, the sheets and pillows were heaped into a mound, the purple Eiderdown splayed across the floor. She motioned toward the bed. We both dropped to the floor, she at the side and me at the foot. No one. No part of a body. Standing back up, I flung open the closet door and jumped to the side. Just rows of running shoes and cowboy boots.

On to the bathroom with the clawfoot tub that could hold three of her. Her boot pushed into the tile floor, her whole body poised to jump away and shoot. She drew back the shower curtain.

Nothing.

We crept, step by step, along the hallway to the guest bedroom. The painting of the one-breasted Amazon looked the same. She still held a sword over a male baby. The child's mother still wept. We bent down to see the underside of the bed. I flung open another closet door.

No one.

My chest was heaving. I leaned against the wall. "He wants to scare you," I said.

"Yeah, well, good luck with that."

We retraced our path down the creaking stairs and past the defaced mural. Polly grasped the pistol with both hands. We reached the first floor. She strode to the front door and locked us in.

"You know what we need?" she said. "Some really good Sumatra."

We walked back through the dining room toward the kitchen. Polly stopped in mid-stride. "Where's Homer?"

The world's ugliest cat would usually greet us by now. Harvey Dean Kogan had killed cats as a teenager. He'd burned cats when we were children. The killer was copying him.

"Homer," she whispered. She collapsed on the floor. The pistol clanked against the pine. "The bastard killed Homer."

The red slashes on the mural above the stairs. What would blood look like when it dried?

My sister began to weep. It had been so long since I'd heard that sound.

A patch of flesh flashed by the kitchen wall. It was an ear, half bitten off. Lemon shaped eyes peered around the corner at us.

Polly jumped to her feet and scooped him up. "You hid," she yelled.

Homer hung in her arms. He fixed his unblinking stare on me. Something about his green eyes seemed amused.

56

I STAYED AT MY in-laws' house that night. Mike and I had checked the windows, doors, and alarm system. He was armed and the police car was parked out front. I draped my arm over Jill as we slept on the pull-out couch. I almost felt as if we'd recovered our old life. Then I remembered the revolver under her pillow. Would we share our bed with a loaded gun for the rest of our lives?

The next morning, at the sunny kitchen table, we ate toast and cereal while the Doobie Brothers loudly accompanied us from Grandpa Mike's stereo. It was the first normal breakfast we'd had in weeks.

Garth clanked something on the table. My spoon fell into the bowl. He held up a pocketknife. This one was blue rather than red like the one my father had given me. Garth's was thicker and had more blades. "Look what Grandpa gave me," he said.

"Grandpa Mike?"

Garth tilted his head at me. What other grandpa did he know?

There was nothing monstrous about a pocketknife. I managed to say something nice. Then forced another spoonful of Cheerios into my mouth. My cell phone rang.

Special Agent Blake said something about Magnolia Thrush.

I motioned Jill to turn down the music and take our children to another room. When it was quiet I said, "What?"

"They found her body in her apartment … this morning."

My elbows collapsed and I had to steady my head with one cupped hand. I saw her behind my eyes, her shy, gap-toothed smile as she held out the mismatched ceramic mugs. Her frail voice was as soft as a breath.

"They think he killed her the day before yesterday."

Right after we'd dropped her off at her apartment. "But why?"

"Betrayal. For abandoning Kogan all those years before. Then she shows up at Stateville and she's working with the FBI."

Magnolia hadn't escaped him or her past. She was murdered because of me.

"Look, I don't think Kogan wanted her killed. She was the only person who loved him as a boy. He protected her anonymity."

Blake said something. His words barely registered.

"What?"

"We have an idea. You're not going to go for it, but I just want you to hear me out."

"An idea about me? About my involvement in this?"

"Of course not," Blake said. "Look, we're running out of time. We have a chance, a slim chance, but a chance to catch Kogan off guard."

"What the hell are you talking about?"

"He doesn't know that his disciple murdered Magnolia. Yet. The prison grapevine hasn't picked it up. The *Chicago Tribune* got a letter from the killer but hasn't published it. We don't have much time."

"What does this have to do with me?"

"What we're thinking is, you could spring the news on him. His son telling him about it might jolt him into giving us something."

They'd keep the news from my father so I could club him with it. In the hope that it would somehow break him? It seemed beyond desperate.

Blake gave a weary, almost husky sigh. "If you get on the G5 tonight you could hit him with it at the crack of dawn, when he's still not awake. The shrinks think it might work."

But the shrinks had forgotten something. Harvey Dean Kogan didn't sleep.

———

He shambled across the prison meeting room's dull floor. His blue shirt and pants hung on him as if he'd lost ten pounds. When he turned his dog eyes on us, the power of what we knew surged through me. I held our secret close, like a concealed knife.

"Where's my sister?" he said.

Polly smiled, but her eyes seethed. She sat next to me. "I've missed you, Pop."

He took in her face and the ear studs, then her black pants and black shirt. He slowly grinned. Lowering himself opposite us, his back to the door, he dropped his manacled hands and they clanked and thudded on the table.

"By God, you look like your mama. But you're not *like* her, are you?"

Polly chuckled. "I'm more like you, Pop. But we both already knew that."

Those unblinking amber eyes locked onto her as if he could hear the thoughts behind her words. "After thirty-one years, you decided it was time to visit."

She shrugged. "I thought we could talk about women."

He sniggered once, like a hiccup. His head swiveled and his eyes locked on me. "Polly's not afraid to look deep down. All the way to the bottom of the well. Your sister was always stronger than you, Tex."

Polly said, "Thanks, Pop. But you forgot something."

She leaned back in the stiff plastic and metal chair. Making him wait. I breathed in her hatred.

She said, "I'm also stronger than you are. So is Mama."

He rubbed his hands together, the chain between the manacles softly jingling. "Polly and Rose, the images and likenesses of God. That's why you're so strong. After all, the two of you healed asthma."

It was like watching a fight, the two opponents circling and feinting. Which made him less wary of me. "Why did he kill my boss?" I said. Let him think this was the news I'd come to tell him.

"Did he?"

"Why?"

He'd cut his nails back to nubs. His thin fingers, even his yellow hands, looked weak. "Maybe he thought she was blocking your promotion."

His mockery couldn't touch me. My fury had boiled down to something more concentrated and potent. "What contact have you had with him, *Pop*?"

He looked down and picked at stray flecks of skin on his left hand. "I can hear your hearts. The blood is rushing through your brains, synapses snapping. Anger gives both of you power."

I said, "You knew the killer, didn't you? Ronny White, the boy on the train."

Amusement filled his eyes. We were inside the frames of his photographs, on ground that he controlled. "Is it that bad, you have to go back forty years?"

"Where'd that mama's boy go after you took his picture?" Polly said.

Kogan's outstretched fingers chafed against one another, the handcuffs chiming. We'd moved him outside the photograph now, but he still thought he controlled us. Good.

"How'd you know him?" I asked.

His unblinking yellow eyes fixed on mine. "We discovered the abyss together."

Abyss. The word seemed tired. "You killed his mother," I said.

"I killed a lot of mothers."

Polly slammed her hand on the table. "But this mother sold out her seven-year-old son. It's the only good thing you did in your sorry life."

His whole face spread into a broad grin: a chasm of caramel-colored teeth. "I guess I'm a hero now," he said.

His taunt hinted at righteousness. I could have appealed to that deluded notion of goodness, but I was done being nice.

"Did you hear that?" I called to the ceiling. "They're going to remember that line, *Pop.* Years from now they'll tell how the Preying Hands thought he was a hero. You'll be their punch line."

Polly smiled at me. My shoulders relaxed. *Probe, evaluate, find the wound, pull it open.*

He said, "Do you know what I hear? I hear those gaping hurts your mama put inside you. You're still just a little boy and a little girl whose mama didn't love them. At least not as much as she loved God."

Polly crossed one black jean leg over the other. Leaned back so he could see her inlaid cowboy boots. "When did you get so boring?" she said.

311

He pointed a bony finger at me, the sibling he thought was weaker. Just wait, I thought.

"The boy was asleep when I killed his mother. The next morning, he wasn't surprised at all to see a stranger there. I fed him cereal and a piece of buttered toast. 'Is today a prize day?' he asked. Such a small, high voice. 'A prize day.'"

I squinted, let the outrage pass through my body. He was nothing but sound. He couldn't affect me, couldn't even touch me.

"After breakfast I took him to see his mama. I'd made her look so beautiful, you couldn't even tell she was an addict. A fresh peroxide rinse and her hair shampooed and blow-dried, her mouth closed to cover those awful teeth."

I pictured Jill's blonde hair and green eyes, Garth's eyes widening and dimming. Forever.

"Her teeth weren't as ugly as yours," Polly said.

He gave a single snicker. "The boy stared at his mama's severed head on that bed. His whole body shook. I told him she couldn't hurt him ever again. I told him to stare deep into her eyes. Look at how honest her eyes had become. Can you see how he started to moan with the truth of it? And then cry? Yes, you can picture that, can't you, Tex? I know your sister sees it—the beautiful grayness, the shadow that joins life and death. The boy was reaching out to touch her hair when I used the chloroform on him. As he faded into unconsciousness, he had that last image of his mother. By the time he woke up, I and his mother were gone. All he remembered was her head lying powerless on the bed. I wanted her head to become part of his dreams. That and the man who saved him."

"You bastard." Polly said it softly. She leaned over the table, her hands squeezed into fists. Maybe she hoped that he'd lay a hand on her. Then she could bite and kick and gouge.

He chafed his cracked palms together. "There's the girl I remember. But you've really got to dress better. No wonder no man wants you."

I said, "You destroyed that boy."

"I saved him. He became a son of God." Kogan stared up at the heavens with feigned piety and pressed his hands together in prayer.

I couldn't hold back my contempt. I unsheathed one of our weapons. "You pretended he was Jonas."

He blinked.

"Jonas seeing your mother's head."

He took two breaths, short and labored. "You think you're so clever. Such a clever little boy." He turned to Polly. "His big dyke sister trying to help."

"And proud of it," Polly said. "What did Ronny White change his name to?"

"Les Filson." His smile burrowed into us like his eyes. "The police will pretend they're near him. They'll be all over the television. But turning up the gas flame won't work."

"It worked on you," Polly said.

His lips and gums were speckled with the metastatic lumps of cancer. And yet he didn't appear in pain. It was my own stomach that was growling and cramping.

"Do you really think I believed all those idiots on TV? When the police said they were a foot away from catching me, you know what I did? I laughed. I laughed for days. Would the Preying Hands let the police trace him to photography chemicals?"

Polly's eyes widened. I could see her mind shaking and whirling. Mama had told us, and the press reported, that the police found him through a photo supply store. Polly and I had believed it our whole lives.

I said it then; my sister needed it. "He killed Magnolia."

313

Our father's face froze around his smile. I yanked out a copy of the letter the *Chicago Tribune* hadn't yet published. Slapped it down in front of him. He was sitting and yet he looked dizzy. As he read, his eyes blinked.

My Dear Public:

Two women betrayed my docent. First was the mother who tortured him. But worse was the sister who abandoned him. Justice served.

Goodbye, Harvey.
Thank you.

"It's a fake. It's just another stupid police trick." His voice had become shrill.

I pulled out the police report and slowly—so he'd have time to dread it—laid the page in front of him. "Her murder will be on the front page of tomorrow's newspapers."

He lowered his head and sucked in ragged breaths.

"Even Jonas didn't love you like she did," I said. "And the last time you saw her, you made her weep."

More yellow seemed to ooze into the whites of his eyes. His mouth had formed into a rigid, cancer-scarred oval. I think at that moment he saw the death of a dream: what his life could have been if he'd escaped with Magnolia.

Polly said, "Ronny White killed the only person who cherished you." She pulled a picture from her lap and set it down in front of him. It was a photo the killer had made of Magnolia.

Harvey Dean Kogan stared at it: the Christmas tree lights that adorned Magnolia's long hair, the candle-wax tears and dollar signs drawn in magic marker on her cheeks. Her own severed thumb protruded from her mouth. It was a copy of the picture of Barb Smith, a prostitute the Preying Hands had killed in Chicago.

Most people would have felt a tinge of sympathy then. But we were riding something deeper. Blacker.

"Look what you did," Polly said. "He dressed up her face like a *whore*."

Kogan leaped to his feet. He backed up, his buttocks hitting the door.

"That's the man who thinks he's your son," I said.

He brought his shackled hands to his face. He pulled the cuffs apart but he could only cover one ear.

I rose. Polly stood beside me. She raised the picture in front of him. "Look at what he made for you," she hissed.

Desperation filled his eyes.

"Who is he?" I yelled. "Give us a name."

"You still need me," he said.

"Who is he?" Polly shouted.

His eyes flicked to the door. "Deputy," he yelled. He raised his face to the ceiling, as if to make the men listening hear better. "I have the legal right to go back to my cell."

"They don't care," I said. "Sit down."

He glared at me. Was that fear in his eyes? He took a step toward us and slowly sank into the chair. Lowered his hands and twisted them inside the cuffs. "He's"—his voice broke—"someone close to you. At the bank."

Polly glanced at me. The elation I felt glinted in her eyes.

"Who close to us at the bank?" I yelled.

"He's more my child than either of you."

He closed his eyes and let the poison of those words sink into us. We shouted at him, but his extraordinary ears had become deaf.

When we'd settled back into the chairs opposite him, he opened his eyes. "You've got the rage, don't you, children? Too bad you don't have a piece of rope or a blade. But that will come later."

Then I understood it. All of it. "You have an agreement with him not to kill us. Not Polly or Mama or me. And not Jill or our children."

His eyes flinched. "Is that what you think?"

"He wasn't supposed to kill Magnolia either. But he doesn't want you as his daddy anymore. If he kills your family, he'll be free of you."

"Tex, I think I know him better than the FBI."

His whole sick scheme coalesced in my mind. As long as I didn't know the name of the murderer, as long as his adopted son roamed free and didn't kill us, I'd have to keep returning. Returning so he could force me to accept that I was like him. As if I were still a child, he would make me submit to his power.

"Don't you see?" I said. "He's going to kill all of us. There's no reason to protect him."

He smiled. His mouth widened and all I saw in those ruined teeth was arrogance. "Has he betrayed me more than you have?"

I don't recall Polly and I walking out, or even shutting the door. What I remember is the weariness that slid like sand over my body. In the hallway, it weighed me down until I held on to Polly and she to me. I thought of Frieda counting in Spanish, of Garth whooshing his superheroes through the air. I thought of Jill sliding her arms around me.

57

AFTER OUR FATHER'S ADMISSION, the FBI dispatched three agents to my bank before Polly and I even left Stateville. Those men were trained to wheedle out more information than I could ever get about our employees and twelve hundred clients.

We took a commercial plane back to San Diego. Polly sat beside me and ordered two Bloody Marys, setting them side by side on the tray table like twins. For a time, she didn't touch them. Then she closed her eyes and took sips. One of the dogmas of her peculiar, Godless religion was that Mama had ignored her suspicions of her husband and burrowed into the delusion that he was a good man. That's why the police needed to catch him by tracing photography chemicals. But our father had just blown up that assumption. For the three-and-a-half-hour flight, as she slowly drained her two Bloody Marys, she retreated into her thoughts.

She only turned to me when the plane touched down in San Diego. "You're the diplomat, you lead the discussion."

We took a taxi directly to Mama's house. It was eleven o'clock by the time we got there, and all the lights were off. Despite Mama's refusal to give in to fear, the front door was locked. I rang the bell five times before the living room light flashed on.

In her nightgown, she motioned us inside. She opened the window in her kitchen to let in some breeze and we sat around her white table. Mama poured us glasses of Diet Coke and sat down. She said, "I don't care how much danger you think there is. I'm not moving out of my house. And you're not staying here."

I'd argue that point later. Rising, I retrieved her second husband's model sailboat from the counter and placed it in the middle of the table. The boat skimmed over an imaginary wave, its sails swelled open.

"What's that for?" Mama said.

"Tonight we need Randall's presence. His calmness." I waited a beat to let her take it in. "We saw Harvey."

Mama's eyes expanded as if we'd stabbed her. Her glass thudded against the table. She must have realized the secret we'd come for.

"Both of you? Both of you did that?"

Polly nodded. "He's pathetic."

Mama took a long drink. Her usually coiffed hair hung down, gray and thin and straggled. "That's how he draws you in. Pity."

"I don't think I've ever pitied that man," Polly said.

I repeated what our father had told us about his arrest, that the police had tried to make him crack by claiming they were within inches of catching him. "He laughed at them," I said.

Mama shrugged. "He *would* say that."

She glanced at Polly, then up to the light fixture and the yellow ceiling. She must have wondered what lies he'd made us believe about her. But I think she was more worried about the truths.

She said, "Listening to that man is like going into his darkroom. It's a place without any light or windows. It's a place where mortal mind takes over your thoughts. Don't you get sucked in."

Polly jerked forward in the chair. "Stop hiding behind Christian Science."

Mama stiffened. She sipped the Coke, the ice tinkling. The drinking glass refracted the lines of her sagging face. Her eyes took in Polly's black shirt and pants, then her cowboy boots. "And what are you hiding behind?"

I heard Polly's slight wheeze and prepared myself for another brawl. But tonight, she didn't grab for her inhaler and brandish it like a weapon in front of Mama's face.

"I'm sorry," Polly said. "That was unfair."

Mama's mouth opened. The apology must have been as unexpected as Polly reciting Mary Baker Eddy.

I said, "All those years, and you never even suspected?"

Mama glared at me, but her eyes held more fear than anger.

"Tell us the truth, Mama," Polly said. "The police didn't really trace the developer chemicals. That was just a story for the press."

Mama stood. She carried her glass to Randall's ancient fridge. The ice maker whirred and plopped more cubes into the Diet Coke. In the kitchen's harsh light, her back looked bent and her shoulders stooped to match her old woman's thin hair.

"You owe us this," Polly said.

Mama's stocking feet swished over the linoleum. The chair shrieked on the tiled floor and she sat down across from us. She inhaled a long breath, as if for strength.

"One day I walked out to his shed and the door was unlocked." She stopped, as if about to walk through that door again.

"What did you find?" My voice was as soft as a nudge.

Mama held the glass between her hands as if she were praying. "Everything was clean and neat, all the tools put away. Harvey made thousands of family pictures, but not a one was there. Just a single black-and-white photograph. This pale girl like a statue with black hair."

I thought of the possibilities: Jenny Winston, Barb Smith, Susanna Lopez.

"You know what I thought?" She glared at Polly. "I thought Harvey was having an affair. That was the worst thing I could imagine."

Polly gave a deep, sad sigh, a sigh that seemed to hold back great swells. "If only that was it."

Mama sipped her Diet Coke. She frowned as if forcing down medicine. "When I showed him the picture, he got so angry. He stood over me with those big hands, but I just yelled right back at him." Her breath came faster, as if she were still marshaling her strength. "He'd taken a photography class. Never mentioned it because I wouldn't approve on account of the money. But he was so proud of that picture. 'She looks perfect,' he said. 'A child of God.'" She stared at Polly, her eyes stricken. "I believed him."

"You *wanted* to believe him." I said it gently. I didn't mean it to hurt her.

She swallowed. Her shoulders dropped as if in surrender. "Later, I found a woman's button in his van. The same false conception took hold of me. But now he made sure his shed was locked. One morning, when he was asleep, I took his keys and made a copy of the one for his padlock. When he went out wandering, I … I snuck inside."

Her eyes entreated me. I felt as if *I'd* forced her into that shed.

"You suspected something," Polly said. "You did what you had to do."

Mama slowly shook her head, as if Polly would never understand. "I got down on my hands and knees and sniffed around the floor like some animal. A board was loose in the corner by his stop-bath tubs. That's where I found it. A big jar. I thought there might be dirty pictures inside." She bowed her head and squeezed her eyes shut.

"Something else was in that jar," I said.

She swallowed. "Some kind of liquid. And floating in the liquid …"

All those years Mama wouldn't tell us what he'd done. All those years she wouldn't even talk about him. Polly and I had to thrash by ourselves through that swamp of shame.

"You found Katherine Miller's hand," I said. "Not the police."

"How could God be in a man who did something like that?"

Polly and I had spent our lives asking how a father could be in a man who did that.

"I'm glad you went to the police," Polly said.

Mama's eyes burst open. She stared at us plaintively. "My daughter was thirteen. My son eight. What might that man have *done* to you?"

"But he didn't," I said. "Because you turned him in."

"You stopped denying who he was," Polly said.

Mama pushed her face into her hands and her whole body seemed to sink into the table. It had taken her thirty-one years to admit it: she'd chosen her children over her faith.

I turned the glass of Diet Coke in my hand. The liquid was as dark as Mama's secrets. All those years she'd kept silent. "Why couldn't you tell us you went to the police?" I said.

She raised her hands hopelessly. "He was my *husband*. He was your *father*. Not some stranger. I told the police he was a murderer … and that he … No mother can talk about that to her children. It was unspeakable."

Instead of telling us, she'd prayed and raised her thoughts back to God. It was the only way she knew to heal our family.

"You tried to erase him from our lives," I said.

She leaned forward over the table as if she were trying to convince us, and herself, all over again. "He was like an illness. The power of what he did could disappear and we could be a family again. The three of us. We just had to push those thoughts out of our minds."

Polly waited until Mama met her eyes before she spoke. "He's a monster. We all loved a monster. But it wasn't our fault."

Mama grimaced. She sipped on the Coke. She ran her nail over the wind-filled sail of Randall's boat, then down the twine halyards to the hull. "We try to be the spirit of God, but each of us has a body that needs food. We reflect perfection but we're still imperfect. And no matter what we do, our children suffer. What's Godly about that?"

I reached over the table and cupped Mama's hand. For the first time I could remember, she seemed heroic.

"Every boy thinks he carries something of his father. But with you, with what your father did, that belief could be so destructive. I didn't want you ever to think you were like him."

"I had to find that out myself, Mama."

She nodded. "I went too far."

"To protect me. To protect Polly. " Then I said it. I, an atheist. "Isn't that the love that comes from God?"

Mama shook her head. There was both joy and sadness in her smile.

The chair squealed. Polly strode to Mama and wrapped her arms around her. Mama stared into her glass of Diet Coke. She bowed her head and her shoulders rounded into Polly's embrace. She was weeping.

58

ON SUNDAY, A MEMORIAL for Elizabeth and Vanessa took place at Kate Sessions Park. The FBI profilers had helped organize it. They calculated a seventy-five percent probability that the killer would show up. Polly had to work, and I didn't want Frieda and Garth anywhere near that park. Only Marta and I went. Along with undercover cops and FBI agents, we were part of a script designed to put pressure on the killer.

More than one hundred people congregated on the road beside a slope of yellow and green grass that overlooked Mission Bay. They stared at a patch of dirt covered with notes and bouquets of flowers. It was where Elizabeth Morton's body had lain in pieces inside a garbage bag.

I stayed at the back of the throng of mourners, the safest place to observe and not be noticed. A baseball cap was pulled down over my face. The last thing I needed was someone to start yelling that I was a murderer. Thirty feet away, Vanessa's husband Bernie looked lost without his wife conducting the crowd around him. Next to him, their daughter glared at me. She still thought I'd killed her mother.

I slipped away and found Marta. A newspaper reporter and photographer saw us and approached. While his colleague snapped pictures, the reporter asked, "Have the charges been dropped?"

Marta said, "Thanks to William's cooperation, our friends at the police department have another suspect. William has also persuaded Harvey Dean Kogan to help"

The reporter drew back. "The Preying Hands?"

"My father understands this monster," I said. "He knows why the man's copying him."

"And why is that?"

"Sorry," Marta said. She pulled my arm and we trudged away.

We'd planned our comments carefully. When the reporter's story hit the press, the killer would think that Kogan had identified him. He'd see the vise closing and panic. Hopefully.

We escaped to the back seat of an SUV with tinted windows. In the front seats sat Detective Lund and District Attorney Jessie Foster. Foster, on the passenger side, looked like she had in court: her eyes unrevealing, her brown hair perfectly in place as if she'd just come from a hair salon. I didn't expect any warmth from her. Marta had persuaded me to file a civil harassment suit against the police. "Show them that an innocent man doesn't take this lying down," she'd said. Our little suit had tainted DA Foster's candidacy for mayor.

"Nice to see you, District Attorney," Marta said. "You too, Kevin."

Foster nodded. "Nice to see you, as well."

Both the attorneys were already lying.

Lund said, "So far, so good."

I thought of what Kogan had told me: turning up the gas flame wouldn't work.

Foster caught my eye. "I want to say how sorry we are that you and your family have to go through this." No admission of a mistake.

"And the charges?" Marta asked.

Foster's eyes hardened even before her head swiveled to Marta. "In good time."

As usual, Marta was ahead of her. "It would be a very nice gesture if you made an announcement today," she said.

Even seated, Foster was several inches taller than Marta. She drew herself up higher and continued to stare. "Today's memorial is for the victims."

"William *is* a victim."

"The dead victims," Foster said.

Marta drummed her nails on the leather seat. They were bright red today. "Okay. But I was hoping we could make an announcement after the memorial. That we were dropping the suit."

Foster's smile was even steelier than Marta's. "I believe you'll be working with both the DA's office and some judges in the future, Counselor. Or are you planning to move out of California?" She pushed open the passenger door and slowly exited the SUV.

After the door shut, Marta said, "Get that grin off your face, Kevin." She flung open the back door and slammed it shut behind her.

Lund turned from the steering wheel. "I think the two people with the biggest balls just left."

I took in the surveillance through the rear window. Two unmarked cars tracked every vehicle that entered the park and all those passing by on the street outside. An undercover cop was posing as a press photographer and snapping pictures of everyone there. I didn't know how many FBI agents were wandering in the crowd.

"This bastard is here somewhere," Lund said. "This is his awards banquet."

I got out of the SUV and pulled down the baseball cap. The only trees I could use as cover were up front by the dais, where Vanessa's upset daughter was brooding. I couldn't risk her bursting into shouts. The back of the crowd was still the safest place. As I surveyed the people, I almost stumbled into Lawrence Massy, the prospect who'd abandoned me. Just seeing those red glasses frames ignited my anger.

"This is so unrelentingly sad," he said.

"The word 'hell' comes more to my mind," I said.

Massy looked into the crowd and frowned. I followed his gaze and saw Bob Morgan, his new account manager. Bullshit Bob handed his card to someone.

"First impressions are often right," Massy said. "Bob is shameless. Maybe that's how they raise men in Michigan, but I'll tell you, Monique was not impressed."

I hadn't known that Bob grew up in the Midwest.

Bob continued to jabber as DA Foster strode to the front of the crowd. She mounted the upraised stage that was set up under the shade of a large oak tree. Elizabeth's parents and Vanessa's husband and daughter got hugs. Foster stepped behind the lectern. Clutching the microphone, she stared hard at the cameras. Her conservative gray suit was perfectly somber. Even Bob stopped talking.

"Today we honor two women who had their lives senselessly and horribly snuffed out. We're here to join with these two families to grieve." Foster nodded at them. "But I also came here to give you a promise. We will give these women justice. The FBI and the San Diego Police Department are working with extraordinary cooperation. Our joint task force is close to finding and punishing this monster. Very, very close."

That was the pressuring statement the FBI had scripted. After hearing Marta and Foster, the press would think the police had a suspect. I looked for a reaction in the people surrounding me. At least fifteen of my clients were in the crowd, but I couldn't see any of them acting strangely. Ambrose stood with her head bowed, fifteen feet away from Bullshit Bob and studiously ignoring him. Bob pushed his hands into his pockets, his lips clasped tightly. His whole body seemed stiff.

Foster was still talking. "The police have to look at everyone. Even innocent people. We made an arrest but have now established that this person had nothing to do with the crime. Today my office will drop the charges against him."

She hadn't mentioned my name—that would be giving in too much to Marta—but everyone knew whom she meant.

Something clunked against the oak tree's branches above the dais. I looked up. The leaves shivered and two objects fell to the road. Shoes the shiny red of lollipops. As they rolled between the dais and the reporters, I recognized them: Vanessa's patent leather red pumps.

Vanessa's daughter screamed. A horde of reporters bent over the red heels. Something was inside them—Vanessa's pale and bloodless feet.

59

I LEFT THE RADIO off as I drove to Jill's parents' house. The whole world was shouting about a pair of Christian Louboutin shoes with Vanessa's feet inside. The police would only say that they fell from a remotely controlled box positioned in a tree. I drew my own conclusion. The killer had graduated from copying the Preying Hands to creating his very own level of depravity. Killing Harvey Dean Kogan's bloodline would be his coronation.

So far, my family seemed safe. For the first time ever, Mama was staying with Polly. Along with three of Polly's ex-military friends. As for Mike's house, he and Jill were armed, of course, and the police car sat out front. The alarm system worked perfectly. I felt they were secure enough for me to spend the nights there. We were trying to stay together as a family as much as we could.

On Monday morning, Jill and our kids clambered into Mike's car. I watched it slide out of the driveway. The police cruiser pulled away and headed in another direction. With his pistol on the seat and his concealed carry permit, Mike took my family to school. He would return to pick them up. This was our new life.

I couldn't get Bullshit Bob out of my mind. Bob who had grown up in Michigan, potentially just a few hours' drive from Stateville. Why had he never married? He'd bragged about his lucky nights, but I'd never seen him with a girlfriend or a date. Not one woman in the office liked him; even Massy's fiancée had found him offensive. Yet Detective Lund had already cleared Bob.

I drove to the bank. I wanted to see who might show up and appear to gloat about the previous day. Unfortunately, gloating was the way Bob usually looked. Press trucks and cameramen had massed at the front of the building. It was just the kind of publicity our clients abhorred. I managed to drive through the back entrance and make my way to the elevator without being recognized. Today the guards kept out everyone but employees and customers. I had an elevator to myself all the way to the tenth floor.

Our reception area looked almost normal: an old mansion's vestibule, a book of opera set designs open on the vintage table. Kathy sat at the antique desk, her usual salad lunch in a bag beside her. For once, her phone wasn't ringing.

"Was Bob out on Wednesday last week?" I asked.

Kathy nodded. "His prospecting day."

"Did anyone talk to him?"

She slowly turned from her computer. "You don't think—"

"Did Ambrose speak with him?"

"Ambrose does her best to *never* speak with him."

Magnolia had been murdered on Wednesday and no one had talked to Bob that day. Someone needed to ask him where he'd been when Elizabeth and Vanessa were killed. I fished Hempel's card from my pocket and called him. I had to leave a voicemail. "I need you to get to the bank right now," I said.

As Kathy put on her headset, she said, "But Bob is just a jerk."

I returned to banking to wait for the detectives to arrive. As usual, Bob stood in his office, selling into his phone. This morning his hair was disheveled and his Pierre Cardin suit mapped with wrinkles. I thought back to the memorial. He'd stiffened after Foster announced the police were close.

"I have to talk to you," Bob yelled to me.

I'd never considered that he might initiate the conversation. I couldn't think of an excuse.

"It will only take a second," he said.

There was no other choice. I sat in the chair in front of his desk.

Bob sat down. "You okay?"

I nodded and quickly—too quickly—said, "How about you?"

"Just trying to get through the day. Then, the week. It changes your outlook on life, I'll tell you." He sighed. "I wanted to discuss Massy. You should be the account manager."

He was giving me Massy? I stalled. "But you wrote up the credit."

"Doesn't matter. I'll put it through and you take him. He prefers you anyway."

Was this some kind of trick?

Bob gave me the loan application and a credit report. "There's a new eight-million-dollar mortgage on his house. Did you know about that?"

I was still trying to figure out why our most ambitious business developer was handing me a loan. He'd never been that generous to anyone before.

"William, did you know anything about that mortgage?"

I reeled back my mind. "Mortgage?"

330

"Eight million dollars."

A hand squeezed my stomach.

Bob said, "I called him about it and he said he just forgot to put it on his loan application."

"Forgot? Eight million dollars?"

"He's buying condos in the Bahamas."

The Bahamas. Where his trust was domiciled. I scanned down the figures on the loan application. No eight million dollar mortgage under Liabilities. His signature at the bottom attested that his financial figures were accurate.

Something about that scrawl struck me. It was jagged, almost vertical, like an EKG. Like Les Filson's signature. I'd never seen Massy's handwriting before because I hadn't ever landed him as a client. He hadn't signed anything.

Bob said, "Maybe he wouldn't have told *me* about his other loan. But you?"

I needed more information. "Did Massy ever meet with Vanessa?"

Bob shook his head. "Couldn't stand her."

"Has anyone actually *met* Massy's fiancée?"

"I haven't met a lot of my clients' girlfriends."

Kogan said that the killer would hate any woman with power. And Bob couldn't have faked the credit report with the mortgage listed on it.

"You look like you're about to get sick," Bob said.

"If you wanted to cash out your real estate and disappear with the money, what would be the quickest and least suspicious way to do it?"

Bob chuckled. "How the hell should I know?"

"Put a mortgage on the biggest thing you own—your house—and transfer out the funds."

Bob collapsed farther into his chair. "Wow. He must have figured he could sell me his story about condos. But not you."

I said, "The second biggest piece of real estate he owns is a storage facility. The one he wants you to finance. He's also got a collection of gems he could hide in his pockets."

I didn't have to spell out the rest. The Bahamas' bank secrecy laws would be tough to breach, even to seize a murderer's cash. In any case, Massy would soon move the money to another offshore territory with even more shatterproof secrecy laws. He'd never make a payment on the mortgage, and the bank would take the collateral. Eight million dollars would be plenty for him to live on anywhere in the world.

I jumped up from the chair. I had to call Lund and Hempel. Right now. Then I thought of one last confirmation. "Do you know where Massy was on Wednesday?"

"I wanted to see him but he was booked up."

"I guess you told him you grew up in Michigan."

"What does that have to do with anything?"

There was no point in revealing the suspicion that information had created for me, or how Massy had planted it. I took out my phone. And stopped. Before I called we had to make sure Massy stayed put.

"I need you to do something," I said.

Bullshit Bob didn't hesitate. It took him about five seconds to think of what he'd say. He dialed and paced with the phone in his hand. "Dr. Massy. How are you, sir?" His voice boomed out the words. Just like any other call. He listened and licked his lips. "I'm really sorry to bother you, but I need one more document signed. I'm trying to present your loan to committee tomorrow." He nodded into the phone. "You're right. Normally a fax or pdf would be okay. But we don't have a fax agreement with you. We have to have an original signature." More silence. "You'll be at home? I'll see you there in about an hour then."

Bob gently set down the phone. He raised his hands in victory.

I was already calling Lund and Hempel.

60

HEMPEL ARRIVED AT THE bank an hour later. In a wrinkled, shiny suit, he looked as ragged as his voice. But that was okay—he wouldn't be posing as a nappy business developer. Although Massy wouldn't talk with a detective, I knew he'd open his door to me. Especially if I brought a copy of our fax agreement for him to sign. And, just to make sure that his loan would go through committee without a hitch, I also brought along the rumpled credit officer we'd just hired.

Hempel and I sneaked out the back door of the bank and managed to escape in his car without the reporters spotting us. We drove to the upper part of La Jolla and parked outside Massy's stucco walls. The gate was locked shut. I pressed the front bell but got no response. We could see the house's closed front door through the wrought iron bars. Evidently San Diego's drought had stopped where we were.

Inside those walls, the plants were blooming, the pear trees and lilacs fully watered.

"Hard to believe somebody with so much money would do this," I said.

Hempel cocked his buzzed-off head at me, his big face puzzled. "I thought you, if anyone, would know. Crazy is crazy, no matter how much freakin' money you have."

He pulled out binoculars from the trunk and stared at the house for a full minute. "I think I heard someone yell inside, didn't you?" His overstuffed eyebrows rose in a question: *Are you with me on this?*

"Definitely."

He reached over the purple trumpet vines, dug his shoes into the wall, and quickly hoisted himself up and over. After a few seconds, he found a button and the gate swung open. We jogged down the unistone driveway. The Maserati was gone from the carport. At the terra cotta brick walkway, we slowed to a walk. I couldn't see anything through the beveled glass of the front door. Hempel rang the bell and it chimed inside. Nothing. He set his ear against the mahogany. Shook his head.

I walked around back to the patio, the kitchen on one side and the pool on the other. The fountain stood empty beside the flower-draped brick walls and arbors. Someone had stripped the tables bare and furled the yellow awning. I couldn't see through the kitchen windows. The door was locked.

Hempel's hoarse voice rose from the corner window. "Look at this."

The overhead light inside illuminated an office I'd never seen. Antique leg irons and handcuffs were mounted to the wall. Just the kind of artwork my father said his admirer would own. On the carpet, file folders had been flung around a dismembered computer.

"He took out the hard drive," Hempel said.

I grabbed the binoculars and trained them on a framed medical degree on the wall. Northwestern Medical School. Chicago was less than fifty miles from Stateville.

"The timing of his med school fits," Hempel said.

Bob's telephone call must have spooked Massy. He'd burned or shredded his financial information. That's why the file folders were empty on the floor.

"Looks like he's about to vanish," Hempel said. "Probably out of the country."

And out of our lives. But in a year, or five years, he would come back. He'd want to give a final artistic touch to my family.

Hempel shook his head. "This feels wacky … all the right stuff where we can see it through the window. Like he *wants* to be caught."

His phone rang and he slid it out of his pocket. "Yeah." The color slid from his broad face. He glanced at me and away.

"What happened?" I said.

Hempel slipped the phone back into his pocket. "Let's go. Right now." He began to run toward his car.

"What's wrong?"

"In the car," he shouted.

We sprinted to the front entrance and through the open gate. Jumped into his car and slammed the doors.

"Tell me!"

"That was Lund. They got a call from Jill's school—she got a text from her father, some kind of emergency with her mom. She and the kids left school. Supposed to meet her dad in the parking lot."

I slammed my hand onto the dashboard. "What happened?"

"Someone went out to the parking lot later. Jill's father was drugged in his car." Hempel set his hand like a slab of beef on my shoulder. "Jill and your kids weren't there. They've disappeared."

61

MY ARM SHOOK AS if it belonged to someone else. Hempel's sad eyes told me I hadn't misunderstood. "He has my whole family?"

"Every police officer in San Diego is looking for them." Something about his sandpaper voice told me how bad it was. "They're still alive. I'm sure of it."

I had to focus. Put thoughts together. Gather ideas into words. "How do you know?"

"This guy never does anything fast." He started the car.

The Preying Hands always had a conversation. He made his victims suffer. Frieda and Garth. Then Jill. I pushed open the door and vomited.

When I swung back inside, Hempel held out a pack of gum. "Take one. It settles your stomach." He shook out a piece. His stubbled head nodded.

I grabbed the gum, unwrapped the paper, and shoved it into my mouth. The cloying minty taste jolted me. But my mind still swirled drunkenly.

Hempel pulled the phone from his pocket and answered. "Got it," he said and hung up. He gunned the engine and pulled the car onto the road. "There's a special unit. We're meeting them at the station in fifteen minutes. Massy won't get far."

I looked back at the iron gate and stucco walls, at the gabled roofs. I should have suspected something. Why hadn't I seen it? "You said Jill got a text. How could she? Mike's phone would have been locked."

"Lund thinks Massy drugged Mike somehow. He used Mike's index finger to open the phone and sent the text. Jill would have recognized her father's car and gone to it without thinking. Maybe she saw him in the front seat and didn't know he was unconscious."

I could imagine the rest. Massy must have forced them into his own vehicle, something no one could identify. Maybe a green van like the Preying Hands had used. He'd shoved Jill and the kids inside.

My whole body was shivering. I tried to still it but couldn't stop the shaking. "Where would he take them?" My voice came out a croak.

Hempel stared through the windshield at the winding road. "Someplace quiet. Out of the way where no one can see."

Someplace quiet. Quiet so he ... I couldn't think about that. Maybe a building. One where he'd set up everything he needed. Oh my God. I forced the images from my mind. I had to wall off those thoughts.

"Go to the bank," I said.

"You think he's there?"

I shook my head. I knew what we had to do. The plan made the rest of my thoughts fall into place. I bit harder on the gum. "There's a reason he shredded his financial statements. The statements have the addresses of the buildings he owns."

Hempel nodded. "The bank has copies."

I snatched out my cell phone and called Bob to tell him what we wanted. Hempel switched on the siren and for ten minutes I listened to it wail inside my head. The two reporters outside the bank must have heard it. They ran to us and I shoved them aside. I had a key to the first floor's back door. We ran down the hallway.

On the tenth floor, Bob waited for us in the boardroom. He'd already spread the financial, tax, and trust statements over the mahogany table. There were hundreds of pages.

I picked up the credit file and said, "Bob, you can leave now. As far as you know, I'm just helping you land this client."

Bob looked at Hempel.

"I'm a detective," Hempel said.

Bob winced. Everyone did when they first heard Hempel's phlegm-filled voice. "You can't give this stuff to the police," Bob said. "You need a court order. If Massy gets off he'll sue the bank. He'll sue you for every stick you own."

"He's got my wife and kids."

Bob swallowed. He slipped off his suit jacket, loosened his silk tie. "What's the plan?"

"He probably has a preferred place he uses over and over," Hempel said. "Somewhere he can keep all his tools."

"Are you sure it's Massy?" Bob said.

Hempel's eyes blazed. "Listen, Bob. As long as you're here, I'd like you to do me a favor. Leave your fucking doubts for later, okay? Can you do that?"

Bob nodded.

I spotted the storage facility. It was in the town of Julian, about an hour and a half outside San Diego. He could hide in any of its units.

"It's harder to get a warrant for Julian," Hempel said.

Bob leafed through another stack and found the rent roll. "We've got bigger problems than that," he said. "There are 183 renters of storage units."

Hempel slammed his palm and the whole table shook. "I'll need a warrant for every goddamn one of those."

I scanned down the names on the rent roll. Nothing popped out. I moved on to the income statement for the C corporation that owned the facility. Just standard revenue designations: leases, cleaning, locks, special services.

I jumped to my feet and paced to the cabinet at the end of the room. *Think.*

"Look at the expenses," Bob said.

The bottom portion of the statement showed a purchase of a Handlon Custom Model 806 T-12 unit. Hempel googled it on his phone. "It's a heavy duty refrigerator," he said. "Mainly for restaurants."

"It could be for foodstuffs," Bob said. "Julian is apple country. Or maybe it's for wine. There are a lot of vacation cottages in that part of the mountains."

I pushed my arm into the table to stop it from shaking. "He doesn't use it for food."

"What are Halsey Eco Green Tech panels?" Bob asked.

Hempel googled them. "Wall panels used in recording studios. Soundproofing."

He passed me another piece of gum. I tore off the paper and crammed it into my mouth. I dug my fingers into my scalp. There had to be a clue. Massy had destroyed his home copies for a reason.

Hempel jerked to his feet. He strode to the window, his jaw hacking at the gum. "I suppose we could surround the storage complex."

"What happens to my family then?"

I flipped through the piles again. Pages and pages slapping onto the mahogany table. The name 928LLC sounded vaguely familiar. It was a limited partnership. I grabbed the rent roll and ran my finger down the 183 names. 928LLC rented unit number 111. A map of the building was jammed into the credit file. I found unit 111—one of the large deluxe ones at the far end. 928LLC. 9-28. I knew then. "My father was arrested on September 28," I said.

"Yes!" Hempel hurried back to the table. "I'll bet this unit has a refrigerator and soundproofing."

I couldn't think about that. I couldn't think about screams, or cameras on tripods, or the grinding squeals of power tools. It was nearly three thirty. Massy'd had my family for four hours. "How fast can you drive to Julian?" I asked Hempel.

"Let's go," Hempel said.

We ran out of the bank to the hallway. But only one elevator was working. While we waited, Hempel telephoned the Sheriff's Department in Julian. He was calling Lund when my cell phone rang.

There was no caller ID. I closed my eyes and tried to slow my heart. When I answered, I only heard his breathing.

"Is this my private banker?" No electronic distortion this time.

Hempel must have seen my body go rigid. He twirled his index finger: *Keep him talking.*

"Where …" My voice cracked. "Where are you?"

"Why don't I hear that famous banker charm? No 'How are you doing?' or 'So nice to hear from you?' You know, we could have been brothers, you and I. But alas, I can only give people eyesight … not vision."

Hempel mouthed words: *Meet him.*

"I want to meet you."

"Of course, you do." Massy laughed. "But you have to be a good little banker, all right? Here's what you're going to do. Go home and wait for instructions on your landline. As of now, no one has been hurt."

"What do you want? Tell me your demands."

He laughed. "One more thing. Let's save the investigators some time. The blood on my kitchen table is O positive."

Jill's blood type.

He giggled. "Guess what? It's not Jill." He disconnected.

What was Polly's blood type? Or Mama's? My God, Garth and Frieda.

Hempel's big hand gripped my shoulder. His eyes bore into mine. All I saw were those terrible hairbrush eyebrows.

"He wants you to panic. That's how he controls you. Don't let him."

The elevator doors opened. We stepped inside and the doors slowly closed. As we rode to the basement I related the conversation. We both knew that Massy couldn't keep my family alive for long. He had to tie them up and the children would start to cry. They'd need water. They'd need a bathroom.

The elevator reached the main floor and we hurried into the hallway. As we jogged toward the back exit Hempel said, "The Sheriff's Department in Julian texted me. They're on their way."

"But as soon as he sees them he's going to—"

"They'll do it quietly. No sirens, just unmarked cars. The FBI helicopter will land miles away. He'll never hear it."

"We have to get there before they do anything."

Hempel stopped. Grabbed my arm. "You think you can go in there and save your family? Be smart, William. Be smarter than *him*."

"What the fuck do you think I'm doing?"

"Go home and wait for his call. You're a banker, you know how to talk. So talk to him."

Was I supposed to just sit at home and wait?

"Blake will brief you," Hempel said. "He'll meet you right here by the door."

"Where are *you* going?"

"To Julian. Kevin and me, we'll make sure this gets done right."

62

I STARED AT THE back hallway of the bank with its two lines of un-marked gray entrances. Massy could be behind such a door. He could be raising his knife over Jill. Over Garth and Frieda. I remembered the loud drone of flies and the metallic smell of blood at Béni-Messous. Then the woman in the burka cut in half and the child on a stake.

I opened the exit door and anchored my mind to the blacktop drive-way on this side of the building. What if Blake couldn't find the back entrance? Suppose he didn't come? I fished out my cell phone and searched for texts and missed calls. Nothing. I pictured our phone ring-ing at home. Over and over. Then nothing.

A car slowly approached. I couldn't see who was inside. The car window opened. A man with ragged ears peered at me from behind the wheel. I ran to the car. Jumped into the front seat.

"Breathe," Blake said.

"He could kill them while I'm on the goddamn phone."

Blake shook his head. His jaw tightened and loosened.

"Why not?"

He stared out the front windshield. "Massy wants to play with you first."

The thought twisted my stomach. I needed a piece of gum. My stomach would explode without it. We pulled onto the highway and I said, "You don't have to drive the speed limit, you know. You're a fucking FBI agent."

The car accelerated under me. It still seemed too slow.

Blake said, "Normally we'd be able to trace Massy's call and tell which storage unit. But he used the internet. Voice Over IP routed through relays."

"Unit 111," I said. "We figured it out from his financials."

He turned. "You're sure?"

I hoped we'd interpreted it correctly.

"He's slipped up," Blake said. "He never guessed you'd figure out the storage site and unit in Julian. We've also searched his house. Percocet and Citalopram were on his nightstand. Sheets and clothes all over the bedroom floor. You know what that means? Our control freak is falling apart. It's just a matter of hours."

Blake's taut face and pulsating jaw muscles belied his confidence. "And I'll let you in on something else. We think Kogan has a phone hidden somewhere in his cell. But we're not searching for it because we have a Stingray at Stateville."

"What the hell is a Stingray?"

"It picks up mobile phone transmissions—voice, cell phone numbers, even emails. If Massy calls him we'll hear every word."

Blake switched lanes and accelerated past two cars. I stared at one of his red, misshapen ears. It looked as if he'd spilled acid on it.

He said, "Look, the one thing we know for sure is that Massy's going to call you. The more he talks, the more he'll start stroking his own ego. Especially if he thinks you're suffering. Then he'll make a mistake."

"He's going to start hurting them while I'm on the phone, isn't he?"

Blake shook his head. "The second he touches your family, you say you're hanging up. He craves an audience."

Could I possibly do that? I fought off more panic. Forced my stomach back down. I looked out the window. We were on a residential street. In the fading light, a palm tree's shadow loomed over someone's dried-out lawn. On his front porch, a man glared at the car. How could I hang up?

We entered the suburban sprawl where I lived. "Do I beg?" I asked. "Do I weep?" As if I'd be able to stop myself.

Blake shook his head. "Try to make a deal. As long as he thinks you've got hope, he can manipulate you. That's how he feels his power. Once you've lost hope, he begins his ritual."

His ritual.

"This is the final period, the final minute. Just stay strong and we'll get this guy."

He pulled into our driveway. I jumped out and we ran past the Bird of Paradise flowers, past the orange tree to the front door. Blake followed me inside. The house was getting dark. I listened for the ring of my house phone. Nothing. We started toward the kitchen. I halted. Something was wrong.

The closet door slid open. Coats whirled and the hangers screamed. Massy leapt out. I saw a glint of metal. It popped. Blake shuddered and fell. Another pop. Pain seared through me. Every muscle cramped. I hit the floor.

Massy stood over me. He bent down. His irises had turned from dark brown to blue. My mind went blank.

63

MY EYES WOULDN'T FOCUS but something about the color of the ceiling looked familiar. Ivory-white. I knew those recessed lights. I made out my office. Blurry figures against the wall to my left. Jill taped to a dining room chair. Something covered her mouth. Her stockings. Frieda and Garth on the floor beside her. Bound and gagged.

Panic hit me like a fist. I struggled against the binding. Pain seared through my head and neck. I remembered Massy bent over me. He must have tasered and then drugged me. Duct tape fixed my arms to a plastic-molded chair. My chair. I relaxed, tried to empty my mind. But I smelled my own sweat and the fear inside it.

He stepped from behind my chair. He'd bleached his hair blond and affixed a blond beard over his jaw and cheeks. The man before me was an older version of Les Filson. His irises gleamed like blue Christmas lights. Contact lenses.

My children whimpered behind their gags. Jill's sad eyes bore into mine. I couldn't read what she was trying to tell me.

"We've got the whole family here," Massy said. "Isn't that nice?" He ran his fingers through his straw hair. "My mother was such a pretty blonde. She had much better hair than mine."

"A beautiful woman with an ugly heart," I said, studying his face for a reaction. Nothing. "Where's Blake?"

"Oh, is that his name? I'm afraid Agent Blake decided to spend eternity in the living room."

He'd killed Blake. He would kill all of us. Kill Garth and Frieda. My throbbing head focused my mind. He had to have a weakness. Everyone did.

"If only your mother had been like Magnolia," I said. "At least Magnolia loved my father."

Massy turned and slapped Jill. Garth and Frieda screamed behind their gags. My body jerked and the pain sliced through me.

"Each time you mention my mother it will get worse," he said.

Garth and Frieda's eyes begged me to do something. Tears streaked their faces. They looked so small bound up on the floor.

"I'm here where you want me," I said. "You don't need them gagged."

"I can take the gags off," Massy said. He turned to them. "But only if you don't cry. Can you do that?"

He didn't worry about them screaming. Maybe removing their gags flattered his sense of control. I could exploit that.

He bent down. He wore blue socks with red diamonds over his soft Italian loafers.

When the gags were untied, Garth and Frieda both wept softly. Words were the only comfort I could give them. "We're just going to talk with this man." To Massy, I said, "Right?"

"The son of the Preying Hands would never hurt children," Massy said.

Garth sniffled and said, "He pretends he's nice."

"Smart boy," Massy said. "You must have some of Grandpa's genes. That's why you wear that Superman shirt."

"It is not," Garth said.

Jill nodded at our boy, feeding him strength. She turned to Massy, her eyes in slits. I sucked in her rage.

He took a few steps and undid the stocking gag around her mouth. I knew the reason. He wanted to hear her scream.

"Leave the children," Jill said. "You only need me."

My brave wife. But I was afraid her courage would only stimulate him. I had to slow things down, give the FBI and police time to realize that Massy wasn't in Julian. They'd try to reach me. They'd come looking. But it would all take so long.

"We have a lot to talk about," I said.

He strode to the desk, where my computer was turned on. He plugged something like a microphone into the USB port and typed on the keyboard.

A high tenor voice on the computer's speaker said, "Hello?"

He was using Voice Over IP so the call couldn't be traced.

"We're all here," Massy said. "William, Garth, Frieda, and even Teacher Jill. It's a family reunion."

"Someone's weeping. Is that a child?" The voice came from Harvey Dean Kogan. He sounded surprised, as if he didn't know that Massy had kidnapped us.

"Harvey, did you think I'd let you die without a retirement party?" One of Massy's Christmas-tree-light eyes winked at me. "Cell phones are illegal at Stateville, of course. But all it takes is money and a cooperative employee. Plenty of those. You can practically hold try-outs."

He and Kogan had talked by phone for months. Maybe years.

"So what do you say about that, little brother?" he went on. "Talk to me."

Blake had said Massy wouldn't start his killing ritual until after I gave up hope of negotiating with him. I had to keep talking. "Would you really hurt your family?" I said. "The man you consider your brother? I can't believe you broke into my house." The Stingray at the prison was sucking up all the voice transmissions. Now the FBI knew where we were. They'd send a SWAT team to our house.

"I *saved* you," my father's voice said from the computer speaker. "That witch of a mother would have killed you without me. You owe me."

"Oh, Harvey. How long have I been repaying that debt? You've become so tiresome. I think the cancer has spread to your anterior frontal lobe."

Kogan had in fact been guiding and molding Massy for years. Years of killing. I looked at Jill. The fury in her eyes buoyed me.

"I'm hot," Frieda said. Her hair was matted to her head.

"Children shouldn't be tied up in this heat," Jill said.

Massy laughed. "So I should let them run outside and yell for help?"

Kogan said, "Do you really think they'll do that with their parents there? Anyone good at this would know better. You're disappointing me, Lawrence."

My father was trying to help us. Bullying Massy, and, at the same time, playing to his exulted sense of control.

Massy smiled and pointed to the microphone plugged into the computer. "Voice scramblers are so cheap these days. Leave it to the Chinese. There must be fifty kinds."

So my father's cell phone and my computer were both masked. Even if the Stingray still allowed the prison to hear me, the cops couldn't decode the words. My voice had been scrambled when I said Massy was at our house. But wouldn't the prison deputies have put electronic surveillance in his cell? If Kogan would just repeat where we were ...

Massy took two steps to Garth and loosened the rags around his arms and feet. "I'll release the boy," he said.

"I'm hot," Frieda said. "Please." She was about to cry.

"Shut up," Massy hissed. He turned to me. "Do they pay you so little at that prissy bank? You can't even afford air conditioning?"

Frieda whimpered. Garth took a step to her and kneeled. He wiped away her tears and the sweat from her hair. He gave her a hug.

"You know, if you run I'll hurt your sister first," Massy said. "Then your mommy and daddy."

Garth stared back at him. Fearless. Even if I ordered him to flee, he wouldn't run. It was as if he'd retreated inside one of his soldier and superhero games.

"You are truly an intriguing boy," Massy said. He returned to the desk.

From the speaker, Harvey said, "If you go through with this, you'll just keep suffering, Lawrence." It was a fatherly voice, the father that Massy yearned for.

"My, you are certainly not the man you used to be," Massy said. "Do you think I'm still a gullible child?"

Garth had leaned over. He slipped something from his sock—the blue pocketknife Mike had given him. Our seven-year-old had hidden

351

it while he was at school. He carried the knife all the time so he'd always be prepared to defend his family. But Massy was a grown man. If Garth attacked, Massy would kill him.

I shook my head at our boy. There had to be another way.

Garth slipped the knife into the waist of his pants, his Superman T-shirt covering it. He had his own plan.

"Our son is so scared, he can't even talk," I said.

Massy turned to Garth. "There's no reason to be frightened."

Jill glanced at me and looked away. "He needs comfort," she said.

Massy smiled sweetly at our boy. "Come here and let me give you a hug."

Garth shook his head. "I want my dad."

Massy studied me, reconfirming how I was trussed to the chair. "Go to him. Give your daddy a last hug."

Garth ran to my chair and threw his arms around me. He climbed on my lap and gripped me harder. When his body covered my bound right side, he stuck the knife between my wrist and the arm of the chair. His hand, hidden by his body, gently sliced the tape.

Massy stared at the computer. From the speaker, my father's calm voice said, "Hurting William and his family was never what we talked about."

He'd helped Massy plan everything.

Rage boiled in my whole body. I focused on the duct tape. As soon as my son cut me free I'd explode. I wouldn't need help from the police.

Massy turned and his fake blue eyes took in my reaction to what my father had just said. I wouldn't give him the satisfaction of looking surprised.

"I always suspected you worked together," I said. "Of course, you killed and cut up Magnolia all on your own." The last part was a reminder aimed at Harvey Dean Kogan.

"A surprise gift for my mentor," Massy said.

Frieda began to cry. Jill whispered, *"Mi querida,"* then other words in Spanish I couldn't understand.

Jill squinted at Massy. "So, your pretend father was the mastermind. You were just a follower." She was goading him, to draw his focus away from Garth and me.

"She thinks I just follow orders," Massy said to the computer. "Tell her whose idea this was."

My father said, "If you hurt them, your mother's hold on you will only get stronger. Her cold eyes will watch you forever."

That was a message to me. Massy's mother was his weakness, the wound we could use. But how?

Massy pointed at Garth. His head was buried in my shoulder. "Superman, come here. I want you beside me when you say hello to your grandfather. The fallen superhero."

Garth began to shake. He stopped cutting. I pushed down my face and touched him with my cheek. The pain in my head was dissolving.

Jill said, "You don't harm children. That's one of your *laws*."

Massy strode toward me. His soft loafers bounced on the carpet. My right arm was almost free, but the other arm and my legs were still taped to the chair. Massy pulled Garth off my lap to stand. He would see the knife.

But Garth's hands were empty. Plastic pressed against the underside of my arm. Garth had turned the knife sideways and wedged it between my wrist and the arm of the seat.

He sat Garth in front of me on a dining room chair between the desk and the floor lamp. "You're going to enjoy this, Harvey. We've got your whole bloodline right here in this room. Except Polly, of course. But she and I will have a chat later."

Our boy's mouth quivered. His arms and legs began to shake and the front of his blue jeans turned dark. As he sobbed, the urine ran down his leg. He was a child trying with all his force to be a man and, like all children, failing.

"There's no need to cry," Massy said. "All superheroes wet themselves. Until someone teaches them their powers. Isn't that right, Harvey?"

"I thought you were a better student than that," my father said.

Massy strode behind my chair. My right arm could break through the tape, but I needed more than one arm. I needed more time. Where were the police?

"Tell me why you want to be my brother," I said.

Instead of answering, Massy stepped in front of the chair and spoke to Garth. "You're a wonderful boy. I think I'm going to adopt you."

I nearly tore through the tape.

Then my mistake hit me. Like a hammer. Why would the FBI bug my father's prison cell when they thought the Stingray would sweep up the entire phone conversation? If the police burst into his cell, Massy would hear it and cut off the connection. Maybe they were listening through the door. But what could they hear? Kogan had the phone jammed to his ear and was speaking quietly.

The police weren't coming.

Unless they'd tried to call Blake's phone. Then they'd realize something had happened to him. At our house. The police just needed time.

"I want to tell you a secret," Massy said to Garth. "A very important secret. Did you know that all superheroes lose their fathers? That's the first step for them to gain their powers."

I said, "That's not true."

"Shut up or I'll gag you."

He wouldn't gag me. He wanted Garth and Frieda to see and hear me die. He wanted Harvey Dean Kogan to hear it.

354

I looked at Jill. She stared into my eyes as if telling me there was a way out. But where? I only had one arm free.

Massy adjusted the shade on the floor lamp. "We need proper lighting for Scene One," he said.

"Stop it," Garth said. His little boy's voice was so small. "Stop it."

"Lawrence!" my father said. "If you do this, I'll tell all the newspapers, all the magazines, all the internet bloggers. 'He was no son of mine,' I'll say."

Massy addressed the computer. "Just listen to yourself, Harvey. You're pathetic. How could I ever think you were my father? I've decided to own the last of your bloodline. Garth—or whatever name I give him—will be mine. All mine. I'll raise him the way your mother raised you."

"I forbid it," my father said.

Frieda moaned. Her eyes filled with tears.

Jill said, *"Te amo."* Then more words in the Spanish that Frieda loved. Our daughter stared at her mother. She took sobbing breaths. She stopped crying.

My own eyes clogged with tears. It was all I could do not to tear through the tape on my right arm.

Massy grasped a metal object on the desk. A scalpel. "It's time to get rid of your pitiful mistake-of-a-son," he said. "What do you think of that, Harvey? Does it make all your senses jingle and jangle?"

"Lawrence, long after you're executed they'll still be talking about the Preying Hands. They'll talk about you too if you stop this."

My father was using anything he could think of to save us. Why wasn't he yelling out our location?

"Pop, do you know where we are?" I said.

"He broke into your house," my father said, his voice loud.

If the prison deputies were listening, they knew where Massy was holding us. They'd deduce what had happened.

355

Massy shook his head at my deception. "Now I have to go faster. And you'll hear it all, Pop."

He took three steps to the office door and closed it. He bent down and tightly wedged a door stopper underneath. Even Garth wouldn't be able to run.

Jill must have seen that my right arm was almost free. I was working the left to be able to rip it from the tape. Her eyes crinkled and her lips formed a kiss.

"Even a bound woman makes you afraid, doesn't she?" Jill said.

My wife was giving me time.

Massy strode to her chair and looked down. "Green irises. Very well formed, almost classical." He raised the scalpel.

Both our children wailed.

I had to do something. Anything. "Call Harvey's wife," I yelled. "The woman who betrayed him. Let her hear."

Massy drew back. He strode toward me and wagged his left finger. "For that bungling attempt, you go first. And as you go, think about what your children will see."

Frieda wailed. He whirled and shouted, "Shut up!" She kept sobbing.

Garth slipped off his chair.

"Perhaps I should do the squealer first."

"You're a terrible photographer, do you know that?" I said. "The Preying Hands thinks you have no talent."

Massy turned slowly and raised the scalpel. "All right, if you insist."

Harvey Dean Kogan's voice rose from the computer. "I can teach you more about the art. William and I both can."

Massy laughed. "Clumsy."

He walked behind me. I tried to tear my legs from the chair. He grabbed my hair and yanked my head back, exposing my neck. Above me, his eyes studied my quivering face. I looked at his long chin and waited. His hand looped in front of me. The scalpel glinted. He brought it down slowly from above. He wanted me to see my own death.

With all my strength, I wrenched my right hand free. The ripping sound of the tape made him glance up. The scalpel froze. I flung up my hand and grabbed his wrist. I pulled it down and jerked forward. My teeth sank into the top of his hand.

Frieda shrieked. Massy yelled. He stepped from behind the chair. His face contorted, he stared at the bloody indentation on his hand, then at me.

Blood dribbled down my chin. I spit out pieces of flesh. Where was the pocketknife? I spotted it on the carpet, out of reach. My eyes darted back to Massy. I had to get him on the ground. Even with one arm. I lunged at him, dragging the chair with me.

He jumped back. The scalpel flew from his bloody hand and bounced under Jill's chair.

I was on my side on the floor. Jill shouted. Frieda screamed. And yet I heard them as if under water. My eyes gauged the distance to him.

Massy glanced over the carpet. He couldn't locate the scalpel. The blood streamed from the top of his hand. He howled.

Garth was kneeling beside Massy's leg. The blue pocketknife stood out rigidly from Massy's loafer. It was stuck in the top of his foot.

Garth crawled to Jill. He picked up the scalpel from under her chair and scurried to me. I grabbed the blade and sliced through the tape on my left arm.

Massy seized the floor lamp from beside the desk. He raised it by the neck over his head. He took two limping steps toward me, his eyes slitted in pain. The knife still stuck out from the top of his shoe. As he swung the lamp down, I jerked the chair over the top of myself and ducked my head under its long back.

The brass lamp thudded against the plastic and shook my whole body. I cut blindly at the tape anchoring my right leg to the base. I didn't have enough time. Massy was standing just beyond my reach. He raised the heavy base of the lamp again.

"Your own mother *hated* you!" Jill's shout cut through the din.

Massy turned toward her and I lunged, digging at the floor with one elbow and my one free leg. I slashed at his Achilles tendon. I felt the heavy pop.

Massy screamed.

I rolled away and the lamp crashed into the carpet beside me. I sawed at the tape binding my other leg to the chair.

Massy wailed. He stood on one foot, the other one flopping from his ankle. He dropped the lamp and fell to his knees. Sat on the floor. His bloody hand yanked the knife from his shoe. He crawled toward Jill and Frieda. Frieda's shriek was the terrible high pitch of a teakettle.

"Your own mother never wanted you!" Jill bellowed.

He stopped. His eyes expanded.

The last tab of duct tape gave way. I grabbed the lamp and jumped to my feet. Massy paused as he extended the knife toward Jill's throat. He looked back at me.

I swung the base of the lamp into his head. There was a crunch.

His body collapsed onto the carpet. I heard a high keening. Like air leaking from a pinched-off balloon. I raised the lamp high over my head. Swung the base down with all my strength. Once, twice, three times, an ax against a block of wood. My wife and children shrieked. Like television sounds from another room.

I stumbled to the computer. My blood-spattered hand reached toward the power button. Over the speaker I heard Harvey Dean Kogan, my father, say, "What happened? William? Lawrence?"

"It's me," I said.

I heard him gasping. Then, "Willy, he was never supposed to hurt you. I just wanted to see you. How can you blame a man for wanting to see his son before he dies?"

I disconnected him.

64

A WEEK AFTER I killed Lawrence Massy, Kevin Lund called. "I want to do you a favor," he said. "Share some things I'm not supposed to."

We huddled in that same miniature, half-paneled interview room on the fourth floor of the police station. The box of Kleenex had disappeared from the table, replaced by two bottles of water. A new plastic trash can sat on the carpet. The old one was probably in an evidence locker awaiting DNA analysis of my vomit.

I looked up at the whiteboard on the wall. A different set of erasures from a different murder smudged its shiny surface. I wondered how many killings had been diagrammed on that board. Fourteen, like the number of women my father had killed? As many as the twenty-four people Lawrence Massy had killed? My father was linked to more deaths than this room had ever considered.

I looked away from the whiteboard. It was too depressing. "Where's Hempel?"

Lund sat across from me in his pressed gray suit, his hair, as usual, perfectly combed. His right hand absently twirled the gold ring on his left. "Just the two of us. No Hempel. No Marta."

Both his deep voice and his smile seemed natural today. A plastic CVS bag lay beside him on the floor. I waited for him to reveal the secret inside.

"I suppose you heard about Poderovsky's family," he said.

"They really were in Hawaii." And not murdered by Jim.

Even Lund's disgust looked real today. "Staying under another man's name." He raised his manicured fingers toward the ceiling. "His wife actually had her child with her while she was with her new man. Some rich people just boggle me."

"Maybe that was why Jim was getting a divorce."

Lund picked up one of the water bottles. Unscrewed the cap and guzzled half of it. He put it down gently on the table. "Massy's storage unit was what we thought it was. Unfortunately."

Every newspaper in the country had reported the inside of that unit. The police had blasted off the steel door and walked in with guns drawn. All they'd seen were power tools and photographic equipment. No people. Until they opened the industrial-sized fridge. Then they found Vanessa. Or parts of her. They found pieces of other victims they hadn't even known about.

"He was planning to take your family there," Lund said.

I nodded. The whole world knew that part of the story.

"Has he tried to contact you?" Lund didn't need to say who.

What could Lund do to me that hadn't already happened? So I told him about my father's phone calls from Stateville. A former inmate whom I'd never met had telephoned from Indiana and begged me to have a heart for a man with cancer.

"And?" Lund asked.

"He's dying."

His brown eyes flared and he shook his head. "Don't talk to that bastard. I don't care how sick he is."

The plastic bag crinkled and Lund placed a small recorder on the table. "This will fortify you. Massy taped his conversations with Kogan. For posterity."

Before I could ponder that absurdity, Lund pushed a button. A baritone voice on the recording said, "What about your *other* son?" Massy sounded timid and uncertain. I almost didn't recognize him.

A high, nasal voice said, "You call that Judas a *son*? He tells everyone his father is dead. He'd sure change his story if the police hunted *him* down."

Even with Lund in front of me, I imagined my father. He leaned over a prison table. An amber gleam flooded from his unblinking eyes.

"What if he were a suspect in a murder?" Massy's pitch had risen, as if he believed that he, and not Harvey Dean Kogan, had conceived of the idea. "A teacher in his wife's school hurt a child."

My father expelled a deep sigh. "I've waited thirty-one years for this."

I heard a terrible longing inside that voice. But not for killing Elizabeth Morton. "Turn it off."

It was clear. All of it. My father had orchestrated her murder. He knew that if Massy copied him, and if all the evidence pointed to me, I'd have to ask for his help. I'd have to visit him before he succumbed to the cancer. Massy had killed Elizabeth so that my father could see his son a last time.

I put my head in my hands. It was so monstrous. And yet so understandable.

"We found a letter from Kogan in Massy's house," Lund said. "It was written to Ronny White."

"Before he changed his name?"

Lund drew out the silence. He rubbed the pale skin beside his gold ring. "Two years after Kogan's arrest."

My mind automatically did the calculation. Twenty-nine years ago. Two years after Mama, Polly, and I had disappeared to California.

Lund pulled a notebook from the pocket of his suit coat. "Amazing how easy it is to get old records. All it takes is the right contacts."

He flicked the pages of the notebook and filled in the sad spaces of Lawrence Massy's life. He started with the social worker reports from each of Ronny's eleven homes. The boy was always odd, always by himself. Not a single family inquired about adopting him. Every report mentioned the pictures that Ronny repeatedly drew of a woman's eyes. No one knew who she was and Ronny wouldn't reveal her. Not to the social workers or to the other children—no matter how much those kids beat him.

When he was fourteen, the police arrested Ronny for cutting up a girl with a razor. She'd called him gay. That's when they summoned the real psychologists. The only thing the professionals agreed on was that Ronny was brilliant. He got all A's in school and no one ever saw him study. This was a boy who could go to college. This was a boy who could rise above his tortured childhood.

The shrinks must have celebrated when he won a scholarship to University of Chicago. But even in a school of eccentric intellectuals, Ronny was twisted. The campus police caught him looking through the windows of a woman's dorm room. If he'd been charged, or if the sex crimes list had existed then, his medical career never would have started. Maybe he would have begun killing sooner. But instead he got to study eyes.

"I keep going back to what Kogan did to him," Lund said. "What kind of monster would subject a child to that?"

But his mother was renting him out to johns for drug money. There was a reason Kogan had showed Ronny her head. "He did it so she'd lose her power over him," I said.

Lund grimaced. "Jesus, William. Listen to yourself."

I twisted off the cap of a water bottle and looked at the whiteboard. It was the only bright thing in that dimly lit room.

"We also talked with Northwestern Medical School," Lund said. "By then he'd changed his name to Lawrence Massy. Massy and the chief eye surgeon did some pro bono work. For guess who?

"Harvey Dean Kogan."

"A detached retina. Seems the boys at Stateville roughed up Kogan and Massy took charge of the surgery."

And saved his hero's sight. But I didn't go there. "How'd he find us?" I asked.

"Probably a PI. Traced your family to San Diego but couldn't find your new name."

"So Ronny moved here from Chicago to find us."

Every time Lund grimaced, I liked him more. I felt as if I were seeing him for the first time.

"He did it for his daddy," he said.

I pictured Ronny White on the Elevated train, Ronny dreaming of a real father, a father who would rescue him. "I'll bet even you feel sorry for that boy," I said.

Instead of answering, Lund fiddled with the recorder. When he found what he was looking for, he said, "Listen to how Kogan manipulated him."

My father's nasal voice rose from the machine. "I killed my first woman to save you, Lawrence. So you'd become my son. So you could find your brother."

Lund turned off the recorder. "Don't tell me Kogan didn't know *exactly* what he was doing."

Massy was a cynical man. He'd suspect that Kogan was lying. But Ronny White? He'd ache for those three sentences to be true. The man was two people.

All that was left was how Massy had found us. He'd built his medical practice while he searched. I could guess what had happened then. My sister started proselytizing about organic farm-to-table food. She and the Haven appeared in the *Union-Tribune*. "Polly" was not a common name. Once Massy identified her, she'd have led him to Mama and me. But he was only interested in the males of our family. He got closer to me by pretending to consider what I was selling at the banks. How he must have savored leading me on. But he had to stop playing that game when Harvey Dean Kogan got cancer.

"Kogan used Massy for at least twenty years," Lund said.

"To find us."

Lund flinched. He shook his head. "They both liked killing."

What if someone snatched away Garth and Frieda and I could never see or talk with them? What if I were about to die? I'd do anything, contemplate crime, just for a word about how they lived their lives. But would I kill to see them again? No.

"Losing his family was worse than being in prison," I told Lund.

"There's absolutely nothing redeemable in that man," Lund said. "Don't go looking for it."

But he'd been Pop to me once. Pop, who built a tree house and a dollhouse and a spring horse. Maybe I was deluding myself, taking him apart and reconstructing him in my own vision. Just as Mama had done.

"Imagine if he'd kept on fathering you," Lund added. "What would he have made you do?"

Even now I think of the red pocketknife he gave me for my seventh birthday. That night when we helped a woman change a tire on a dark road. We stared at her in the van's headlight beams and he taught me the signs of fear on her face. But he never hurt her. Or me.

Lund drew back as if he could hear the dangerous sympathy corrupting my thoughts. He was a decent man. That deep announcer's voice, his impeccable dress, and all his ruses had blinded me to him. Today he was trying to protect me. We were meeting alone so he could reveal this side of himself.

"You're planning to talk with him, aren't you?" he said.

I was quiet.

"He'll persuade you to visit him again."

"He's dying."

"He'll still use you. It'll be his last, destructive act."

Lund leaned forward in the chair. Ever the detective, he had held something back. His last bit of persuasion.

"Let me tell you something else that was in that letter to Ronny White. Kogan said he started teaching him the art of killing when Ronny was fifteen. Think about that. It means your father sought out Ronny before he was arrested. Maybe he started communicating with him soon after killing the boy's mother. He might have met with him several times."

There it was. My father's ultimate betrayal. Even while I'd lived with him, he'd cultivated Ronny White as a son. And yet . . . I could comprehend it. He saw the boy as a version of himself. Or of his brother, Jonas. Maybe during one of those meetings my father gave Ronny a copy of the picture of Polly and me. He'd pointed out Alice White's double-exposed head at the bottom of the soybean field. "She can't hurt any of my children," he would have said.

"It was the ultimate power," Lund said. "He killed Ronny White's mother and created a son."

Because my father had created Ronny White, he preferred him over me. That was what Kevin Lund wanted me to believe.

"My father tried to convince Massy to let us go," I said.

"William, don't go there."

"The deal was that Massy wouldn't hurt us. My father didn't know he'd betray him."

"*Betray* him?"

"He has his own moral code."

Lund sighed, rotated the gold ring around his finger. "Those are your speculations. Those are human interpretations."

"And Harvey's not human?"

"No."

He was wrong. All his photographs seemed intimately bound to pain and desperation. Harvey Dean Kogan, my father, was human. But that didn't mean I forgave him.

65

I'M A "HERO." A man who grew up with the devil and slew a serial killer to save his family. Every customer and prospect I meet wants an appointment—even the women. It's been over two years since I killed Lawrence Massy and my business keeps building. For the first time, my loan production numbers have steamed past those of Bullshit Bob. I've personally raised our bank's share price, which makes our new CEO talk about stock options and a bigger office with a bigger window. Executive recruiters are calling. After thirty-one years of trying to escape my father's stigma, he's made me almost as famous as he is. There's something sickening about that.

There was also something sick about the envelope I received at my office a few months ago. It was addressed to *Preying Hands II*. My fan had sent me exquisitely drawn pen and ink sketches of dismembered women. That's why our family's phone is unlisted. Even our email addresses are confidential.

Jill and I started over in a new house with no name on the door or mailbox. We live in Leucadia, close to Jill's parents. Mama complains about how much farther away we are. We pretend to sympathize. As for our old house, plenty of crazies were interested in purchasing it. They wanted to live where the "real" son of the Preying Hands was martyred. I never want to meet the man who bought it.

Polly was the first to go public about growing up with Harvey Dean Kogan. It was the only way to control the story. The *Union-Tribune* did a Sunday article with photos of her restaurant and even Homer the cat. Newspapers from as far away as Sydney, Australia, picked it up. Polly hates the publicity as much as I do. Every week a few tourists show up at the Haven to meet the Preying Hands' daughter. Polly suggests that they find another restaurant. Sometimes she manages not to shout.

Homer's skin is wrinkling like an old man's and the small bit of fuzz on his face has started to turn gray. At some point he confirmed our friendship by dropping a kill at my feet. He even lets me rub his scarred stomach. I stare into those green eyes and see something cold and yet familiar. We've grown to a kind of understanding.

Jill has returned to an almost normal teaching life. Her colleagues and the older kids know the whole story of how she fought off a serial killer. The sixth graders are in awe. But her third graders don't understand what she had to do with Ms. Morton's death. Jill intends to keep it that way. We hope that in a few years she'll once again be what she was before: a remarkable teacher.

We both worry about Garth and Frieda. No one knows with any certainty how Massy affected them. We're committed to extended counseling, but children don't want to talk about how they witnessed a man try to cut up their father. And then watched their father beat him to death. The experts say it will take time for our kids to "process" the "incidents." My optimistic wife thinks our children are resilient enough to fully recover. But I know that what happened will taint their childhoods, just as my father's crimes irrevocably shattered mine. As sad as it makes me, I've learned that some wounds can't be cured; they have to be lived with.

The police never returned my vape pen and the marijuana extract. They gave back everything else though—even the copies of Harvey Dean Kogan's victim pictures and the pocketknife he gave me. Jill helped me burn the pictures. We rented a boat so Garth and I could throw our pocketknives into Mission Bay.

I now understand why Mama forbade Polly and me to see ourselves in our father's image. She refused to let the thought of his murders exist in our family. That absolute belief in our goodness was an act of love. I intend to pass that gift on to my children.

Which brings me to my final secret, the one that took me until last night to admit to Jill. Even now, the truth of it hides in recesses of myself I don't want to uncover. But I have to. If for nothing else, to free myself from what happened.

Jill and I were sitting on our new couch in our new house. I'd sucked down two glasses of pinot noir to fortify me. "Remember Béni-Messous and the *Time* magazine photo?" I said.

The truth is, I saw fifteen men's corpses on the road through that Algerian village. Their killers had placed their heads on top of their chests. I aimed my Nikon but knew that no newspaper would publish such a grisly photograph. I needed something more indirect, more stylized to make my name as a photojournalist. Colonel Laribi helped me compose the shot. His soldiers placed the men's heads in a neat line on a white wall that paralleled the road. Laribi's men used blood to write in Arabic on the wall: "God is great." I photographed the backs of those heads. The dead men seemed to stare into the houses where their wives and children lay slaughtered. That staged scene became the photo I'm famous for.

As she listened, Jill squinted. Then her eyes softened. Can anyone sympathize like my wife?

She put her arms around me. "It's time you forgave yourself," she said. "For what you did. And for what he did."

My father. Harvey Dean Kogan. The Preying Hands. I never did journey back to visit him. Never spoke by phone. Even now I sometimes see Pop with the eyes of the child who adored him. But I'm a dad, a man who must protect his children. That means walling off the love I once felt for my father.

I imagine that he died alone on one of those gurneys the prisons use for lethal injections. But cancer is a slower form of execution. Perhaps, as it claimed him, he was alone and terrified—like his victims. Or maybe kindly doctors or inmates caressed his hair and said that he had God inside him. Maybe a kind of grace—even goodness—floated down like a hand to touch his yellow forehead.

Maybe.

Photo © Michael Prine Jr.

About the Author

Like the protagonist of *Murderabilia*, Carl Vonderau was a private banker who grew up in a religious family. His banking career took him to the US, Canada, Latin America, and North Africa. He did business in Spanish, French, and Portuguese. Now a full-time writer, Carl also devotes his time to helping nonprofits. He lives with his wife in San Diego. *Murderabilia* is his first novel.

WWW.MIDNIGHTINKBOOKS.COM

From the gritty streets of New York City to sacred tombs in the Middle East, it's always midnight somewhere. Join us online at any hour for fresh new voices in mystery fiction.

At midnightinkbooks.com you'll also find our author blog, new and upcoming books, events, book club questions, excerpts, mystery resources, and more.

MIDNIGHT INK ORDERING INFORMATION

Order Online:
• Visit our website www.midnightinkbooks.com, select your books, and order them on our secure server.

Order by Phone:
• Call toll-free within the U.S. at
  1-888-NITE-INK (1-888-648-3465)
• We accept VISA, MasterCard, American Express, and Discover
• Canadian customers must use credit cards

Order by Mail:
Send the full price of your order (MN residents add 6.875% sales tax) in U.S. funds, plus postage & handling to:

> Midnight Ink
> 2143 Wooddale Drive
> Woodbury, MN 55125-2989

Postage & Handling:

Standard (US). If your order is:
> $30.00 and under, add $6.00
> $30.01 and over, FREE STANDARD SHIPPING

AK, HI, PR: $16.00 for one book plus $2.00 for each additional book.

International Orders: Including Canada
> $16.00 for one book plus $3.00 for each additional book

Orders are processed within 12 business days. Please allow for normal shipping time.
Postage and handling rates subject to change.